DECADENCE FROM DEDALUS

the Child of Pleasure

Gabriele D'Annunzio

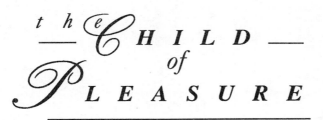

the **CHILD**
of
PLEASURE

translated by Georgina Harding

DEDALUS

Published in the UK by Dedalus Ltd
Langford Lodge, St Judith's Lane, Sawtry, Cambs, PE17 5XE

ISBN 0 946626 60 X

First published in Italy in 1889 as Il Piacere
Dedalus edition 1991

Printed in England by Clays Ltd, St. Ives plc.

A C.I.P. listing for this title is available on request.

Dedalus would like to express its gratitude to David Blow for his help
in originating the Decadence from Dedalus series.

Also by Gabriele D'Annunzio:

BOOK I

CHAPTER I

ANDREA SPERELLI dined regularly every Wednesday with his cousin the Marchesa d'Ateleta.

The salons of the Marchesa in the Palazzo Roccagiovine were much frequented. She attracted specially by her sparkling wit and gaiety and her inextinguishable good humour. Her charming and expressive face recalled certain feminine profiles of the younger Moreau and in the vignettes of Gravelot. There was something Pompadouresque in her manner, her tastes, her style of dress, which she no doubt heightened purposely, tempted by her really striking resemblance to the favourite of Louis xv.

One Tuesday evening, in a box at the Valle Theatre, she said laughingly to her cousin, 'Be sure you come to-morrow, Andrea. Among the guests there will be an interesting, not to say *fatal*, personage. Forewarned is forearmed—Beware of her spells—you are in a very weak frame of mind just now.'

He laughed. 'If you don't mind, I prefer to come unarmed,' he replied, 'or rather in the guise of a victim. It is a character I have assumed for many an evening lately, but alas, without result so far.'

'Well, the sacrifice will soon be consummated, *cugino mio.*'

'The victim is ready!'

The next evening, he arrived at the palace a few minutes earlier than usual, with a wonderful gardenia in his buttonhole and a vague uneasiness in his mind. His *coupé* had to stop in front of the entrance, the portico being occupied by another carriage, from which a lady was alighting. The liveries, the horses, the ceremonial which accompanied her arrival all proclaimed a great position. The Count caught a glimpse of a tall and graceful figure, a scintillation of diamonds in dark hair and a slender foot on the step. As he went upstairs he had a back view of the lady.

She ascended in front of him with a slow and rhythmic movement; her cloak, lined with fur as white as swan's-down, was unclasped at the throat, and slipping back, revealed her shoulders, pale as polished ivory, the shoulder-blades disappearing into the lace of the corsage with an indescribably soft and fleeting curve as of wings. The neck rose slender and round, and the hair, twisted into a great knot on the crown of her head, was held in place by jewelled pins.

The harmonious gait of this unknown lady gave Andrea such sincere pleasure that he stopped a moment on the first landing to watch her. Her long train swept rustling over the stairs; behind her came a servant, not immediately in the wake of his mistress on the red carpet, but at the side along the wall with irreproachable gravity. The absurd contrast between the magnificent creature and the automaton following her brought a smile to Andrea's lips.

In the anteroom while the servant was relieving her of her cloak, the lady cast a rapid glance at the young man who entered.

The servant announced—' Her Excellency the Duchess of Scerni!' and immediately afterwards—'Count Sperelli-Fieschi d'Ugenta!' It pleased Andrea that his name should be coupled so closely with that of the lady in question.

In the drawing-room were already assembled the Marchese and Marchesa d'Ateleta, the Baron and Baroness d'Isola and Don Filippo del Monte. The fire burned cheerily on the hearth, and several low seats were invitingly disposed within range of its warmth, while large leaf plants spread their red-veined foliage over the low backs.

The Marchesa advanced to meet the two new arrivals with her delightful ready laugh.

'Ah,' she said, 'a happy chance has forestalled me and made it unnecessary for me to tell you one another's names. Cousin Sperelli, make obeisance before the divine Elena.'

Andrea bowed profoundly. The Duchess held out her hand with a frank and graceful gesture.

' I am very glad to know you, Count,' she said, looking him full in the face. 'I heard so much about you last summer at Lucerne from one of your friends—Giulio Musellaro. I must confess I was rather curious——Besides, Musellaro lent me your exquisite "Story of the Hermaphrodite" and made me a present of your etching "Sleep"—a proof copy—a real gem. You have a most ardent admirer in me—please remember that.'

She spoke with little pauses in between. Her voice was so warm and insinuating in tone that it almost had the effect of a caress, and her glance had that unconsciously voluptuous and disturbing expression which instantly kindles the desire of every man on whom it rests.

'Cavaliere Sakumi!' announced the servant, as the eighth and last guest made his appearance.

He was one of the secretaries to the Japanese Legation, very small and yellow, with prominent cheek-bones and long, slanting, bloodshot eyes over which the lids blinked incessantly. His body was disproportionately large for his spindle legs, and he turned his toes in as he walked. The skirts of his coat were too wide, there was a multitude of wrinkles in his trousers, his necktie bore visible evidence of an unpractised hand. It was as if a *daimio* had been taken out of one of those cuirasses of iron and lacquer, so like the shell of some monstrous crustacean, and thrust into the clothes of a European waiter. And yet, with all his ungainliness and apparent stupidity there was a glint of malice in his slits of eyes and a sort of ironical cunning about the corners of his mouth.

Arrived in the middle of the room, he bowed low. His gibus slipped from his hand and rolled over the floor.

At this, the Baroness d'Isola, a tiny blonde with a cloud of

fluffy curls all over her forehead, vivacious and grimacing as
a young monkey, called to him in her piping voice :

'Come over here, Sakumi—here, beside me.'

The Japanese cavalier advanced with a succession of bows
and smiles.

' Shall we see the Princess Issé this evening ? ' asked Donna
Francesca d'Ateleta, who had a mania for gathering in her
drawing-rooms all the most grotesque specimens of the exotic
colonies of Rome, out of pure love of variety and the
picturesque.

The Asiatic replied in a barbarous jargon, a scarcely
intelligible compound of English, French, and Italian.

For a moment everybody was speaking at once—a chorus
through which now and then the fresh laughter of the
Marchesa rang like silver bells.

'I am sure I have seen you before—I cannot remember
when and I cannot remember where, but I am certain I have
seen you,' Andrea Sperelli was saying to the duchess as he stood
before her. ' When I saw you going upstairs in front of me,
a vague recollection rose up in my mind, something that took
shape from the rhythm of your movements as a picture grows
out of a melody. I did not succeed in making the recollection clear, but when you turned round, I felt that your profile
answered incontestably to that picture. It could not have
been a divination, therefore it must have been some obscure
phenomenon of memory. I must have seen you somewhere
before—who knows—perhaps in a dream—perhaps in another
world, a previous existence——'

As he pronounced this last decidedly hackneyed, not to
say silly remark, Andrea laughed frankly as if to forestall the
lady's smile, whether of incredulity or irony. But Elena
remained perfectly serious. Was she listening, or was she
thinking of something else ? Did she accept that kind of
speech, or was she, by her gravity, amusing herself at his
expense ? Did she intend assisting him in the scheme of
seduction he had begun with so much care, or was she going
to shut herself up in indifference and silence ? In short, was

she or was she not the sort of woman to succumb to his attack? Perplexed, disconcerted, Andrea examined the mystery from all sides. Most men, especially those who adopt bold methods of warfare, are well acquainted with this perplexity which certain women excite by their silence.

A servant threw open the great doors leading to the dining-room.

The Marchesa took the arm of Don Filippo del Monte and led the way.

'Come,' said Elena, and it seemed to Andrea that she leaned upon his arm with a certain abandon—or was it merely an illusion of his desire?—perhaps. He continued in doubt and suspense, but every moment that passed drew him deeper within the sweet enchantment, and with every instant he became more desperately anxious to read the mystery of this woman's heart.

'Here, cousin,' said Francesca, pointing him to a place at one end of the oval table, between the Baron d'Isola and the Duchess of Scerni with the Cavaliere Sakumi as his *vis-à-vis*. Sakumi sat between the Baroness d'Isola and Filippo del Monte. The Marchesa and her husband occupied the two ends of the table, which glittered with rare china, silver, crystal and flowers.

Very few women could compete with the Marchesa d'Ateleta in the art of dinner giving. She expended more care and forethought in the preparation of a menu than of a toilette. Her exquisite taste was patent in every detail, and her word was law in the matter of elegant conviviality. Her fantasies and her fashions were imitated on every table of the Roman upper ten. This winter, for instance, she had introduced the fashion of hanging garlands of flowers from one end of the table to the other, on the branches of great candelabras, and also that of placing in front of each guest, among the group of wine glasses, a slender opalescent Murano vase with a single orchid in it.

'What a diabolical flower!' said Elena Muti, taking up the vase and examining the orchid which seemed all blood-stained and deformed.

Her voice was of such rich full *timbre* that even her most trivial remarks acquired a new significance, a mysterious grace, like that King of Phrygia whose touch turned everything to gold.

'A symbolical flower—in your hands,' murmured Andrea, gazing at his neighbour, whose beauty in that attitude was really amazing.

She was dressed in some delicate tissue of palest blue, spangled with silver dots which glittered through antique Burano lace of an indefinable tint of white inclining to yellow. The flower, like something evil generated by a malignant spell, rose quivering on its slender stalk out of the fragile tube which might have been blown by some skilful artificer from a liquid gem.

'Well, I prefer roses,' observed Elena, replacing the orchid with a gesture of repulsion, very different from her former one of curiosity. She then joined in the general conversation.

Donna Francesca was speaking of the last reception at the Austrian Embassy.

'Did you see Madame de Cahen?' asked Elena. 'She had on a dress of yellow tulle covered with humming birds with ruby eyes—a gorgeous dancing bird-cage. And Lady Ouless —did you notice her?—in a white gauze skirt draped with sea-weed and little red fishes, and under the sea-weed and fish another skirt of sea-green gauze—Did you see it?—a most effective aquarium!' and she laughed merrily.

Andrea was at a loss to understand this sudden volubility. These frivolous and malicious things were uttered by the same voice which, but a few moments, ago had stirred his soul to its very depths; they came from the same lips which, in silence, had seemed to him like the mouth of the Medusa of Leonardo, that human flower of the soul rendered divine by the fire of passion and the anguish of death. What then was the true essence of this creature? Had she perception and consciousness of her manifold changes, or was she impenetrable to herself and shut from her own mystery? In her expression, her manifestation of herself, how much was

artificial and how much spontaneous? The desire to fathom
this secret pierced him even through the délight experienced by the proximity of the woman whom he was
beginning to love. But his wretched habit of analysis for
ever prevented him losing sight of himself, though every
time he yielded to its temptation he was punished, like Pysche
for her curiosity, by the swift withdrawal of love, the frowns of
the beloved object and the cessation of all delights. Would
it not be better to abandon oneself frankly to the first ineffable sweetness of new-born love? He saw Elena in the
act of placing her lips to a glass of pale gold wine like liquid
honey. He selected from among his own glasses the one the
servant had filled with the same wine, and drank at the same
moment that she did. They replaced their glasses on the
table together. The similarity of the action made them turn
to one another, and the glance they exchanged inflamed them
far more than the wine.

'You are very silent,' said Elena, affecting a lightness
of tone which somewhat disguised her voice. 'You have
the reputation of being a brilliant conversationalist—exert
yourself therefore a little!'

'Oh cousin! cousin!' exclaimed Donna Francesca with a
comical air of commiseration, while Filippo del Monte
whispered something in his ear.

Andrea burst out laughing.

'Cavaliere Sakumi; we are the silent members of this party
—we must wake up!'

The long narrow eyes of the Asiatic—redder than ever now
that the wine had kindled a deeper crimson on his high cheek-
bones—glittered with malice. All this time he had done
nothing but gaze at the Duchess of Scerni with the ecstatic
look of a *bonze* in presence of the divinity. His broad flat
face, which might have come straight out of a page of O-kou-
sai, the great classical humorist, gleamed red among the
chains of flowers like a harvest moon.

'Sakumi is in love,' said Andrea in a low voice, and leaning
over towards Elena.

' With whom ? '

' With you—have you not observed it yet ? '

' No.'

' Well, look at him.'

Elena looked across at him. The amorous gaze of the disguised *daimio* suddenly affected her with such ill-disguised mirth that the Japanese felt deeply hurt and humiliated.

' See,' she said, and to console him she detached a white camellia and threw it across the table to the envoy of the Rising Sun,—' find some comparison in praise of me ! '

The Oriental carried the flower to his lips with a ludicrous air of devotion.

' Ah—ah—Sakumi ! ' cried the little Baroness d'Isola, ' you are unfaithful to me ! '

He stammered a few words while his face flamed. Everybody laughed unrestrainedly, as if the foreigner had been invited solely to provide entertainment for the other guests. Andrea turned laughing towards Elena.

Her head was raised and a little thrown back, and she was gazing furtively at the young man under her eyelashes with one of those indescribably feminine glances which seem to absorb—almost one would say drink in—all that is most desirable, most delectable in the man of their choice. The long lashes veiled the soft dark eyes which were looking at him a little sidelong, and her lower lip had a scarcely perceptible tremor. The full ray of her glance seemed to rest upon his lips as the most attractive point about him.

And in truth his mouth was very attractive. Pure and youthful in outline and rich in colouring, a little cruel when firmly closed, it reminded one irresistibly of that portrait of an unknown gentleman in the Borghese gallery, that profound and mysterious work of art in which the fascinated imagination has sought to recognise the features of the divine Cesare Borgia depicted by the divine Sanzio. As soon as the lips parted in a smile the resemblance vanished, and the square, even dazzlingly white teeth lit up a mouth as fresh and jocund as a child's.

The moment Andrea turned, Elena withdrew her eyes, though not so quickly but that the young man caught the flash. His delight was so poignant that it sent the blood flaming to his face.

'She is attracted by me!' he thought to himself, inwardly exulting in the assurance of having found favour in the eyes of this rare creature. 'This is a joy I have never experienced before!' he said to himself.

There are certain glances from a woman's eye which a lover would not exchange for anything else she can offer him later. He who has not seen that first love-light kindle in a limpid eye has never touched the highest point of human bliss. No future moment can ever approach that one.

The conversation around them grew more animated, and Elena asked him—'Are you staying the winter in Rome?'

'The whole winter—and longer,' was Andrea's reply, to whom the simple question seemed to open up a promise.

'Ah, then you have set up a home here?'

'Yes, in the Casa Zuccari—*domus aurea.*'

'At the Trinità de' Monti?—Lucky being!'

'Why lucky?'

'Because you live on a spot I have a great liking for.'

'You are quite right. I always think—don't you?—that there the most perfect essence of Rome is concentrated as in a cup.'

'Quite true! I have hung up my heart—both Catholic and Pagan—as an *ex-voto* between the obelisk of the Trinità and the column of the Conception.'

She laughed as she spoke. A sonnet to this suspended heart rose instantly to his lips, but he did not give it utterance, for he was in no mood to continue their conversation in this light vein of false sentiment, which broke the sweet spell she had been weaving about him. He was silent therefore.

She, too, remained a moment pensive, and then threw herself with renewed vivacity into the general conversation, prodigal of wit and laughter, flashing her teeth and her *bon mots* at all in

turn.   Francesca was retailing spicily a piece of gossip about
the Princess di Ferentino on the subject of a recent, and
somewhat risky, adventure of hers with Giovanella Daddi.

'By the by—the Ferentino announces another charity
bazaar for Epiphany,' said the Baroness d'Isola.   'Does
anybody know anything about it yet?'

'I am one of the patronesses,' said Elena Muti.

'And you are a most valuable patroness,' broke in Don
Filippo del Monte, a man of about forty, almost bald, a keen
sharpener of epigrams, whose face seemed a sort of Socratic
mask; the right eye was for ever on the move, and flashed
with a thousand changing expressions, while the left remained
stationary and glazed behind the single eye-glass, as if
he used the one for expressing himself and the other for
seeing.   'At the May bazaar, you brought in a perfect shower
of gold.'

'Oh, the May bazaar—what a mad affair that was!'
exclaimed the Marchesa.

While the servants were filling the glasses with iced
champagne, she added, 'Do you remember, Elena, our stalls
were close together?'

'Five louis d'or a drink—five louis d'or a bite!' Don
Filippo called, in the voice of a street-hawker.   Elena and
the Marchesa burst out laughing.

'Why yes, of course, Filippo, you cried the wares,' said
Donna Francesca.   'Now what a pity you were not there,
cugino mio!   For five louis you might have eaten fruit out of
which I had had the first bite, and have drunk champagne
out of the hollow of Elena's hands for five more.'

'How scandalous!' broke in the Baroness d'Isola, with a
horrified grimace.

'Ah, Mary, I like that!   And did you not sell cigarettes
that you lighted up first yourself for a louis?' cried Francesca
through her laughter.   Then she became suddenly grave.
'Every deed, with a charitable object in view, is sacred,' she
observed sententiously.   'By merely biting into fruit, I
collected at least two hundred louis.'

'And you?' Andrea Sperelli turned to Elena with a constrained smile—'With your human drinking-cup—how much did you get?'

'I?—oh, two hundred and seventy louis.'

Everybody was full of fun and laughter, excepting the Marchese d'Ateleta, who was old, and afflicted with incurable deafness; was padded and painted—in a word, artificial from head to foot. He was very like one of the figures one sees at a wax work show. From time to time—usually the wrong one—he would give vent to a little dry cackling laugh, like the rattle of some rusty mechanism inside him.

'However,' Elena resumed, 'you must know, that after a certain point in the evening, the price rose to ten louis, and at last, that lunatic of a Galeazzo Secinaro came and offered me a five hundred lire note, if I would dry my hands on his great golden beard!'

As was ever the case at the d'Ateletas', the dinner increased in splendour towards the end; for the true luxury of the table is shown in the dessert. A multitude of choice and exquisite things, delighting the eye no less than the palate, were disposed with consummate art in various crystal and silver-mounted dishes. Festoons of camellias and violets hung between the vine-wreathed eighteenth century candelabras, round which sported fairies and nymphs, and on the wall-hangings more fairies and nymphs, and all the charming figures of the pastoral mythology—the Corydons, the Phylises, the Rosalinds—animated with their sylvan loves one of those sunny Cytherean landscapes originated by the fanciful imagination of Antoine Watteau.

The slightly erotic excitement, which is apt to take hold upon the spirits at the end of a dinner graced by fair women and flowers, betrayed itself in the tone of the conversations, and the reminiscences of this bazaar, at which the ladies—urged on by a noble spirit of emulation in collecting the largest sums—employed the most unheard of audacities to attract buyers.

'And did you accept it?' asked Andrea of the Duchess.

' I sacrificed my hands on the altar of Benevolence,' she replied. ' Twenty-five louis more to my account ! '

' *All the perfumes of Arabia will not sweeten this little hand.*' He laughed as he quoted Lady Macbeth's words, but, in reality, his heart was sore with a confused, ill-defined pain, that bore a strong resemblance to jealousy. And suddenly he became aware of something excessive, almost— it might be—a touch of the courtesan, defacing the manners of the great lady. Certain inflections of her voice, certain tones of her laughter, here a gesture, there an attitude, certain glances, exhaled a charm that was perhaps a trifle too Aphrodisiac. She was, besides, somewhat over-lavish with the visible favours of her graces, and the air she breathed was continually surcharged with the desire she herself excited.

Andrea's heart swelled with bitterness ; he could not take his eyes off Elena's hands. Out of those hands, so delicately, ideally white and transparent, with their faint tracery of azure veins—from those rosy hollowed palms, wherein a chiromancer would have discovered many an intricate crossing of lines, ten, twenty different men had drunk at a price. He could *see* the heads of these unknown men bending over her and drinking the wine. But Secinaro was one of his friends —a great handsome jovial fellow, imperially bearded like a very Lucius Verus, and a most formidable rival to have. He felt as if the dinner would never come to an end.

' You are such an innovator,' Elena was saying to Donna Francesca, as she dipped her fingers into warm water in a pale blue finger-glass rimmed with silver, ' Why do you not revive the ancient fashion of having the water offered to one after dinner with a basin and ewer ? The modern arrangement is very ugly, do you not think so, Sperelli ? '

Donna Francesca rose. Every one followed her example. Andrea, with a bow, offered his arm to Elena and she looked at him without smiling as she slowly laid her hand on his arm. Her last words were gaily and lightly spoken, but her gaze was so grave and profound that the young man felt it sink into his very soul.

'Are you going to the French Embassy to-morrow evening?'
she asked him.

'Are you?' Andrea asked in return.

'I am.'

'So am I.'

They smiled at one another like two lovers.

'Sit down,' she added as she sank into a seat.

The seat was far from the fire, with its back to the curve
of a grand piano which was partially draped in some rich
stuff. At one end of the divan, a tall bronze crane held in
his beak a tray hanging by three chains like one side of a pair
of scales, and on it lay a new book and a little Japanese
scimitar—a *waki-gashi*—the scabbard and hilt encrusted
with silver chrysanthemums.

Elena took up the book, which was only half cut, read the
title, and then replaced it on the tray which swung to and fro.
The scimitar fell to the ground. As both she and Andrea
stooped to pick it up, their hands met. She straightened
herself up and examined the beautiful weapon with some
curiosity, retaining it in her hand while Andrea talked about
the new novel, insinuating into his remarks general argu-
ments upon love; and her fingers wandered absently over
the chasing of the weapon, her polished nails seeming a
repetition of the delicate gems that sparkled in her rings.

Presently, after a pause, Elena said without looking at him :
'You are very young—have you often been in love?'

He answered by another question—'Which do you consider the truest, noblest way of love—to imagine you have
discovered every aspect of the eternal Feminine combined in
one woman, or to run rapidly over the lips of woman as you
run your fingers over the keys of a piano, till, at last, you
find the sublime chord of harmony?'

'I really cannot say—and you?'

'Nor I either—I am unable to solve the great problem
of sentiment. However, by personal instinct, I have followed
the latter plan and have now, I fear, struck the grand chord
—judging, at least, by an inward premonition.'

'You fear?'

'*Je crains ce que j'espère.*'

He instinctively employed this language of affected sentiment to cloak his really strong emotion, and Elena felt herself
caught by his voice as in a golden net and drawn forcibly
out of the life surrounding them.

'Her Excellency the Princess di Micigliano!' announced
a footman.

'Count di Gissi!'

'Madame Chrysoloras!'

'The Marchese and the Marchesa Massa d'Albe!'

The rooms began to fill rapidly. Long shimmering trains
swept over the deep red carpet, white shoulders emerged
from bodices starred with diamonds, embroidered with pearls,
covered with flowers, and in nearly every coiffure glittered
those marvellous hereditary gems for which the Roman
nobility are so much envied.

'Her Excellency the Princess of Ferentino!'

'His Excellency the Duke of Grimiti!'

The guests formed themselves in various groups, the rally-
ing points of gossip and of flirtation. The chief group,
composed exclusively of men, was in the vicinity of the
piano, gathered round the Duchess of Scerni, who had risen
to her feet, the better to hold her own against her besiegers.
The Princess of Ferentino came over to greet her friend with
a reproach.

'Why did you not come to Nini Santamarta's to-day?
We all expected you.'

She was tall and thin with extraordinary green eyes sunk
deep in their shadowy sockets. Her dress was black, the
bodice open in a point back and front, and in her hair, which
was *blond cendré*, she wore a great diamond crescent like
Diana. She waved a huge fan of red feathers hastily to and
fro as she spoke.

'Nini is at Madame Van Hueffel's this evening.'

'I am going there later on for a little while, so I shall see
her,' answered the Duchess.

'Oh, Ugenta,' said the Princess turning to Andrea, 'I was looking for you to remind you of our appointment. To-morrow is Thursday and Cardinal Immraet's sale begins at twelve. Will you fetch me at one?'

'I shall not fail, Princess.'

'I simply must have that rock crystal.'

'Then you must be prepared for competition.'

'From whom?'

'My cousin for one.'

'And who else?'

'From me,' said Elena.

'You?—Well, we shall see.'

Several of the gentlemen asked for further enlighten-ment.

'It is a contest between ladies of the 19th century for a rock crystal vase which belonged to Niccolò Niccoli,' Andrea explained with solemnity; 'a vase, on which is engraved the Trojan Anchises untying one of the sandals of Venus Aphrodite. The entertainment will be given gratis, at one o'clock to-morrow afternoon, in the Public Sale-rooms of the Via Sistina. Contending parties—the Princess of Ferentino, the Duchess of Scerni and the Marchesa d'Ateleta.'

Everybody laughed, and Grimiti asked, 'Is betting permitted?'

'The odds! The odds!' yelled Don Filippo del Monte, imitating the strident voice of the bookmaker Stubbs.

The Princess gave him an admonitory tap on the arm with her red fan, but the joke seemed to amuse them hugely and the betting began at once. Hearing the bursts of laughter, other ladies and gentlemen joined the group in order to share the fun. The news of the approaching contest spread like lightning and soon assumed the proportions of a society event.

'Give me your arm and let us take a turn through the rooms,' said Elena to Andrea Sperelli.

As soon as they were in the west room, away from the

noisy crowd, Andrea pressed her arm and murmured, 'Thanks.'

She leaned on him, stopping now and again to reply to some greeting. She seemed fatigued, and was as pale as the pearls of her necklace. Each gentleman addressed her with some hackneyed compliment.

'How stupid they all are! it makes me feel quite ill,' she said.

As they turned, she saw Sakumi was following them noiselessly, her camellia in his buttonhole, his eyes full of yearning, not daring to come nearer. She thew him a compassionate smile.

'Poor Sakumi!'

'Did you not notice him before?' asked Andrea.

'No.'

'While we were sitting by the piano, he was in the recess of the window, and never took his eyes off your hands when you were playing with the weapon of his native country—now reduced to being a paper-cutter for a European novel.'

'Just now, do you mean?'

'Yes, just now. Perhaps he was thinking how sweet it would be to perform *Hara-Kiri* with that little scimitar, the chrysanthemums on which seemed to blossom out of the lacquer and steel under the touch of your fingers.'

She did not smile. A veil of sadness, almost of suffering, seemed to have fallen over her face; her eyes, faintly luminous under the white lids, seemed drowned in shadow, the corners of her mouth drooped wearily, her right arm hung straight and languid at her side. She no longer held out her hand to those who greeted her; she listened no longer to their speeches.

'What is the matter?' asked Andrea.

'Nothing—I must go to the Van Hueffels' now. Take me to Francesca to say good-bye, and then come with me down to my carriage.'

They returned to the first drawing-room, where Luigi Gulli, a young man, swarthy and curly-haired as an Arab, who had left his native Calabria in search of fortune, was executing, with much feeling, Beethoven's sonata in C♯ minor. The Marchesa d'Ateleta, a patroness of his, was standing near the piano, with her eyes fixed on the keys. By degrees, the sweet and grave music drew all these frivolous spirits within its magic circle, like a slow-moving but irresistible whirlpool.

'Beethoven!' exclaimed Elena in a tone of almost religious fervour, as she stood still and drew her arm from Andrea's.

She had halted beside one of the great palms and, extending her left hand, began very slowly to put on her glove. In that attitude her whole figure, continued by the train, seemed taller and more erect ; the shadow of the palm veiled and, so to speak, spiritualised the pallor of her skin. Andrea gazed at her in ·a kind of rapture, increased by the pathos of the music.

As if drawn by the young man's impetuous desire, Elena turned her head a little, and smiled at him—a smile so subtle, so spiritual, that it seemed rather an emanation of the soul than a movement of the lips, while her eyes remained sad and as if lost in a far away dream. Thus overshadowed they were verily the eyes of the Night, such as Leonardo da Vinci might have imagined for an allegorical figure after having seen Lucrezia Crevelli at Milan.

During the second that the smile lasted, Andrea felt himself absolutely alone with her in the crowd. An immense wave of pride flooded his heart.

Elena now prepared to put on the other glove.

'No, not that one,' he entreated in a low voice.

She understood, and left her hand bare.

He was hoping to kiss that hand before she left. And suddenly he had a vision of the May Bazaar, and the men drinking champagne out of those hollowed palms, and for the second time that night he felt the keen stab of jealousy.

'We will go now,' she said, taking his arm once more.

The sonata over, conversation was resumed with fresh vigour. Three or four new names were announced, amongst them that of the Princess Issé, who entered smiling, with funny

little tottering steps, in European dress, her oval face as
white and tiny as a little *netske* figurine.   A stir of curiosity
ran round the room.

'Good-night, Francesca,' said Elena, taking leave of her
hostess, 'I shall see you to-morrow.'

'Going so soon?'

'I am due at the Van Hueffels'.   I promised to go.'

'What a pity!   Mary Dyce is just going to sing.'

'I must go—good-bye!'

'Well, take this, and good-bye.   Most amiable of cousins,
please look after her.'

The Marchesa pressed a bunch of double violets into her
hand and hurried away to receive the Princess Issé very
graciously.   Mary Dyce, in a red dress, slender and undulating as a tongue of fire, began to sing.

'I am so tired!' murmured Elena, leaning wearily on
Andrea's arm.   'Please ask for my cloak.'

He took her cloak from the attendant, and in helping her
to put it on, touched her shoulder with the tips of his fingers,
and felt her shiver.   The words of one of Schumann's songs
was borne to them on Mary Dyce's passionate soprano,
Ich kann's nicht fassen, nicht glauben!

They descended the stairs in silence.   A footman preceded
them to call the duchess's carriage.   The stamping of the
horses rang through the echoing portico.   At every step,
Andrea felt the pressure of Elena's arm grow heavier; she
held her head high, and her eyes were half closed.

'As you ascended these stairs, my admiration followed
you, unknown to you.   Now, as you come down, my love
accompanies you,' he said softly, almostly humbly, faltering
a little between the two last words.

She made no reply, but she lifted the bunch of violets to
her face, and inhaled the perfume.   In so doing, the wide
sleeve of her evening cloak slipped back over her arm beyond
the elbow, thrilling the young man's senses almost beyond
control.   His lips trembled, and he with difficulty restrained
the burning words that rose to them.

The carriage was standing at the foot of the great stairway; a footman held open the door.

'To Madame Van Hueffel's,' said the duchess to him, while Andrea helped her in.

The man left the door and returned to his seat beside the coachman. The horses stamped, striking out sparks from the stones.

'Take care!' cried Elena, holding out her hand to the young man. Her eyes and her diamonds flashed through the gloom.

'Oh, to be in there with her in the shadow—to press my lips to her satin neck under the perfumed fur of her mantle!'

'Take me with you!' he would like to have cried.

But the horses plunged. 'Oh, take care!' Elena repeated.

He kissed her hand—pressing his lips to it as if to leave the mark of his burning passion. He closed the door and the carriage rolled rapidly away under the porch, and out to the Forum.

And thus ended Andrea Sperelli's first meeting with the Duchess of Scerni.

CHAPTER II

THE gray deluge of democratic mud, which swallows up so
many beautiful and rare things, is likewise gradually engulfing
that particular class of the old Italian nobility in which from
generation to generation were kept alive certain family traditions of eminent culture, refinement and art.

To this class, which I should be inclined to denominate
Arcadian because it shone with greatest splendour in the
charming atmosphere of the eighteenth century life, belonged
the Sperelli. Urbanity, hellenism, love of all that was exquisite,
a predilection for out-of-the-way studies, an æsthetic curiosity,
a passion for archæology, and an epicurean taste in gallantry
were hereditary qualities of the house of Sperelli. An
Alessandro Sperelli brought in 1466 to Frederic of Aragon,
son of Ferdinand King of Naples, and brother to Alfonso
Duke of Calabria, a manuscript in folio containing the 'less
rude' poems of the old Tuscan writers which Lorenzo de
Medici had promised him at Pisa in 1465; and in concert
with the most erudite scholars of his time, that same
Alessandro wrote a Latin elegy on the death of the divine
Simonetta—sad and melting numbers after the manner of
Tibullus. Another Sperelli—Stefano,—was during the same
century in Flanders, in the midst of all the pomp, the
extravagant elegance, the almost fabulous magnificence of
the court of Charles the Bold, Duke of Burgundy, where he
remained, having allied himself with a Flemish family. A
son of his, named Giusto, learned painting under the direction
of Gossaert, in whose company he came to Italy in the suite
of Philip of Burgundy, the ambassador of the Emperor

Maximilian to Pope Julius II. in 1508. He settled in Florence, where the chief branch of his family continued to flourish, and had for his second master Piero di Cosimo, that jocund and facile painter and vivid and harmonious colourist, under whose brush the pagan deities came to life again. This Giusto was by no means a mediocre artist, but he consumed all his forces in the vain effort to reconcile his primary Gothic education with the newly awakened spirit of the Renaissance. Towards the middle of the seventeenth century the Sperelli family migrated to Naples. There a Bartolomeo Sperelli published in 1679 an astrological treatise: *De Nativitatibus*; in 1720 a Giovanni Sperelli wrote for the theatre an opera bouffe entitled *La Faustina* and also a lyrical tragedy entitled *Progne*; 1756 a Carlo Sperelli brought out a book of amatory verses in which much licentious persiflage was expressed with the Horatian elegance so much affected at that period. A better poet, and moreover a man of exquisite gallantry, was Luigi Sperelli, attached to the court of the *lazzaroni* king of Naples and his queen Caroline. His Muse was very charming, and affected a certain epicurean melancholy. He loved much and with a fine discrimination, and had innumerable adventures—some of them famous—as, for instance, that with the Marchesa di Bugnano who poisoned herself out of jealousy, and with the Countess of Chesterfield who died of consumption, and whom he mourned in a series of odes, sonnets and elegies—very moving, if perhaps somewhat overladen with metaphor.

Count Andrea Sperelli-Fieschi d'Ugenta, sole heir to the family, carried on its traditions. He was, in truth, the ideal type of the young Italian nobleman of the nineteenth century, a true representative of a race of chivalrous gentlemen and graceful artists, the last scion of an intellectual line.

He was, so to speak, thoroughly impregnated with art. His early youth, nourished as it was by the most varied and profound studies, promised wonders. Up to his twentieth year, he alternated between severe study and long journeys, in company with his father, and could thus complete his extraordinary æsthetic education under paternal direction, without the restrictions and constraints imposed by tutors. And it was to his father that he owed his taste for everything pertaining to art, his passionate cult of the Beautiful, his paradoxical disdain of prejudice, and his keen appetite for the sensuous.

That father, who had grown up in the midst of the last expiring splendours of the Bourbon court of Naples, understood life on a large scale, was profoundly initiated into all the arts of the voluptuary, combined with a certain Byronic leaning towards fantastic romanticism. His marriage had occurred under *quasi* tragic circumstances, the finale of a mad passion; then, after disturbing and undermining the conjugal peace in every possible fashion, he had separated from his wife, and, keeping his son always with him, had travelled about the whole of Europe.

Andrea's education had thus been a living one; that is to say, derived less from books than from the study of life as he had seen it. His mind was corrupted not only by over-refined culture, but also by actual experiments, and in him curiosity grew keener in proportion as his knowledge grew wider. From the beginning, he had ever been prodigal of his powers, for the great nervous force with which nature had endowed him was inexhaustible in providing him with the treasures he dispensed so lavishly. But the expansion of that energy caused in him the destruction of another force: the moral one, which his own father had not scrupled to repress in him. And he never perceived that his whole life was a steady retrogression of all his faculties, of his hopes, his joys—a species of gradual renunciation—and that the circle was slowly but inexorably narrowing round him.

Among other fundamental maxims his father had given him the following: You must *make* your own life as you would any other work of art. The life of a man of intellect should be of his own designing. Herein lies the only true superiority.

Again: Never, let it cost what it may, lose the mastery

over yourself even in the most intoxicating rapture of the senses. *Habere non haberi* is the rule from which the man of intellect should never swerve.

And again—Regret is the idle pastime of an unoccupied mind. The best method, therefore, to avoid regret is to keep the mind constantly occupied with new fancies, fresh sensations.

Unfortunately, however, these *voluntary* axioms, which from their ambiguity might just as easily be interpreted as lofty moral rules, fell upon an *involuntary* nature ; that is to say, one in which the will power was extremely feeble.

Another seed sown by the paternal hand had borne evil fruit in Andrea's spirit—the seed of sophistry. Sophistry, said this imprudent teacher, is at the bottom of all human pleasure or pain. Therefore, quicken and multiply your sophisms and you quicken and multiply your own pleasure or your own pain. It is possible that the whole science of life consists in obscuring the truth. The word is a very profound matter in which inexhaustible treasure is concealed for the man who knows how to use it. The Greeks, who were artists in words, were the most refined voluptuaries of antiquity. The sophists flourished in the greatest number during the age of Pericles, the Golden Age of pleasure.

This germ had found a favourable soil in the unhealthy culture of the young man's mind. By degrees, insincerity— rather towards himself than towards others—became such a habit of Andrea's mind, that finally he was incapable of being wholly sincere or of regaining dominion over himself.

The death of his father left him alone at the age of twenty, master of a considerable fortune, separated from his mother, and at the mercy of his passions and his tastes. He spent fifteen months in England. His mother married again, and he returned to Rome from choice.

Rome was his passion—not the Rome of the Cæsars, but the Rome of the Popes—not the Rome of the Triumphal Arches, the Forums, the Baths, but the Rome of the Villas, the Fountains, the Churches. He would have given all the

Colosseums in the world for the Villa Medici, the Campo
Vaccino for the Piazza di Spagna, the Arch of Titus for the
Fountain of the Tortoises. The princely magnificence of the
Colonnas, the Dorias, the Barberinis, attracted him far more
than the ruins of imperial grandeur. It was his dream to
possess a palace crowned by a cornice of Michael Angelo's,
and with frescos by the Carracci like the Farnese palace—a
gallery of Raphaels, Titians and Domenichini like the
Borghese ; a villa like that of Alessandro Albani, where deep
shadowy groves, red granite of the East, white marble from
Luni, Greek statues and Renaissance pictures should weave an
enchantment round some sumptuous amour of his. In an
album of ' Confessions ' at his cousin's, the Marchesa d'Ateleta,
against the question—' What would you most like to be ?' he
had written, ' A Roman prince.'

Arriving in Rome about the end of September, he set up
his ' home ' in the Palazzo Zuccari, near the Trinità de' Monti,
where the obelisk of Pius VI. marks with its shadow the
passing hours. The whole of October was devoted to fur-
nishing them. When the rooms were all finished and decorated
to his taste, he passed some days of invincible melancholy
and loneliness in his new abode. It was a St. Martin's
summer, a ' Springtime of the Dead,' calmly sad and sweet, in
which Rome lay all golden, like a city of the Far East, under
a milk-white sky, diaphanous as the firmament reflected in
Southern seas.

All this languor of atmosphere and light, in which things
seemed to lose their substance and reality, oppressed the
young man with an infinite weariness, an inexpressible sense
of discontent, of discomfort, of solitude, emptiness and home-
sickness, mostly, no doubt, the result of the change of
climate and customs.

It was just this, that he was entering upon a new phase of
life. Would he find therein the woman and the work capable
of dominating his heart and becoming an object in life to
him ? Within himself he felt neither the conviction of power
nor the presage of fame or happiness. Though penetrated,

impregnated with art, as yet he had not produced anything remarkable. Eager in the pursuit of pleasure and of love, he had never yet really loved or really enjoyed whole-heartedly. Tortured by aspirations after an Ideal, and abhorring pain both by nature and education, he was vulnerable on every side, accessible to pain at every point.

In the tumult of his conflicting inclinations, he had lost all guiding will-power and moral perception. Will, in abdicating, had yielded the sceptre to instinct and the æsthetic sense was substituted for the moral. But, it was nevertheless precisely to his æsthetic sense—in him most subtle and powerful—that he owed a certain strength and equilibrium of mind, so that one might say his existence was a perpetual struggle between contrary forces, enclosed within the limits of that equilibrium. Men of intellect, educated in the cult of the beautiful, preserve a certain sense of order even in their worst depravities. The conception of the beautiful is, so to speak, the axis of their being, round which all their passions revolve.

Over this sadness, the recollection of Constance Landbrooke still floated like a faded perfume. His love for Conny had been a very delicate affair, for she was a very sweet little creature. She was like one of Lawrence's creations, with all the dainty feminine graces so dear to that painter of furbelows and laces and velvets, of lustrous eyes and pouting lips, a very re-incarnation of the little Countess of Shaftesbury. Lively, chattering, never still, lavish of infantile diminutives and silvery peals of laughter, easily moved to sudden caresses and as sudden melancholies and quick bursts of anger, she contributed to her share of love a vast amount of movement, much variety and many caprices. But Conny Landbrooke's melodious twitterings had left no more mark on Andrea's heart than the light musical echo left in one's ear for a time by some gay ritornella. More than once in some pensive hour of twilight melancholy, she had said to him with a mist of tears before her eyes—'I know you do not love me.' And in truth he did not love her, she did not by any means satisfy his longings. His ideal was less northern in character. Ideally he felt himself attracted by those courtesans of the sixteenth century, over whose faces there would appear to be drawn some indefinable veil of sorcery, some transparent mask of enchantment, some divine nocturnal spell.

The moment Andrea set eyes on the Duchess of Scerni, he said to himself—' *This* is my Ideal Woman ! ' and his whole soul went out to her in a transport of joy, in the presentiment of the future.

CHAPTER III

THE next day the public sale-room of the Via Sistina was thronged with fashionable people, come to look on at the famous contest.

It was raining hard; the light in the low-roofed damp rooms was dull and gray. Along the walls were ranged various pieces of carved furniture, several large diptychs and triptychs of the Tuscan school of the fourteenth century; four pieces of Flemish tapestry representing the Story of Narcissus hung from ceiling to floor; Metaurensian majolicas occupied two long shelves; stuffs—for the most part ecclesiastical—lay spread out on chairs or heaped up on tables; antiquities of the rarest kind—ivories, enamels, crystals, engraved gems, medals, coins, breviaries, illuminated manuscripts, silver of delicate workmanship were massed together in high cabinets behind the auctioneer's table. A peculiar musty odour, arising from the clamminess of the atmosphere and this collection of ancient things, pervaded the air.

When Andrea Sperelli entered the room with the Princess di Ferentino, he looked about him rapidly with a secret tremor—Is *she* here? he said to himself.

She was there, seated at the table between the Cavaliere Davila and Don Filippo del Monte. Before her on the table lay her gloves and her muff, to which a little bunch of violets was fastened. She held in her hand a little bas-relief in silver, attributed to Caradosso Foppa, which she was examining with great attention. Each article passed from hand to hand along the table while the auctioneer proclaimed its merits in a loud voice, those standing behind the line of chairs leaning over to look.

The sale began.

'Make your bids, gentlemen! make your bids!' cried the auctioneer from time to time.

Some amateur encouraged by this cry bid a higher sum with his eye on his competitors. The auctioneer raised his hammer.

'Going—Going—Gone!'

He rapped the table. The article fell to the last bidder. A murmur went round the assemblage, then the bidding recommenced. The Cavaliere Davila, a Neapolitan gentleman of gigantic stature and almost femininely gentle manners, a noted collector and connoisseur of majolica, gave his opinion on each article of importance. Three lots in this sale of the Cardinal's effects were really of 'superior' quality: the Story of Narcissus, the rock-crystal goblet, and an embossed silver helmet by Antonio del Pollajuolo presented by the City of Florence to the Count of Urbino in 1472 for services rendered during the taking of Volterra.

'Here is the Princess,' said Filippo del Monte to the Duchess.

Elena rose and shook hands with her friend.

'Already in the field!' exclaimed the Princess.

'Already.'

'And Francesca?'

'She has not come yet.'

Four or five young men—the Duke of Grimiti, Roberto Casteldieri, Ludovico Barbarisi, Gianetto Rutolo—drew up round them. Others joined them. The rattle of the rain against the windows almost drowned their voices.

Elena held out her hand frankly to Sperelli as to everybody else, but somehow he felt that that handshake set him at a distance from her. Elena seemed to him cold and grave. That instant sufficed to freeze and destroy all his dreams; his memories of the preceding evening grew confused and dim, the torch of hope was extinguished. What had happened to her?—She was not the same woman. She was wrapped in the folds of a long otter-skin coat, and wore a toque of the same fur on her head. There was something hard, almost contemptuous, in the expression of her face.

'The goblet will not come on for some time yet,' she observed to the Princess, as she resumed her seat.

Every object passed through her hands. She was much tempted by a centaur cut in a sardonyx, a very exquisite piece of workmanship, part, perhaps, of the scattered collection of Lorenzo the Magnificent. She took part in the bidding, communicating her offers to the auctioneer in a low voice without raising her eyes to him. Presently the competition stopped ; she obtained the intaglio for a good price.

'A most admirable acquisition,' observed Andrea Sperelli from behind her chair.

Elena could not repress a slight start. She took up the sardonyx and handed it to him to look at over her shoulder without turning round. It was really a very beautiful thing.

'It might be the centaur copied by Donatello,' Andrea added.

And in his heart, with his admiration for the work of art, there rose up also a sincere admiration for the noble taste of the lady who now filled all his thoughts. 'What a rare creature both in mind and body !' he thought. But the higher she rose in his imagination, the further she seemed removed from him in reality. All the security of the preceding evening was transformed into uneasiness, and his first doubts reawoke. He had dreamed too much last night with waking eyes, bathed in a felicity that knew no bounds, while the memory of a gesture, a smile, a turn of the head, a fold of her raiment held him captive as in a net. Now all this imaginary world had tumbled miserably about his ears at the touch of reality. In Elena's eyes there had been no sign of that special greeting to which he had so ardently looked forward ; she had in no wise singled him out from the crowd, had offered him no mark of favour. Why not ? He felt himself slighted, humiliated. All these fatuous people irritated him, he was exasperated by the things which seemed to engross Elena's attention, and more particularly by Filippo del Monte, who leaned towards her every now and then to whisper something to her—scandal no doubt.   The Marchesa d'Ateleta now arrived, cheerful as ever.   Her laugh, out of the centre of the circle of men who hastened to surround her, caused Don Filippo to turn round.

'Ah—so the trinity is complete!' he exclaimed, rising from his seat.

Andrea instantly slipped into it at Elena Muti's side.   As the subtle perfume of the violets reached him, he murmured—

'These are not those of last night, are they?'

'No,' she answered coldly.

In all her varying moods, changeful and caressing as the waves of the sea, there always lay a hidden menace of rebuff. She was often taken with fits of cold restraint.   Andrea held his tongue, bewildered.

'Make your bids, gentlemen,' cried the auctioneer.

The bids rose higher.   Antonio del Pollajuolo's silver helmet was being hotly contested.   Even the Cavaliere Davila entered the lists.   The very air seemed gradually to become hotter; the feverish desire to possess so beautiful an object seemed to spread like a contagion.

In that year the craze for *bibelots* and *bric-à-brac* reached the point of madness.   The drawing-rooms of the nobility and the upper middle classes were crammed with curios; every lady must needs cover the cushions of her sofas and chairs with some piece of church vestment, and put her roses into an Umbrian ointment pot, or a chalcedony jar.   The sale-rooms were the favourite meeting-places, and every sale crowded.   It was the fashion for the ladies when they dropped in anywhere for tea in the afternoon, to enter with some such remark as—'I have just come from the sale of the painter Campos' things.   Tremendous bidding!   Such Hispano-Moresque plaques!   I secured a jewel belonging to Maria Leczinska.   Look!'

The bidding continued .   Fashionable purchasers crowded round the table, vieing with each other in artistic and critical comparisons between the Giottoesque Nativities and Annuncia-

tions. Into this atmosphere of mustiness and antiquity the
ladies brought the perfume of their furs, and more especially
of the violets which each one wore on her muff, according to
the then prevailing charming fashion, and their presence
diffused a delicious air of warmth and fragrance. Outside,
the rain continued to fall, and the light to fade. Here and
there a little flame of gas struggled feebly with such daylight
as remained.

'Going—going—gone!' The stroke of the hammer put
Lord Humphrey Heathfield in possession of the Florentine
helmet. The bidding then began for smaller articles, which
passed in turn from hand to hand down the long table.
Elena handled them carefully, examined them, and placed
them in front of Andrea without remark. There were
enamels, ivories, eighteenth century watches, Milanese gold-
smiths' work of the time of Ludovico the Mcor, Books of
Hours inscribed in gold letters on pale blue vellum. These
precious things seemed to increase in value under the touch
of Elena's fingers; her little hands had a faint tremor of
eagerness when they came in contact with some specially
desirable object. Andrea watched them intently, and his
imagination transformed every movement of her hands into a
caress. 'But why did she place each thing upon the table
instead of passing it to him?'

He forestalled her next time by holding out his hand.
And from thenceforth the ivories, the enamels, the ornaments
passed from the hands of the lady to those of her lover, to
whom they communicated an ineffable thrill of delight. He
felt that thus some particle of the charm of the beloved
woman entered into these objects, just as a portion of the
virtue of the magnet enters into the iron. It was, in truth,
the magnetic sense of love—one of those acute and profound
sensations which are rarely felt but at love's beginning, and
which, differing essentially from all others, seem to have no
physical or moral seat, but to exist in some neutral element of
our being—an element that is intermediate, and the nature of
which is unknown.

'Here again is a rapture I have never felt before,' thought Andrea.

A kind of torpor seemed creeping over him. Little by little, he was losing consciousness of time and place.

'I recommend this clock to your notice,' Elena was saying to him, with a look the full significance of which he did not for the first moment understand.

It was a small Death's-head, carved in ivory with extraordinary power and anatomical skill. Each jaw was furnished with a row of diamonds, and two rubies flashed from the deep eye-sockets. On the forehead was engraved, *Ruit Hora*; and on the occiput, *Tibi, Hippolyta*. It opened like a box, the hinging being almost imperceptible, and the ticking inside lent an indescribable air of life to the diminutive skull. This sepulchral jewel, the offering of some unknown artist to his mistress, had doubtless marked many an hour of rapture, and served as a warning symbol to their amorous souls.

Could a lover wish for anything more exquisite and more suggestive? 'Has she any special reason for recommending this to me?' thought Andrea, all his hopes reviving on the instant. He threw himself into the bidding with a sort of fury. Two or three others bid against him, notably Giannetto Rutolo, who, being in love with Donna Ippolita Albonico, was attracted by the dedication: *Tibi, Hippolyta*.

Presently Rutolo and Sperelli were left alone in the contest. The bidding rose higher than the actual value of the article, which forced a smile from the auctioneer. At last, vanquished by his adversary's determination, Giannetto Rutolo was silent.

'Going—going—— !'

Donna Ippolita's lover, a little pale, cried one last sum. Sperelli named a higher—there was a moment's silence. The auctioneer looked from one to the other, then he raised his hammer and slowly, still looking at the two—'Going—going—gone!'

The Death's-head fell to the Conte d'Ugenta. A murmur ran round the room. A sudden flood of light burst through the windows, lit up the gleaming gold backgrounds of the triptychs, and played over the sorrowfully patient brow of the Siennese Madonna and the glittering steel scales on the Princess di Ferentino's little grey hat.

'When is the goblet coming on?' asked the princess impatiently.

Her friends consulted the catalogue. There was no hope of the goblet for that day. The unusual amount of competition made the sale go slowly. There was still a long list of smaller articles—cameos, medallions, coins. Several antiquaries and Prince Stroganow disputed each piece hotly. The rest felt considerably disappointed. The Duchess of Scerni rose to go.

'Good-bye, Sperelli,' she said. 'I shall see you again this evening—perhaps.'

'Why perhaps?'

'I do not feel well.'

'What is the matter?'

She turned away without replying, and took leave of the others. Many of them followed her example and left with her. The young men were making fun of the 'spectacle manqué.' The Marchesa d'Ateleta laughed, but the princess was evidently thoroughly out of temper. The footmen waiting in the hall called for the carriages as if at the door of a theatre or concert hall.

'Are you not coming on to Laura Miano's?' Francesca asked the duchess.

'No, I am going home.'

She waited on the pavement for her brougham to come up. The rain was passing over; patches of blue were beginning to appear between the great banks of white cloud; a shaft of sunshine made the wet flags glitter. Flooded by this pale rose splendour, her magnificent furs falling in straight symmetrical folds to her feet, Elena was very beautiful. As Andrea caught a glimpse of the inside of her brougham, all cosily lined with white satin like a little boudoir, with its shining silver foot-warmer for the comfort of her small feet, his dream of the preceding evening came back to him—'Oh, to be there with her alone, and feel the warm perfume of her breath mingling with the violets—behind the mist-dimmed windows through which one hardly sees the muddy streets, the gray houses, the dull crowd !'

But she only bowed slightly to him at the door, without even a smile, and the next moment the carriage had flashed away in the direction of the Palazzo Barberini, leaving the young man with a dim sense of depression and heartache.

She only said 'perhaps,' so it was quite possible that she would not be at the Palazzo Farnese that evening. What should he do then ? The thought that he might not see her was intolerable; already every hour he passed far from her weighed heavily on his spirits. 'Am I then so deeply in love with her already?' he asked himself. His spirit seemed imprisoned within a circle in which the phantoms of all his sensations in presence of this woman surged and wheeled around him. Suddenly there would emerge from this tangle of memory, with singular precision, some phrase of hers, an inflection of her voice, an attitude, a glance, the seat where they had sat, the finale of the Beethoven sonata, a burst of melody from Mary Dyce, the face of the footman who had held back the *portière*—anything that happened to have caught his attention at the moment—and these images obscured by their extreme vividness the actual life around him. He pleaded with her; said to her in thought what he would say to her in reality by and by.

Arrived in his own rooms, he ordered tea of his man-servant, installed himself in front of the fire and gave himself up to the fictions of his hope and his desire. He took the little jewelled skull out of its case and examined it carefully. The tiny diamond teeth flashed back at him in the firelight, and the rubies lit up the shadowy orbits. Behind the smooth ivory brow time pulsed unceasingly—*Ruit Hora*. Who was the artist who had contrived for his Hippolyta so superb and bold a fantasy of Death, at a period too when the masters of enamelling had been wont to ornament with tender idylls the little watches destined to warn Coquette of the time of the rendezvous in the parks of Watteau? The modelling gave evidence of a masterly hand—vigorous and full of admirable style; altogether it was worthy of a fifteenth century artist as forcible as Verrocchio.

'I recommend this clock to your consideration.' Andrea could not help smiling a little at Elena's words uttered in so peculiar a tone after so cold a silence. He was assured that she intended him to put the construction upon her words which he had afterwards done, but then why retire into impenetrable reserve again—why take no further notice of him —what ailed her? Andrea lost himself in a maze of conjecture. Nevertheless, the warm atmosphere of the room, the luxurious chair, the shaded lamp, the fitful gleams of firelight, the aroma of the tea—all these soothing influences combined to mitigate his pain. He went on dreamingly, aimlessly, as if wandering through a fantastic labyrinth. With him reverie sometimes had the effect of opium—it intoxicated him.

'May I take the liberty of reminding the Signor Conte that he is expected at the Casa Doria at seven o'clock,' observed his valet in a subdued and discreet murmur, one of his offices being to jog his master's memory. 'Everything is ready.'

He went into an adjoining octagonal room to dress, the most luxurious and comfortable dressing-room any young man of fashion could possibly desire. On a great Roman sarcophagus, transformed with much taste into a toilet table, were ranged a selection of cambric handkerchiefs, evening gloves, card and cigarette cases, bottles of scent, and five or six fresh gardenias in separate little pale blue china vases— all these frivolous and fragile things on this mass of stone, on which a funeral *cortège* was sculptured by a masterly hand !

CHAPTER IV

At the Casa Doria, speaking of one thing and another, the Duchess Angelieri remarked—'It seems that Laura Miano and Elena Muti have quarrelled.'

'About Giorgio perhaps?' returned another lady laughing.

'So they say. The story began this summer at Lucerne——'

'But Laura was not at Lucerne.'

'Exactly—but her husband was——'

'I believe it is a pure invention,' broke in the Florentine countess Donna Bianca Dolcebuono—'Giorgio is in Paris now.'

Andrea heard it all in spite of the chattering of the little Contessa Starnina, who sat at his right hand, and never gave him a moment's peace. Bianca Dolcebuono's words did little to ease the smart of his wound. At least, he would have liked to know the whole story. But the Duchess Angelieri did not resume the thread of her discourse, and other conversations crossed and recrossed the table under the great gorgeous roses from the Villa Pamfili.

Who was this Giorgio? A former lover? Elena had spent part of the summer at Lucerne,—she had just come from Paris. After the sale she had refused to go to Laura Miano's. A fierce desire assailed him to see her, to speak to her again. The invitation at the Palazzo Farnese was for ten o'clock—half past ten found him there waiting anxiously.

He waited long. The rooms filled rapidly; the dancing began. In the Carracci gallery the divinities of fashionable Rome vied in beauty with the Ariadnes, the Galateas, the Auroras, the Dianas of the frescos; couples whirled past;

heads glittering with jewels drooped or raised themselves, bosoms panted, the breath came fast through parted crimson lips.

' You are not dancing, Sperelli? ' asked Gabriella Barbarisi, a girl brown as the *oliva speciosa*, as she passed him on the arm of her partner, fanning herself and smiling to show a dimple she had at the corner of her mouth.

' Yes—later on,' Andrea responded hastily—' later on.'

Heedless of introductions or greetings, his torment increased with every moment of this fruitless expectation, and he roamed aimlessly from room to room. That 'perhaps' made him sadly afraid that Elena would not come. And supposing she really did not? When was he likely to see her again? Donna Bianca Dolcebuona passed, and, almost without knowing why, he attached himself to her side, saying a thousand agreeable things to her, feeling some slight comfort in her society. He had the greatest desire to speak to her about Elena, to question her, to reassure himself; but the orchestra struck up a languorous mazurka and the Florentine countess was carried off by her partner.

Thereupon, Andrea joined a group of young men near one of the doors—Ludovico Barbarisi, the Duke di Beffi, Filippo del Gallo and Gino Bomminaco. They were watching the couples, and exchanging observations not over refined in quality. One of them turned to Andrea as he came up.

' Why, what has become of you this evening? Your cousin was looking for you a moment ago. There she is dancing with my brother now.'

' Look! ' exclaimed Filippo del Gallo—' the Albonico has come back, she is dancing with Giannetto.'

' The Duchess of Scerni came back last week,' said Ludovico ; ' what a lovely creature ! '

' Is she here? '

' I have not seen her yet.'

Andrea's heart stopped beating for a moment, fearing that something would be said against her by one or other of these malicious tongues. But the passing of the Princess Issé on the arm of the Danish Minister diverted their attention. Nevertheless, his desire for further knowledge was so intense, that it almost drove him to lead back the conversation to the name of his lady-love. But he was not quite bold enough. The mazurka was over; the group broke up. 'She is not coming! She is not coming!' His secret anxiety rose to such a pitch that he half thought of leaving the place altogether; the contact of this laughing, careless throng was intolerable.

As he turned away, he saw the Duchess of Scerni entering the gallery on the arm of the French ambassador. For one instant their eyes met, but that one glance seemed to draw them to each other, to penetrate to the very depths of their souls. Both knew that each had only been looking for the other, and at that moment there seemed to fall a silence upon both hearts, even in the midst of the babel of voices, and all their surroundings to vanish and be swept away by the force of their own absorbing thought.

She advanced along the frescoed gallery where the crowd was thinnest, her long white train rippling like a wave over the floor behind her. All white and simple, she passed slowly along, turning from side to side in answer to the numerous greetings, with an air of manifest fatigue and a somewhat strained smile which drew down the corners of her mouth, while her eyes looked larger than ever under the low white brow, her extreme pallor imparting to her whole face a look so ethereal and delicate as to be almost ghostly. This was not the same woman who had sat beside him at the Ateleta's table, nor the one of the Sale Rooms, nor the one standing waiting for a moment on the pavement of the Via Sistina. Her beauty at this moment was of ideal nobility, and shone with additional splendour among all these women heated with the dance, over-excited and restless in their manner. The men looked at her and grew thoughtful; no mind was so obtuse or empty that she did not exercise a disturbing influence upon it, inspire some vague and indefinable hope. He whose heart was free imagined with a thrill what such a woman's love would be; he who loved already conceived a vague regret, and dreamed of raptures hitherto unknown; he who bore a wound dealt by some woman's jealousy or faithlessness suddenly felt that he might easily recover.

Thus she advanced amid the homage of the men, enveloped by their gaze. Arrived at the end of the gallery, she joined a group of ladies who were talking and fanning themselves excitedly under the fresco of Perseus turning Phineus to stone. They were the Princess di Ferentino, Hortensa Massa d'Alba, the Marchesa Daddi-Tosinghi and Bianca Dolcebuono.

'Why so late?' asked the latter.

'I hesitated very much whether to come at all—I don't feel well.'

'Yes, you look very pale.'

'I believe I am going to have neuralgia badly again, like last year.'

'Heaven forefend!'

'Elena, do look at Madame de la Boissière,' exclaimed Giovanella Daddi in her queer husky voice; 'doesn't she look like a camel with a yellow wig!'

'Mademoiselle Vanloo is losing her head over your cousin,' said Hortensa Massa d'Alba to the Princess as Sophie Vanloo passed on Ludovico Barbarisi's arm. 'I heard her say just now when they passed me in the mazurka—*Ludovic, ne faites plus ça en dansant; je frissonne toute——*'

The ladies laughed in chorus, fluttering their fans. The first notes of a Hungarian waltz floated in from the next room. The gentlemen came to claim their partners. At last Andrea was able to offer Elena his arm and carry her off.

'I thought I should have died waiting for you! If you had not come I should have gone to find you—anywhere. When I saw you come in I could scarcely repress a cry. This is only the second evening I have met you, and yet I feel as if I had loved you for years. The thought of you and you alone is now the life of my life.'

He uttered his burning words of love in a low voice, looking straight before him, and she listened in a similar attitude, apparently quite impassive, almost stony. Only a sprinkling of people remained in the gallery. Between the busts of the Cæsars along the walls, lamps with milky globes shaped like lilies shed an even, tempered light. The profusion of palms and flowering plants gave the whole place the look of a sumptuous conservatory. The music floated through the warm-scented air under the vaulted roof and over all this mythology like a breeze though an enchanted garden.

'Can you love me?' he asked; 'tell me if you think you can ever love me.'

'I came only for you,' she returned slowly.

'Tell me that you will love me,' he repeated, while every drop of blood seemed to rush in a tumult of joy to his heart.

'Perhaps——' she answered, and she looked into his face with that same look which, on the preceding evening, had seemed to hold a divine promise, that ineffable gaze which acts like the velvet touch of a loving hand. Neither of them spoke; they listened to the sweet and fitful strains of the music, now slow and faint as a zephyr, now loud and rushing like a sudden tempest.

'Shall we dance?' he asked with a secret tremor of delight at the prospect of encircling her with his arm.

She hesitated a moment before replying. 'No; I would rather not.'

Then, seeing the Duchess of Bugnare, her aunt, entering the gallery with the Princess Alberoni and the French ambassadress, she added hurriedly, 'Now—be prudent, and leave me.'

She held out her gloved hand to him and advanced alone to meet the ladies with a light firm step. Her long white train lent an additional grace to her figure, the wide and heavy folds of brocade serving to accentuate the slenderness of her waist. Andrea, as he followed her with his eyes, kept repeating her words to himself, 'I came for you alone—I came for you alone!' The orchestra suddenly took up the waltz measure with a fresh impetus. And never, through all his life, did he forget that music, nor the attitude of the woman he loved, nor the sumptuous folds of the brocade trailing over the floor, nor the faintest shadow on the rich material, nor one single detail of that supreme moment.

CHAPTER V

ELENA left the Farnese palace very soon after this, almost
stealthily, without taking leave of Andrea or of any one else.
She had therefore not stayed more than half an hour at the
ball. Her lover searched for her through all the rooms in
vain. The next morning, he sent a servant to the Palazzo
Barberini to inquire after the duchess, and learned from him
that she was ill. In the evening he went in person, hoping
to be received ; but a maid informed him that her mistress
was in great pain and could see no one. On the Saturday,
towards five o'clock, he came back once more, still hoping for
better luck.

He left his house on foot. The evening was chill and
gray, and a heavy leaden twilight was settling over the city.
The lamps were already lighted round the fountain in the
Piazza Barberini like pale tapers round a funeral bier, and the
Triton, whether being under repair or for some other reason,
had ceased to spout water. Down the sloping roadway came
a line of carts drawn by two or three horses harnessed in
single file, and bands of workmen returning home from the
new buildings. A group of these came swaying along arm in
arm, singing a lewd song at the pitch of their voices.

Andrea stopped to let them pass. Two or three of the
debased, weather-beaten faces impressed themselves on his
memory. He noticed that a carter had his hand wrapped
in a blood-stained bandage, and that another, who was
kneeling in his cart, had the livid complexion, deep sunken
eyes and convulsively contracted mouth of a man who has
been poisoned. The words of the song were mingled with

44

guttural cries, the cracking of whips, the grinding of wheels, the jingling of horse bells and shrill discordant laughter.

His mental depression increased. He found himself in a very curious mood. The sensibility of his nerves was so acute that the most trivial impression conveyed to them by external means assumed the gravity of a wound. While one fixed thought occupied and tormented his spirit, the rest of his being was left exposed to the rude jostling of surrounding circumstances. Groups of sensations rushed with lightning rapidity across his mental field of vision, like the phantasmagoria of a magic lantern, startling and alarming him. The banked-up clouds of evening, the form of the Triton surrounded by the cadaverous lights, this sudden descent of savage looking men and huge animals, these shouts and songs and curses aggravated his condition, arousing a vague terror in his heart, a foreboding of disaster.

A closed carriage drove out of the palace garden. He caught a glimpse of a lady bowing to him, but he failed to recognise her. The palace rose up before him, vast as some royal residence. The windows of the first floor gleamed with violet reflections, a pale strip of sunset sky rested just above it; a brougham was turning away from the door.

'If I could but see her!' he thought to himself, standing still for a moment. He lingered, purposely to prolong his uncertainty and his hope. Shut up in this immense edifice she seemed to him immeasurably far away—lost to him.

The brougham stopped, and a gentleman put his head out of the window and called—'Andrea!'

It was the Duke of Grimiti, a near relative of his.

'Going to call on the Scerni?' asked the duke with a significant smile.

'Yes,' answered Andrea, 'to inquire after her—she is ill, you know.'

'Yes, I know—I have just come from there. She is better.'

'Does she receive?'

'Me—no. But she may perhaps receive you.' And

Grimiti laughed maliciously through the smoke of his cigarette.

'I don't understand,' Andrea answered coldly.

'Bah!' said the duke. 'Report says you are high in favour. I heard it last night at the Pallavicinis', from a lady, a great friend of yours—give you my word!'

Andrea turned on his heel with a gesture of impatience.

'*Bonne chance!*' cried the duke.

Andrea entered the portico. In reality he was delighted and flattered that such a report should be circulated already. Grimiti's words had suddenly revived his courage like a draught of some cordial. As he mounted the steps, his hopes rose high. He waited for a moment at the door to allow his excitement to calm down a little. Then he rang.

The servant recognised him and said at once: 'If the Signor Conte will have the kindness to wait a moment I will go and inform *Mademoiselle.*'

He nodded assent, and began pacing the vast ante-chamber, which seemed to echo the violent beating of his heart. Hanging lamps of wrought iron shed an uncertain light over the stamped leather panelling of the walls, the carved oak chests, the antique busts on pedestals. Under a magnificently embroidered baldachin blazed the ducal arms: a unicorn on a field gules. A bronze card-tray, heaped with cards, stood in the middle of a table, and happening to cast his eye over them, Andrea noticed the one which Grimiti had just left lying on the top—*Bonne chance!*—The ironical augury still rang in his ears.

Mademoiselle now made her appearance. 'The duchess is feeling a little better,' she said. 'I think the Signor Conte might see her for a moment. This way, if you please.'

She was a woman past her first youth, rather thin and dressed in black, with a pair of gray eyes that glittered curiously under the curls of her false fringe. Her step and her movements generally were light, not to say furtive, as of one who is in the habit of attending upon invalids or of executing secret orders.

'This way, Signor Conte.'

She preceded Andrea though the long flight of dimly-lighted rooms, the thick soft carpets deadening every sound ; and even through the almost uncontrollable tumult of his soul, the young man was conscious of an instinctive feeling of repulsion against her, without being able to assign an adequate reason for it.

Arrived in front of a door concealed by two pieces of tapestry of the Medicean period, bordered with deep red velvet, she stopped.

'I will go first and announce you. Please to wait here.'

A voice from within, which he recognised as Elena's, called, 'Christina !'

At the sound of her voice coming thus unexpectedly, Andrea began to tremble so violently that he thought to himself—'I am sure I am going to faint.' He had a dim presentiment of some more than mortal happiness in store for him which should exceed his utmost expectations, his wildest dreams—almost beyond his powers to support. She was there—on the other side of that door. All perception of reality deserted him. It seemed to him that he had already imagined—in some picture, some poem—a similar adventure, under the self-same circumstances, with these identical surroundings and enveloped in the same mystery, but of which *another*—some fiction of his own brain—was the hero. And now, by some strange trick of the imagination, the fictitious was confounded with the real, causing him an indescribable sense of confusion and bewilderment. On each of the pieces of tapestry was a large symbolical figure—Silence and Slumber—two Genii, tall and slender, which might have been designed by Primaticcio of Bologna, guarding the door. And he —he himself—stood before the door waiting, and on the other side of it was his divine lady. He almost thought he could hear her breathe.

At last Mademoiselle returned.   Holding back the heavy draperies she smiled, and in a low voice said :

'Please go in.'

She effaced herself, and Andrea entered the room.

He noticed first of all that the air was very hot, almost stifling, and that there was a strong odour of chloroform. Then, through the semi-darkness, he became aware of something red—the crimson of the wall paper and the curtains of the bed—and then he heard Elena's languid voice murmuring, 'Thank you so much for coming, Andrea—I feel better now.'

He made his way to her with some difficulty, being unable to distinguish things very clearly in the half light.

She smiled wanly at him from among the pillows out of the gloom.   Across her forehead and round her face, like a nun's wimple, lay a band of white linen which was scarcely whiter than the cheeks it encircled, such was her extreme pallor. The outer angles of her eyelids were contracted by the pain of her inflamed nerves, the lower lids quivering spasmodically from time to time, and the eyes were dewy and infinitely melting, as if veiled by a mist of unshed tears under the trembling lashes.

A flood of pity and tenderness swept over the young man's heart when he came close to her and could see her clearly. Very slowly she drew one hand from under the coverlet and held it out to him.   He bent over it till he half knelt on the edge of the couch and rained kisses thick and fast upon that burning, fevered hand, and the white wrist with its hurrying pulse.

'Elena—Elena—my love ! '

Elena had closed her eyes, as if to resign herself more wholly to the ecstasy that penetrated to the most hidden fibre of her being.   Then she turned her hand over that she might feel those kisses on her palm, on each finger, all round her wrist, on every vein, in every pore.

'Enough ! ' she murmured at last, opening her eyes again, and passed her languid hand softly over Andrea's hair.

Her caress, though light, was so ineffably tender, that to

the lover's soul it had the effect of a rose leaf falling into a full cup of water. His passion brimmed over. His lips trembled under a confused torrent of words which rose to them but which he could not express. He had the violent and divine sensation as of a new life spreading in widening circles round him beyond all physical perception.

'What bliss!' said Elena, repeating her fond gesture, and a tremor ran through her whole person, visible through the coverlet.

But when Andrea made as if to take her hand again—'No,' she entreated, 'do not move—stay as you are, I like to have you so.'

She gently pressed his head down till his cheek lay against her knee. She gazed at him a little, still with that caressing touch upon his head, and then in a voice that seemed to faint with ecstasy she murmured, lingering over the syllables—

'How I love you!'

There was an ineffable seduction in the way she pronounced the words—so liquid, so enthralling on a woman's lips.

'Again!' whispered her lover, whose senses were languishing with passion under the touch of those hands, the sound of that caressing voice. 'Say it again—go on speaking.'

'I love you,' repeated Elena, noticing that his eyes were fixed upon her lips, and being perhaps aware of the fascination that emanated from them while pronouncing the words.

With a sudden movement she raised herself from the pillows, and taking Andrea's head between her two hands, she drew him to her, and their lips met in a long and passionate kiss.

Afterwards she fell back again, and lying with her arms stretched straight along the coverlet at her sides, she gazed at Andrea with wide open eyes, while one by one the great tears gathered slowly, and silently rolled down her cheeks.

'What is it, Elena—tell me—What is it?' asked her lover, clasping her hands and leaning over her to kiss away the tears.

She clenched her teeth and bit her lips to keep back the sobs.

'Nothing—nothing—go now, leave me—please! You shall see me to-morrow—go now.'

Her voice and her look were so imploring that Andrea obeyed.

'Goodbye,' he said, and kissed her tenderly on the lips, carrying away upon his own the taste of her salt tears. 'Goodbye! Love me—and do not forget.'

As he crossed the threshold, he seemed to hear her break into sobs behind him. He went on a little unsteadily, like a man who is not sure of his sight. The odour of chloroform lingered in his nostrils like the fumes of an intoxicating vapour ; but, with every step he took, some virtue seemed to go out of him, to be dissipated in the air. The rooms lay empty and silent before him. 'Mademoiselle' appeared at a door without any warning sound of steps or rustle of garments, like a ghost.

'This way, Signor Conte, you will not be able to find your way.'

She smiled in an ambiguous and irritating manner, her gray eyes glittering with ill-concealed curiosity. Andrea did not speak. Once more the presence of this woman annoyed and disturbed him, arousing an undefined sense of repulsion and anger in him.

No sooner was he outside the door than he drew a deep breath like a man relieved from some heavy burden. The gentle splash of the fountain came through the trees, broken now and then by some clearer, louder sound ; the whole firmament glittered with stars, veiled here and there by long trailing strips of cloud like tresses of pale hair ; carriage lamps flitted rapidly hither and thither, the life of the great city sent up its breath into the keen air, bells were ringing far and near. . At last, he had the full consciousness of his overwhelming felicity.

CHAPTER VI

THUS began for them a bliss that was full, frenzied, for ever changing and for ever new; a passion that wrapped them round and rendered them oblivious of all that did not minister immediately to their mutual delight.

'What a strange love!' Elena said once, recalling those first days—her illness, her rapid surrender—'My heart was yours from the first moment I saw you.'

She felt a certain pride in the fact.

'And when, on that evening, I heard my name announced immediately after yours,' her lover replied, 'I don't know why, but I suddenly had the firm conviction that my life was bound to yours—for ever!'

And they really believed what they said. Together they re-read Goethe's Roman elegy—*Lass dich, Geliebte, nicht reu'n, dass du mir so schnell dich ergeben!*—Have no regrets, my Beloved, that thou didst yield thee so soon—'Believe me, dearest, I do not attribute one base or impure thought to you. Cupid's darts have varying effects—some inflict but a slight scratch, and the poison they insinuate lingers for years before it really touches the heart, while others, well feathered and armed with a sharp and penetrating point, pierce to the heart's core at once and send the fever racing through the blood. In the old heroic days of the loves of the gods and goddesses desire followed upon sight. Think you that the goddess of Love considered long in the grove of Ida that day Anchises found favour in her eyes? And Luna?—had she hesitated, envious Aurora would soon have wakened her handsome shepherd.'

For them, as for Faustina's divine singer, Rome was

illumined by a new light. Wherever their footsteps strayed
they left a memory of love. The forgotten churches of the
Aventine—Santa Sabina with its wonderful columns of Parian
marble, the charming garden of Santa Maria del Priorata, the
campanile of Santa Maria in Cosmedin piercing the azure
with its slender rose-coloured spire grew to know them well.
The villas of the cardinals and the princes—the Villa Pamfili mirrored in its fountains and its lakes, all sweetness
and grace, where every shady grove seems to harbour some
noble idyll ; the Villa Albani, cold and silent as a church,
with its avenues of sculptured marble and centenarian trees ;
where in the vestibules, under the porticos and between the
granite pillars, Caryatides and Hermes, symbols of immobility,
gaze at the immutable symmetry of the verdant lawns ; and
the Villa Medici—like a forest of emerald green spreading
away in a fairy tale, and the Villa Ludovici—a little wild—
redolent of violets, consecrated by the presence of that Juno
adored by Goethe in the days when the plane-trees and the
cypresses, that one might well have thought immortal, had
already begun to tremble with the foreboding of sale and
death—all the patrician villas, the crowning glory of Rome,
became well acquainted with their love. The picture and
sculpture galleries too—the room in the Borghese where,
before Correggio's 'Danae' Elena smiled as at her own reflection ; and the Mirror Room, where her image glided among
the Cupids of Ciro Ferri and the garlands of Mario de' Fiori ;
the chamber of Heliodorus, where Raphael has succeeded in
making the dull walls throb and palpitate with life ; and the
apartments of the Borgias, where the great fantasia of Pentu-
ricchio unfolds its marvellous web of history, fable, dreams,
caprices and audacities ; and the Galatea Room, through
which is diffused an ineffable freshness, a perennial serenity
of light and grace ; and the room where the Hermaphrodite,
that gentle monster, offspring of the loves of a nymph and a
demi-god, extends his ambiguous form amidst the sparkle of
polished stone—all these unfrequented abodes of Beauty were
well acquainted with them.

They echoed fervently the sublime cry of the poet—*Eine Welt zwar bist du, O Rom!* Thou art a world in thyself, oh Rome! But as without love the world would not be the world, so Rome without love would not be Rome, and the stairway of the Trinità, glorified by the slow ascension of the Day, became the Stairway of Felicity by the ascent of Elena the Fair on her way to the Palazzo Zuccari.

'At times,' Elena said to him, 'my feeling for you is so delicate, so profound, that it becomes——how shall I describe it?—maternal almost!'

Andrea laughed, for she was his senior by barely three years.

'And at times,' he rejoined, 'I feel the communion of our spirits to be so chaste that I could call you sister while I kiss your hands.'

These fallacious ideas of purity and loftiness of sentiment were but the reaction after more carnal delights, when the soul experiences a vague yearning for the ideal. At such times too, the young man's aspirations towards the art he so much loved were apt to revive. The desire to give pleasure to his mistress by his literary or artistic efforts drove him to work. He accordingly wrote *La Simona*, and executed his two engravings: *The Zodiac* and *Alexander's Bowl*.

For the execution of his art, he chose by preference, the most difficult, exact, and incorruptible vehicles—verse and engraving; and he aimed at adhering strictly to, and reviving, the traditional Italian methods, by going back to the poets of the *stil novo*, and the painters who were precursors of the Renaissance. His tendencies were essentially towards form; his mind more occupied by the expression of his thought than the thought itself. Like Taine, he considered it a greater achievement to write three really fine lines, than to win a pitched battle. His *Story of the Hermaphrodite* imitated in its structure Poligiano's *Story of Orpheus* and contained lines of extraordinary delicacy, power and melody, particularly in the choruses of hybrid monsters—the Centaurs, Sirens and Sphinxes. His new tragedy, *La Simona*, of moderate length, possessed a most singular charm. Written and rhymed though it was, on the ancient Tuscan rules, it might have been conceived by an English poet of Elizabeth's time, after a story from the *Decameron,* and it breathed something of the strange and delicious charm of certain of the minor dramas of Shakespeare.

On the frontispiece of the single copy, the author had signed his work : A. S. CALCOGRAPHUS AQUA FORTI SIBI TIBI FECIT.

Copper had greater attractions for him than paper, nitric acid than ink, the graving-tool than the pen. One of his ancestors before him, Giusto Sperelli, had tried his hand at engraving. Certain plates of his, executed about 1520, showed distinct evidences of the influence of Antonio del Pollajuolo by the depth and acidity, so to speak, of the design. Andrea used the Rembrandt method *a tratti liberi* and the *maniera nera* so much affected by the English engravers of the school of Green, Dixon, and Earlom. He had formed himself on all models, had studied separately the effects sought after by each engraver, had schooled himself under Albrecht Dürer and Parmigianino, Marc' Antonio and Holbein, Hannibal Carracci, MacArdell, Guido, Toschi and Audran ; but once his copper plate before him, his one aim was to light up, by Rembrandtesque effects, the elegance in design of the fifteenth-century Florentines of the second generation, such as Botticelli, Ghirlandajo and Filippino Lippi.

One of Andrea's most precious possessions was a bed-cover of finest silk in faded blue, round the border of which circled the twelve signs of the Zodiac, each with its appropriate legend : Aries, Taurus, Gemini, Cancer, Leo, Virgo, Libra, Scorpio, Sagittarius, Capricornus, Aquarius, Pisces—in gothic characters. A flaming golden sun occupied the centre ; the animal figures, drawn in somewhat archaic style, as one sees in mosaics, were extraordinarily brilliant. The whole thing was worthy to grace an Emperor's bed, and had, in fact, formed part of the trousseau of Bianca Maria Sforza, niece of Ludovico the Moor, when she espoused the Emperor Maximilian.

One of the engravings represented Elena asleep under this celestial counterpane. The rounded limbs appeared outlined under the silken folds, the head thrown carelessly back towards the edge of the couch, the hair rippling in a torrent to the floor, one arm hanging down, the other stretched along her side. The parts which were left uncovered, the face, the neck, the shoulders, and the arms, were extremely luminous, and the stile had reproduced most effectively the glitter of the embroidery in the half-light and the mysterious quality of the symbols. A tall white hound, Famulus, brother to the one which lays its head on the knee of the Countess of Arundel in Rubens' picture, stretched his muzzle towards the lady, guarding her slumbers, and was designed with much felicitous boldness of foreshortening. The background of the room was sumptuous and shadowy.

The other engraving referred to an immense silver basin which Elena had inherited from her aunt Flaminia.

This basin was historical, and was known as Alexander's Bowl. It had been given to the Princess of Bisenti by Caesar Borgia on his departure for France, when he went to carry the Papal Bill of divorce and dispensation to Louis xii. The design for the figures running round it and the two which rose over the edge at either side were attributed to Raphael.

It was called the Bowl of Alexander because it purported to be a reproduction of the prodigious vessel out of which the famous King of Macedonia was wont to drink at his splendid festivals. Groups of archers surrounded its base, their bows stretched, in the admirable attitudes of those painted by Raphael aiming their arrows at Hermes in the fresco of that room in the Borghese decorated by John of Bologna. They were in pursuit of a great Chimera, which emerged over the edge of the bowl in guise of a handle, while on the opposite side bounded the youthful Bellerophon, his bow at full stretch against the monster. The ornaments of the base and the edge were of rare elegance. The inside was gilded, the metal sonorous as a bell, and weighed three hundred pounds. Its shape was extremely harmonious.

Never had Andrea Sperelli experienced so intensely both the delight and the anxiety of the artist who watches the blind and irreparable action of the acid ; never before had he brought so much patience to bear upon the delicate work of the dry point. The fact was, that like Lucas of Leyden, he was a born engraver, possessed of an admirable knowledge, or, more properly speaking, a rare instinct as to the most minute particularity of time and degree, which may aid in varying the efficacy of the acid on copper. It was not only practice, industry, and intelligence, but more especially this inborn, well-nigh infallible instinct which warned him of the exact instant at which the corrosion had proceeded far enough to give such and such a value to the shadows as, in the artist's intention, the engraving required. It was just this triumph of mind over matter, this power of infusing an æsthetic spirit into it, as it were, this mysterious correspondence between the throb of his pulses and the progressive gnawing of the acid that was his pride, his torment, and his joy.

In his dedication of these works to her, Elena felt herself deified by her lover as was Isotta di Rimini by the medals which Sigismondo Malatesta caused to be struck in her honour ; and yet, on those days when Andrea was at work, she would become moody and taciturn, as if under the influence of some secret grief, or she would give way to such sudden bursts of tenderness, mingled with tears and half-suppressed sobs, that the young man was startled and, not understanding her, became suspicious.

One evening, they were returning on horseback from the Aventine down the Via di Santa Sabina, their eyes still filled with a vision of imperial palaces flaming under the setting sun that burned red through the cypresses and seemed to cover them with golden dust. They rode in silence, for Elena seemed out of spirits, and her depression had communicated itself to her lover. As they passed the church of Santa Sabina, Andrea reined up his horse.

'Do you remember?' he said.

Some fowls, picking about peacefully in the grass, skurried away at the barking of Famulus. The whole place was as quiet and unassuming as the purlieus of a village church, but the walls had that singular luminous glow which the buildings of Rome seem to give out at 'Titian's hour.'

Elena drew up beside him.

'That day—how long ago it seems now!' she said with a little tremor in her voice.

In truth, the memory of it had already dropped away into the gulf of time as if their love had endured for years. Elena's words raised that illusion in Andrea's mind, but, at the same time, a certain uneasiness. She began recalling the details of their visit to Santa Sabina one afternoon in January under a prematurely mild sun. She dwelt insistently upon the most trivial incidents, breaking off from time to time as if following a separate train of thought, distinct from the words she uttered. Andrea fancied he caught a note of regret in her voice. Yet, what had she to regret? Surely their love had many a sweeter day before it still—the Spring had come again to Rome. Doubting and perplexed, he ceased to listen to her. The horses went on down the hill at a walk, side by side, snorting noisily from time to time, and putting their heads together, as if exchanging confidences. Famulus sped on before, or bounded after them, perpetually on the gallop.

'Do you remember,' Elena went on, 'do you. remember the Brother who came to open the gates for us when we rang the bell?'

'Yes—yes.'

'And how perfectly aghast he looked when he saw who it was? He was such a little, little red-faced man without any beard. When he went to get the keys of the church, he left us alone in the vestibule—and you kissed me—do you remember?'

'Yes.'

'And all those barrels in the vestibule! And the smell of wine while the Brother was explaining the legends carved on

the cypress-wood door. And then about the Madonna of the
Rosary—do you remember?—his explanation made you laugh,
and I could not help laughing too, and the poor man was so
put out, that he would not open his mouth again, not even to
thank you at the last——'

There was a little pause. Then she began again.

'And at Sant' Alexio, where you would not let me look at
the cupola through the keyhole. How we laughed then
too!'

Renewed silence. Along the road towards them came a
party of men carrying a coffin, and followed by a hired
conveyance full of tearful relatives. They were on their way
to the Jewish cemetery. It was a grim and silent funeral.
The men with their hooked noses and rapacious eyes were all
as like one another as brothers. The two horses separated to
let the procession pass, keeping close to the wall on either
side, and the lovers looked at each other across the dead,
their spirits sinking lower with every moment.

When presently they rejoined one another, Andrea said—
'Tell me—what is the matter? What is on your mind?'

She hesitated a moment before replying, keeping her eyes
on her horse's neck and stroking it with the end of her riding
whip, irresolute and very pale.

'You have something on your mind,' persisted the young
man.

'Very well then—yes—and I had better tell you and get it
over. I am going away next Wednesday. I do not know
for how long—perhaps for a long time—perhaps for ever. I
cannot say. We must break with one another. It is entirely
my fault. But do not ask me why—do not ask me anything,
I entreat you—I could not answer you.'

Andrea looked at her incredulously. The thing seemed
to him so utterly impossible that it did not affect him
painfully.

'Of course you are only joking, Elena?'

She shook her head; there was a lump in her throat, and
she could not speak. She suddenly set her horse into a trot.

Behind them the bells of Santa Sabina and Santa Prisca began to ring through the twilight. They trotted on in silence, awakening the echoes under the arches and among the temples—all the solitary and desolate ruins on their way. They passed San Giorgio in Velabo on their left, which still retained a gleam of rosy light on its campanile; they passed the Roman Forum, the Forum of Nerva already full of blue shadow like that which hovers over the glaciers at night, and stopped at last at the Arco dei Pantani, where their grooms and carriages awaited them.

Hardly was Elena out of the saddle, than she held out her hand to Andrea without meeting his eyes. She seemed in a great hurry to be gone.

'Well?' said Andrea as he helped her into the carriage.

'To-morrow—not this evening—I cannot——'

CHAPTER VII

THE Campagna stretched away before them under an ideal light, as a landscape seen in dreams, where the objects seem visible at a great distance by virtue of some inward irradiation which magnifies their outlines.

The closed carriage rolled along smoothly at a brisk trot; the walls of ancient patrician villas, grayish-white and dim, slid past the windows with a continuous and gentle motion. Great iron gateways came in view from time to time, through which you caught a glimpse of an avenue of lofty beech trees, or some verdant cloister inhabited by antique statues, or a long green arcade pierced here and there by a laughing ray of pale sunshine.

Wrapped in her ample furs, her veil drawn down, her hands encased in thick chamois leather gloves, Elena sat and mutely watched the passing landscape. Andrea breathed with delight the subtle perfume of heliotrope exhaled by the costly fur, while he felt Elena's arm warm against his own. They felt themselves far from the haunts of men—alone—although from time to time the black carriage of a priest would flit past them, or a drover on horseback, or a herd of cattle.

Just before they reached the bridge she said—'Let us get out here.'

Here in the open country the light was translucent and cold as the waters of a spring, and when the trees waved in the wind their undulation seemed to communicate itself to all the surrounding objects.

She clung close to his arm, stumbling a little on the uneven ground. 'I am going away this evening,' she said,—'this is the last time——'

There was a moment's silence; then in plaintive tones, and with frequent pauses in between, she began to speak of the necessity of her departure, the necessity of their rupture. The wind wrenched the words from her lips, but she continued in spite of it, till Andrea interrupted her by seizing her hand.

'Don't!' he cried—'be quiet.'

They walked on struggling against the fierce gusts of wind.

'Don't go—don't leave me! I want you—want you always.'

He had managed to unfasten her glove and laid hold of her bare wrist with a caressing insistent clasp that was full of tormenting desire.

She threw him one of those glances that intoxicate like wine. They were quite near the bridge now, all rosy under the setting sun. The river looked motionless and steely throughout its sinuous length. Reeds swayed and shivered on the banks, and some stakes, fixed in the clay of the river-bed to fasten nets, shook with the motion of the water.

He then endeavoured to move her by reminiscences. He recalled those first days—the ball at the Farnese palace, a certain hunting party out in the Campagna, their early morning meetings in the Piazza di Spagna in front of the jewellers' windows, or in the quiet and aristocratic Via Sistina when she came out of the Barberini palace followed by the flower girls offering her baskets of roses.

'Do you remember—do you remember?'

'Yes.'

'And that evening—quite at the beginning, when I brought in such a mass of flowers.—You were alone—beside the window—reading. You remember?'

'Yes—yes.'

'I came in. You scarcely turned your head and you spoke quite harshly to me—what was the matter?—I do not know. I laid the flowers upon the tables and waited. You spoke of trivial things at first, with indifference—without interest. I thought to myself bitterly—"She is tired of me already—she does not love me." But the scent of the flowers was

very strong—the room was full of it. I can see you now—
how you suddenly seized the whole mass in your two hands
and buried your face in it, drinking in the perfume. When
you lifted it again all the blood seemed to have left your face,
and your eyes were swimming in a kind of ecstasy——'

'Go on—go on!' said Elena feverishly, as she leaned over
the parapet fascinated by the rushing waters below.

'Afterwards, you remember on the sofa—I smothered you
in flowers—your face, your bosom, your shoulders, and you
raised yourself out of them every moment to offer me your
lips, your throat, your half closed lids. And between your
skin and my lips I felt the rose leaves soft and cool. I
kissed your throat and a shiver ran through you, and you put
out your hands to keep me away.—Oh, then—your head was
sunk in the cushions, your breast hidden under the roses,
your arms bare to the elbow—nothing in this world could be
so dear and sweet as the little tremor of your white hands
upon my temples—do you remember?'

'Yes—go on.'

He went on with ever-increasing fervour. Carried away
by his own eloquence, he was hardly conscious of what he
said. Elena, her back turned to the light, leaned nearer and
nearer to him. Under them the river flowed cold and silent ;
long slender rushes, like strands of hair, bent with every gust
and trailed on the surface of the water.

He had ceased to speak, but they were gazing into one
another's eyes and their ears were filled with a low continuous murmur which seemed to carry away part of their life's
being—as if something sonorous had escaped from their very
brains and were spreading away in waves of sound till it filled
the whole air about them.

Elena rose from her stooping posture. 'Let us go on,'
she said. 'I am so thirsty—where can we get some water?'
They crossed the bridge to a little inn on the other side, in
front of which some carters were unharnessing their horses
with much lively invective. The setting sun lit up the group
of men and beasts vividly.

The people at the inn showed not the faintest sign of surprise at the entry of the two strangers. Two or three men shivering with ague, ˉmorose and jaundiced, were crouching round a square brazier. A red-haired bullock-driver was snoring in a corner, his empty pipe still between his teeth. A pair of haggard, ill-conditioned young vaga-bonds were playing at cards, fixing one another in the pauses with a look of tigerish eagerness. The woman of the inn, corpulent to obesity, carried in her arms a child which she rocked heavily to and fro.

While Elena drank the water out of a rude earthenware mug, the woman, with wails and plaints, drew her attention to the wretched infant.

'Look, signora mia—look at it!'

The poor little creature was wasted to a skeleton, its lips purple and broken out, the inside of its mouth coated with a white eruption. It looked as if life had abandoned the miserable little body, leaving but a little substance for fungoid growths to flourish in.

'Feel, dear lady,—its hands are icy cold. It cannot eat, it cannot drink—it does not sleep any more——'

The mother broke into loud sobs. The ague-stricken men looked on with eyes full of utter prostration, while the sound of the weeping only drew an impatient movement from the two youths.

'Come away—come away!' said Andrea, taking Elena by the arm and dragging her away, after throwing a piece of money on the table.

They returned over the bridge. The river was lighted up by the flames of the dying day, and in the distance the water looked smooth and glistening as if great spots of oil or bitumen were floating on it. The Campagna, stretching away like an ocean of ruins, was of a uniform violet tint. Nearer the town the sky flushed a deep crimson.

'Poor little thing!' murmured Elena in a tone of heartfelt compassion, and pressing closer to Andrea.

The wind had risen to a gale. A flock of crows swept

across the burning heavens, very high up, croaking hoarsely.

A sudden passionate exaltation suddenly filled the souls of the two at sight of this vast solitude. Something tragic and heroic seemed to enter into their love and the hill-tops of their passion to catch the blaze of the stormy sunset. Elena stood still.

'I can go no further,' she gasped.

The carriage was still at some distance, standing motionless where they had left it.

'A little further, Elena, just a step or two! Shall I carry you?'

Then, seized with a sort of frenzy, he burst out again— Why was she going away? Why did she want to break with him? Surely their destinies were indissolubly knit together now? He could not live without her—without her eyes, her voice, the constant thought of her. He was saturated through and through with love of her—his whole blood was on fire as with some deadly poison. Why was she running away from him?—He would hold her fast—would suffocate her on his heart first——No—it could not, must not be—never!

Elena listened, with bent head to meet the blast, but she did not answer. Presently she raised her hand and beckoned to the coachman. The horses pawed and pranced as they started.

'Stop at the Porta Pia,' she called to the man, and entered the carriage with her lover. Then she turned and with a sudden gesture yielded herself to his desire, and he kissed her greedily—her lips, her brow, her hair, her eyes—rapidly, without giving himself time to breathe.

'Elena! Elena!'

A vivid gleam of crimson light reflected from the red brick houses penetrated the carriage. The ringing trot of several horses came nearer along the road.

Leaning against her lover's shoulder with ineffable tenderness she said—'Good-bye, dear love—good-bye—good-bye!'

As she raised herself again, ten or twelve red-coated

horsemen passed to right and left of the carriage returning from a fox hunt. One of them, the Duke di Beffi, bent low over his saddle to peer in at the window as he rode by.

Andrea said no more. His whole soul was weighed down by hopeless depression. The first impulse of revolt over, the childish weakness of his nature almost led him to give way to tears. He wanted to cast himself at her feet, to humble himself, to beg and entreat, to move this woman to pity by his tears. He felt giddy and confused; a subtle sensation of cold seemed to grip the back of his head and penetrate to the roots of his hair.

'Good-bye,' repeated Elena for the last time, and the carriage stopped under the archway of the Porta Pia to let him get out.

CHAPTER VIII

THEIR final farewells *au grand air*, by Elena's desire, did nothing towards dissipating Andrea's suspicions. 'What could be her secret reasons for this abrupt departure?' He tried in vain to penetrate the mystery; he was oppressed with doubt and fear.

During the first days, the anguish of his loss was so cruelly poignant that he thought he must die of it. His jealousy, lulled to sleep by the persistent ardour of Elena's affection, awoke now with redoubled vigour, and the suspicion that a man was at the bottom of this enigmatical affair increased his sufferings a hundredfold. Sometimes he would be seized with sullen anger against the absent woman, a bitter rancour, almost a desire for revenge, as if she had mystified and duped him in order to give herself to another. Then again he would feel that he did not long for her, did not love her any more, had never loved her. But these fits of oblivion were but of short duration. The Spring had come again to Rome in a riot of colour and sunshine. The city of limestone and brick absorbed the light as a parched forest the rain, the papal fountains rose into a limpid sapphire sky, the Piazza di Spagna was fragrant as a rose-garden, and above the great flight of steps, alive with little children, the Trinità de' Monti shone in a blaze of gold.

Excited by the re-awakened beauty of Rome, all that still remained of Elena's fascination in his blood and his spirit revived and re-kindled. He was stirred to his very depths by sudden invincible pain, by implacable inward tumults, by indefinable languors, almost like some strange renewal of his adolescence.

Andrea's liaison with Elena Muti had been perfectly well known, as sooner or later every adventure and every flirtation becomes known in Roman society, or the society of any other city for the matter of that. Precautions are useless. To the initiated a look, a gesture, a smile suffices to betray the secret. Besides which, in every society there are certain persons who make it their business in life to ferret out and follow up the traces of a love affair with an assiduity only to be equalled by the hunter of rare game. They are ever on the watch, though not apparently so ; never, by any chance, miss a murmured word, the faintest smile, a tremor, a blush, a lightning glance. At balls or any large gatherings, where there is more probability of imprudence, they are ubiquitous, with ear stretched to catch a fragment of dialogue, and eye keenly on the watch to note a stolen hand-clasp, a tremulous sigh, the nervous pressure of delicate fingers on a partner's shoulder.

One such terrible trapper, for example, was Don Filippo del Monte. But to tell the truth, Elena Muti did not trouble herself overmuch about what society said of her, covering her every audacity with the mantle of her beauty, her wealth, and her ancient name ; and she went on her way serenely, surrounded by adulation and homage, by reason of a certain good-natured tolerance which is one of the most pleasing qualities of Roman society, amounting almost to an article of faith.

In any case, Andrea's connection with the Duchess of Scerni had instantly raised him enormously in the estimation of the women. An atmosphere of favour surrounded him, and his successes became astonishing. Moreover, he owed something to his reputation as a mysterious artist, and two sonnets which he wrote in the Princess di Ferentino's album became famous, in which, as in an ambiguous diptych, he lauded in turn a diabolical and an angelic mouth—the one that destroys souls and the other that sings ' Ave ! '

He responded, without a moment's hesitation, to every advance. No longer restrained by Elena's complete dominion over him, his energies returned to their original state of disorder. He passed from one liaison to another with incredible frivolity, carrying on several at the same time, and weaving without scruple a great net of deceptions and lies, in which to catch as much prey as possible. The habit of duplicity undermined his conscience, but one instinct remained alive, implacably alive in him—the repugnance at all this which attracted without holding him captive. His will, as useless to him now as a sword of indifferently tempered steel, hung as if at the side of an inebriated or paralysed man.

One evening, at the Dolcebuonos', when he had outstayed the rest of the guests in the drawing-room, full of flowers and still vibrating with a *Cachoucha* of Raff's, he had spoken of love to Bianca. He did it almost without thinking, attracted instinctively by the reflected charm of her being a· friend of Elena's. Maybe too, that the little germ of sympathy sown in his heart by her kindly championship at the dinner in the Doria palace was now bearing fruit. Who can say by what mysterious process some contact—whether spiritual or material—between a man and a woman may generate and nourish in them a sentiment which, latent and unsuspected for long, may suddenly wake to life through unforeseen circumstances? It is the same phenomenon so often encountered in our mental world, when the germ of an idea or a shadowy fancy suddenly reappears before us after a long interval of unconscious development as a finished picture, a complex thought. The same law governs all the varying activities of our being; and the activities of which we are conscious form but a small part of the whole.

Donna Bianca Dolcebuono was the ideal type of Florentine beauty, such as Ghirlandajo has given us in the portrait of Giovanna Tornabuoni at Santa Maria Novella. Her face was fair and oval, with a broad white brow, a sweet and expressive mouth, a nose a trifle *retroussé*, and eyes of that deep

hazel so dear to Firenzuola.   She was fond of wearing her
hair parted and arranged in full puffs half way over her
cheeks in the quaint old style.   Her name suited her admirably, for into the artificial life of fashionable society she
brought a great natural sweetness of temper, much indulgence for the failings of others, courtesy accorded impartially
to high and low, and a most melodious voice.

On hearing Andrea's hackneyed phrases, she exclaimed in
graceful surprise—

'What, have you forgotten Elena so soon?'

Then after a few days of engaging hesitation, it pleased
her to yield to his solicitations, and she often spoke of Elena
to the faithless young lover, but with perfect frankness and
without jealousy.

'But why did she go away sooner than usual this year?'
she asked him one day with a smile.

'I have no idea,' answered Andrea, not without a touch of
impatience and bitterness.

'Then it is all over between you—quite over?'

'For pity's sake, Bianca, let us talk about ourselves,' he
retorted sharply.   The subject disturbed and irritated him.

She remained pensive for a moment, as if seeking to un-
ravel some enigma, then she smiled and shook her head with
a little fugitive shadow of melancholy in her eyes.

'Such is love!' she sighed, and returned Andrea's kisses.

In her he seemed to possess all those charming women of
whom Lorenzo the Magnificent sang:

> 'And on every side we find,
> Absence, as men say, estranges,
> Fancy ranges as the eye ranges,
> Out of sight is out of mind.
>
> Love departs and is not love:
> As from sight the eye departs
> Even so do hearts from hearts;
> And at other hands we prove
> Fancies rove as the eyes rove,
> Parted pleasures come again.'

When the summer came, and she was on the point of

leaving Rome, she said to him, without seeking to conceal her gentle emotion—

'When we meet again I know you will not love me any more. That is love. But think of me always as a friend.'

He did not love her, certainly ; nevertheless during the heat and tedium of the days that followed, certain cadences of that dulcet voice returned to him like a haunting melody, suggesting visions of a garden, fresh with splashing fountains, where Bianca wandered in company with other fair women playing on the viol and singing as in a vignette of the ' Dream of Polyphilo.'

And Bianca passed and was succeeded by others—sometimes two at a time ; but it was finally the little ivory Death's-head which had belonged to the Cardinal Immenraet, the funereal jewel dedicated to an unknown Ippolita, that suggested to him the caprice of tempting Donna Ippolita Albonico.

CHAPTER IX

DONNA IPPOLITA ALBONICO had a great air of princely
nobility in her whole person, and bore some resemblance to
Maria Maddalena of Austria, wife of Cosimo II. of Medici,
whose portrait by Suttermans is at Florence in the possession
of the Corsinis. She affected a sumptuous style of dress
—brocades, velvets, laces—and the high Medici collars
which seemed the most appropriate setting to her superb and
imperial head.

One day at the races, when seated beside her, Andrea was
suddenly seized with the whim to get her to promise to come
to the Palazzo Zuccari and receive the mysterious little clock
dedicated to her namesake. Hearing his audacious words,
she frowned, wavering between curiosity and prudence; but
as he, nothing daunted, persevered in the attack, an irrepressible smile quivered on her lips. Under the shadow of
her large hat with its white plumes, and with her lace-flounced
parasol as a back-ground, she was marvellously handsome.

'*Tibi, Hippolyta!* Then you will come? I shall be on
the look-out for you all the afternoon, from two o'clock till
evening—Is that settled?'

'You must be mad!'

'What have you to fear? I swear that I will not rob Your
Majesty of so much as a glove. You shall remain seated as
on a throne, as befits your regal state, and even in taking a
cup of tea, you shall not lay aside the invisible sceptre you
carry for ever in your imperial right hand. On these conditions is the grace accorded?'

'No.'

But she smiled nevertheless, flattered by this exaltation of the regal aspect of her beauty, wherein she gloried. And Sperelli continued to tempt her, always in a tone of banter or entreaty, but adding to the seduction of his voice a gaze so subtle, so penetrating and disturbing that, at length, Donna Ippolita, half offended and blushing faintly, said to him—

'I will not have you look at me like that.'

Few persons besides themselves remained upon the stand. Ladies and gentlemen strolled up and down across the grass, along the barrier, or surrounded the victorious horse or the yelling bookmakers, under the inconstant rays of the sun that came and went between the floating archipelago of clouds.

'Let us go down,' she said, unaware of Giannetto Rutolo leaning with watchful eyes upon the railing of the staircase.

As they passed him, Sperelli called back over his shoulder—

'Addio, Marchese—see you again soon. Our race is on directly.'

Rutolo bowed profoundly to Donna Ippolita, and a deep flush rose suddenly to his face. He seemed to have caught a touch of derision in Sperelli's greeting. Leaning on the railing, he followed the retreating couple with hungry eyes. He was obviously suffering.

'Rutolo, be on your guard!' said the Contessa di Lucoli with a malicious laugh as she passed down the stairs on the arm of Don Filippo del Monte.

The blow struck home. Donna Ippolita and the Conte d'Ugenta having penetrated as far as the umpire's stand were now retracing their steps. The lady held her sunshade over her shoulder, twirling the handle languidly in her fingers; the white cupola stood out round her head like a halo, and the lace frills rose and fluttered incessantly. Within this revolving circle, she laughed from time to time at what her companion said, and a delicate flush stained the noble pallor of her face. Sometimes they would both stand still.

Under pretext of examining the horses now entering the race-course, Giannetto turned his field-glass upon the two.

His hands trembled visibly. Every smile, every movement, every glance of Ippolita's was a sword-thrust in his heart. When he dropped his glass, he was deadly pale. He had surprised a look in the eyes that met Sperelli's which he knew full well of old. Everything seemed crumbling to ruins around him. The love of years was over—irrevocably lost— slain by that glance. The sun was the sun no longer, life was not life any more.

The grand stand was rapidly refilling; the signal for the third race was about to be given. The ladies stood up on their seats. A murmur ran along the tiers like a breeze over a sloping garden. The bell rang. The horses started like a flight of arrows.

'I shall ride in your honour, Donna Ippolita,' said Andrea Sperelli as he took leave of her to get ready for the next race, which was for gentlemen riders—' *Tibi, Hippolyta, Semper !* '

She pressed his hand warmly for luck, never remembering that Giannetto Rutolo was also among the competitors. When, a moment later, she noticed him going down the stairs, pale and alone, the unconcealed cruelty of indifference shone in her beautiful dark eyes. The old love had fallen away from her like a useless garment, and had given place to the new. This man was nothing to her, had no claims of any kind upon her now that she no longer loved him. It is inconceivable how quickly a woman regains entire possession of her own heart once she has ceased to love a man.

'He has stolen her from me!' he thought to himself, as he made his way to the Jockey Club tent, and the grass seemed to give beneath his feet like sand. At a little distance in front of him walked the other with a firm and elastic step. In his long gray overcoat his tall and shapely figure had that peculiar and inimitable air of elegance which only breeding can give. He was smoking, and Giannetto Rutolo, coming up behind him, caught the delicate aroma of the cigarette with every puff, causing him an intolerable nausea as if it had been poison.

The Duke di Beffi and Paolo Caligaro were at the entrance,

already in racing dress. The duke was making gymnastic movements to test the elasticity of his leather breeches and the strength of his knees. Little Caligaro was execrating last night's rain, which had made the ground heavy.

'You have a very good chance with *Miching Mallecho*, I consider,' he remarked to Sperelli when he came up.

Giannetto Rutolo heard this forecast with a bitter pang. He had founded a vague hope on the event of his own victory. He represented to himself the advantage he might gain over his enemy by a victorious race and a successful duel. As he changed his clothes his every movement betrayed his preoccupation.

'Here is a man who before getting on horseback sees the grave open before him,' said the duke, laying his hand on the young man's shoulder with a serio-comic air—'*Ecce homo novus.*'

Andrea Sperelli, who felt in the best of spirits at that moment, gave vent to one of those frank bursts of laughter which were the most engaging trait of his youth.

'What are you laughing at?' demanded Rutolo, lividly pale, glaring at him from under frowning brows.

'It seems to me, my dear fellow,' returned Sperelli unmoved, 'that you are a little out of temper——'

'And if I am?'

'You are at liberty to think what you like about my laughing.'

'Then I think it is idiotic.'

Sperelli bounded to his feet and made a stride forward with uplifted whip. By a miracle, Paolo Caligaro managed to catch his arm. Violent words followed. Don Marc Antonio Spada appeared upon the scene and heard the altercation.

'That's enough, boys—you both know what you have to do to-morrow—you 've got to ride now.'

The two adversaries finished their dressing in silence and then went out. The news of the quarrel had already spread through the enclosure and up to the grand stand, increasing the excitement of the race. With a refinement of perfidy, the Contessa di Lucoli repeated it to Donna Ippolita.

The latter gave no sign of inward perturbation. 'I am sorry to hear that,' was her only comment, 'I thought they were friends.'

The crowd surged round the bookmakers. *Miching Mallecho*, the horse of the Conte d'Ugenta, and *Brummel*, that of the Marchese Rutolo, were the favourites; then came the Duke di Beffi's *Satirist* and Caligaro's *Carbonilla*. However, the best judges had not overmuch confidence in the two first, thinking that the nervous excitement of their riders must inevitably tell upon the racing.

But Andrea Sperelli was perfectly calm, not to say gay.

His sense of superiority over his rival gave him assurance; moreover, his romantic taste for any adventure savouring of peril, inherited from his Byronic father, shed a halo of glory round the situation, and all the inborn generosity of his young blood awoke at the prospect of danger.

With a beating heart, he went forward to meet his horse as to a friend who was bringing him the news of some great good fortune. He stroked its nose fondly, and the glances of the animal's eye, an eye that flashed with the inextinguishable fire of noblest breeding, intoxicated him like a woman's magnetic gaze.

'Mallecho,' he whispered as he caressed the horse, 'this is a great day—we must win!'

His trainer, a little red-faced man, who was engaged in scrutinising the other horses as they were led past by their grooms, answered in his rough husky voice,—'There's no doubt but you will!'

Miching Mallecho was a superb bay from the stables of the Baron de Soubeyran, and combined extreme elegance of build with extraordinary strength of muscle. His fine and shining coat, under which the tracery of veins was distinctly visible on chest and flank, seemed almost to exhale a fiery vapour, so intense was the creature's vitality. A splendid jumper, he had often carried his master in the hunting-field over every obstacle of the Roman countryside, irrespective of the nature of the ground, never refusing the highest gate, the most forbidding wall, for ever at the tail of the hounds. A word from his rider had more effect on him than the spur, a caress made him quiver with delight.

Before mounting, Andrea carefully examined every strap and buckle, then with a smile he vaulted into the saddle. As he watched his master move away the trainer expressed his confidence in an eloquent gesture.

A crowd of bettors pressed round the indicator. Andrea felt that every eye was upon him. Gazing eagerly at the stand to the right, he tried to catch sight of Ippolita Albonico, but could distinguish no one among the multitude of ladies. The Marchesa d'Ateleta, who had heard of the quarrel, made him a sign of reproof from afar.

'How is the betting on Mallecho?' he asked of Ludovico Barbarisi.

As he moved towards the starting-post, he reflected calmly on the means he would employ for winning, and considered his three rivals critically, calculating the strength and science of each of them. Paolo Caligaro was a tricky devil, as thoroughly versed in all the knavery of the stable as any jockey; but Carbonilla, although fast, had little staying power. The Duke di Beffi, a rider of the 'haute école' style, who had come off victorious in more than one race in England, was mounted on an animal of uncertain temper which would probably refuse some of the jumps. Giannetto Rutolo, on the contrary, was riding a well-bred and well-trained horse, but though he was a very capable rider he was too impetuous; moreover, this was the first time he had taken part in a public race. Besides, he must be in a terrible state of nervous irritation, as was apparent from numerous signs.

As he looked at him, Andrea thought to himself—'I have no doubt that my victory to-day would influence the course of the duel to-morrow. In both instances, he will lose his head—it behoves me to keep calm on both fields——' Then

—'I wonder what Donna Ippolita feels about it?' There seemed to be an unusual silence round about him. With his eye he measured the distance that separated him from the first hurdle; he noticed a shining stone on the course; he observed that Rutolo was watching him, and a tremor ran through him from head to foot.

The bell gave the signal, but Brummel was off too soon and the start was no good. The second time too they made a false start, and again through Brummel's fault. Sperelli and the duke exchanged a furtive smile.

The third start was successful. Brummel instantly detached himself from the group and swept along by the palings. The other three horses followed abreast for a moment or so, and cleared the first hurdle and then the second very well. Each of the three riders played a different game. The Duke di Beffi tried to keep with the group, so that Satirist might be induced to follow the example of the other horses at the obstacles; Caligaro moderated Carbonilla's pace in order to save up her strength for the last five hundred yards. Sperelli increased his speed gradually with the intention of catching up with his adversary in the neighbourhood of the most difficult obstacle. In effect, Mallecho soon distanced his two companions and began to press Brummel very closely.

Rutolo heard the rapidly approaching hoof-thuds behind him and was seized with such nervousness that his sight seemed to fail him. Everything swam before his eyes as if he were on the point of swooning. He made a frightful effort to keep his spurs at his horse's sides, overcome by terror at the thought that his senses might leave him. There was a muffled roar in his ears, and through that roar he caught the hard, clear sound of Andrea Sperelli's 'Hi!'

More susceptible to the voice than any other mode of urging, Mallecho simply devoured the intervening space; he was not more than two or three lengths behind Brummel— was on the point of joining—of passing him.

'Hi!'

A high barrier intersected the course. Rutolo actually did

not see it, having lost all sense of his surroundings, and only preserved a furious instinct to remain glued to his horse and force it along, never mind how.   Brummel jumped, but receiving no aid from his rider, caught his hind legs against the barrier, and came down so awkwardly on the other side that the rider lost his stirrups, without, however, coming out of the saddle, and he continued to run.   Andrea Sperelli now took the lead, Giannetto Rutolo, without having recovered his stirrups, being second, with Paolo Caligaro close upon his heels; the duke, retarded by a refusal from Satirist, came last.   In this order they passed the grand stand.   They heard a confused clamour but it soon died away.

The spectators held their breath in suspense.   From time to time, somebody would remark aloud on the various incidents of the running.   At every change in the order of the horses numerous exclamations sounded through the continuous murmur, and the ladies thrilled visibly.   Donna Ippolita Albonico, mounted on a seat, with her hands on the shoulders of her husband who stood below her, watched the race with marvellous self-control and without a trace of apparent emotion, unless the over-tight compression of her lips and a scarcely perceptible furrow between her brows might have revealed the effort to an observant eye.   At a certain moment, however, she drew her hands away from her husband's shoulder, fearful of betraying herself by some involuntary movement.

'Sperelli is down!' announced the Contessa di Lucoli in a loud voice.

Mallecho, in jumping, had slipped on the wet grass and come down on his knees, but recovered himself in an instant. Andrea had gone over his head, but was none the worse, and with lightning rapidity was back in the saddle as Rutolo and Caligaro came up with him.   Brummel performed prodigies, in spite of the wounded leg, and showed the quality of his blood.   Carbonilla was at last putting out all her speed, guided with consummate skill by her rider.   There were still about eight hundred yards to the winning post.

Sperelli saw victory escaping him and gathered up all his forces to grasp it again. Standing in the stirrups, bent low over his horse's neck, he uttered from time to time that short, sharp, ringing word which always acted so effectively upon the noble creature. While Brummel and Carbonilla, fatigued by the heaviness of the ground, began to lose the pace, Mallecho steadily increased the vehemence of his rush and had nearly reconquered his former position, scenting victory already with his fiery nostrils. Flying over the last obstacle, he passed Brummel — his head was level with Carbonilla's shoulder—a hundred yards from the post he skirted the barrier—on—on—leaving Caligaro's black mare ten lengths behind. The bell rang—a furious clapping of hands, like the pelting of hail-stones, and then a dull roar spread through the great crowd on the green sward under the flood of brilliant sunshine.

As he entered the enclosure, Andrea Sperelli thought to himself—'Fortune is with me to-day, but how will it be to-morrow?' And feeling the breath of triumph surge round him, a vague sense of resentment rose up in him against the possibilities of the morrow. He would have preferred to face it to-day and get it over, that he might enjoy a double victory and then taste the fruit offered to him by the hand of Ippolita Albonico. He was possessed, for the moment, by that inexplicable intoxication which results—with certain men of intellect—from the exercise of their physical powers, the experience of their courage and the revelation of their inherent brutality. The substratum of primitive ferocity which exists at the bottom of most of us rushes to the surface, on occasion, with curious vehemence, and under the skin-deep varnish of modern civilisation, our hearts swell sometimes with a nameless sanguinary fury, and visions of carnage rise up before us. Inhaling the hot and acrid exhalations of his horse, Andrea Sperelli felt that none of the delicate perfumes affected by him up till now, had ever afforded him such intense enjoyment.

He had scarcely quitted the saddle, before he found

himself surrounded by friends of both sexes, eager to congratulate him.   Mallecho, breathing hard, smoking and covered with foam, snorted and stretched his neck, shaking the bridle.   His sides rose and fell with a deep continuous movement, as if they must burst; his muscles vibrated under skin like a bow-string after the shot; his eyes, dilated and bloodshot, had the cruel glare of those of a beast of prey; his coat, now showing great patches of darker colour, ran down with rivulets of perspiration.   The incessant trembling of his whole body was pitiable to see, like the suffering of a human being.

'Poor fellow!' murmured one of the ladies.

Andrea examined his knees to see if he had taken any hurt from his fall.   They were sound.   Then patting him softly on the neck, he said in an indefinable tone of gentleness—'Go, Mallecho, go——'

And he followed him with his eyes till he disappeared.

Directly he had changed his clothes, he went in search of Ludovico Barbarisi and the Baron di Santa Margherita.

Both instantly accepted the office of arranging preliminaries with Rutolo.   He begged them to hasten matters as much as possible.

'Fix it all by this evening.   To-morrow by one o'clock I absolutely must be free.   But let me sleep till nine to-morrow morning.   I dine with the Ferentinos, then I shall look in at the Palazzo Giustiniani, and after that I shall go to the Club, but it will be late—You will know where to find me.   Many thanks, my dear fellows, and *a rividerci.*'

He repaired to the grand stand, but avoided approaching Donna Ippolita at once.   He smiled, feeling every feminine eye upon him.   Many a fair hand was held out, many a sweet voice called him familiarly—'Andrea'—some of them even a little ostentatiously.   The ladies who had bet upon his horses told him the amount of their winnings, others asked curiously if he were really going to fight.

It seemed to him that in one day he had reached the summit of adventurous glory.   He had come out victor in

a record race, had gained the graces of a new love, magnificent and serene as a Venetian Dogaressa, had provoked a man
to mortal combat and now was passing calm and courteous—
but neither more so nor less than usual—amid the openly
adoring smiles of all these fair women.

'See the conquering hero comes!' cried Ippolita's husband with outstretched hand and pressing Andrea's with
unusual warmth.

'Yes, indeed; quite a hero!' echoed Donna Ippolita in
the superficial tone of necessary compliment, affecting igno-
rance of the real drama.

Sperelli bowed and passed on, feeling strangely embarrassed
by Albonico's excessive friendliness. A suspicion crossed
his mind that he was grateful to him for having provoked a
quarrel with his wife's lover, and the cowardice of the man
brought a supercilious smile to his lips.

Returning from the races on the Prince di Ferentino's mail
coach, he espied Giannetto Rutolo tearing back to Rome in
a little two-wheeled trap behind a great fast-trotting roan;
bending forward with head down, a cigar between his teeth
and utterly regardless of the injunctions of the police to keep
in the line. Rome rose up before them, black against a
band of saffron light, and in the violet sky above that light
the statues on the Basilica of San Giovanni stood out ex-
aggeratedly large. And Andrea then fully realised the pain
he was inflicting on this man's soul.

CHAPTER X

At the Palazzo Giustiniani that evening, Andrea said to Ippolita Albonico, 'Well then, it is a fixed thing that I expect you to-morrow between two and five?'

She would like to have said: 'Then you are not going to fight to-morrow?' but she did not dare.

'I have promised,' she replied.

A minute or two afterwards, her husband came up to Andrea and taking his arm with much effusion, began asking particulars about the duel. He was a youngish man, slim, with very thin fair hair and colourless eyes and projecting teeth. He had a slight stammer.

'Well, well—so it is to come off to-morrow, is it?'

Andrea could not repress his disgust, and let his arm hang loosely at his side to show that he was in no mood for these familiarities. Seeing the Baron di Santi Margherita enter the room, he disengaged himself quickly.

'Excuse me, Count,' he said, 'I want to speak to Santa Margherita.'

The Baron met him with the assurance that all was in order.

'Very good—at what hour?'

'Half-past ten at the Villa Sciarra. Rapiers and fencing-gloves, *à outrance.*'

'Whom else have you got for seconds?'

'Roberto Casteldieri and Carlo de Souza. We settled everything as quickly as possible, avoiding formalities. Giannetto had got his seconds already. We arranged the proceedings at the Club without any fuss. Try not to be too late in going to bed—you must be dead tired.'

But, heedless of this good advice, on leaving the Palazzo Giustiniani, Andrea betook himself to the Club, where Santa Margherita came upon him at two o'clock in the morning, and, forcing him to leave the card-tables, bore him off on foot to the Palazzo Zuccari.

'My dear boy,' he said reproachfully as they walked along, 'you are really foolhardy. In a case like this, the smallest imprudence might lead to fatal results. To preserve his full strength and activity, a good swordsman should have as much care for his person as a tenor has for his voice. The wrist is as delicate an organ as the throat—the articulations of the legs as sensitive as the vocal chords. The mechanism suffers from the smallest disturbance; the instrument gets out of gear and will not answer to the player. After a night of play or drink, Camillo Agrippa himself could not thrust straight, and his parries were neither sure nor rapid. An error of a hair's breadth will suffice to let three inches of steel into one's body.' They were at the top of the Via Condotti, and in the distance they could see the Piazza di Spagna, lighted up by the full moon, the stairway bathed in silver, and the Trinità de' Monti rising into the soft blue.

'Certainly,' continued the Baron, 'you have great advantages over your adversary, amongst others, a cool head—also you have been out before. I saw you in Paris in your affair with Gauvaudan—you remember? A grand duel that! You fought like a god!'

Andrea laughed, much gratified. The praise of this un rivalled duellist made his heart swell with pride, and infused fresh vigour into his muscles. Instinctively, he grasped his walking stick, and repeated the famous pass which pierced the arm of the Marquis de Gauvaudan the previous winter.

'Yes,' he said, 'it was a direct return hit after a parry of " contre de tierce." '

'On the floor, Giannetto Rutolo is a skilful swordsman, but in the open he gets confused. He has only been out once before with my cousin Cassibile, and he came off badly. He does far too much of the one, two,—one, two, three business

in attacking.   Stop thrusts and hits with a *half volte* would be
useful to you.   It was just in that way that my cousin touched
him in the second round.   And those thrusts are your special
forte.   Keep a sharp look-out and try to keep your distance.
And do not forget that you have to do with a man whom, as
I hear, you have robbed of his mistress, and to whom you
lifted your whip.'

They had reached the Piazza di Spagna.   The Barcaccia
splashed and gurgled softly, glistening under the moon that
was mirrored in its waters.   Four or five hackney carriages
stood in a line with their lamps lighted.   From the Via del
Babuino came a tinkle of bells, and the dull tramp of hoofs,
as of a herd in motion.

At the foot of the steps the Baron took leave of him.

'Good-bye then, till to-morrow.   I shall be with you a
little before nine with Ludovico.   You must make a pass or
so, just to unstiffen the muscles.   We will see about the
doctor.   Off with you now and get a good sleep.'

Andrea mounted the steps.   At the first broad landing, he
stood still to listen to the tinkle of the approaching bells.
In truth, he did feel rather tired, and even a little heartsick.
Now that the excitement called up by the conversation on
fencing, and the recollection of his former doughty deeds in
that line had subsided, a sense of dissatisfaction had come
upon him, confusedly, as yet, and mingled with doubt and
regret.   After being on the stretch throughout the violent
feverish incidents of the day, his nerves relaxed under the
balmy influences of the spring night.   Why should he,
without any excuse of passion, out of mere caprice, from pure
vanity and arrogance, have taken pleasure in awakening the
hatred, and deeply wounding the heart of a fellow man?
The thought of the horrid pain that must be torturing his
adversary filled him with a sort of compassion.   Elena's
image flashed before him, and he called to mind the anguish
he had endured the year before, what time he had lost her—
his jealousy, his anger, his nameless torments.   Then, as
now, the nights were serene and calm, and filled with

perfume, and yet how they weighed upon his spirit! He inhaled the fragrant breath of the roses blooming in the little gardens about, and watched the flock of sheep passing through the Piazza below.

The mass of thick white fleece advanced with a continuous undulating motion, a compact and unbroken surface, like a muddy wave pouring over the pavement. A sharp quavering bleat would mingle with the tinkling bells to be answered by other voices, fainter and more timid; from time to time, the mounted shepherds, riding at either side or behind the flock, gave a sharp word of command, or used their long staves. The splendour of the moonlight lent to this passage of flocks through the midst of the slumbering city the mystery of things seen in a dream.

Andrea recalled one serene February night when, on coming away from a ball at the English Embassy, he and Elena had met a flock of sheep in the Via Venti Settembre which obliged their carriage to stop. Elena, her face pressed to the window, watched the sheep crowding against the carriage wheels, and pointed to the little lambs with childish delight; and he with his face close to hers, his eyes half closed, listened to the pattering hoofs, the bleating, the tinkling bells.

Why should these recollections of Elena come back to him just now?—He resumed his way slowly up the steps, his feet heavy with fatigue, his knees giving way beneath him. Suddenly the thought of death flashed across his mind. 'What if I were killed, or received such a wound as to maim me for life?' But his thirst for life and pleasure caused his whole being to revolt against such a sinister possibility. 'I *must* come off victorious!' he said to himself. And he began reviewing all the advantages that would fall to him from this second victory: the prestige of his success, the fame of his prowess, Ippolita's kisses, new loves, new pleasures, the gratification of new whims.

Presently, however, he bethought him of the necessary precautions for insuring his bodily vigour. He went to bed

and slept soundly till he was awakened by the arrival of his
seconds; took his customary shower-bath; had a strip of
linoleum laid down and invited Santa Margherita and then
Barbarisi to exchange a few passes with him, during which
he executed with precision several stop thrusts.

' In capital form!' the Baron congratulated him.

Sperelli then took two cups of tea and some biscuits,
donned a very easy pair of trousers, comfortable shoes with
low heels and a very slightly starched shirt; he prepared his
gloves by moistening the palm slightly and rubbing in pow-
dered resin; arranged a leather strap for fastening the guard
to his wrist; examined the blade and the point of both
rapiers; omitted no precaution, no detail.

When all was to his satisfaction—'Let us be going now,'
he said; 'better be on the ground before the others. What
about the doctor?'

'He will be waiting for us there.'

On the way down stairs they met Grimiti, who had come
on behalf of the Marchesa d'Ateleta.

' I shall follow you to the Villa and then bring the news
as quickly as possible to Francesca,' said he.

They all went down together. The Duke jumped into his
buggy and the others entered a closed carriage. Andrea
made no show of indifference or good spirits—to make
jokes before engaging in a serious duel seemed to him
execrably bad taste—but he was perfectly calm. He smoked
and listened composedly to Santa Margherita and Barbarisi,
who were discussing—apropos of a recent case in France—
whether it was legitimate or not to use the left hand against
an adversary. Now and again, he leaned forward to look out
of the window.

On this May morning Rome shone resplendent under the
caressing sun. Here a fountain lit up with its silvery laughter
a little piazzetta still plunged in shadow; there the open gates
of a palace disclosed a vista of courtyard with a background
of portico and statues; from the baroque architecture of a
brick church hung the decorations for the month of Mary.

Under the bridge, the Tiber gleamed and glistened as it hurried away between the gray-green houses towards the island of San Bartolomeo. After a short ascent, the whole city spread out before them, immense, imperial, radiant, bristling with spires and columns and obelisks, crowned with cupolas and rotundas, clean cut out of the blue like a citadel.

'*Ave Roma, moriturus te salutat!*' exclaimed Andrea Sperelli, throwing away the end of his cigarette. 'Though, to tell the truth, my dear fellows,' he added, 'a sword-thrust would decidedly inconvenience me this morning.'

They had reached the Villa Sciarra, already partially profaned by the builders of modern houses, and were passing through an avenue of tall and slender laurels bordered by hedges of roses. Santa Margherita, putting his head out of the window, caught sight of another carriage standing in the drive before the villa.

'They are waiting for us,' he said.

He consulted his watch — ten minutes yet to the hour agreed upon. He got out of the carriage and went across with the other seconds and the surgeons to the opponents. Andrea stayed behind in the avenue. He went over, in his own mind, certain points of attack and defence he hoped to employ successfully, but the miracles of light and shadow playing fitfully through the interlacing laurels distracted his attention. While his mind was occupied with the position of the wound he intended inflicting, his eyes were attracted by the reeds shivering in the morning breeze, and the trees, tender as the amorous allegories of Petrarch, sighed gently over a head that was wholly absorbed in plans of dealing a mortal blow.

Barbarisi came to call him.

'Everything is ready,' he said. 'The caretaker has opened the villa for us—we have the rooms on the ground floor at our disposal—most convenient. Come and undress.'

Andrea followed him. While he undressed, the two surgeons opened their surgical cases and displayed the array of glittering steel instruments within. One of them was a youngish man, pale, bald, and with feminine hands and a hard mouth, with a continual and visible contraction of the lower jaw, which was extraordinarily developed. The other was a thickset man of mature years with a freckled face, bushy red beard and the neck of an ox. The one seemed the antithesis of the other, and their disparity excited Sperelli's curiosity and attention. They set out upon a table bandages and carbolic acid for disinfecting the weapons. The smell of the acid diffused itself through the room.

As soon as Sperelli was ready, he went out accompanied by his second and the surgeons. Once again, the view of Rome seen through the laurels attracted his eyes and made his heart beat fast. He was full of impatience. He wished he could put himself on guard at that very instant, and hear the signal for the attack. He seemed to have the decisive thrust, the victory in his hand.

'Ready?' asked Santa Margherita advancing to meet him.

'Quite ready.'

The spot chosen for the encounter was a path at the side of the villa, in the shade, and covered with fine rolled gravel. Rutolo was already stationed there, at the further end, with Roberto Casteldieri and Carlo di Souza. Everybody wore a grave, not to say solemn, air. The two adversaries were placed opposite to one another and their eyes met. Santa Margherita, who had the direction of the combat, noticed that Rutolo's shirt was very stiffly starched and the collar too high. He remarked upon it to Casteldieri who exchanged a few words with his principal, and Sperelli saw the blood rush to his adversary's face while he proceeded resolutely to divest himself of his shirt. Andrea with cold composure followed his example. He then turned up his trousers and Santa Margherita handed him the glove, the strap and the rapier. He armed himself with scrupulous care, and shook his weapon slightly to see that he had it well in hand. The movement brought out the play of his biceps very visibly,

bearing witness to long practice of the arm and the strength
it had thereby acquired.

When the two combatants measured their swords for
the distance, that of Giannetto Rutolo shook convulsively.
After the usual set phrases as to the honour and good faith
of the combatants, Santa Margherita gave the word in a
ringing powerful voice.

'Gentlemen—on guard!'

The duellists threw themselves on guard simultaneously;
Rutolo, with a stamp of the foot, Sperelli, bending forward
lightly. Rutolo was of medium height, very slender, all
nerves, with an olive face, to which the curled moustaches
and the little pointed beard à la Charles I. in Van Dyck's
pictures lent a certain piquant and dashing air. Sperelli
was taller, more dignified, admirable of attitude, calm and
collected, perfectly balanced between grace and strength, his
whole person proclaiming the *grand seigneur*. They looked
each other full in the eye, and each experienced a curious
internal thrill at the sight of the bare flesh against which
he pointed his sharp blade. Through the silence came the
fresh murmur of the fountain mingled with the rustle of the
breeze among the climbing rose-bushes, where innumerable
yellow and white roses nodded their fragrant heads.

'Play!' cried the Baron.

Andrea was prepared for an impetuous attack from Rutolo,
but the latter did not move. For about a minute, they stood
watching each other closely without ever crossing swords,
almost motionless. Sperelli bending his knees still more, on
guard with the point low, assumed the tierce guard and
sought to provoke his adversary by the insolent challenge of
his eyes and by stamping his foot. Rutolo made a step
forward with a menace of straight thrust, accompanying it
with a cry after the manner of certain Sicilian fencers. The
duel began.

Sperelli avoided any decisive movement, restricting himself
to parrying only, forcing his opponent to discover his intentions, to exhaust all his methods, to bring out his whole

repertoire of sword-play. His parries were neat and rapid, never yielding a foot of ground, admirable in precision, as if he were taking part in a fencing match in the school with blunt foils; whereas Rutolo attacked him warmly, accompanying each thrust with a hoarse cry like that of the wood-cutters when they use their hatchets.

'Halt!' cried Santa Margherita, whose vigilant eye marked every flash of the blades.

He went up to Rutolo. 'You are touched, if I am not mistaken,' he said.

True, Rutolo had a scratch on the forearm, but so slight that there was no need even of sticking-plaster. Nevertheless, he was breathing hard, and his livid pallor bore witness to his suppressed anger.

'I know my man thoroughly now,' whispered Sperelli with a smile to Barbarisi. 'You watch the second round. I mean to pink him on the right breast.'

As he spoke, he absently rested the point of his rapier on the ground. The bald young surgeon with the strong jaw immediately came up to him with a sponge soaked in carbolic acid and proceeded to purify the weapon again.

'Good heavens!' Andrea exclaimed in a low voice to Barbarisi, 'he has all the air of a *jettatore*. This rapier is certain to break.'

A thrush began to sing somewhere in the trees. Here and there a rose scattered its petals on the breeze. Some low-lying fleecy clouds rose to meet the sun, broke up into airy flakes and gradually dispersed.

'On guard!'

Conscious of his inferiority, Rutolo determined to hamper his opponent's play, to attack him at close quarters and so break his continuity of action. For this he enjoyed the advantage of shorter stature and a frame which, being wiry, thin and flexible, offered but little mark to the other's weapon.

Andrea foresaw that Rutolo would adopt this plan. He stood on guard, bent like a taut bow, watching for the right moment.

'Halt!' cried Santa Margherita.

A streak of blood showed on Rutolo's breast. The rapier had penetrated, just under the right breast, almost to the rib. The surgeons hurried over, but the wounded man instantly turned to Casteldieri, and with a tremor of anger in his voice said roughly:—

'It is a mere scratch. I shall go on.'

He refused to go inside to have the wound dressed. The bald doctor, after squeezing the small hole, which scarcely bled, and sponging it with antiseptic lotion, applied a simple piece of lint and said:—

'You may go on now.'

At Casteldieri's invitation, the Baron gave the word without delay for the third round.

'On guard!'

Sperelli perceived his danger. Directly in front of him stood his adversary, his knees firmly bent, masked, as it were, behind his rapier, his whole strength resolutely collected for one supreme effort. His eyes had a singular glitter, and the calf of his left leg quivered perceptibly under the excessive tension of the muscles. This time, in order to avoid the shock of his opponent's impetus, Andrea determined to throw himself to one side and repeat the thrust which Cassibile had employed so successfully, the white patch of lint on Rutolo's breast serving him as a mark. It was there he proposed wounding him again, but, this time, the rapier should enter the intercostal space and not be deterred by the rib. The silence all about them deepened, the spectators felt the homicidal desire that animated the two men, and were seized with apprehension, their hearts sinking at the thought that doubtless they would have to carry away a dead or dying man. The sun, veiled by fleecy cloudlets, shed a milky light over the scene, the trees rustled fitfully, the thrush sang on invisible.

'Play!'

Rutolo charged his adversary with a double derobe. Sperelli parried and returned, giving way a step. Rutolo followed up furiously with a rush of rapid thrusts, nearly all

in the low line, without uttering the usual cries.   Sperelli,
nothing daunted by this onslaught, and wishing to avoid an
actual hand-to-hand fight, parried vigorously, and returned
with such directness that he might, had he so wished, have
run his adversary through the body each time.   Rutolo's leg
was bleeding near the groin.

'Halt !' cried Santa Margherita the moment he perceived it.

But in the same instant Sperelli, parrying low quarte and
not encountering his adversary's blade, received a thrust full
in the breast.   He fell back into Barbarisi's arms and fainted.

'Wound penetrating the thorax through the fourth intercostal space on the right side with superficial wound of the
lung,' pronounced the bull-necked surgeon, after his examina-
tion in the room to which they had conveyed the wounded
man.

BOOK II

CHAPTER I

CONVALESCENCE is a purification, a new birth. Never is life so sweet as after the pangs of physical suffering, and never is the human soul so inclined towards purity and faith as after having had a glimpse into the abyss of death.

After his terrible wound, after a long, slow, agonising struggle, Andrea Sperelli came back to life renewed in body and spirit—like another man, like a creature risen out of the icy waters of death, with a mind swept bare of all that has gone before. The past had receded into the dim perspective, the troubled waters had calmed, the mud sunk to the bottom; his soul was cleansed. He returned to the bosom of Mother Nature, and he felt her re-inforce him maternally with goodness and with strength.

The guest of his cousin at her villa of Schifanoja, Andrea returned to life again in sight of the sea. The convalescent drew his breath in harmony with the deep, calm breath of the ocean; his mind was tranquillised by the serenity of the horizon. Little by little, in these hours of enforced idleness and retirement, his spirit expanded, bloomed out, erected itself slowly, like the grass trodden under foot on the pathway, and he returned to truth and simple faith, became natural and free of heart, open to the knowledge and disposed to the contemplation of pure things.

August was drawing to a close. An ecstatic serenity reigned over the sea; the waters were so transparent that they repeated every image with absolute fidelity, and their ultimate line melted so imperceptibly into the sky that the two elements seemed as one, impalpable and supernatural.

The wide amphitheatre of hills, clothed with olives, oranges and pines and all the noblest forms of Italian vegetation, embraced the silent sea, and seemed not a multiplicity of things, but a single vast object under the all-pervading sunshine.

Lying on the grass, or sitting on a rock or under a tree, the young man felt the river of life flow within him; as in a trance, he seemed to feel the whole universe throb and palpitate in his breast; in a species of religious rapture, he felt that he possessed the infinite. That which he experienced was ineffable, divine. The vista before him opened out by degrees into a profound and long continued vision, the branches of the trees overhead supported the firmament, filling the blue, and shining like the garlands of immortal poets. And he gazed and listened and breathed with the sea and the earth, placid as a god.

Where were now all his vanities and his cruelties, his schemes and his duplicities? What had become of all his loves and his illusions, his disappointments and his disgusts, and the implacable reaction after pleasure? He remembered none of them. His spirit had renounced them all, and with the absence of desire, he had found peace.

Desire had abandoned its throne and intellect was free to follow its proper course, and reflect the objective world purely from the outside point of view; things appeared clearly and precisely under their true form, in their true colours, in all their real significance and beauty; every personal sentiment was in abeyance.

'*Die Sterne, die begehrt man nicht—Man freut sich ihrer Pracht.*'

One desires not the stars, but rejoices in their splendour—and for the first time in his life the young man really recognised the poetic harmony of summer skies at night.

These were the last nights of August, and there was no moon. Innumerable in the deep starry vault, the constellations throbbed and palpitated with ardent life. The two Bears, Hercules, Cassiopeia, glittered with so rapid a palpitation that they seemed almost to approach the earth, to penetrate the terrestrial atmosphere. The Milky Way flowed wide like a regal aërian river, a confluence of the waters of Paradise, over a bed of crystal between starry banks. Brilliant meteors cleft the motionless air from time to time, gliding lightly and silently as a drop of water over a sheet of glass. The slow and solemn respiration of the sea sufficed to measure the peace of the night without disturbing it, and the pauses were almost sweeter than the music.

In every aspect of the things around him he beheld some analogy to his own inner life. The landscape became to him a symbol, an emblem, a sign to guide him through the labyrinthine passes of his own soul. He discovered secret affinities between the visible life around him and the intimate life of his desires and memories. 'To me, high mountains are a *feeling.*'—and as the mountains were to Byron, so the sea was to him a *sentiment.*

Oh, that limpid September sea ! Calm and guileless as a sleeping child, it lay outstretched beneath the pearly sky— now green, the delicate and precious green of malachite, the little red sails upon it like flickering tongues of fire, now intensely—almost one might call it heraldically—blue, and veined with gold like lapis-lazuli, with pictured sails upon it as in a church procession. At other times, it took on a dull metallic lustre as polished silver mingled with the greenish-yellow tint of ripe lemons, indefinable, strange and delicate, and the sails would come crowding like the wings of the cherubim in the background of a Giotto picture.

Forgotten sensations of early youth came back to him, that impression of freshness which the salt breath of the sea infuses into young blood, the indescribable effects produced by the changing lights and shadows, the tints, the smell of the salt water upon the unsullied soul. The sea was not only a delight to his eyes, but also an inexhaustible well-spring of peace, a magic fount of youth wherein his body regained health, and his spirit nobility. The ocean had for him the mysterious attraction of a mother country, and he abandoned himself to it with filial confidence, as a feeble

child might sink into the arms of an omnipotent mother.
And he received comfort and encouragement; for who ever
confided his pain, his yearnings or his dreams to her in
vain?

For him the sea had ever a profound word, some sudden
revelation, some unlooked for enlightenment, some unexpected
significance. She revealed to him, in the secret recesses of
his soul, a wound still gaping though quiescent, and she made
it bleed again, but only to heal it with balm that was doubly
sweet. She reawakened the dragon that slumbered within
him, till he felt once more the terrible grip of its claws, and
then she slew it once for all and buried it deep in his heart
never to rise again. No corner of his being but lay open to
the great Consolatrix.

But at times, under the continuous dominion of this influence, under the persistent tyranny of this fascination, the convalescent was conscious of a sort of bewilderment and fear, as
if both the dominion and fascination were insupportable to his
weak state. The incessant colloquy between him and the
sea gave him a vague sense of prostration, as if the sublime
language were beyond his restricted powers, so eager to
grasp the meaning of the incomprehensible.

But this period of visions, of abstractions, of pure con-
templativeness was of short duration. By degrees, he began
to resume his attitude of self-consciousness, to recover the
sensation of his personality, to return to his original frame of
mind. One day at the hour of high noon, the vast and
terrible silence when all life seems suspended, a sudden
glimpse into his own heart revealed shuddering abysses, inextinguishable desires, ineffaceable memories, accumulations
of suffering and regret—all the wretchedness he had gone
through, all the inevitable scars of his vices, all the results of
his passions. He seemed to be witnessing the shipwreck of
his whole life. A thousand voices cried to him for succour,
imploring aid, cursing death—voices that he knew, that he
had listened to in days gone by. But they cried and im-
plored and cursed in vain, feeling that they were perishing,

choked by the hungry waves; then the voices grew faint, broken, irrecognisable—and died away into silence.

He was alone. Of all his youth, of all his boasted fulness of inner life, of all his ideality, not a vestige remained; within —a black and yawning abyss, around him—impassive nature, endless source of pain to solitary souls. Every hope was dead, every voice mute, every anchor gone—what use was life?

Suddenly the image of Elena rose up before him, then that of other women whom he had known and loved. Each of them smiled a hostile smile, and each one, as she vanished, seemed to carry away something of him—what, he could not definitely say. An unspeakable distress weighed upon him, an icy breath of age swept over him, a tragic, warning voice rang through his heart—Too late! Too late!

All his recent comfort and peace seemed now a vain delusion, a dream that had flown, a pleasure enjoyed by some other spirit. Every wound he had ruthlessly dealt to his soul's dignity bled afresh; every degradation he had inflicted upon his conscience started out and spread like a leprosy. Every violation he had committed upon his ideality roused an endless, despairing, terrible remorse in him. He had lied too flagrantly, had deceived, debased himself beyond all power of redress. He loathed himself and all his evil works—Shame! Shame! Nothing could wipe out those dishonouring stains, no balm could ever heal those wounds, he must for ever endure the torment of that self-loathing.—Shame!——

His eyes filled with tears, and dropping his head upon his arms he abandoned himself to the weight of his misery, prostrate as a man who has no hope of salvation.

With the new day, he awoke to new life, one of those awakenings, so fresh and limpid, that are only vouchsafed to adolescence in its triumphant springtide. It was a marvellous morning—only to breathe the air was pure delight. The whole earth rejoiced in the living light; the hills were wrapped about with a diaphanous silvery veil and seemed to quiver with life, the sea appeared to be traversed by rivulets of milk, by rivers of crystal and of emerald, by a thousand currents forming the rippling intricacies of a watery labyrinth. A sense of nuptial joy and religious grace emanated from the concord between earth and sky.

And he breathed and gazed and listened, not a little surprised. During his sleep the fever had left him. He had slumbered, lulled by the voice of the waters as if by the voice of a faithful friend—and he who sleeps to the sound of that lullaby enjoys a repose that is full of healing peace.

He gazed and listened mutely, fondly, letting the flood of immortal life penetrate to his heart's core. Never had the sacred music of a great master—an Offertory of Haydn, a Te Deum of Mozart—produced in him the emotion caused now by the simple chimes of the distant village churches, as they greeted the rising of the sun into the heavens. His soul swelled and o'erflowed with unspeakable emotion. Some vision, vague but sublime, hovered over him like a rippling veil through which gleamed the splendour of the mysterious treasure of ultimate felicity. Up till now, he had always known exactly what he wished for, and had never found any pleasure in desiring vainly. Now, he could not have named his desire, but he had no doubts that the thing longed for was infinitely sweet, since the very act of wishing was bliss. The words of the Chimera in 'The King of Cyprus'—old world, half-forgotten verses, recurred to him with all the force of a caressing appeal—

> 'Would'st thou fight?
> Would'st kill? would'st thou behold rivers of blood?
> Great heaps of gold? white herds of captive women?
> Slaves? other, and far other spoils? Would'st thou
> Bid marble breathe? Would'st thou set up a temple?
> Would'st fashion an immortal hymn? Would'st (hearken,
> Hearken, O youth, hearken!)—would'st thou divinely
> Love?'

He smiled faintly to himself. 'Whom should I love?—Art?—a woman?—what woman?' Elena seemed far removed from him, lost to him, a stranger—dead. The others

—still further off, dead for evermore.   Therefore he was free.
But why renew a pursuit so useless and so perilous?   Why
stretch out his hand again towards the tree of knowledge?
'The tree of knowledge has been plucked—all's known!' as
Byron said in Don Juan.   What he desired, at the bottom of
his heart, was to give himself freely, gratefully to some higher
and purer being.   But where to find that being was the
question.

Truly his salvation in the future lay rather in the practice
of caution, prudence, sagacity.   His tone of mind seemed to
him admirably expressed in a sonnet of a contemporary poet,
whom, from a certain affinity of literary tastes and similar
æsthetic education, he particularly affected—

> ' I am as one who lays himself to rest
> Under the shadow of a laden tree ;
> Above his head hangs the ripe fruit, and he
> Is weary of drawing bow or arbalest.
>
> He shakes not the fair bough that lowliest
> Droops, neither lifts he hand, nor turns to see ;
> But lies, and gathers to him indolently
> The fruits that drop into his very breast.
>
> In that juiced sweetness, over-exquisite,
> He bites not deep ; he fears the bitterness ;
> Yet sets it to his lips, that he may smell,
>
> Sucks it with pleasure, not with greediness,
> And he is neither grieved nor glad at it.
> This is the ending of the parable.'

Art!   Art!   She was the only faithful mistress—forever
young—immortal ; there was the Fountain of all pure joys,
closed to the multitude but freely open to the elect ; that was
the precious Food which makes a man like unto a god !   How
could he have quaffed from other cups after having pressed
his lips to that one?—how have followed after other joys
when he had tasted that supreme one?

'But what if my intellect has become decadent?—if my

hand has lost its cunning? What if I am no longer *worthy*?'
He was seized with such panic at the thought, that he set
himself wildly to find some immediate means of proving to
himself the irrational nature of his fears. He would instantly
compose some difficult verses, draw a figure, engrave a plate,
solve some problem of form. Well—and what then? Might
not the result be entirely fallacious? The slow decay of
power may be imperceptible to the possessor—that is the
terrible thing about it. The artist who loses his genius little
by little is unaware of his progressive feebleness, for as he
loses his power of production he also loses his critical faculty,
his judgment. He no longer perceives the defects of his
work—does not know that it is mediocre or bad. That is
the horror of it! The artist who has fallen from his original
high estate is no more conscious of his failings than the
lunatic is aware of his mental aberration.

Andrea was seized with terror. Better—far better be dead!
Never, as at this moment, had he so fully grasped the divine
nature of that *gift*, never had the *spark* of genius appeared to
him so sacred. His whole being was shaken to its foundations by the mere suggestion that that gift might be destroyed,
that spark extinguished. Better to die!

He lifted his head and shook off his inertia, then he went
down to the park and walked slowly under the trees, unable
to form a definite plan. A light breeze rippled through the
tree tops, now and again the leaves rustled as if a band of
squirrels were passing through them; patches of blue sky
gleamed between the branches like eyes beneath their lids.
Arrived at a favourite spot of his, a sort of tiny *lucus* pre-
sided over by a four-fronted Hermes plunged in quadruple
meditation, he stopped and seated himself on the grass, with
his back against the pedestal of the statue and his face turned
to the sea. Before him the tree-trunks, straight but of uneven height, like the pipes of the great god Pan, intercepted
his view of the sea; all around him the acanthus spread the
exquisite grace of its foliage, symmetrical as the capitals of
Callimachus.

He thought of the words of Salamis in the *Story of the Hermaphrodite*,

> ' Noble acanthus, in the woods of Earth
> Tokens of peace, high-flowering coronals,
> Of most pure form ; O ye, the slender basket
> That Silence weaves with light, untroubled hand
> To gather up the flowers of woody dreams,
> What virtue have ye poured on this fair youth
> Out of those dusky and sweet-smelling leaves?
> Naked he sleeps ; his arm supports his head.'

Other lines came back to him, and yet others—a riot of verse. His soul was filled with the music of rhymes and rhythmic measures. He was overjoyed ; coming to him thus spontaneously and unexpectedly, this poetic agitation caused him inexpressible happiness. And he gave ear to the music, delighting himself in rich imagery, in rare epithets, in the luminous metaphors, the exquisite harmonies, the subtle refinements which distinguished his metrical style and the mysterious artifices of the endecasyllabic verse learned from the admirable poets of the fourteenth century, and more especially from Petrarch. Once more the magic spell of versification subjugated his soul, and he felt the full force of the sentiment of a contemporary poet—Verse is everything !

A perfect line of verse is absolute, immutable, deathless. It encloses a thought as within a clearly marked circle which no force can break ; it belongs no more to the poet, it belongs to all and yet to none, as do space, light, all things intransitory and perpetual. When the poet is about to bring forth one of these deathless lines he is warned by a divine torrent of joy which sweeps over his soul.

Andrea half closed his eyes to prolong this delicious tremor which with him was ever the forerunner of inspiration, and more especially of poetic inspiration, and he determined in a moment upon the metrical form into which he would pour his thoughts, like wine into a cup—the sonnet.

While composing Andrea studied himself curiously. It was long since he had made verses. Had this interval of idleness been harmful to his technical capacities? It seemed to him that the lines, rising one by one out of the depths of his brain, had a new grace. The consonance came of itself, and ideas were born of the rhymes. Then suddenly some obstacle would intercept the flow, a line would rebel and the whole verse would be displaced like a shaken puzzle; the syllables would struggle against the constraint of the measure; a musical and luminous word which had taken his fancy had to be excluded by the severity of the rhythm, do what he would to retain it, and the verse was like a medal which has turned out imperfect through the inexperience of the caster, who has not calculated the proper quantity of metal necessary for filling the mould. With ingenious patience he poured the metal back into the crucible and began all over again. Finally the verse came out full and clear, and the whole sonnet lived and breathed like a free and perfect creature.

Thus he composed—now slow, now fast—with a delight never felt before. As the day grew, the sea cast luminous darts between the trees as between the columns of a jasper portico. Here Alma Tadema would have depicted a Sappho with hyacinthine locks, seated at the foot of the marble Hermes, singing to a seven-stringed lyre and surrounded by a chorus of maidens with locks of flame, all pallid and intent, drinking in the pure harmony of the verses.

Having accomplished the four sonnets, he heaved a sigh and proceeded to recite them silently but with inward emphasis. Then he wrote them on the quadrangular pedestal of the Hermes, one on each surface in the following order—

I

' Four-fronted Hermes, to thy four-fold sense
Have these my marvellous tidings been made known?
Suave spirits, singing on their way, have flown
Forth from my heart, light-hearted ; and from thence

Have cast forth every foul intelligence,
And every foul stream dammed, and overthrown
The old unguarded bridges, stone by stone,
And quenched the flame of my impenitence.

Singing, the spirits ascend ; I know the voice,
The hymn ; and, inextinguishable and vast,
Delighting laughters from my heart arise.

Pale, but a king, I bid my soul rejoice
To hearken my heart's laughter, as at last
Low in the dust the conquered evil lies.

II

The glad soul laughs, because its loves have fled,
Because the conquered evil bites the dust
Which into intertangled fires had thrust,
As into fiery thickets, feet now led

Into the circle human sorrows tread ;
It leaves the treacherous labyrinths of lust,
Where the fair pagan monsters lure the just,
In hyacinth robes, a novice, garmented.

Now may no Sphinx with golden nails ensnare,
No Gorgon freeze it out of snaky folds,
No Siren lull it on a sleepy coast ;

But, at the circle's summit, see, a fair
White woman, in the act of worship, holds
In her pure hands the sacrificial Host.

III

Beyond all harm, all ambush, and all hate,
Tranquil of face, and strong at heart, she stands,
And knows till death, and scorns, and understands
All evil things that on her passage wait.

Thou hast in ward and keeping every gate,
The winds breathe sweetness at thy sweet commands,
Might'st thou but take, when with these restless hands
I lay at thine untroubled feet my fate !

Even now there shines before me in thy meek
And holy hands the Host, like to a sun.
Have I attained, have I then paid the price ?

She, that is favourable to all that seek,
Lifting the Host, declares : *Now is begun*
And ended the eternal sacrifice !

IV

For I, she saith, *am the unnatural Rose,*
I am the Rose of Beauty.   I instil
The drunkenness of ecstasy, I fill
The spirit with my rapture and repose.

Sowing with tears, sorrowful still are those
That with much singing gather harvest still.
After long sorrow, this my sweetness will
Be sweeter than all sweets thy spirit knows.

So be it, Madonna ; and from my heart outburst
The blood of tears, flooding all mortal things,
And the immortal sorrow be yet whole ;

Let the depths swallow me, let there as at first
Be darkness, so I see the glimmerings
Of light that rain on my unconquered soul !

Die XII. Septembris MDCCCLXXXVI.'

CHAPTER II

SCHIFANOJA was situated on the heights at that point where the chain of hills, after following the curving coast line, took a landward bend and sloped away towards the plain. Notwithstanding that it had been built in the latter half of the eighteenth century—by the Cardinal Alfonso Carafa d'Ateleta —the villa showed a certain purity of architectural design. It was a square building of two stories, with arched colonnades alternating with the apartments, which imparted to the whole edifice a look of lightness and grace. It was a real summer palace, open on all sides to the breath of the sea. At the side towards the sloping gardens, a wide hall opened on to a noble double flight of steps leading to a platform like a vast terrace, surrounded by a stone balustrade and adorned by two fountains. At either end of this terrace, other flights of steps interrupted by more terraces led by easy stages almost to the sea, affording a full view from the level ground of their sevenfold windings through superb verdure and masses of roses. The special glories of Schifanoja were its cypresses and its roses. Roses were there of every kind and for every season, enough '*pour en tirer neuf ou dix muytz d'eaue rose*' as the poet of the *Vergier d'honneur* would have said. The cypresses, sharp-pointed and sombre, more hieratic than the Pyramids, more enigmatic than the obelisks, were in no respect inferior either to those of the Villa d'Este, or the Villa Mondragone or any of the giants growing round the glorious Roman villas.

The Marchesa d'Ateleta was in the habit of spending the summer and part of the autumn at Schifanoja ; for, though a

thorough woman of the world, she was fond of the country
and its freedom, and liked to keep open house there for her
friends. She had lavished every care and attention upon
Andrea during his illness; had been to him like an elder
sister, almost a mother, and untiring in her devotion. She
cherished a profound affection for her cousin, was ever ready
to excuse or pardon, was a good and frank friend to him,
capable of understanding many things, always at his beck and
call, always cheerful, always bright and witty. Although she
had overstepped the thirties by a year, she had lost nothing
of her youth, vivacity and great personal charm, for she possessed the secret of Madame de Pompadour's fascination,
that '*beauté sans traits*' which lights up with unexpected
graces. Moreover, she possessed that rare gift commonly
called tact. A fine feminine sense of the fitness of things
was an infallible guide to her. In her relations with a host
of acquaintances of either sex she always succeeded in steering her course discreetly; she never committed an error of
taste, never weighed heavily on the lives of others, never
arrived at an inopportune moment nor became importunate,
no deed or word of hers but was entirely to the point. Her
treatment of Andrea during the somewhat trying period of his
convalescence was beyond all praise. She did her utmost to
avoid disturbing or annoying him, and, what is more, managed
that no one else should; she left him complete liberty, pretended not to notice his whims and melancholies; never
worried him with indiscreet questions; made her company
sit as lightly as possible on him at obligatory moments, and
even went so far as to refrain from her usual witty remarks
in his presence to save him the trouble of forcing a smile.

Andrea recognised her delicacy and was profoundly
grateful.

Returning from the garden with unwonted lightness of
heart on that September morning after writing his sonnets
on the Hermes, he encountered Donna Francesca on the
steps, and, kissing her hand, he exclaimed in laughing
tones :

'Cousin Francesca, I have found the Truth and the Way!'
'Alleluja!' she returned, lifting up her fair rounded arms,
—'Alleluja!'

And she continued on her way down to the garden while
Andrea went on to his room with heart refreshed.

A little while afterwards there came a gentle knock at the
door and Francesca's voice asking—'May I come in?'

She entered with the lap of her dress and both arms full of
great clusters of dewy roses, white, yellow, crimson, russet
brown. Some were wide and transparent like those of the
Villa Pamfili, all fresh and glistening, others were densely
petalled, and with that intensity of colouring which recalls the
boasted magnificence of the dyes of Tyre and Sidon; others
again were like little heaps of odorous snow, and gave one a
strange desire to bite into them and eat them. The infinite
gradations of red, from violent crimson to the faded pink of
over-ripe strawberries, mingled with the most delicate and
almost imperceptible variations of white, from the immaculate
purity of freshly fallen snow to the indefinable shades of new
milk, the sap of the reed, dull silver, alabaster and opal.

'It is a *festa* to-day,' she said, her laughing face appearing
over the flowers that covered her whole bosom up to the
throat.

'Thanks! Thanks!' Andrea cried again and again as he
helped her to empty the mass of bloom on to the table, all
over the books and papers and portfolios—'*Rosa rosarum!*'

Her hands once free, she proceeded to collect all the vases
in the room and fill them with roses, arranging each cluster
with rare artistic skill. While she did so, she talked of a
thousand things with her usual blithe volubility, almost as if
compensating herself for the parsimony of words and laughter
she had exercised up till now, out of regard for Andrea's
taciturn melancholy.

Presently she remarked, 'On the 15th we expect a
beautiful guest, Donna Maria Ferrès y Capdevila, the
wife of the Plenipotentiary for Guatemala. Do you know
her?'

' I think not.'

' No, I do not suppose you could. She only returned to
Italy a few months ago, but she will spend next winter in
Rome because her husband has been appointed to that post.
She is a very dear friend of mine—we knew each other as
children, and were three years together at the Convent of
the Annunciation in Florence. She is younger than I am.'

' Is she an American?'

' No, an Italian. She is from Sienna. She comes of the
Bandinelli family, and was baptized with water from the
" Fonte Gaja." For all that, she is rather melancholy by
nature, but very sweet. The story of her marriage is not
a very cheerful one. Ferres is a most unsympathetic
person. However, they have a little girl—a perfect darling
—you will see; a little white face with enormous eyes and
masses of dark hair. She is very like her mother—Look,
Andrea, is not that rose just like velvet? And this—I
could eat it — look — it is like glorified cream. How
delicious ! '

She went on picking out the different roses and chatting
pleasantly. A wave of perfume, intoxicating as century-old
wine, streamed from the massed flowers ; some of the petals
dropped and hung in the folds of Francesca's gown ; beneath
the window the dark shaft of a cypress pierced the golden
sunshine, and through Andrea's memory ran persistently, like
a phrase of music, a line from Petrarch :—

> ' *Così partia le rose e le parole.*'

Two days afterwards he repaid his cousin by presenting her
with a sonnet curiously fashioned on an antique model and
inscribed on vellum with illuminated ornaments in the style
of those that enliven the missals of Attavante and of Liberale
of Verona.

> ' Ferrara, for its d'Estes glorious,
>   Where Cossa strove in triumphs to recall
>   Cosimo Tura's triumphs on the the wall,
>   Saw never feast more fair and plenteous.

Monna Francesca plucked and bore to us
Such store of roses, and so shed on all,
That heaven had lacked for such a coronal
The little angels it engarlands thus.

She spoke, and shed the roses in such showers,
And such a loveliness was seen in her,
This, said I, *is some Grace the sun discloses.*

I trembled at the sweetness of the flowers.
A verse of Petrarch mounted in the air :
She scatters words and scatters with them roses.'

CHAPTER III

ON the following Wednesday, the 15th of September, the new guest arrived.

The Marchesa, accompanied by Andrea and her eldest son, Fernanindo, drove over to Rovigliano, the nearest station, to meet her. As they drove along the road shadowed by lofty poplars, the Marchesa spoke to Andrea of her friend with much affection.

'I think you will like her,' she remarked in conclusion.

Then she began to laugh as if at some sudden thought.

'Why do you laugh?' asked Andrea.

'I am making a comparison.'

'What comparison?'

'Guess.'

'I can't.'

'Well, I was thinking of another introduction I gave you about two years ago, which I accompanied by a delightful prophecy—you remember?'

'Ah—ha——'

'And I laughed because this time again there is an unknown lady in question and this time too I may play the part of——an involuntary providence.'

'Oh—oh!'

'But this case is very different, or rather the difference lies in the heroine of the possible drama.'

'You mean——'

'That Maria Ferrès is a *turris eburnea.*'

'And I am now a *vas spirituale.*'

'Ah yes, I had forgotten that you had, at last, found the

Truth and the Way—" The glad soul laughs because its loves have fled——" '

'What—you are quoting my verses?'

'I know them by heart.'

'How sweet of you!'

'However, I confess, my dear cousin, that your "fair white woman" holding the Host in her pure hands seems to me a trifle suspicious. She has, to my mind, too much of the air of a hollow shape, a robe without a body inside it, at the mercy of whatever soul, be it angel or demon, that chooses to enter it and offer you the communion.

'But this is sacrilege—rank sacrilege!'

'Ah, you had better take care! Watch that figure and use plenty of exorcisms——But there, I am prophesying again! Really, it seems a weakness of mine.'

'Here we are at the station.'

They both laughed, and all three entered the little station to wait for the train, which was due in a few minutes. Fernandino, a sickly-looking boy of twelve, was carrying a bouquet which he was to present to Donna Maria. Andrea, put in excellent spirits by his little conversation with his cousin, took a tea-rose from the bouquet and stuck it in his button-hole, then cast a rapid glance over his light summer clothes and noticed with complaisance that his hands had become whiter and thinner since his illness. But he did it all without reflection, simply from an instinct of harmless vanity which had suddenly awakened in him.

'Here comes the train,' said Fernandino.

The Marchesa hurried forward to greet her friend, who was already leaning out of the carriage window waving her hand and nodding. Her head was enveloped in a large gray gauze veil which half covered her large black hat.

'Francesca! Francesca!' she cried with a little tremor of joy in her voice.

The sound of that voice made a singular impression on Andrea—it reminded him vaguely of a voice he knew—but whose?

Donna Maria left the carriage with a rapid and light step, and with a pretty grace raised her veil above her mouth to kiss her friend. Suddenly Andrea was struck by the profound charm of this slender, graceful, veiled woman of whose face he saw only the mouth and chin.

'Maria, let me present my cousin to you—Count Andrea Sperelli-Fieschi d'Ugenta.'

Andrea bowed. The lady's lips parted in a smile that was rendered mysterious from the rest of the face being concealed by the veil.

The Marchesa then introduced Andrea to Don Manuel Ferrès y Capdevila ; then, stroking the hair of the little girl who was gazing at the young man with a pair of wide-open, astonished eyes, 'This is Delfina,' she said.

In the carriage, Andrea sat opposite to Donna Maria and beside her husband. She kept her veil down still ; Fernandino's bouquet lay in her lap and from time to time she raised it to her face to inhale the perfume while she answered the Marchesa's questions. Andrea was right ; there were tones in her voice exactly like Elena's. He was seized with impatient curiosity to see her face—its expression and colouring.

'Manuel,' she was saying, 'has to leave on Friday. He will come back for me later on.'

'Much later, let us hope,' said Donna Francesca cordially. 'A month, at the very least, eh, Don Manuel? The best plan would be to wait and all go on the same day. We are at Schifanoja till the first of November.'

'If my mother were not expecting me, nothing would delight me more than to stay with you. But I have promised faithfully to be in Sienna for the 17th of October—Delfina's birthday.'

'What a pity ! on the 20th there is the Festival of the Donations at Rovigliano—so very beautiful and peculiar.'

'What is to be done? If I do not keep my promise, my mother will be dreadfully disappointed. She adores Delfina.'

The husband took no part whatever in the conversation,

he seemed a very taciturn man. He was of middle height, inclined to be stout and bald, and his skin of a most peculiar hue—something between green and violet, in which the whites of the eyes gleamed as they moved like the enamel eyes of certain antique bronze heads. His moustache, which was harsh and black and cut evenly like the bristles of a brush, shadowed a coarse and sardonic mouth. He appeared to be about forty, or rather more. In his whole appearance there was something disagreeably hybrid and morose, that indefinable air of viciousness which belongs to the later generations of bastard races brought up in the midst of moral disorder.

'Look, Delfina—orange trees, all in flower!' exclaimed Donna Maria, stretching out her hand to pluck a spray as they passed.

Near Schifanoja, the road lay between orange groves, the trees being so high that they afforded a pleasant shade, through which the sea-breeze sighed and fluttered, so laden with perfume that one might almost have quaffed it like a draught of cool water.

Delfina was kneeling on the carriage seat and leaned out to catch at the branches. Her mother wound an arm about her to keep her from falling out.

'Take care! Take care! You will tumble — wait a moment till I untie my veil. Would you mind helping me, Francesca?'

She bent her head towards her friend to let her unfasten the veil from her hat, and in doing so the bouquet of roses fell at her feet. Andrea promptly picked them up, and as he rose from his stooping position, he at last saw her whole face uncovered.

It was an oval face, perhaps the least trifle too long, but hardly worth mentioning—that aristocratic oval which the most graceful portrait painters of the fifteenth century were rather fond of exaggerating. The refined features had that subtle expression of suffering and lassitude which lends the human charm to the Virgins of the Florentine *tondi* of the time of Cosimo. A soft and tender shadow, the fusion of

two diaphanous· tints—violet and blue, lay under her eyes,
which had the leonine irises of the brown-haired angels.
Her hair lay on her forehead and temples like a heavy crown,
and was gathered into a massive coil on her neck. The
shorter locks in front were thick and waving as those that
cover the head of the Farnese Antinous. Nothing could
exceed the charm of that delicate head, which seemed to
droop under its burden as under some divine chastisement.

'Dio mio!' she sighed, endeavouring to lighten with her
hands the weight of tresses gathered up and compressed
under her hat. 'My head aches as if I had been hanging by
the hair for an hour. I cannot keep it fastened up for long
together, it tires me so. It is a perfect slavery.'

'Do you remember at school,' broke in Francesca, 'how
we were all wild to comb your hair? It led to furious
quarrels every day. Fancy, Andrea—at last it came to
bloodshed! Oh, I shall never forget the scene between
Carlotta Fiordelise and Gabreilla Vanni. It got to be sheer
monomania. To comb Maria Bandinelli's hair was the one
ambition in life of every school-girl there—big or little.
The epidemic spread through the whole school, and resulted
in scoldings, punishments, and finally threats to have your
hair cut off. Do you remember, Maria? Our very souls
were enthralled by the magnificent black plait that hung
like a rope to your heels!'

Donna Maria smiled a mournful, dreamy smile. Her lips
were slightly parted, the upper one projecting the least little
bit beyond the under one; the corners of her mouth drooped
plaintively, the soft curve losing itself in shadow which gave
her an expression both sad and kind, but with a dash of that
pride which reveals the moral elevation of those who have
suffered much and been strong.

To Andrea the story of these girls enamoured of a plait
of hair, enflamed with passion and jealousy, wild to pass a
comb or their fingers through the living treasure, seemed a
charming and poetic episode of convent life, and in his
imagination, this woman with the sumptuous hair became

vaguely illumined like the heroine of some Christian legend of the childhood of a saint destined for martyrdom and future canonisation. At the same time, it struck him what rich and varied lines might be afforded to the design of a female figure by the undulating masses of that black hair.

Not that it was really black, as Andrea perceived next day at dinner, when a ray of sunshine touched the lady's head, bringing out sombre violet lights, reflections as of tempered steel or burnished silver. Notwithstanding its density too, it was perfectly light, each hair seeming to stand apart as if permeated by and breathing the air. Her conversation revealed keen intelligence and a delicate mind, much refinement of taste and pleasure in the æsthetic. She possessed abundant and varied culture, a vivid imagination, and the rich, descriptive language of one who has seen many lands, lived under widely different climes, known many people. To Andrea, she seemed to exhale some exotic charm, some strange fascination, some spell born of the phantoms of the far off things she had looked upon, the scenes she still preserved before her mind's eye, the memories that filled her soul; as if she still bore about her some traces of the sunshine she had basked in, the perfumes she had inhaled, the strange dialects she had heard—all the magic of these countries of the Sun.

That evening, in the great room opening off the hall, she went over to the piano, and opening it, she said : ' Do you still play, Francesca ? '

' Oh, no,' replied the Marchesa, ' I have not practised for years. I feel that listening to others is decidedly preferable. However, I affect to be a patroness of Art, and during the winter I gladly preside at the execution of a little good music. Is that not so, Andrea ? '

' My cousin is too modest, Donna Maria ; she does something more than merely patronise—she is a reviver of good taste. Only last February, thanks to her, we were made acquainted with a quintett, a quartett, and a trio of Boccherini, and besides that with a quartett of Cherubini—music that was well-nigh forgotten, but admirable and always new. Boccherini's adagios and minuets are deliciously fresh; only the finales seem to me a trifle antiquated. I am sure you must know something of his.'

'I remember having heard one of his quintetts four of five years ago at the Conservatoire in Brussels, and I thought it magnificent—in the very newest style and full of unexpected episodes. I remember perfectly that in certain passages the quintett was reduced to a duet by employing the unison, but the effects produced by the difference in the tone of the instruments was something marvellous! I cannot recall anything the least like it in other instrumental compositions.'

She discussed music with all the subtlety of a true connoisseur, and in describing the sentiments aroused in her by some particular composition, or the entire work of a master, she expressed herself most felicitously.

'I have played and heard a great deal of music,' she said, 'and of every symphony, every sonata, every nocturne I have a separate and distinct picture, an impression of shape and colour, of a figure, a group, a landscape, so that each of my favourite compositions has a name corresponding to the picture;—for instance, the Sonata of the Forty Daughters-in-law of Priam; the Nocturne of the Sleeping Beauty in the Wood, the Gavotte of the Yellow Ladies, the Gigue of the Mill, the Prelude of the Drops of Water, and so on.'

She laughed softly, a laugh which surprised one with its ineffable grace on that plaintive mouth.

'You remember, Francesca, the multitude of notes with which we afflicted the margins of our favourite pieces at school. One day, after a most serious consultation, we changed the title of every piece of Schumann's we possessed, and each title had a long explanatory note. I have the papers still. Now, when I play the *Myrthen* or the *Album-blätter*, all these mysterious annotations are quite incomprehensible to me; my emotions and my point of view have changed completely, but there is a delicate pleasure in comparing the sentiments of the present with those of the

past, the new picture and the old. It is a pleasure very
similar to that of re-reading one's diary, only perhaps rather
more mournful and intense. A diary is generally the descrip-
tion of real events, a chronicle of days happy or otherwise,
the gray or rosy traces left by time in its flight; the notes
written in youth on the margin of a piece of music are, on
the contrary, fragments of the secret poems of a soul that is
just breaking into bloom, the lyric effusions of our ideality as
yet untouched, the story of our dreams. What language?
What a flow of words! You remember, Francesca?'

She talked with perfect freedom, even with a touch of
spiritual exaltation, like a person long condemned to inter-
course with inferiors, who has the irresistible desire to open
her mind and heart to a breath of the higher life. Andrea
listened to her and was conscious of a pleasing sense of
gratitude towards her. It seemed to him that in speaking
of these things in his presence, she offered him a kindly
proof of friendship, and permitted him to draw nearer to her.
He thereby caught a glimpse of her inner world, less through
the actual words she uttered than by the modulations of her
voice. And again he recognised the accents of *the other*.

It was an ambiguous voice, a voice with double chords in
it, so to speak. The more virile tones, deep and slightly
veiled, would soften, brighten, become feminine, as it were,
by a transition so harmonious that the ear of the listener
was at once surprised, delighted, and perplexed by it. The
phenomenon was so singular that it sufficed by itself to
occupy the mind of the listener independently of the sense of
the words, so that after a few minutes the mind yielded to
the mysterious charm and remained suspended between
expectation and desire to hear the sweet cadence, as if
waiting for a melody played upon an instrument. It was the
feminine note in this voice which recalled *the other*.

'You sing?' asked Andrea half shyly.

'A little,' she replied.

'Then please sing a little,' entreated Donna Francesca.

'Very well, but I can only give you a sort of idea of the

music, for, during the last year, I have almost lost my voice.'

In the adjoining room, Don Manuel was silently playing cards with the Marchese d'Ateleta. In the drawing-room the light of the lamps shone softly red through a great Japanese shade. The sea-breeze, entering through the pillars of the hall, shook the high Karamanieh curtains and wafted the perfume of the garden on its wings. Beyond the pillars was a vista of tall cypresses, massive and black as ebony against a diaphanous sky throbbing with stars.

'As we are on the subject of old music,' said Donna Maria seating herself at the piano, 'I will give you an air of Paisiello's out of *Nina Pazza*, an exquisite thing.'

She accompanied herself as she sang. In the fervour of the song, the two tones of her voice blended into one another like two precious metals combining to make a single one— sonorous, warm, caressing, vibrating. ·Paisiello's melody— simple, pure and spontaneous, full of delicious languor and winged sadness, with a delicately light accompaniment— issued from that plaintive mouth and rose with such a flame of passion that the convalescent was moved to the depths of his being, and felt the notes drop one by one through his veins, as if all the blood in his body had stopped in its course to listen. A cold shiver stirred the roots of his hair, shadows, thick and rapid, passed before his eyes, he held his breath with excitement. In the weak state of his nerves his sensations were so poignant that it was all he could do to keep back his tears.

'Oh, dearest Maria!' exclaimed Donna Francesca, kissing her fondly on the hair when she stopped.

Andrea could not utter a word; he remained seated where he was, with his back to the light and his face in shadow.

'Please go on,' said Francesca.

She sang an Arietta by Antonio Salieri, then she played a Toccata by Leonardo Leo, a Gavotte by Rameau, a Gigue by Sebastian Bach. Under her magic fingers the music of the eighteenth century lived again—so melancholy in its dance airs, that sound as if they were intended to be danced to in a languid afternoon of a Saint Martin's summer, in a deserted park, amid silent fountains and statueless pedestals, on a carpet of dead roses by pairs of lovers on the point of ceasing to love one another.

CHAPTER IV

'Let down a rope of your hair to me that I may climb up,' Andrea called laughingly from the terrace below to Donna Maria, where she stood between two pillars of the loggia opening out of her rooms.

It was morning, and she had come out into the sun to dry her wet hair, which hung round her like a heavy mantle, and accentuated the soft pallor of her face. The black border of the vivid orange-coloured awning hung above her head like a frieze, such as one sees round the antique Greek vases of the Campagna. Had she had a garland of narcissus on her brows and at her side a great nine-stringed lyre with bas-reliefs of Apollo and a greyhound, she might have been taken for a pupil of the school of Mytilene, or a Lesbian musician in repose as imagined by a Pre-Raphaelite.

'You send me up a madrigal,' she answered in the same playful tone, but drawing back a little from view.

'Very well, I will go and write one in your honour on the marble balustrade of the lowest terrace. Come down and read it when you are ready.'

Andrea proceeded slowly to descend the steps leading to the lower level. In that September morning his soul seemed to dilate with every breath he drew. A certain sanctity seemed to pervade the air; the sea shone with a splendour of its own, as if the sources of magic rays lay in its depths; the whole landscape was steeped in sunshine.

He stood still from time to time. The thought that Donna Maria was perhaps watching him from the loggia disturbed him curiously, made his heart beat fast and flutter timidly,

as if he were a boy in love for the first time. It was unspeakable bliss merely to breathe the same warm and limpid air
that she did. An immense wave of tenderness flooded his
heart and communicated itself to the trees, the rocks, the
sea, as if to beings who were his friends and confidants. He
was filled with a desire to worship humbly and purely; to
bend his knee and clasp his hands and offer up to some one
this vague mute adoration which he would have been at a
loss to explain. He felt as if the goodness of all created
things was being poured out upon him and mingling with all
he possessed of goodness into one jubilant stream.

'Can it be that I love her?' he asked himself. But he
dared not look closely into his soul, lest the delicate enchantment should disperse and vanish like a dream at break of
day.

'Do I love her? And what does she think? And if she
comes alone, shall I tell her that I love her?' He took
pleasure in thus asking himself questions which he did not
answer, intercepting the reply of his heart by another question,
prolonging his uncertainty—at once so tormenting and so
sweet. 'No, no—I shall not tell her that I love her. She is
far above all the others.'

Arrived at the lowest terrace, he turned round and looked
up, and there in the loggia, in the full blaze of the sun, he
could just make out the indistinct outline of a woman's form.
Had she followed him with her eyes and her thoughts down
the long flights of steps? A childish impulse made him
suddenly pronounce her name aloud on the deserted terrace.
'Maria! Maria!' he repeated, listening to his own voice. No
word, no name had ever seemed to him so sweet, so melodious, so caressing. How happy he would be if she would only
allow him to call her Maria, like a sister.

This woman—so spiritual, so soulful—inspired him with
the highest sentiment of devotion and humility. If he had
been asked what he considered the sweetest possible task, he
would have answered in all sincerity—'To obey her.'
Nothing in the world would have mortified him so much as

to be accounted by her a commonplace man. By no other
woman had he so ardently desired to be praised, admired,
understood, appreciated in his tastes, his cultivation, his
artistic aspirations, his ideals, his dreams, all the noblest
parts of his spirit and his life. And his highest ambition was
to fill her heart.

She had now been ten days at Schifanoja, and in those ten
days how entirely she had subjugated him ! They had
conversed sometimes for hours seated on the terrace or on
one of the numerous marble benches scattered about the
grounds or in the long rose-bordered avenues, while Delfina
sped like a little gazelle through the winding paths of the
orange groves. In her conversation she displayed a charming
flow of language, many gems of delicate yet keen observation,
occasionally affording glimpses of her inner self with a
candour that was full of grace ; and when speaking of her
travels, she would often, by a single picturesque phrase, call
up before Andrea's eyes wide vistas of distant lands and seas.
On his part, he did his utmost to show himself to the best
advantage, to impress upon her the wide range of his culture,
the refinement of his taste, the exquisite keenness of his
susceptibilities, and his heart swelled with pride when she
said in tones of unfeigned sincerity after reading his *Story of
the Hermaphrodite*—

' No music has ever carried me away like this poem, nor
has any statue ever given me such an impression of harmonious beauty. Certain lines haunt me persistently, and will
continue to do so for long, I am sure—they are so intense.'

As he sat now on the marble balustrade, he was thinking
of these words of hers. Donna Maria was no longer in the
loggia, the awning concealed the whole space between the
pillars. Perhaps she would soon be down—should he write
the madrigal he had promised her ? But even the slight
effort necessary for writing the lines thus in hot haste seemed
intolerable to him here in the wide and opulent garden,
blossoming under the September sunshine in a sort of
magical Spring. Why disturb these rare and delicious

emotions by a hurried search after rhymes? why reduce this far reaching sentiment to a brief metrical sigh?

He resolved to break his promise and remained as he was, idly watching the sails on the distant horizon, like fiery torches outshining the sun.

But as time went on, he grew restless and nervous, turning round every minute to see if a feminine form had not appeared between the columns of the vestibule which gave access to the steps—'Was this then a love tryst? Did he expect her to join him here for some secret interview? Had she any idea of his agitation?'

His heart gave a great throb—it was she!

She was alone. Slowly she descended the steps, and when she reached the first terrace she stopped beside the fountain. Andrea followed her intently with his eyes; her every movement, every attitude sent a delicious thrill through him, as if each one of them had some special significance, were a form of individual expression. Thus she passed down the succession of steps and terraces, appearing and disappearing, now completely hidden by the rose-bushes, now only her head or her rounded bust visible above them. Sometimes the thickly interlaced boughs hid her for several minutes, then, where the bushes were thinner, the colour of her dress would show through them and the pale straw of her hat would catch the sunlight. The nearer she came the more slowly she walked, loitering among the verdant shrubs, stopping to gaze at the cypresses, stooping to gather a handful of fallen leaves. From the last terrace but one, she waved her hand to Andrea standing waiting for her at the foot of the steps, and threw down to him the leaves she had gathered, which first rose fluttering in the air like a cloud of butterflies and then floated down—now fast, now slow,—noiseless as snow-flakes on the stones.

'Well?' she asked, leaning over the balustrade, 'what have you got for me?'

Andrea bent his knee to the step and lifted his clasped hands.

'Nothing!' he was obliged to confess. 'I implore you to

forgive me ; but, this morning, you and the sun together
filled the whole world for me with sweetness and light.
Adoremus ! '

The confession was perfectly sincere, as was the adoration
also, though both were uttered in a tone of banter. Donna
Maria evidently felt the sincerity, for she coloured slightly as
she said with peculiar earnestness—

' No—don't—please don't kneel.'

He rose, and she offered him her hand, adding, ' I will
forgive you this time because you are an invalid.'

She wore a dress of a curious indefinable dull rusty red,
one of those so-called æsthetic colours one meets with in the
pictures of the Early Masters or of Dante Gabriel Rossetti.
It was arranged in a multitude of straight regular folds beginning immediately under the arms, and was confined at the
waist by a wide blue-green ribbon, of the pale tinge of a
faded turquoise, that fell in a great knot at her side. The
sleeves were very full and soft, and were gathered in closely
at the wrist. Another ribbon of the same shade, but much
narrower, encircled her neck and was tied at the left side in
a small bow, and a similar ribbon fastened the end of the
prodigious plait which fell from under her straw hat, round
which was twined a wreath of hyacinths like that of Alma
Tadema's Pandora. A great Persian turquoise, her sole
ornament, shaped like a scarabeus and engraved with talis-
manic characters, fastened her dress at the throat.

' Let us wait for Delfina,' she said, ' and then, what do you
say to our going as far as the gate of the Cybele ? Would
that suit you ? '

She was full of delicate consideration for the convalescent.
Andrea was still very pale and thin, which made his eyes look
extraordinarily large, the somewhat sensual expression of his
mouth forming a singular and not unattractive contrast to the
upper part of his face.

' Yes,' he replied, ' and I am deeply grateful to you.'
Then, after a moment's hesitation—' Do you mind if I am
rather silent this morning ? '

'Why do you ask me that?'

'Because I feel as if I had lost my tongue and could find nothing to say; and yet silence becomes burdensome and annoying if it is prolonged. That is why I ask if, during our walk, you will allow me to be silent and only listen to you.'

'Why, then, we will be silent together,' she said with a little smile.

She looked up towards the villa with evident impatience— 'What a long time Delfina is!'

'Was Francesca up when you came out?' asked Andrea.

'Oh no, she is incredibly lazy—ah, there is Delfina, do you see her?'

The little girl came hurrying down, followed by her governess. Though not visible on the flight of steps, she appeared upon the terraces which she traversed at a run, her hair floating over her shoulders in the breeze from under a broad-brimmed straw hat wreathed with poppies. On the last step she opened her arms wide to her mother and covered her face with kisses. After this she said—'Good morning, Andrea,' and presented her forehead to his kiss with childlike and adorable grace.

She was a fragile creature, highly strung and vibrating as an instrument fashioned of sentient material, her flesh so delicately transparent as to seem incapable of concealing or even veiling the radiance of the spirit that dwelt within it like a flame in a precious lamp.

'Heart's dearest!' murmured her mother, gazing at her with a look in which was concentrated all the tenderness of a soul wholly occupied by this one absorbing affection. But at those words, that look, that caress, Andrea felt a sudden stab of jealousy, something like a rebuff, as if her heart were turning away from him, eluding him, becoming inaccessible.

The governess asked permission to return to the villa, and the three turned into a path bordered by orange-trees. Delfina ran on in front with her hoop, her straight slender little legs in their long black stockings, moving with rhythmic grace.

'You seem a little out of spirits now,' said Donna Maria to her companion, 'and only a little while ago, when you came down, you seemed so bright. Is something troubling you? —do you not feel so well?'

She put these questions in an almost sisterly manner, soberly and kindly, inviting his confidence. A timid desire, a vague temptation assailed the invalid to slip his arm through hers, and let her lead him in silence through the flickering shadows and the perfumes, over the flower-strewn ground, down the pathways measured off at intervals by ancient moss-grown statues. He seemed, all at once, to have returned to the first days of his illness, those never-to-be-forgotten days of happy languor and semi-unconsciousness, and felt as if he had great need of a friendly support, an affectionate, a familiar arm. The desire grew so intense that the words which would give it voice rushed to his lips. However he merely replied—

'No, Donna Maria, thank you, I feel quite well. It is only that the September weather rather affects me.'

She looked at him as if she rather doubted the sincerity of his reply; but, to avoid an awkward silence after his evasive remark, she asked—

'Which of the neutral months do you like best—April or September?'

'Oh, September. It is more feminine, more discreet, more mysterious—like a Spring seen in a dream. Then all the plants slowly lose their vital forces, and, at the same time, some of their reality. Look at the sea over there—has it not more the appearance of an atmosphere than of a solid mass of water? And never, to my mind, does the union of sea and sky seem so mystical, so profound as in September.'

They had very nearly reached the end of the path. Why should Andrea be suddenly seized with a tremor of nervous fear on approaching the spot where, a fortnight ago, he had written the sonnets on his deliverance? Why this struggle between hope and anxiety lest she should discover them and read them? Why did some of the lines keep running in his

mind to the exclusion of others, as if they expressed his
actual sentiments at that moment, his aspirations, the new
dream he carried in his heart?

'I lay at thine untroubled feet my fate!'

It was true! It was true! He loved her, he laid his
whole life at her feet—was conscious of but one desire—
humble and absorbing—to be the earth between her footsteps.

'How beautiful it is here!' exclaimed Donna Maria, as
she entered the demesne of the four-fronted Hermes, into
the paradise of the acanthus. 'But what a strange scent!'

The whole air was full of the odour of musk, as from the
unseen presence of some musk-breathing insect or animal.
The shadows were deep and mysterious, the rays of light
which pierced the foliage, already touched by the finger of
autumn, seemed like shafts of moonlight shining through
the storied windows of a cathedral. A mixed sentiment,
partly Pagan, partly Christian, seemed to emanate from this
sylvan retreat, as from a mythological picture painted by an
early Christian artist.

'Oh look, look, Delfina!' her mother exclaimed in the
excited tones of one who suddenly comes upon a thing of
beauty.

Delfina had skilfully woven little sprays of orange blossom
into a garland, and now, with the fancifulness of childhood,
she was eager that it should encircle the head of the marble
deity. She could not reach it, but did her best to accomplish
her object by standing on tiptoe and stretching her arm to its
utmost extent ; her slender, elegant and vivacious little figure
offering a striking contrast to the rigid, square and solemn
form of the statue, like a lily-stem against an oak. All her
efforts were, however, fruitless.

Smilingly, her mother came to her aid. Taking the wreath
from the child's hand, she placed it on the pensive brows of
the god. As she did so, her eyes fell involuntarily upon the
inscriptions.

'Who has been writing verses here.—You?' she asked,

turning to Andrea in surprise and pleasure. 'Yes—I recognise your hand.'

Forthwith, she knelt upon the grass to read with eager
curiosity. While Donna Maria read the words in a low voice,
Delfina leaned upon her mother's shoulder, one arm about
her neck, cheek pressed to cheek. The two figures thus
bending over the pedestal of the tall flower-wreathed statue,
in the uncertain light, surrounded by the emblematical
acanthus, formed a group so harmonious in line and colouring
that the poet stood a moment lost in pure æsthetic pleasure
and admiration.

But the next moment the old obscure sense of jealousy
was upon him once more. The fragile little creature clinging
to the mother, indissolubly connected with her mother's very
being, seemed to him an enemy, an insurmountable obstacle
rising up against his love, his desires, his hopes. He was not
jealous of the husband, but he was of the daughter. It was
not the body but the soul of this woman that he longed
to possess, and to possess it wholly, undivided, with all its
tenderness, all its joys, its hopes, its fears, its pain, its dreams
—in short the sum total of her spiritual being, and be able
to say—'I am the life of her life.'

But instead, it was the daughter who possessed all this
incontestably, absolutely, continuously. When her idol left
her side, even for a short time, the mother seemed to miss
some essential element of her existence. Her face was
instantaneously and visibly transfigured when, after a brief
absence, that childish voice fell upon her ear once more. At
times, unconsciously and as if by some occult correspondence,
some law of common vital accordance, she would repeat
a gesture of the child's, a smile, an attitude, a pose of the
head. Again, when the child was in repose or asleep, she
had moments of contemplation so intense that she seemed
to have lost all sense of her surroundings and to have
absorbed herself into the creature she was contemplating.
When she spoke to her darling, every word was a caress,
and the plaintive lines vanished from her mouth. Under the

child's kisses, her lips quivered and her eyes filled with ineffable happiness like the eyes of an ecstatic at a beatific vision. If she happened to be conversing with other people or listening to their talk, she would appear to have sudden lapses of attention, momentary absence of mind, and this was for her daughter—for her—always for her.

Who could ever break that chain? Could any one ever succeed in conquering a part—even the very smallest atom of that heart? Andrea suffered as under an irreparable loss, some forced renunciation, some shattered hope. At this moment, this very moment, was not the child stealing something from him?

For Delfina was playfully constraining her mother to remain upon her knees. She hung with all her weight round Donna Maria's neck, crying through her laughter—

'No—no—no—you shall not get up!'

And whenever her mother opened her mouth to speak, she clapped her little hands over it to prevent her, made her laugh, bandaged her eyes with the long plait—played a hundred pranks.

Watching her, Andrea felt, that by all this playful commotion, she was dispelling from her mother all that his verses had possibly instilled into her mind.

When, at last, Donna Maria succeeded in freeing herself from her darling tyrant, she saw his annoyance in his face, and hastened to say—'Forgive me, Andrea, Delfina is sometimes taken with these fits of wildness.'

With a deft hand she re-arranged the disordered folds of her dress. There was a faint flush under her eyes and her breath came quickly.

'And forgive her too,' she continued with a smile to which the unwonted animation of colour lent a singular light, 'out of consideration for her unconscious homage, for it was she who had the happy inspiration to place a nuptial wreath over your verses which sing of nuptial communion. That sets a seal upon the alliance.'

'My thanks both to you and to Delfina,' answered Andrea.

It was the first time she had called him by his Christian name, and the unexpected familiarity, combined with her gentle words, restored his confidence. Delfina had run off down one of the paths.'

'These verses are a spiritual record, are they not?' Donna Maria resumed. 'Will you give them to me that I may not forget them?'

His natural impulse was to answer—'They are yours by right to-day, for they speak of you and to you——' But he only said—

'You shall have them.'

They continued their way towards the Cybele, but as they were leaving the little enclosure, Donna Maria suddenly turned round towards the Hermes as if some one had called her; her brow seemed heavy with thought.

'What are you thinking about?' Andrea asked her almost timidly.

'I was thinking about you,' she replied.

'What were you thinking about me?'

'I was thinking of your past life, of which I know nothing whatever. You have suffered greatly?'

'I have greatly sinned.'

'And loved much?'

'I do not know. Perhaps it was not love that I felt. Perhaps I have yet to learn what love is—really I cannot say.'

She did not answer. They walked on in silence for a little way. To their right, the path was bordered by high laurels, alternating at regular intervals with cypress trees, and in the background, through the fluttering leaves, the sea rippled and laughed, blue as the flower of the flax. On their left ran a kind of parapet like the back of a long stone bench, ornamented throughout its whole length with the Ateleta shield and arms and a griffin alternately, under each of which again was a sculptured mask through whose mouth a slender stream of water fell into a basin below, shaped like a sarcophagus and ornamented with mythological subjects in low relief. There must have been a hundred of these mouths, for the walk was called the avenue of the Hundred Fountains, but many of them were stopped up by time and had ceased to spout, while others did very little. Many of the shields were broken and moss had obliterated the coats of arms; many of the griffins were headless and the figures on the sarcophagi appeared through a veil of moss like fragments of silver work through an old and ragged velvet cover. On the water in the basins—more green and limpid than emerald —maiden-hair waved and quivered, or rose leaves, fallen from the bushes overhead, floated slowly while the surviving waterpipes sent forth a sweet and gurgling music that played over the murmur of the sea like the accompaniment to a melody.

'Do you hear that?' said Donna Maria, standing still to listen, attracted by the charm of the sound. 'That is the music of salt and of sweet waters!'

She stood in the middle of the path, finger on lip, leaning a little towards the fountains, in the attitude of one who listens and fears to be disturbed. Andrea, who was next the parapet, turned and saw her thus against a background of delicate and feathery verdure such as an Umbrian painter would have given to an Annunciation or a Nativity.

'Maria!' he murmured, his heart filling with fond adoration, 'Maria!—Maria——!'

It afforded him untold pleasure to mingle the soft accents of her name with the music of the waters. She did not look at him, but she laid her finger on her lips as a sign to him to be silent.

'Forgive me,' he said, unable to control his emotion—'but I cannot help myself—it is my soul that calls to you.'

A strange nervous exaltation had taken possession of him, all the hill-tops of his soul had caught the lyric glow and flamed up irresistibly; the hour, the place, the sunshine, everything about them suggested love—from the extreme limits of the sea to the humble little ferns of the fountains —all seemed to him part of the same magic circle whose central point was this woman.

'You can never know,' he went on in a subdued voice as if fearful of offending her—'You can never know how absolutely my soul is yours.'

She grew suddenly very pale, as if all the blood in her veins had rushed to her heart. She did not speak, she did not look at him.

'Delfina!' she cried, with a tremor of agitation in her voice.

There was no answer; the little girl had wandered off among the trees at the end of the long avenue.

'Delfina,' she repeated, louder than before, in a sort of terror.

In the pause that followed her cry the songs of the two waters seemed to make the silence deeper.

'Delfina!'

There was a rustling in the leaves as if from the passage of a little kid, and the child came bounding through the laurel thicket, carrying in her hands her straw hat heaped to the brim with little red berries she had gathered. Her exertions and the running had brought a deep flush to her cheeks, broken twigs were sticking in her frock, and some leaves hung trembling in the meshes of her ruffled hair.

'Oh mamma, come quick—do come with me!'

She began dragging her mother away—'There is a perfect forest over there—heaps and heaps of berries! Come with me, mamma, do come——'

'No, darling, I would rather not—it is getting late.'

'Oh, do come!'

'But it is late.'

'Come! Come!'

Donna Maria was obliged to give in and let herself be dragged along by the hand.

'There is a way of reaching the arbutus wood without going through the thicket,' said Andrea.

'Do you hear, Delfina? There is a better way.'

'No, mamma, I want you to come with me.'

Delfina pulled her mother along towards the sea through

the laurel thicket, and Andrea followed, content to be able to gaze without restraint at the beloved figure in front of him, to devour her with his eyes, to study her every movement and her rhythmic walk, interrupted every moment by the irregularities of the path, the obstacles presented by the trees and their interlaced branches. But while his eyes feasted on these things, his mind was chiefly occupied in recalling the one attitude, the one look—oh, that pallor, that sudden pallor just now when he had proffered those few low words! And the indefinable tone of her voice when she called Delfina.

'Is it far now?' asked Donna Maria.

'No, no, mamma, we are just there—here it is!'

As they neared the spot a sort of shyness came over Andrea. Since those words of his he had not met Maria's eye. What did she think? What were her feelings? What would her eyes say when, at last, she looked at him?

'Here it is!' cried the little girl.

The laurels had grown thinner, affording a freer view of the sea, and the next moment the mass of arbutus flushed rosy-red before them like a forest of coral with large tassels of blossom at the end of their branches.

'What a glory!' murmured Maria.

The marvellous wilderness bloomed and bore fruit in a deep and sunny space curved like an amphitheatre, in which all the delicious sweetness of that aromatic shore seemed gathered up and concentrated. The stems, tall and slender, crimson for the most part, but here and there yellow, bore great shining green leaves, all motionless in the calm air. Innumerable tassels of blossom, like sprays of lily-of-the-valley, white and dewy, hung from the young boughs, while the maturer ones were loaded with red or orange-yellow fruit. And all this wondrous pomp of blossom and fruit, of green leaves and rosy stems displayed against the brilliant blue of the sea, like a garden in a fairy tale, intense and fantastic as a dream.

'What a marvel!'

Donna Maria advanced slowly, no longer led by Delfina, who, wild with delight, rushed about with no thought but for stripping the whole wood.

Andrea plucked up his courage.

'Can you forgive me?' he asked anxiously. 'I did not mean to offend you. Indeed, seeing you so far above me, so pure, so unapproachable, I thought that never in this world could I reveal my secret to you, never ask anything of you, never put myself in your way. Since ever I saw you, I have thought of you night and day, but without hope, without any definite end in view. I know that you do not love me, that you never can love me. And yet, believe me, I would renounce every promise that life may have in store for me, just for the hope of living in a little corner of your heart——'

She continued to advance slowly under the sun-flecked trees, while the delicate tassels of pink and white blossom swayed gently above her head.

'Believe me, Maria—only believe me! If I were bidden at this moment to give up every desire and every ambition, the dearest memories of the past and the most flattering promises of the future, and to live solely in the thought of and for you—without a to-morrow, without a yesterday, without other ties or attachments, far from the world, lost to everything but you, till death—to all eternity—I would not hesitate for one instant. You have looked at me and talked to me, have smiled and answered; you have sat at my side pensive and silent; side by side with me you have lived your own inner life, that inscrutable and inaccessible existence of which I know nothing—can never know anything—and your soul has taken full and absolute possession of mine to its deepest depths, but without ever a thought, without being aware of it, as the ocean swallows up a river.—What is my love to you? What is any one's love to you? The word has too often been profaned, and the sentiment too often a make-believe.—I do not offer you love. But surely you will not refuse the humble tribute of devotion that my spirit offers up to a being nobler and higher than itself.'

She walked on at the same slow pace, her head bent, her face bloodless, towards a seat at the further end of the wood and facing the sea.

It was a wide semicircle of white marble with a back running round the entire length and, for sole ornamentation, a lion's paw at each end as a support. It recalled those antique seats on which, in some island of the Archipelago or in Greece or Pompeii, ladies reclined and listened to a reading from the poets, under the shade of the oleanders, within sight of the sea. Here the arbutus cast the shadow of its blossom and its fruit, and in contrast to the marble, the coral of the stems seemed more vivid than elsewhere.

'I care for everything that interests you; you possess all those things after which I am seeking. Pity from you would be more precious to me than passionate love from any other woman. Your hand upon my heart—I know—would cause a second youth to spring up in me far purer than the first and stronger. The ceaseless vacillation which makes up the sum of my inner life would find rest and stability in you. My unsatisfied and restless spirit, harried by a perpetual warfare between attraction and repulsion, eternally and irremediably alone, would find in yours a haven of refuge against the doubts which contaminate every ideal, and weaken the will. There are men more unfortunate, but I doubt if in the whole wide world there was ever one less happy than I.'

He was making use of Obermann's words as his own. In the sort of sentimental intoxication to which he had worked himself up, all his melancholy broodings surged to his lips, and the mere sound of his own voice—with a little quiver of humble entreaty in it—served to augment his emotions.

'I do not venture to tell you all my thoughts. At your side, during the few days since I first met you, I have had moments of oblivion so complete as almost to make me feel that I was back in the first days of my convalescence, when the sense of another world was still present with me. The past, the future were obliterated—as if the former had never been, and the latter never would be. The whole world was without form and void. Then, something like a dream, dim but stupendous, rose upon my soul—a fluttering veil, now impenetrable, now transparent, and yielding intermittent glimpses of a splendid but unattainable treasure. What did you know or care about me in such moments? Doubtless your spirit was far away from me. And yet, your mere bodily presence was sufficient to intoxicate me—I felt it flowing through my veins like blood, taking hold upon my soul with superhuman force——'

She sat silent and motionless, gazing straight before her, her figure erect, her hands rigidly clasped in her lap, in the attitude of one who makes a supreme effort to brace himself against his own weakness. Only her mouth—the expression of the lips she vainly strove to keep firm—betrayed a sort of anguished rapture.

'I dare not tell you all I feel.—Maria, Maria, can you forgive me?—say that you forgive me.'

Two little hands came suddenly from behind the seat and clasped themselves over the mother's eyes, and a voice panting with fun and mischief cried—

'Guess who it is—guess who it is!'

She smiled, and allowed herself to be drawn backwards by Delfina's clinging fingers, and instantly, with preternatural clearness, Andrea saw that smile wipe away all the obscure, delicious pain from her lips, efface every sign that might be construed into an avowal, put to flight the least lingering shadow of uncertainty that he might possibly have converted into a gleam of hope. He sat there like a man who has expected to drink from an overflowing cup and suddenly finds it has nothing but the empty air to offer to his thirsty lips.

'Guess!'

The little girl covered her mother's head with loud, quick kisses, in a kind of frenzy, even hurting her a little.

'I know who it is—I know who it is,' cried Donna Maria —'Let me go!'

'What will you give me if I do?'

'Anything you like.'

'Well, I want a pony to carry back my berries to the house. Come and see what a heap I have collected.'

She ran round the seat and pulled her mother by the hand. Donna Maria rose rather wearily, and as she stood up she closed her eyes for a moment as if overcome by sudden giddiness. Andrea rose too, and both followed in Delfina's wake.

The mischievous child had stripped half the wood of fruit. The lower branches had not a single berry left. With the aid of a stick, picked up goodness knows where, she had reaped a prodigious harvest and then piled up the fruit into one great heap, so intense in colouring against the dark soil, that it looked like a heap of glowing embers. The flowers had apparently not attracted her; there they hung, white and pink and yellow and translucent, more delicate than the flowering locks of the acacia, more graceful than the lily-of-the-valley, all bathed in dim golden light.

'Oh Delfina! Delfina!' exclaimed Donna Maria, looking round upon the devastation, 'what have you done!'

The child laughed and clapped her hands with glee in front of the crimson pyramid.

'You will have to leave it all here.'

'No—no——'

At first she refused, but she thought for a moment, and then said, half to herself with beaming eyes: 'The doe will come and eat them.'

She had probably noticed the beautiful creature moving about in the park, and the thought of having collected so much food for it pleased her and fired her imagination, already full of stories in which deer are beneficent and powerful fairies who repose on silken cushions and drink from jewelled cups. She remained silent and absorbed, picturing to herself the beautiful tawny animal browsing on the fruit under the flowering trees.

'Come,' said Donna Maria, 'it is getting late.'

Holding Delfina by the hand, she walked on till they came to the edge of the wood. Here she stopped to look at the sea, which, catching the reflection of the clouds, was like a vast undulating, glittering sheet of silk.

Without a word, Andrea plucked a spray of blossom, so full that the twig it hung from bent beneath its weight, and offered it to Donna Maria. As she took it from his hand she looked at him, but she did not open her lips.

They passed on down the avenue, Delfina talking, talking incessantly; repeating the same things over and over again, infatuated about the doe, inventing long monotonous tales in which she ran one fairy story into another, losing herself in labyrinths of her own creation, as if the sparkling freshness of the morning air had gone to her head. And round about the doe she grouped the children of the king, Cinderellas, fairy queens, magicians, monsters—all the familiar personages of those imaginary realms, crowding them in tumultuously with the kaleidoscopic rapidity of a dream. Her prattle sounded like the warbling of a bird; full of sweet modulations, with now and then a rapid succession of melodious notes that were not words,—a continuation of the wave of music already set in motion, like the vibrations of a string during a pause—when in the childish mind, the connection between the idea and its verbal expression met with a momentary interruption.

The other two neither spoke nor listened. To them the little girl's bird-like twittering covered the murmur of their own thoughts, and if Delfina stopped for a moment's breathing space, they felt as strangely perturbed and apprehensive as if the silence might disclose or lay bare their souls.

The avenue of the Hundred Fountains stretched away before them in diminishing perspective; a peacock, perched upon one of the shields, took flight at their approach, scattering the rose leaves into a fountain below. A few steps further on, Andrea recognised the one beside which Donna Maria had stood, and listened to the music of the waters.

In the retreat of the Hermes the smell of musk had

evaporated. The statue, all pensive under its garland, was flecked with patches of sunshine which filtered through the surrounding foliage. Blackbirds piped and answered one another.

Taken with a sudden fancy, Delfina exclaimed, 'Mamma, I want the wreath again.'

'No, leave it there—why should you take it away?'

'I want it for Muriella.'

'But Muriella will spoil it.'

'Do, please, give it me.'

Donna Maria looked at Andrea. He slowly went up to the statue, lifted the wreath and handed it to Delfina. In the exaltation of their spirits, this simple little episode had all the mysterious significance of an allegory—was in some way symbolical. One of his own lines ran persistently in Andrea's head—

'Have I attained, have I then paid the price?'

The nearer they approached the end of the pathway, the fiercer grew the pain at his heart; he would have given half his life for a word from the woman he loved. A dozen times she seemed on the point of speaking, but she did not.

'Look, mamma, there are Fernandino and Muriella and Ricardo,' cried Delfina, catching sight of Francesca's children; and she started off running towards them and waving her wreath.

'Muriella! Muriella! Muriella!'

CHAPTER V

MARIA FERRÈS had always remained faithful to her girlhood's habit of setting down daily in her journal the passing thoughts, the joys, the sorrows, the fancies, the doubts, the aspirations, the regrets and the hopes—all the events of her spiritual life as well as the various incidents of her outward existence, compiling thereby a sort of Itinerary of the Soul which she liked occasionally to study, both for guidance on the path still to be pursued and also to follow the traces of things long dead and forgotten.

Perpetually denied, by force of circumstances, the relief of self-expansion, enclosed within the magic circle of her purity as in a tower of ivory for ever incorruptible and inaccessible, she found solace and refreshment in the daily outpourings she confided to the white pages of her private book. Therein she was free to make her moan, to abandon herself to her griefs, to seek to decipher the enigma of her own heart, to interrogate her conscience; here she gained courage in prayer, tranquillised herself by meditation, laid her troubled spirit once more in the hands of the Heavenly Father. And from every page shone the same pure light—the light of Truth.

.   .   .   .

'*September* 15*th* (Schifanoja).—How tired I feel! The journey was rather fatiguing and the unaccustomed sea air makes my head ache at first. I need rest, and I already seem to have a foretaste of the sweetness of sleep and the happiness of awaking in the morning in the house of a friend and to the pleasures of Francesca's cordial hospitality at Schifanoja with its lovely roses and its tall cypress trees. I shall wake up

142

to the knowledge that I have some weeks of peace before me
—twenty days, perhaps even more, of congenial intellectual
companionship.   I am very grateful to Francesca for her
invitation.   To see her again was like meeting a sister.   How
much and how profoundly I have changed since the dear old
days in Florence !

'Speaking to-day of my hair, Francesca began recalling
stories of our absurd childish passions and melancholies in
those days; of Carlotta Fiordelise and Gabriella Vanni and
various incidents of that distant school life which seems to me
now as though I had never lived it, but only read it of it in
some old forgotten book or seen it in a dream.   My hair has
not fallen, but for every hair of my head there has been a
thorn in my destiny.

'But why let my sad thoughts get the upper hand over me
again?   And why let memory cause me pain?   It is useless
to lament over a grave which never gives back its dead.
Would to Heaven I could remember that, once for all !

'Francesca is still young, and has retained the frank and
charming gaiety which, in our school days, exercised such a
strange fascination over my somewhat gloomy temperament.
She has one great and rare virtue : though she is light-hearted
herself, she can enter into the troubles of others and knows
how to lighten them by her kindly sympathy and pity.   She
is above all things a woman of high intelligence and refined
tastes, a perfect hostess and a friend who never palls upon
one.   She is perhaps a trifle too fond of witty *mots* and
sparkling epigrams, but her darts are always tipped with gold,
and she aims them with inimitable grace.   Among all the
women of the great world I have ever known there is certainly
not one to compare with her, and of all my friends, she is the
one I care for most.

'Her children are not like her, they are not handsome.
But the youngest, Muriella, is a dear little thing, with the
sweet laugh and the eyes of her mother.   She did the honours
of the house to Delfina with all the air of a little lady ; she
has certainly inherited her mother's perfect manner.

'Delfina seems to be happy. She has already explored the greater part of the grounds, as far as the sea, and has run down all the flights of steps. She came to tell me about all the wonderful things she had seen—panting, swallowing half the words, her eyes looking almost dazzled. She spoke continually of her new friend Muriella—a pretty name that sounds still prettier from her lips.

'She is fast asleep. When her eyes are closed, her lashes cast a long, long shadow on her cheeks. Francesca's cousin was struck by their length this evening and quoted a beautiful line from Shakespeare's Tempest on Miranda's eye-lashes.

'The scent of the flowers is too strong in this room. Delfina was anxious to keep the bouquet of roses by her bedside, but now that she is asleep I shall take them away and put them out into the loggia in the fresh air.

'I am tired, and yet I have written four pages ; I am sleepy, and yet I would gladly prolong this languor of soul, lulled by I know not what unwonted sense of tenderness diffused around me. It is so long—so long—since I have felt myself surrounded by a little kindness !

'I have just carried the vase of roses into the loggia and stayed there a few moments to listen to the voices of the night, moved by the regret of losing in the blindness of sleep the hours that pass under so beautiful a sky. How strange is the harmony between the song of the fountains and the murmur of the sea ! The cypresses seemed to be the pillars of the firmament ; the stars shining just above them tipped their summits with fire.

'*September* 16*th.*—A delightful afternoon, spent almost entirely in conversation with Francesca in the loggia, on the terraces, in the avenues, at the various points of outlook of this villa, which looks as if it had been built by a princely poet to drown a grief. The name of the Palace at Ferrara suits it admirably.

'Francesca gave me a sonnet of Count Sperelli's to read— a trifle, but of rare literary charm, and inscribed on vellum.

Sperelli has a mind of a very high order, and is most intense. To-day at dinner, he said several very beautiful things. He is recovering from a terrible wound received in a duel in Rome last May. In all his actions, his looks, his words, there is that affectionate and charming licence which is the prerogative of the convalescent, of those who have newly escaped the clutches of death. He must be very young, but he has gone through much and lived fast. He bears the evidences of it. . . . A charming evening of conversation and music all by ourselves after dinner. I talked too much, or, at any rate, with two much eagerness. But Francesca listened and encouraged me, and so did Count Sperelli. That is just the delightful part of a conversation not on common subjects—to feel the same degree of warmth animating the minds of all present. Only then do one's words have the true ring of sincerity and give real pleasure, both to the speaker and the hearer.

'Francesca's cousin is a most cultivated judge of music. He greatly admires the masters of the eighteenth century, Domenico Scarlatti being his special favourite. But his most ardent devotion is reserved for Sebastian Bach. He does not care much for Chopin, and Beethoven affects him too profoundly and perturbs his spirit.

'He listened to me with a singular expression, almost as if dazed or distressed. I nearly always addressed myself to Francesca, but I felt his eyes upon me with an insistence which embarrassed but did not offend me. He must still be weak and ill and a prey to his nerves. Finally he asked me —"Do you sing?" in the same tone in which he would have said—"Do you love me?"

'I sang an air of Paisiello's and another by Salieri, and I played a little eighteenth century music. I was in good voice and my touch on the piano happy.

'He gave me no word of thanks or praise, but remained perfectly silent. I wonder why?

'Delfina was in bed by that time. When I went upstairs afterwards to see her, I found her asleep, but with her eye-

lashes wet as if with tears. Poor darling! Dorothy told me
that my voice could be heard distinctly up here, and that
Delfina had wakened from her first sleep and begun to sob,
and wanted to come down.

'She is asleep again now, but from time to time her little
bosom heaves with a suppressed sob which sends a vague
distress into my own heart, and a desire to respond to that
involuntary sob, to this grief which sleep cannot assuage.
Poor darling!

'Who is playing the piano downstairs, I wonder? With
the soft pedal down, some one is trying over that gavotte of
Rameau's, so full of bewitching melancholy, that I was
playing just now. Who can it be? Francesca came up with
me—it is late.

'I went out and leaned over the loggia. The room opening
into the vestibule is dark, but there is light in the room
next to it, where Manuel and the Marchese are still playing
cards.

'The gavotte has stopped, some one is going down the steps
into the garden.

'Why should I be so alert, so watchful, so curious? Why
should every sound startle me to-night?

'Delfina has wakened and is calling me.

'*September* 17*th.*—Manuel left this morning. We accom-
panied him to the station at Rovigliano. He will return
about the 10th of October to fetch me, and we all go on to
Sienna, to my mother. Delfina and I will probably stay at
Sienna till after the New Year. I shall see the Loggia of the
Pope and the Fonte Gaja, and my beautiful black and white
Cathedral once more—that beloved dwelling-place of the
Blessed Virgin, where a part of my soul has ever remained
to pray in a spot that my knees know well.

'I always have a vision of that spot clearly before me, and
when I go back I shall kneel on the exact stone where
I always used to. I know it as well as if my knees had left
a deep hollow there. And there too I shall find that portion
of my soul which still lingers there in prayer beneath the

starry blue vault above, which is mirrored in the marble floor like a midnight sky in a placid lake.

'Assuredly nothing there is changed. In the costly chapel, full of palpitating shadow and mysterious gloom, alive with the glint of precious marble, the lamps burned softly, all their light seemingly gathered into the little globe of oil that fed the flame as into some limpid topaz. Little by little, under my intent gaze, the sculptured stone grew less coldly white, took on warm ivory tints, became gradually penetrated by the pallid life of the celestial beings, and over the marble forms crept the faint transparency of angelic flesh.

'Ah, how fervent and spontaneous were my prayers then! When I absorbed myself in meditation, I seemed to be walking through the secret paths of my soul as in a garden of delight, where nightingales sang in the blossoming trees and turtle-doves cooed beside the running waters of Grace divine.

'*September 18th.*—A day of nameless torture. Something seems to be forcing me to gather up, to re-adjust, to join together the fragments of a dream, half of which is being confusedly realised outside of me, and the other half going on equally confusedly in my own heart. And try as I will, I cannot succeed in piecing it completely together.

'*September 19th.*—Continued torture. Long ago, some one sang to me but never finished the song. Now some one is taking up the strain at the point where it broke off, but meanwhile, I have forgotten the beginning. And my spirit loses itself in vain gropings after the old melody, nor can it find any pleasure in the new.

'*September 20th.*—To-day, after lunch, Andrea Sperelli invited me and Francesca to come to his room and look at some drawings that had arrived for him yesterday from Rome.

'It would not be too much to say that an entire Art has passed before our eyes to-day—an art studied and analysed by the hand of a master draughtsman. I have never experienced a more intense pleasure.

'The drawings are Sperelli's own work—studies, sketches, notes, mementos of every gallery in Europe; they are, so to speak, his breviary, a wonderful breviary 'n which each of the Old Masters has his special page, affording a condensed example of his manner, bringing out the most lofty and original beauties of his work, the *punctum saliens* of his entire productions. In going through the large collection, not only have I received a distinct impression of the various schools, the movements, the influences which have combined to develop the art of painting in various countries, but I feel that I have had a glimpse into the spirit, the essential meaning of the art of each individual painter. I am as if intoxicated with art, my brain is full of lines and figures, but in the midst of the apparent confusion there stand out clearly before me the women of the early masters, those never-to-be-forgotten heads of Saints and Virgins which smiled down upon my childish piety in old Sienna from the frescoes of Taddeo and Simone.

'No masterpiece of art, however advanced and brilliant, leaves upon the mind so strong and enduring an impression. All these slender forms, delicate and drooping as lily-buds, these grave and noble attitudes for receiving a flower offered by an angel, placing the fingers on an open book, bending over the Holy Infant, or supporting the body of Christ; in the act of blessing, of agonising, of ascending into Heaven— all these things, so pure, so sincere, so profoundly touching, affect the soul to its depths and imprint themselves for ever on the memory.

'Thus, one by one, the women of the Early Masters passed in review before us. Francesca and I were seated on a low couch with a great stand before us, on which lay the portfolio containing the drawings which the artist, seated opposite, slowly turned over, commenting on each in succession. I watched his hand as he took up a sheet and placed it with peculiar care on the other side of the portfolio, and each time I felt a sort of thrill, as if that hand were going to touch me.—Why?—

' Presently, his position doubtless becoming uncomfortable, he knelt on the floor, and in that attitude continued turning over the drawings. In speaking, he nearly always addressed himself to me, not at all with the air of imparting instruction, but as if discussing the pictures with a person as familiar with the subject as he was himself; and, at the bottom of my heart, I was conscious of a sense of complacency mingled with gratitude. Whenever I exclaimed in admiration, he looked at me with a smile which I can still see, but cannot define. Two or three times, Francesca rested her arm on his shoulder in unconscious familiarity. Looking at the head of the first-born of Moses, copied from Botticelli's fresco in the Sistine Chapel, she said—"It has a look of you when you are in one of your melancholy moods."—And when we came to the head of the Archangel Michael from Perugino's Madonna of Pavia, she remarked—"It is a little like Giulia Moceto, is it not?" He did not answer, but only turned the page over rather sooner than usual. Upon which she added with a laugh—"Away with the pictures of sin!"

' This Giulia Moceto is, I suppose, some one he was once in love with. The page once turned, I had a wild, unreasoning desire to look at the Michael again and examine the face more closely. Was it merely artistic curiosity?

' I cannot say, I dare not pry into my heart, I prefer to temporise, to deceive myself; I have not the courage to face the battle, I am a coward.

' And yet the present is so sweet. My imagination is as excited as if I had drunk strong tea. I have no desire to go to bed. The night is soft and warm as if it were August, the sky is cloudless but dimly veiled, the breathing of the sea comes slow and deep, but the fountains fill up the pauses. The loggia attracts me—shall we go out and dream a little, my heart and I?—dream of what?

' The eyes of the Virgins and the Saints pursue me—deep-set, long and narrow, with meekly downcast lids, from under which they gaze at one with that charmed look—innocent as the dove, and yet a little side-long like the serpent. "Be

ye harmless as doves and wise as serpents," said Our
Lord—

'Yes, be wise—go, say your prayers, and then, to bed and
sleep——

'*September 21st.*—Alas, must the heavy task ever painfully
begin again from the beginning, the steep path be climbed,
the battle that was won fought over again!

'*September 22nd.*—He has given me one of his poems, *The
Story of the Hermaphrodite,* the twenty-first of the twenty-five
copies, printed on vellum and with two proof engravings of
the frontispiece.

'It is a remarkable work, enclosing a mystic and profound
idea, although the musical element predominates, entrancing
the soul by the unfamiliar magic of its melody, which
envelopes the thoughts that shine out like a glister of gold
and diamonds through a limpid stream. Certain lines
pursue me incessantly and will continue to do so for long, no
doubt—they are so intense . . . Every day and every hour
he subjugates me more and more, mind and soul—against
my will, despite my resistance. His every word and look,
his slightest action sinks into my heart.

'*September 23rd.*—When we converse with one another, I
sometimes feel as if his voice were an echo of my soul. At
times, a sudden wild frenzy comes over me, a blind desire, an
unreasoning impulse to make some remark, utter some word
that would betray my secret weakness. I only save myself
from it by a miracle, and then there falls an interval of silence,
during which I am shaken with inward terror. Then, when
I do speak again, it is to say something trivial in the lightest
tone I can command, but I feel as if a flame were rushing
over my face—that I am going to blush. If he were to seize
this moment to look me boldly in the eyes, I should be lost!

'I played a good deal this evening, chiefly Bach and
Schumann. As on the first evening, he sat in a low chair
to the right but a little behind me. From time to time, at
the end of each piece, he rose and leaned over me, turning
the pages to point out another Fugue or Intermezzo. Then

he would sit down again and listen, motionless, profoundly absorbed, his eyes fixed on me, forcing me to *feel* his presence.

' Did he understand, I wonder, how much of myself, of my thoughts and griefs found voice in the music of others ?

' It is a threatening night. A hot moist wind blows over the garden and its dull moaning dies away in the darkness only to begin again more loudly. The tops of the cypresses wave to and fro under an almost inky sky in which the stars burn with feeble ray. A band of clouds spans the heavens from side to side, ragged, contorted, blacker than the sky, like the tragic locks of a Medusa. The sea is invisible through the darkness, but it sobs as if in measureless and uncontrollable grief—forsaken and alone.

' Why this unreasoning terror ? The night seems to warn me of approaching disaster, a warning that finds its echo in a dim remorse within my heart.

' But I always take comfort from my daughter, she heals my fever like some blessed balm.

' She is asleep now, shaded from the lamp which shines with the soft radiance of the moon. Her face—white with dewy freshness of a white rose, seems half buried in the masses of her dark hair. One would think the eyelids were too delicately transparent to veil the splendour of her eyes. As I lean over her and gaze at her, all the sinister voices of the night are silenced for me, and the silence is measured only by her gentle respiration.

' She feels the vicinity of her mother. The longer I contemplate her, the more does she assume in my eyes the aspect of some ethereal creature, of a being formed of " such stuff as dreams are made of."

' She shall grow up nourished and enwrapped by the flame of my love—of my great, my *only* love——

' *September 24th.*—I can form no resolve—I can decide upon no plan of action. I am simply abandoning myself a little to this new sentiment, shutting my eyes to the distant peril, and my ears to the warning voice of conscience, with the shuddering temerity of one who, in gathering violets, ventures too near the edge of a precipice at the foot of which roars a hungry torrent.

'He shall never know anything from my lips, I shall never know anything from his. Our two souls will mount together, for a brief space, to the mountain-tops of the Ideal, will drink side by side at the perennial fountains, and then each go on its separate way, encouraged and refreshed.

'How still the air is this afternoon! The sea has the faint milky-blue tints of the opal, of Murano glass, with here and there a patch like a mirror dimmed by a breath.

'I am reading Shelley, a favourite poet with him, that divine Ariel feeding upon light and speaking with the tongues of angels. It is night——

'*September* 25*th.*——*Mio Dio! Mio Dio!* His voice when he spoke my name—the tremor in it—oh, I thought my heart was breaking in my bosom, and that I must inevitably lose consciousness.—"You will never know," he said—"never know how utterly my soul is yours."

'We were in the avenue of the fountains—I was listening to the sound of the water; but from that moment, I heard nothing more. Everything around me seemed to flee away, carrying my life with it, and the earth to open beneath my feet. I made a superhuman effort to control myself. Delfina's name rose to my lips and I was seized with a wild impulse to fly to her for protection, for safety. Three times I cried that name, but in the intervals my heart ceased to beat and the breath died away upon my lips.

'*September* 26*th.*—Was it true? Was it not merely some illusion of my overwrought and distracted spirit? Why should that hour yesterday seem to me so far away, so *unreal*?

'He spoke a second time, at greater length, close to my side while I walked on under the trees as in a dream.— Under the trees was it? It seemed to me rather that I was walking through the hidden pathways of my soul, among flowers born of my imagination, listening to the words of an invisible spirit that yet was part of myself.

'I can still hear the sweet and dreadful words—"I would renounce all that the future may hold for me to live in a small corner of your heart—Far from the world, wholly lost in the thought of you—until death, to all eternity"—And again—"Pity from you would be far dearer to me than love from any other woman. Your mere presence suffices to intoxicate me—I feel it flowing into my veins like my life's blood and filling my soul with rapture beyond all telling."

'*September 27th.*—When he gathered the spray of blossom at the entrance to the wood and offered it to me, did I not, in my heart, call him—*Life of my life?*

'When, in the avenue, we passed again by the fountain where he first spoke to me, did I not call him *Life of my life?*

'When he took the wreath from off the Hermes and gave it back to my child, did he not give me to understand that the woman exalted in these verses had fallen from her high estate, and that I, I alone, was all his hope? And once more I called him *Life of my life.*

'*September 28th.*—How long I have been in finding peace!

'From that moment onwards, what hours of struggle and travail I have had, how painfully I have striven to penetrate the real state of my mind, to see things in their true light, bring a calm and fair judgment to bear upon what has happened, to recognise and determine upon my duty! But I continually evaded myself, my mind became confused, my will was but a broken reed on which to lean, every effort was vain. By a sort of instinct, I have avoided being alone with him, kept close to Francesca or my child, or stayed here in my room as in a haven of refuge. When my eyes did meet his, I seemed to read in them a profound and imploring sadness. Does he not know how deeply, deeply, deeply I love him?

'He does not know it, nor ever will. That is my firm resolve—that is my duty. Courage!

'Help me, oh my God!

'*September 29th.*—Why did he speak? Why did he break

the enchanted silence in which I let my soul be steeped, almost without regret or fear? Why tear away the veil of uncertainty and put me face to face with his unveiled love? Now I have no further excuse for temporising, for deluding myself. The danger is there—certain, undeniable, manifest— it attracts me to its dizzy edge like a precipice. One moment of weakness, of languor, and I am lost.

'I ask myself—am I sincere in my pain and regret at this unexpected revelation? How is it that I think perpetually of those words? And why, when I repeat them to myself, does a wave of ineffable rapture sweep over my soul? Why do I thrill to the heart's core at the imagined prospect of hearing more—more such words?

'Night. The agitation of my soul takes the forms of questions, riddles—I ask myself endless questions to which I never have an answer. I have not had the courage to look myself through and through—to form a really bold and honest resolution. I am pusillanimous, I am a coward. I shrink from pain, I want to suffer as little as possible, I prefer to temporise, to hang back, to resort to subterfuges, to wilfully blind myself instead of courageously facing the risks of a decisive battle.

'The fact of the matter is this—that I am *afraid* of being alone with him, of having a serious conversation with him, and so my life is reduced to a series of petty schemes and manœuvrings and pretexts for avoiding his company. Such devices are unworthy of me. Either I must renounce this love altogether, and he shall hear my sad but firm resolve, or I shall accept it, in so far as it is pure, and he will receive my spiritual consent.

'And now I ask myself—What do I really want? Which of the two paths am I to choose? Must I renounce—shall I accept?

'My God! my God! answer Thou for me—light up the path before me!

'To renounce is like tearing out a piece of my heart with my own hands. The agony would be supreme, the wrench would exceed the limits of the endurable. But, by God's grace, such heroism would be crowned by resignation, would be rewarded by that sweet and holy calm which follows upon every high moral impulse, every victory of the soul over the dread of suffering.

' I shall renounce—my daughter shall keep possession of my whole life, of my whole soul. That is the path of duty, and I will walk in it.

' Sow in tears, oh mourning souls, that ye may reap with songs of gladness !

' *September* 30*th.*—I feel somewhat calmer in writing these pages. I regain, at least for the moment, some slight balance of mind. I can look my misfortune more clearly in the face, and my heart seems relieved as if after confession.

' Oh, if I could but go to confession !—could implore counsel and help of my old friend and comforter, Dom Luigi !

' What sustains me most of all in my tribulation, is the thought that in a short time I shall see him again and be able to pour out all my griefs and fears to him, show him all my wounds, ask of him a balm for all my ills, as I used to in the days when his benign and solemn words would call up tears of tenderness to my eyes, that knew not then the bitterness of other tears or—more terrible by far—the burning pain of dry-eyed misery.

' Will he understand me still ? Can he fathom the deep anguish of the woman as he understood the vague and fitful melancholy of the girl ? Shall I ever again see him lean towards me in pity and consolation, that gentle brow, crowned with silvery locks, illumined with purity and holiness, and sanctified by the hand of the Lord ?

' In the chapel, after mass, I played on the organ music of Bach and of Cherubini. I played the same prelude as the other evening.

' A soul weeps and moans, weighed down with anguish, weeps and moans and cries to God, asking His pardon, imploring His aid, with a prayer that rises to heaven like a tongue of fire. It cries and it is heard—its prayer is answered; it receives light from above, utters songs of gladness, reaches at length the haven of Peace and Truth and rests in the Lord——

'The organ is not large nor is the chapel, but, nevertheless, my soul expanded as in a basilica, soared up as under some vast dome, and touched the pinnacle of high Heaven where blazes the Sign of Signs in the azure of Paradise, in the sublime ether.

'Night. Alas! nothing is of any avail—nothing gives me one hour, one minute, one second's respite. Nothing can ever cure me, no dream of my mind can ever efface the dream of my heart.—All has been in vain; this anguish is killing me. I feel that my hurt is mortal, my heart pains me as if some one were actually crushing it, were tearing it to pieces. My agony of mind is so great that it has become a physical torment—atrocious, unbearable. I know perfectly well that I am overwrought, nervous—the victim of a sort of madness; but I cannot get the upper hand over myself, cannot pull myself together, cannot regain control of my reason. I cannot—I simply cannot!

'So this, then, is love!

'He went off somewhere this morning on horseback accompanied by a servant before I saw him, and I spent the whole morning in the chapel. When lunch time came he had not returned. His absence caused me such misery that I myself was astonished at the violence of my pain. I came up to my room afterwards, and to ease my heart I wrote a page of my journal, a devotional page, seeking to revive my fainting spirit at the glowing memory of my girlhood's faith. Then I read a few pieces, here and there, of Shelley's *Epipsychidion*, after which I went down into the park looking for Delfina. But no matter what I did, the thought of him was ever present with me, held me captive and tortured me relentlessly.

'When, at last, I heard his voice again, I was on the first terrace. He was speaking to Francesca in the vestibule. She came out and called to me to come up.

'I felt my knees giving way beneath me at each step. He held out his hand to me and he must have noticed the trembling of mine, for I saw a sudden gleam flash into his eyes. We all three sat down on low cane lounges in the vestibule, facing the sea. He complained of feeling very tired, and smoked while he told us of his ride. He had gone as far as Vicomile, where he had made a halt.

'Vicomile, he said, possesses three wonderful treasures—a pine wood, a tower, and a fifteenth-century monstrance. Imagine a pine wood, between the sea and the hill, interspersed by a number of pools that multiply the trees indefinitely; a campanile in the old rugged Lombardy style that goes back to the eleventh century—a tree-trunk of stone, as it were, covered with sculptured sirens and peacocks, serpents and griffins and dragons—a thousand and one monsters and flowers; and a silver-gilt monstrance all enamelled, engraved and chased—Gothico-Byzantine in style and form with a fore-taste of Renaissance, the work of Gallucci, an almost unknown artist, but who was the great forerunner of Benvenuto Cellini——

'He addressed himself all the time to me. Strange how exactly I remember every word he says! I could set down any conversation of his, word for word, from beginning to end; if there were any means of doing so, I could reproduce every modulation of his voice.

'He showed us two or three little sketches he had made, and then began again describing the wonders of Vicomile with that warmth with which he always speaks of beautiful things and that enthusiasm for art which is one of his most potent attractions.

'"I promised the Canonico to come back to-morrow. We will all go, will we not, Francesca? Donna Maria ought to see Vicomile!"

'Oh, my name on his lips! If it were possible, I could reproduce the very movements of his lips in uttering each syllable of those two words—Donna Maria——But what I never could express is my own emotion on hearing it; could

never explain the unknown, undreamed-of sensation awakened
in me by the presence of this man.

'We sat there till dinner-time. Contrary to her usual habit,
Francesca seemed a little pensive and out of spirits. There
were moments when heavy silence fell upon us. But between
him and me there then occurred one of those *silent colloquies*
in which the soul exhales the Ineffable and hears the murmur
of its thoughts. He said things to me then that made me
sink back against the cushions of my chair faint with rapture
—things that his lips will never repeat to me, that my ears
will never hear.

'In front of us, the cypresses, tipped with fire by the setting
sun, stood up tall and motionless like votive candles. The
sea was the colour of aloe leaves, dashed here and there with
liquid turquoise; there was an indescribable delicacy of
varying pallor—a diffusion of angelic light, in which each
sail looked like an angel's wing upon the waters. And the
harmony of faint and mingled perfumes seemed like the soul
of the declining day.

'Oh sweet and tranquil death of September!

'Another month ended, lost, dropped away into the abyss
of Time—Farewell!

'I have lived more in this last fortnight than in fourteen
years; and not one of my long weeks of unhappiness has
ever equalled in sharpness of torture this one short week of
passion. My heart aches, my head swims; in the depths of
my being, I feel a something obscure and burning—a something that has suddenly awakened in me like a latent disease,
and now begins to creep through my blood and into my soul
in spite of myself, baffling every remedy—desire.

'It fills me with shame and horror as at some dishonour,
some sacrilege or outrage; it fills me with wild and desperate
terror as at some treacherous enemy who will make use of
secret paths to enter the citadel which are unknown to
myself.

'And here I sit in the night watches, and while I write these
pages, with all the feverish ardour that lovers put into their

love-letters, I cease to listen to the gentle breathing of my child. She sleeps in peace; she little knows how far away from her her mother's spirit is!

'*October 1st.*—I see much in him that I did not observe before. When he speaks, I cannot take my eyes off his mouth—the play of his lips and their colouring occupies my attention more than the sound or the sense of his words.

'*October 2nd.*—To-day is Saturday—just a week since the never-to-be-forgotten day, the 25th of September.

'By some strange chance, although I no longer avoid being alone with him—for I am anxious now for the dread and heroical moment—by some strange chance, that moment has not yet occurred.

'Francesca has always been with me the whole day long. This morning we had a ride along the road to Rovigliano, and we spent the best part of the afternoon at the piano. She made me play some sixteenth-century dance music, and then Clementi's famous Toccata and two or three Caprices of Scarlatti's, and, after that, I had to sing certain songs from Schumann's *Frauenliebe*—what contrasts!

'Francesca has lost much of her old gaiety, she is not as she used to be in the first days of my stay here. She is often silent and preoccupied, and when she does laugh or make fun, her gaiety seems to me very forced. I said to her once. "Is something worrying you?"

'"Why?" she answered with assumed surprise.

'"Because you seem to me a little out of spirits lately."

'"Out of spirits? oh, no, you are quite mistaken," she answered, and she laughed, but with an involuntary note of bitterness. This troubles me and causes me a vague sense of uneasiness.

'We are going to Vicomile to-morrow afternoon.

'He asked me—"Would it tire you too much to come on horseback? In that way we could cut right through the pine wood!"

'So we are going to ride and Francesca will join us. The others, including Delfina, will come in the mail-coach.

' What a strange state of mind I am in this evening ! I feel a kind of dull and angry bitterness at the bottom of my heart, without knowing why—am impatient with myself, my life, the whole world—my nervous irritation rises, at times, to such a pitch, that I am seized with an insane desire to scream aloud, to dig my nails into my flesh, to bruise my fingers against the wall—any physical suffering would be better than this intolerable mental discomfort, this unbearable wretchedness. I feel as if I had a burning knot in my bosom, that my throat were closed by a sob I dared not give vent to—I am icy cold and burning hot by turns and, from time to time, a sudden pang darts through me, an irrational terror that I can neither shake off nor control. Thoughts and images flash suddenly across my brain, coming from I know not what ignoble depths of my soul.

' *October 3rd.*—How weak and miserable is the human soul, how utterly defenceless against the attacks of all that is least noble and least pure in us, and that slumbers in the obscurity of our unconscious life, in those unexplored abysses where dark dreams are born of hidden sensations !

' A dream can poison a whole soul, a single involuntary thought is sufficient to corrupt and break down the force of will.

' We are just starting for Vicomile. Delfina is in raptures.

' It is the festival of Our Lady of the Rosary. Courage, my heart !

' *October 4th.*—I found no courage.

' Yesterday was so full of trifling incidents and great emotions, so joyful and so sad, so strangely agitating that I am almost at a loss when I try to remember it all. And yet all—all other recollections pale and vanish before the one.

' After having visited the tower and admired the monstrance, we prepared to return home at about half-past five. Francesca was tired and preferred going back in the coach to getting on horseback again. We followed them for a while, riding behind or beside them, while Delfina and Muriella waved long flowering bulrushes at us, laughing and threatening us with their splendid spears.

'The evening was calm, not a breath of wind stirred. The sun was sinking behind the hill at Rovigliano in a sky all rosy-red, like a sunset in the Far East.

'When we came in sight of the pine-wood, he suddenly said to me : "Shall we ride through it ? "

'The high road skirted the wood, describing a wide curve, at one part of which it almost touched the sea-shore. The wood was already growing dark and was full of deep-green twilight, but under the trees the pools gleamed with a pure and intense light, like fragments of a sky far fairer than the one above our heads.

'Without giving me time to answer, he said to Francesca. "We are going to ride through the wood and shall join you at the other side, on the high road, by the bridge "—and he reined in his horse.

'Why did I consent—why did I follow him ? There was a sort of dazzle before my eyes. I felt as if I were under the influence of some nameless fascination, as if the landscape, the light, this incident, the whole combination of circumstances were not new to me, but things that had all happened to me before, in another existence, and were now only being repeated. The impression is quite indescribable. My will seemed paralysed. It was as when some incident of one's life reappears in a dream, but with added details that differ from the real circumstances. I shall never be able to adequately describe even a part of this strange phenomenon.

'We rode in silence at a foot's pace ; the cawing of the rooks, the dull beat of the horses' hoofs and their noisy breathing in no way disturbed the all-pervading peace that seemed to grow every minute deeper and more magical.

'Ah, why did he break the spell we ourselves had woven ?

'He began to speak ; he poured out upon me a flood of burning words—words which, in the silence of the wood, frightened me because they carried with them an impression of something preternatural, something indefinably weird and

compelling. He was no longer the humble suppliant of that
morning in the park, spoke no more of his diffident hopes,
his half-mystical aspirations, his incurable sense of sorrow.
This time he did not beg and entreat. It was the voice of
passion, full of audacity and virile power, a voice I did not
know in him.

' "You love me, you love me—you cannot help but love me
—tell me that you love me!"

' His horse was close beside mine. I felt him brush me ;
I almost felt the breath of his burning words upon my cheek,
and I thought I must swoon with anguish and fall into his
arms.

' "Tell me that you love me," he repeated obstinately,
relentlessly. " Tell me that you love me ! "

' Under the terrible strain of his insistent voice, I believe
I answered wildly—whether with a cry or a sob, I do not
know—

' " I love you, I love you, I love you ! " and I set my horse
at a gallop down the narrow rugged path between the crowded
tree-trunks, unconscious of what I was doing.

' He followed me crying—" Maria, Maria, stop—you will
hurt yourself."

' But I fled blindly on. I do not know how my horse
managed to keep clear of the trees, I do not know why I
was not thrown ; I am incapable of retracing my impressions
in that mad flight through the dark wood, past the gleaming
patches of water. When at last I came out upon the road,
near the bridge, I seemed to have come out of some
hallucination.

' " Do you want to kill yourself? " he said almost fiercely.
We heard the sound of the approaching carriage and turned
to meet it. He was going to speak to me again.

' "Hush, for pity sake," I entreated, for I felt I was at the
end of my forces.

' He was silent. Then, with an assurance that stupefied
me, he said to Francesca—" Such a pity you did not come !
It was perfectly enchanting."

'And he went on talking as quietly and unconcernedly as if nothing had happened, even with a certain amount of gaiety. I was only too thankful for his dissimulation which screened me, for if I had been obliged to speak, I should inevitably have betrayed myself, and for both of us to have been silent would doubtless have aroused Francesca's suspicions.

'A little further on, the road wound up the hill towards Schifanoja. Oh, the boundless melancholy of the evening! A new moon shone in the faintly-tinted, pale-green sky, where my eyes, and perhaps mine alone, detected a lingering rosy tinge—that same rosy light that gleamed upon the pools down in the pine wood.

'*October 5th.*—He knows now that I love him, and knows it from my own lips. Nothing is left for me but flight—this is what I have come to!

'When he looks at me now, there is a strange gleam in the depths of his eyes that was not there before. To-day, while Francesca was absent for a moment, he took my hand and made as if he would kiss it. I managed to draw it away, but I saw his lips tremble; I caught, as it were, the reflection of the kiss that never left his lips, and the image of that kiss haunts me now—it haunts me—haunts me——

'*October 6th.*—On the 25th of September, on the marble seat in the arbutus wood, he said to me—"I know you do not love me and that you never will love me!" And on the 3rd of October—"You love me—you love me—you cannot help but love me——"

'In Francesca's presence, he asked if I would allow him to make a study of my hands, and I consented. He will begin to-day.

'I am nervous and frightened, as if I were going to expose my hands to some nameless ordeal.

'Night. It has begun, the slow, sweet, unspeakable torture.

'He drew with red and black chalk. My right hand lay on a piece of velvet; near me on the table stood a Corean vase, yellow and spotted like the skin of a python, and in the

vase was a group of orchids, those grotesque flowers for
which Francesca has so curious a predilection.

'When I felt that I could no longer bear the ordeal, I
looked at the flowers to distract my thoughts, and their
strange, distorted shapes carried me to the distant countries
of their birth, giving me a moment's respite from my haunting grief.   He went on drawing in silence; his eyes passing
continually from the paper to my hand.   Two or three
times he looked at the vase ; at last, rising from his chair,
he said—"Excuse me"—and lifting the vase, he carried it
away and placed it on another table.   I do not know why.

'After that, he resumed his drawing with much greater
freedom, as if relieved of an annoyance.

'I cannot describe the sensation produced in me by his
eyes.   I felt as if not my hand, but a part of my soul were
laid bare to his scrutinising gaze, that his eyes pierced to
its very depths, exploring its most secret recesses.   Never
had my hand felt so alive, so expressive, so responsive to my
heart, revealing so much that I would fain have kept secret.
Under his gaze I felt it quiver imperceptibly but continuously, and the tremor spread to my innermost veins.
When his gaze grew too intense, I was seized with an instinctive desire to withdraw my hand altogether, arising from
a sense of shame.

'Now and then, he would stop drawing and sit for quite an
appreciable time with his eyes fixed, and then I had the
impression that he was absorbing something of me through
his pupils, or that he was caressing me with a touch that
was softer than the velvet beneath my hand.   At other times,
while he bent over the drawing, transferring maybe into the
lines what he had taken from me, a faint smile played round
his mouth, so faint that I only just caught it.   I do not know
why, but that smile sent a pang of delight thrilling through
my heart.   Once or twice, I saw the image of a kiss appear
again upon his lips.

'At last, curiosity got the better of me and I said—"Well
—what is it?"

' Francesca was at the piano with her back turned to us, her fingers wandering over the keys, trying to remember Rameau's Gavotte *of the Yellow Ladies* that I have played so often, and which will always be connected in my mind with my stay at Schifanoja. She muffled the notes with the soft pedal and broke off frequently. These interruptions and gaps in the melody which was so familiar to me and which my ear filled up each time, in advance, added immeasurably to my distress. All at once, she struck one note hard several times in succession as if under the spur of some nervous irritation; then she started up and came and bent over the drawing.

' I looked at her—I understood it all.

' This last drop was wanting in my cup of bitterness. God had still this last and cruelest trial of all reserved for me.— His will be done !

' *October 7th.*—I have now but one thought, one desire—to fly from here—to escape.

' I have come to the end of my strength. This love is crushing me, is killing me, and the unexpected discovery I have made increases my wretchedness a thousandfold. What are her feelings towards me? What does she think? So she loves him too?—and since when? Does he know it? Or has he no suspicion of the fact?

' *Mio Dio ! Mio Dio !* I believe I am going out of my mind—all my strength of will is forsaking me. At long intervals there comes a pause in my torment, as when the wild elements of the tempest hold their breath for a moment, only to break forth again with redoubled fury. I sit then in a kind of stupor, with heavy head and my limbs feeling as bruised and tired as if I had been beaten, and while my pain gathers itself up for a fresh onslaught, I do not succeed in collecting sufficient strength to resist it.

' What does she think of me? What does she think? How much does she know?

' Oh, to be misjudged by her—my best, my dearest friend

—the one to whom I have always been able to open my heart! This is my crowning grief, my bitterest trial—

'I must speak to her before I go. She must know all from me, I must know all from her—that is only right and just.

'Night. About five o'clock she proposed a drive along the Rovigliano road. We two went alone in the open carriage. I was trembling with agitation as I said to myself—"Here is my opportunity for speaking to her." But my nervousness deprived me of every vestige of courage. Did she expect me to confide in her? I cannot tell.

'We sat silent for a long while, listening to the steady trot of the horses, looking at the trees and the meadows by the side of the road. From time to time, by a brief remark or a sign, she drew my attention to some detail of the autumnal landscape.

'All the witchery of the Autumn concentrated itself into this hour. The slanting rays of the evening sun lit up the rich and sombre harmonies of the dying foliage. Gold, amber, saffron, violet, purple, sea-green—tints the most faded and the most violent mingled in one deep strain, not to be surpassed by any melody of Spring, however sweet.

'"Look," she said, pointing to the acacias, "would you not say they were in flower?"

'At last, after an interval of silence, to make a beginning I said: "Manuel is sure to be here by Saturday. I expect a telegram from him to-morrow, and we shall leave by the early train on Sunday. You have been very good to me while I have been with you——I am deeply grateful to you."

'My voice broke, a flood of tenderness swelled my heart. She took my hand and clasped it tight without speaking or looking at me. We remained silent for a long time, holding one another by the hand.

'Presently she asked—"How long will you be with your mother?"

'"Till the end of the year, I hope—perhaps longer."

'"As long as that?"

'We fell silent again. By this time, I felt I should never have the courage to face an explanation; besides which, I felt that it was less necessary now. Francesca seemed to have come back to me, to understand me, to be once more the sweet kind sister of old. My sorrow drew out her sadness as the moon attracts the waters of the ocean.

'"Listen!" she said.

'The sound of women's voices, singing, floated over to us from the fields, a slow song, full and solemn as a Gregorian chant. Further on, we came in sight of the singers. They were coming away from a field of dried sun-flowers; walking in single file like a religious procession, and the sunflowers on their long leafless stalks, their great discs stripped of their halo of petals and their wealth of seed, were like liturgic emblems or monstrances of pale gold.

'My emotion waxed greater. The song spread wide through the evening air. We passed through Rovigliano, where the lamps were beginning to twinkle, and came out again upon the high road. The church bells rang softly behind us. A moist breeze rustled in the trees that cast a faint blue shadow on the white road, and in the air a shadow as liquid as water.

'"Are you not cold?" she asked me, and she ordered the footman to spread a rug over us, and told the coachman to turn homewards.

'In the belfry at Rovigliano, a bell tolled with deep slow strokes as for some solemn rite, and the wave of sound seemed to send a wave of cold through the air. With a simultaneous movement, we drew closer to one another, settling the rug more warmly over our knees, and a shiver ran through us both. The carriage entered the town at a walk.

'"What can that bell be ringing for?" she murmured in a voice that hardly seemed like her own.

'I answered—"I fancy it must be for the Viaticum."

'And in fact, a little further on we saw the priest just entering a door while a clerk held the canopy over him, and two others stood upon the threshold, straight as candelabra, holding up lighted lanterns. A single window of the house was lighted up, the one behind which the dying Christian was awaiting Extreme Unction. Faint shadows flitted across the brightness of that pale yellow square on which was outlined the whole mysterious drama of Death.

' The footman bent down from the box and asked in a low voice—" Who is it ? "

' The person addressed answered in dialect and mentioned a woman's name.

' I would have liked to muffle the sound of the carriage wheels upon the stones, to have made our passage a silent one past the spot where a soul was about to take flight. Francesca, I am sure, shared my feeling.

' The carriage turned into the road to Schifanoja and the horses set off at a brisk trot. The moon, ringed by a halo, shone like an opal in the milk-white sky. A train of cloud rose out of the sea and stretched away by degrees in spiral form, like a trail of smoke. The somewhat stormy sea drowned all other sounds with its roar. Never, I think, did a heavier sadness weigh upon two spirits.

' I felt something wet upon my cold cheek, and turning to Francesca to see if she noticed that I was crying, I met her eyes—they were full of tears. And so we sat, side by side, with mute, convulsively closed lips, clasping one another's hand, the tears rolling silently drop by drop over our cheeks, both knowing that they were for him.

' As we neared Schifanoja I dried my eyes, and she did the same, each striving to hide her own weakness.

' He was standing in the hall with Delfina and Muriella looking out for us. Why did I feel a sudden vague distrust of him, as if some instinct warned me of hidden danger? What troubles are in store for me in the future? Shall I be able to escape from the passion that attracts and blinds me?

' And yet, those few tears have given me much relief! I feel less broken, less scorched, more self-confident; and it affords me an indescribable fond pleasure to retrace again, for myself alone, that last drive, while Delfina sleeps, made happy by the storm of kisses I rained upon her face, and while the moon that so lately saw me weep smiles sadly through the window panes.

'*October 8th*—Did I sleep last night—did I wake? I could not say. Through my brain, like thick dark shadows, flitted terrifying thoughts, insupportable images of torment; and my heart gave sudden throbs and bounds, and I would find myself staring wide-eyed into the darkness, not knowing whether I had just awakened from a dream or whether I had never been asleep at all. And this state of semi-consciousness—infinitely more unbearable than real sleeplessness—continued throughout the night.

'Nevertheless, when I heard my little girl's morning call, I did not answer, but pretended to be sound asleep, so that I need not rise, so that I might remain a few minutes longer in bed and thus retard for a while the inexorable certainty of the realities of life. The torments of thought and imagination seemed to me less cruel than those, so impossible to foresee, which awaited me in these last two days.

'A little while later, Delfina came in on tip-toe, holding her breath. She looked at me and then whispered to Dorothy, with a little fond tremor in her voice—

'"She is fast asleep! We will not wake her!"

'Night. I do not believe I have a spark of life left in me. As I came upstairs I felt, at each step, as if every drop of blood had left my veins. I am as weak as one at the point of death.

'Courage! courage!—only a few hours more. Manuel will be here to-morrow morning. We shall leave on Sunday, and on Monday I shall be with my mother.

'Just now, I returned him two or three books he had lent me. In the volume of Shelley I underlined with my nail the last two lines of a certain verse and put a mark in the page—

> "And forget me, for I *can never*—
> Be thine!"

'*October 9th.*—Night. All day long he has sought an

opportunity for speaking to me. His distress is evident.
And all day long I have done my utmost to avoid him,
so that he might not sow fresh seeds of pain, of desire, of
regret and remorse in my heart. And I have triumphed—I
was strong and brave—My God, I thank Thee !

'This night is the last. To-morrow we leave—all will be
over.

'All will be over? A voice out of the depths cries unto
me—I do not understand its words, but I know that it tells
me of coming disaster, unknown but inevitable, mysterious
and inexorable as death. The future is lugubrious as a
cemetery full of open graves, ready to receive the dead, with
here and there a flicker of pale torches which I can scarce
distinguish, and I know not if they are there to lure me on
to destruction or to show me to a path of safety.

'I have re-read my Journal slowly, carefully, from the 15th
of September, the day of my arrival. What a difference
between the first entry and the last !

'I wrote :—I shall wake up in the house of a friend, to the
enjoyment of Francesca's cordial hospitality, in Schifanoja,
where the roses are so fair and the cypresses so tall and
grand. I shall wake with the prospect of some weeks of
peace before me—twenty days or more of congenial intellectual companionship—Alas ! where is that promised peace !
But the roses, the beautiful roses, were they, too, faithless to
their promise ? Did I perhaps, on that first night in the
loggia, open my heart too wide to their seductive fragrance
while Delfina slept ? And now the October moon floods the
sky with its cold radiance, and through the closed windows
I see the sharp points of the cypresses, all sombre and
motionless, and on that night they seemed to touch the stars.

'Of that prelude there is but one phrase which finds a place
in this sad finale : So many hairs on my head, so many
thorns in my woeful destiny !

'I am going, and what will he do when I am far away ?
What will Francesca do ?

'The change in Francesca still remains incomprehensible,

inexplicable—an enigma that torments and bewilders me.
She loves him—but since when?—and does he know it?
Confess, oh, my soul, to this fresh misery. A new poison is
added to that already infecting me—I am jealous!

'But I am prepared for any suffering, even the most
horrible; I know well the martyrdom that awaits me; I know
that the anguish of these days is as nought compared to that
which I must face presently, the terrible cross on which my
soul must hang. I am ready. All I ask, oh my God, is a
respite, a short respite for the hours that remain to me here.
To-morrow I shall have need of all my strength.

' How strangely sometimes the incidents of one's life repeat
themselves! This evening in the drawing-room, I seemed
to have gone back to the 16th of September, when I first
played and sang and my thoughts began to occupy themselves with him. This evening again I was seated at the
piano, and the same subdued light illumined the room, and
next door Manuel and the Marchese were at the card-table.
I played the Gavotte *of the Yellow Ladies*, of which Francesca
is so fond and which I heard some one trying to play on the
16th of September while I sat up in my room and began my
nightly vigils of unrest.

' He, I am sure, is not asleep. When I came upstairs, he
went in and took the Marchese's place opposite to my husband. Are they playing still? Doubtless he is thinking and
his heart aches while he plays. What are his thoughts?—
what are his sufferings?

' I cannot sleep. I shall go out into the loggia. I want to
see if they are still playing, or if he has gone to his room.
His windows are at the corner, in the second story.

' It is a clear, mild night. There are lights still in the card-
room. I stayed a long time in the loggia looking down at
the light shining out against the cypresses and mingling with
the silvery whiteness of the moon. I am trembling from
head to foot. I cannot describe the almost tragic effect of
those lighted windows behind which the two men are playing,
opposite to one another, in the deep silence of the night,

scarcely broken by the dull sob of the sea. And they will perhaps play on till morning, if he will pander so far to my husband's terrible failing. So we shall all three wake till the dawn and take no rest, each a prey to his own passion.

'But what is he really thinking of? Of what nature is his pain? What would I not give, at this moment, to see him, to be able to gaze at him till the day breaks, even if it were only through the window, in the night dews, trembling, as I do now, from head to foot. The maddest, wildest thoughts rush through my brain like flashes of lightning, dazzling and confusing me. I feel the prompting of some evil spirit to do some rash and irreparable thing, I feel as if I were treading on the edge of perdition. It would, I feel, lift the great weight from my heart, would take this suffocating knot from my throat if, at this moment, I could cry aloud, into the silence of the night, with all the strength of my soul—"I love him! I love him! I love him!"'

BOOK III

CHAPTER I

Two or three days after the departure of the Ferrès, Sperelli and his cousins returned to Rome, Donna Francesca, contrary to her custom, wishing to shorten her stay at Schifanoja.

After a brief stay at Naples, Andrea reached Rome on the 24th of October, a Sunday, in the first heavy morning rain of the Autumn season. He experienced an extraordinary pleasure in returning to his apartments in the Casa Zuccari, his tasteful and charming *buen retiro*. There he seemed to find again some portion of himself, something he had missed. Nothing was altered; everything about him retained, in his eyes, that indescribable look of life which material objects assume, amongst which one has lived and loved and suffered. His old servants, Jenny and Terenzio, had taken the utmost care of everything, and Stephen had attended to every detail likely to conduce to his master's comfort.

It was raining. Andrea went to the window and stood for some time looking out upon his beloved Rome. The piazza of the Trinità de' Monti was solitary and deserted, left to the guardianship of its obelisk. The trees along the wall that joins the church to the Villa Medici, already half stripped of their leaves, rustled mournfully in the wind and the rain. The Pincio alone still shone green, like an island in a lake of mist.

And as he gazed, one sentiment dominated all the others in his heart; the sudden and lively re-awakening of his old love for Rome—fairest Rome—that city of cities, immense, imperial, unique—like the sea, for ever young, for ever new, for ever mysterious.

'What time is it?' Andrea asked of Stephen.

It was about nine o'clock. Feeling somewhat tired, he determined to have a sleep: also, that he would see no one that day and spend the evening quietly at home. Seeing that he was about to re-enter the life of the great world of Rome, he wished, before taking up the old round of activity, to indulge in a little meditation, a slight preparation; to lay down certain rules, to discuss with himself his future line of conduct.

'If any one calls,' he said to Stephen, 'say that I have not yet returned; and let the porter know it too. Tell James I shall not want him to-day, but he can come round for orders this evening. Bring me lunch at three—something very light—and dinner at nine. That is all.

He fell asleep almost immediately. The servant woke him at two and informed him that, just before twelve o'clock, the Duke of Grimiti had called, having heard from the Marchesa d'Ateleta that he had returned to town.

'Well?'

'Il Signor Duca left word that he would call again in the afternoon.'

'Is it still raining? Open the shutters wide.'

The rain had stopped, the sky was lighter. A band of pale sunshine streamed into the room and spread over the tapestry representing *The Virgin with the Holy Child and Stefano Sperelli,* a work of art brought by Giusto Sperelli from Flanders in 1508. Andrea's eyes wandered slowly over the walls, rejoicing in the beautiful hangings, the harmonious tints; and all these things so familiar and so dear to him seemed to offer him a welcome. The sight of them afforded him intense pleasure, and then the image of Maria Ferrès rose up before him.

He raised himself a little on the pillows, lit a cigarette and abandoned himself luxuriously to his meditations. An unwonted sense of comfort and well-being filled his body, while his mind was in its happiest vein. His thoughts mingled with the rings of smoke in the subdued light in which all forms and colours assume a pleasing vagueness.

Instead of reverting to the days that were past, his thoughts carried him forward into the future.—He would see Donna Maria again in two or three months—perhaps much sooner; there was no saying. Then he would resume the broken thread of that love which held for him so many obscure promises, so many secret attractions. To a man of culture, Donna Maria Ferrès was the Ideal Woman, Baudelaire's *Amie avec des hanches*, the perfect *Consolatrix*, the friend who can hold out both comfort and pardon. Though she had marked those sorrowful lines in the volume of Shelley, she had, most assuredly, said very different words in her heart. 'I can never be thine!' Why *never*? Ah, there had been too much passionate intensity for that in the voice in which she answered him that day in the wood at Vicomile—'I love you! I love you! I love you!'

He could hear her voice now, that never-to-be-forgotten voice!

Stephen knocked at the door. 'May I remind the Signor Conte that it is three o'clock?'

Andrea rose and passed into the octagonal room to dress. The sun shone through the lace window screens and sparkled on the Hispano-Mauresque tiles, the innumerable toilet articles of crystal and silver, the bas-reliefs on the antique sarcophagus; its dancing reflections imparting a delightful sense of movement to the air. He felt in the best of spirits, completely cured, full of the joy and the vivacity of life. He was inexpressibly happy to be back in his home once more. All that was most frivolous, most capricious, most worldly in him awoke with a bound. It was as if the surrounding objects had the power to evoke in him the man of former days. His sensual curiosity, his elasticity, his ubiquity of mind reappeared. He already began to feel the necessity of expansion, of mixing in the world of pleasure and with his friends.

He discovered that he was very hungry, and ordered the servant to bring the lunch at once. He rarely dined at home, but for special occasions—some *recherché* lunch or private little supper—he had a dining-room decorated with eighteenth century Neapolitan tapestries which Carlo Sperelli had ordered of Pietro Dinanti in 1766 from designs by Storace. The seven wall panels represented episodes of Bacchic love, the portières and the draperies above the doors and windows having groups of fruit and flowers. Shades of gold—pale or tawny—predominated, and mingling with the warm, pearly flesh-tints and sombre blues, formed a harmony of colour that was both delicate and sumptuous.

'When the Duke of Grimiti comes back, show him up,' he said to the servant.

Into this room too, the sun, sinking towards the Monte Mario, shot his dazzling rays. You could hear the rumble of the carriages in the piazza of the Trinità de' Monti. The rain over, it looked as if all the luminous gold of the Roman October were spread out over the city.

'Open the window,' he said to the servant.

The noise of the carriage wheels was louder now, a soft damp breeze stirred the curtains lightly.

'Divine Rome!' he thought as he looked at the sky between the wide curtains.

An irresistible curiosity drew him to the open window.

Rome appeared, all pearly gray, spread out before him, its lines a little blurred like a faded picture, under a Claude Lorrain sky, sprinkled with ethereal clouds, their noble grouping lending to the clear spaces between an indescribable delicacy, as flowers lend a new grace to the verdure which surrounds them. On the distant heights the gray deepened gradually to amethyst. Long trailing vapours slid through the cypresses of the Monte Mario like waving locks through a comb of bronze. Close by, the pines of the Monte Pincio spread their sun-gilded canopies. Below, on the piazza, the obelisk of Pius VI. looked like a pillar of agate. Under this rich autumnal light everything took on a sumptuous air.

Divine Rome!

He feasted his eyes on the prospect before him. Looking down, he saw a group of red-robed clerics pass along by the church; then the black coach of a prelate with its two black, long-tailed horses; then other open carriages containing ladies and children. He recognised the Princess of Ferentino with Barbarella Viti, followed by the Countess of Lucoli driving a pair of ponies and accompanied by her great Danish hound. A perturbing breath of the old life passed over his spirit, awakening indeterminate desires in his heart.

He left the window and returned to his lunch. The sun shone on the wall and lit up a dance of satyrs round a Silenus.

'The Duke of Grimiti and two other gentlemen,' announced the servant.

The Duke entered with Ludovico Barbarisi and Giulio Musellaro. Andrea hastened forward to meet them and they greeted him warmly.

'You, Giulio!' exclaimed Sperelli, who had not seen his friend for more than two years. 'How long have you been in Rome?'

'Only a week. I was going to write to you to Schifanoja, but thought I would rather wait till you came back. And how are you? You are looking a little thin, but very well. It was only when I got back to Rome that I heard of your affair; otherwise, I would certainly have come from India to offer you my services. At the beginning of May, I was at Padmavati in the Bahara. What a heap of things I have to tell you!'

'And so have I!'

They shook hands heartily a second time. Sperelli seemed overjoyed. None of his friends were so dear to him as Musellaro, for his noble character, his keen and penetrating mind and rare culture.

'Ruggiero—Ludovico—sit down. Giulio, will you sit here?'

He offered them tea, cigarettes, liqueurs. The conversation grew very lively. Grimiti and Barbarisi gave the news of Rome, especially the more spicy items of society gossip. The aroma of the tea mingled with that of the tobacco.

'I have brought you a chest of tea,' said Musellaro to Sperelli, 'and much better tea too than your famous Kien Loung used to drink.'

'Ah, do you remember, in London, how he used to make tea after the poetical method of the Great Emperor?'

'I say,' said Grimiti, 'do you know that the fair Clara Green is in Rome? I saw her on Sunday at the Villa Borghese. She recognised me and stopped her carriage to speak to me. She is as lovely as ever. You remember her passion for you, and how she went on when she thought you were in love with Constance Landbrooke? She instantly asked for news of you.'

'I should be very pleased to see her again. Does she still dress in green and wear sunflowers in her hat?'

'Oh no. She has apparently abandoned the æsthetic for good and all. She goes in for feathers now. On Sunday, she was wearing an enormous hat à la Montpensier with a perfectly fabulous feather in it.'

'The season is in full swing, I suppose?'

'Earlier than usual this year, both as to saints and sinners.

'Which of the saints are already in Rome?'

'Almost all—Giulia Moceto, Barbarella Viti, the Princess of Micigliano, Laura Miano, the Marchesa Massa d'Alba, the Countess Lucoli——'

'I saw her just now from the window, driving. And I saw your cousin too with Barbarella Viti.'

'My cousin is only here till to-morrow, then she goes back to Frascati. On Wednesday, she gives a kind of garden party at the villa in the style of the Princess of Sagan. Costume is not absolutely *de rigueur*, but the ladies will all wear Louis xv. or Directoire hats. We are going.'

'You are not leaving Rome again so soon, I hope?' Grimiti asked of Sperelli.

'I shall stay till the beginning of November. Then I am going to France for a fortnight to see about some horses. I shall be back in Rome about the end of the month.'

'Talking of horses,' said Ludovico, 'Leonetto Lanza wants to sell *Campomorto.* You know it—a magnificent animal, a first-rate jumper. That would be something for you.'

'How much does he want for it?'

'Fifteen thousand lire, I think.'

'Well, we might see ——'

'Leonetto is going to be married directly. He got engaged this summer at Aix-les-Bains.'

'I forgot to tell you,' said Musellaro, 'that Galeazzo Secinaro sends you his remembrances. We travelled back from India together. If you only knew of all Galeazzo's doughty deeds on the journey! He is at Palermo now, but he will be in Rome in January.'

'And Gino Bomminaco begs to be remembered to you,' added Barbarisi.

'Ah, ha!' exclaimed the duke with a burst of laughter, 'you should get Gino to tell you the story of his adventure with Donna Giulia Moceto. You are, I fancy, in a position to give us some details on the subject of Donna Giulia.'

Ludovico, too, began to laugh.

'Oh, I know,' broke in Musellaro, 'you have made the most tremendous conquests in Rome. *Gratulator tibi!*'

'But tell me—do tell me about this adventure,' asked Andrea with impatient curiosity.

These subjects excited him. Encouraged by his friends, he launched forth into a discourse on female beauty, displaying the profound knowledge and fervour of a connoisseur, taking a pleasure in using the most highly-coloured expressions, with the subtle distinctions of an artist and a libertine. Indeed, had any one taken the trouble to write down the conversation of the four young men within these walls, hung with the voluptuous scenes of the Bacchic tapestries, it might well have formed the *Breviarium arcanum* of upper-class corruption at the end of the nineteenth century.

The shades of evening were falling, but the air was still permeated with light as a sponge absorbs the water.

Through the windows, one caught a glimpse of the horizon and a band of orange against which the cypresses of the Monte Mario stood out sharply like the teeth of a great ebony rake.   Ever and anon, came the cawing of the rooks, assembling in groups on the roof of the Villa Medici before descending on the Villa Borghese and into the narrow Valley of Sleep.

'What are you going to do this evening?' Barbarisi asked Andrea.

'I really don't know.'

'Well, then, come with us—dinner at eight, at Doney's, to inaugurate his new restaurant at the Tea'.u Nazionale.'

'Yes, come with us, do come with us!' entreated Giulio Musellaro.

'Besides the three of us,' continued the duke, 'there will be Giulia Arici, Bébé Silva and Maria Fortuna—That reminds me—capital idea!—you bring Clara Green.'

'A capital idea!' echoed Ludovico Barbarisi.

'And where shall I find Clara Green?'

'At the Hotel de l'Europe, close by, in the Piazza di Spagna.   A note from you would put her in the seventh heaven.   She is certain to give up any other engagement she may have.'

Andrea was quite agreeable to the plan.

'But it would be better if I called on her,' he said. 'She is pretty sure to be in now.   Don't you think so, Ruggiero?'

'Well, dress quick and come out with us now.'

Clara Green had just come in.   She received Andrea with childish delight.   No doubt she would have preferred to dine alone with him, but she accepted the invitation without hesitating, wrote a note to excuse herself from a previous engagement, and sent the key of her box at the theatre to a lady friend.   She seemed overjoyed.   She told him a string of sentimental stories and vowed that she had never been able to forget him; holding Andrea's hands in hers while she talked.

'I love you more than words can say, Andrew.'

She was still young. With her pure and regular profile, her pale gold hair parted and knotted very low on her neck, she looked like a beauty in a Keepsake. A certain affectation of æstheticism clung to her since her liaison with the poet-painter Adolphus Jeckyll, a disciple in poetry of Keats, in painting of Holman Hunt; a composer of obscure sonnets, a painter of subjects from the *Vita Nuova*. She had sat to him for a *Sibylla Palmifera* and a *Madonna with the Lily*. She had also sat to Andrea for a study of the head of Isabella in Boccaccio's story. Art therefore had conferred upon her the stamp of nobility. But, at bottom, she possessed no spiritual qualities whatsoever; she even became tiresome in the long-run by reason of that sentimental romanticism so often affected by English *demi-mondaines* which contrasts so strangely with the depravity of their licentiousness.

'Who would have thought that we should ever be together again, Andrew?'

An hour later, Andrea left her and returned to the Palazzo Zuccari by the little flight of steps leading from the Piazza Mignanelli to the Trinità. The murmur of the city floated up the solitary little stairway through the mild air of the October evening. The stars twinkled in a cool pure sky. Down below, at the Palazza Casteldelfino, the shrubs inside the little gate cast vague uncertain shadows in the mysterious light, like marine plants waving at the bottom of an aquarium. From the palace, through a lighted window with red curtains, came the tinkle of a piano. The church bells were ringing. Andrea felt his heart suddenly grow heavy. The recollection of Donna Maria came back to him with a rush, filling him with a dim sense of regret, almost of remorse. What was she doing at this moment? Thinking? Suffering? Deep sadness fell upon him. He felt as if something in the depths of his heart had taken flight—he could not define what it was, but it affected him as some irreparable loss.

He thought of his plan of the morning—an evening of

solitude in the rooms to which some day perhaps she might come, an evening, sad yet sweet, in company with remembrances and dreams, in company with her spirit, an evening of meditation and self-communings. In truth, he had kept well to his promises! He was on his way to a dinner with friends and *demi-mondaines* and, doubtless, would go home with Clara Green afterwards.

His regret was so poignant, so intolerable, that he dressed with unwonted rapidity, jumped into his brougham and arrived at the hotel before the appointed time. He found Clara ready and waiting, and offered her a drive round the streets of Rome to pass the time till eight o'clock

They drove through the Via del Babuino, round the obelisk in the Piazza del Popolo, along the Corso and to the right down the Via della Fontanella di Borghese, returning by the Montecitorio to the Corso which they followed as far as the Piazza di Venezia and so to the Teatro Nazionale. Clara kept up an incessant chatter, bending, every other minute, towards her companion to press a kiss on the corner of his mouth, screening the furtive caress behind a fan of white feathers which gave out a delicate odour of 'white rose.' But Andrea appeared not to hear her, and even her caress only drew from him a slight smile.

' *Che pensi ?* ' she asked, pronouncing the Italian words with a certain hesitation which was very taking.

'Nothing,' returned Andrea, taking up one of her ungloved hands and examining the rings.

' *Chi lo sa !* ' she sighed, throwing a vast amount of expression into these three words, which foreign women pick up at once, because they imagine that they contain all the pensive melancholy of Italian love. ' *Chi lo sa !* '

With a sudden change of humour, Andrea kissed her on the ear, slipped an arm round her waist and proceeded to say a host of foolish things to her. The Corso was very lively, the shop windows resplendent, newspaper-vendors yelled, public and private vehicles crossed the path of their carriage ; all the stir and animation of Roman evening life was in

full swing from the Piazza Colonna to the Piazza di
Venezia.

It was ten minutes past eight by the time they reached
Doney's. The other guests were already there. Andrea
Sperelli greeted the assembled company, and taking Clara
Green by the hand—

'This,' he said, 'is Miss Clara Green, *ancilla Domini,
Sibylla palmifera, candida puella.*'

'*Ora pro nobis!*' replied Musellaro, Barbarisi, and Grimiti
in chorus.

The women laughed though they did not understand. Clara
smiled, and slipping out of her cloak appeared in a white dress,
quite simple and short, with a V-shaped opening back and
front, a knot of sea-green ribbon on her left shoulder, and
emeralds in her ears, perfectly unabashed by the triple
scrutiny of Giulia Arici, Bébé Silva and Maria Fortuna.

Musellaro and Grimiti were old acquaintances; Barbarisi
was introduced.

Andrea proceeded—'Mercedes Silva, surnamed Bébé—
chica pero qualsa.

'Maria Fortuna, a veritable *Fortuna publica* for our Rome
which has the good fortune to possess her.'

Then, turning to Barbarisi—'Do us the honour to present
us to this lady who is, if I am not mistaken, the divine Giulia
Farnese.'

'No—Arici,' Giulia broke in.

'Oh, I beg your pardon, but really, to believe that, I
should have to call upon all my powers of credulity and to
consult Pinturicchio in the Fifth Room.'

He uttered these absurdities with a grave smile, amusing
himself by bewildering and teasing these pretty fools. In the
demi-monde he adopted a manner and style entirely his own,
using grotesque phrases, launching the most ridiculous para-
doxes or atrocious impertinences under cover of the ambiguity
of his words; and all this in most original language, rich in a
thousand different flavours, like a Rabelaisian *olla podrida*, full
of strong spices and succulent morsels.

'Pinturicchio,' asked Giulia turning to Barbarisi; 'who's that?'

'Pinturicchio,' exclaimed Andrea, 'oh, a sort of feeble house-painter who once took it into his head to paint your picture on a door in the Pope's apartments. Never mind him—he is dead.'

'Dead? How?'

'In a most appalling manner! His wife's lover was a soldier from Perugia in garrison at Sienna—ask Ludovico— he knows all about it, but has never liked to tell you, for fear of hurting your feelings. Allow me to inform you, Bébé, that the Prince of Wales does not begin to smoke till between the second and third courses—never sooner. You are anticipating.'

Bébé Silva had lighted a cigarette and was eating oysters, while she let the smoke curl through her nostrils. She was like a restless schoolboy, a little depraved hermaphrodite; pale and thin, the brightness of her eyes heightened by fever and kohl, with lips that were too red, and short and rather woolly hair that covered her head like an astrachan cap. Fixed tightly in her left eye was a single eyeglass; she wore a high stiff collar, a white necktie, an open waistcoat, a little black coat of masculine cut and a gardenia in her button-hole. She affected the manners of a dandy and spoke in a deep husky voice. And just therein lay the secret of her attraction— in this imprint of vice, of depravity, of abnormity in her appearance, her attitudes and her words. *Sal y pimienta.*

Maria Fortuna, on the contrary, was of somewhat bovine type, a Madame de Parabère with a tendency to stoutness.

Like the fair mistress of the Regent, she possessed a very white skin, one of those opaque white complexions which seem only to flourish and improve on sensual pleasure. Her liquid violet eyes swam in a faint blue shadow; and her lips, always a little parted, disclosed a vague gleam of pearl behind their soft rosy line, like a half-opened shell.

Giulia Arici took Andrea's fancy very much on account of her golden-brown tints and her great velvety eyes of that soft deep chestnut that sometimes shows tawny gleams. The somewhat fleshy nose, and the full, dewy scarlet, very firm lips gave the lower part of her face a frankly animal look. Her eye-teeth, which were too prominent, raised her upper lip a little and she continually ran the point of her tongue along the edge to moisten it, like the thick petal of a rose running over a row of little white almonds.

'Giulia,' said Andrea with his eyes on her mouth, 'Saint Bernard uses, in one of his sermons, an epithet which would suit you marvellously. And I'll be bound you don't know this either.'

Giulia laughed her sonorous rather vacant laugh, exhaling, in the excitement of her hilarity, a more poignant perfume, like a scented shrub when it is shaken.

'What will you give me,' continued Andrea, 'if I extract from the holy sermon a voluptuous motto to fit you?'

'I don't know,' she replied laughing, holding a glass of Chablis in her long slender fingers. 'Anything you like.'

'The substantive of the adjective.'

'What?'

'We will come back to that presently. The word is: *linguatica*—Messer Ludovico, you can add this clause to your litanies—' *Rosa linguatica, glube nos.*'

'What a pity,' said Musellaro, 'that you are not at the table of a sixteenth-century prince, sitting between a Violante and an Imperia with Pietro Aretino, Giulio Romano, and Marc' Antonio!'

CHAPTER II

The year was dying gracefully. A late wintry sun filled the sky over Rome with a soft, mild, golden light that made the air feel almost spring-like. The streets were full as on a Sunday in May. A stream of carriages passed and repassed rapidly through the Piazza Barberini and the Piazza di Spagna, and from thence a vague and continuous rumble mounted to the Trinità de' Monti and the Via Sistina and even faintly reached the apartments of the Palazzo Zuccari.

The rooms began slowly to fill with the scent exhaled from numberless vases of flowers. Full-blown roses hung their heavy heads over crystal vases that opened like diamond lilies on a golden stem, similar to those standing behind the Virgin in the *tondo* of Botticelli in the Borghese Gallery. No other shape of vase is to be compared with this for elegance; in that diaphanous prison, the flowers seemed to etherealise and had more the air of a religious than an amatory offering.

For Andrea Sperelli was expecting Elena Muti.

He had met her only yesterday morning in the Via Condotti, where she was looking at the shops. She had returned to Rome a day or two before, after her long and mysterious absence. They had both been considerably agitated by the unexpected encounter, but the publicity of the street compelled them to treat one another with ceremonious, almost cold politeness. However, he had said with a grave, half-mournful air, looking her full in the eyes—'I have much to say to you, Elena; will you come to my rooms to-morrow? Everything is just as it used to be—nothing is

188

changed.' To which she replied quite simply—'Very well, I will come. You may expect me about four o'clock. I too have something to say to you—but leave me now.'

That she should have accepted the invitation so promptly, without demur, without imposing any conditions or seemingly attaching the smallest importance to the matter, roused a certain vague suspicion in Andrea's mind. Was she coming as friend or lover?—to renew old ties or to destroy all hope of such a thing for ever? What vicissitudes had not occurred in this woman's soul during the last two years? Of that he was necessarily ignorant, but he had carried away with him the thrill of emotion called up in him by Elena's glance when they suddenly met in the street and he bent his head in greeting before her. It was the same look as of old—so tender, so deep, so infinitely seductive from under the long lashes.

Everything in the arrangement of the rooms showed evidences of special loving care. Logs of juniper wood burned brightly on the hearth; the little tea-table stood ready with its cups and saucers of Castel-Durante majolica, of antique shape and inimitable grace, whereon were depicted mythological subjects by Luzio Dolci, with lines from Ovid underneath in black characters and a running hand. The light from the windows was tempered by heavy curtains of red brocade embroidered all over with silver pomegranates, trailing leaves and mottos. The declining sun, as it caught the window-panes, cast the shadow of the lace blinds on the carpet.

The clock of the Trinità struck half-past three. He had half an hour still to wait. Andrea rose from the sofa where he had been lying and opened one of the windows; he wandered aimlessly about the room, took up a book, read a few lines and threw it down again; looked about him unde-cidedly as if searching for something. The suspense was so trying that he felt the necessity of rousing himself, of counteracting his mental disquietude by physical means. He went over to the fireplace, stirred up the logs and put on a fresh one. The glowing mass collapsed, sending up a shower of sparks, and part of it rolled out as far as the fender. The flames broke into a quantity of little tongues of blue fire, springing up and disappearing fitfully, while the broken ends of the log smoked.

The sight brought back certain memories to him. In days gone by Elena had been fond of lingering over this fireside. She expended much art and ingenuity in piling the wood high on the fire-dogs, grasping the heavy tongs in both hands and leaning her head slightly back to avoid the sparks. Her hands were small and very supple, with that tendril-like flexibility, so to speak, of a Daphne at the very first onset of the fabled metamorphose.

Scarcely were these matters arranged to her satisfaction than the logs would catch and send forth a sudden blaze, and the warm ruddy light would struggle for a moment with the icy gray shades of evening filtering through the windows. The sharp fumes of the burning wood seemed to rise to her head, and facing the glowing mass Elena would be seized with fits of childish glee. She had a rather cruel habit of pulling all the flowers to pieces and scattering them over the carpet at the end of each of her visits and then stand ready to go, fastening a glove or a bracelet, and smile in the midst of the devastation she had wrought.

Nothing was changed since then. A host of memories were associated with these things which Elena had touched, on which her eyes had rested, and scenes of that time rose up vividly and tumultuously before him. After nearly two years' absence, Elena was going to cross his threshold once more. In half an hour, she would be seated in that chair —a little out of breath at first, as of yore—would have removed her veil—be speaking. All these familiar objects would hear the sound of her voice again—perhaps even her laugh—after two long years.

'How shall I receive her—what shall I say?'

He was quite sincere in his anxiety and nervousness, for he had really begun to love this woman once more, but the expression of his sentiments, whether verbal or otherwise, was ever with him such an artificial matter, so far removed from truth and simplicity, that he had recourse to these preparations from pure habit even when, as was the case now, he was sincerely and deeply moved.

He tried to imagine the scene beforehand, to compose some phrases; he looked about him in the room, considering where would be the most appropriate spot for the interview. Then he went over to a looking-glass to see if his face were as pale as befitted the occasion, and his gaze rested complacently on his forehead, just where the hair began at the temples and where, in the the old days, Elena was often wont to press a delicate kiss. In matters of love, his vitiated and effeminate vanity seized upon every advantage of personal grace or of dress to heighten the charm of his appearance, and he knew how to extract the greatest amount of pleasure therefrom. The chief reason of his unfailing success lay in the fact that, in the game of love, he shrank from no artifice, no duplicity, no falsehood that might further his cause. A great portion of his strength lay in his capacity for deception.

'What shall I do—what shall I say when she comes?'

His mind was all undecided and yet the minutes were flying. Besides, he had no idea in what frame of mind Elena might arrive.

It wanted but two or three minutes now to the hour. His excitement was so great that he felt half suffocated. He returned to the window and looked out at the steps of the Trinità. She used always to come up those steps, and when she reached the top, would halt for a moment before rapidly crossing the square in front of the Casa Casteldelfina. Through the silence, he often heard the tapping of her light footsteps on the pavement below.

The clock struck four. The rumble of carriage wheels came up from the Piazza di Spagna and the Pincio. A great many people were strolling under the trees in front of the Villa Medici. Two women seated on a stone bench beside the church were keeping watch over some children playing

round the obelisk, which shone rosy red under the sunset, and
cast a long, slanting, blue-gray shadow.

The air freshened as the sun sank lower. Farther off, the
city stood out golden against the colourless clear sky, which
made the cypresses on the Monte Mario look jet black.

Andrea started. A shadow stole up the little flight of
steps beside the Casa Casteldelfina leading up from the
Piazzetta Mignanelli. It was not Elena ; it was some other
lady, who slowly turned the corner into the Via Gregoriana.

' What if she did not come at all?' he said to himself as he
left the window. Coming away from the colder outside air
he felt the warmth of the room all the more cosy, the scent of
the burning wood and the roses more piercing sweet, the
shadow of the curtains and portières more delightfully
mysterious. At that moment the whole room seemed on the
alert for the arrival of the woman he loved. He imagined
Elena's sensations on entering. It was hardly possible that
she should be able to resist the influence of these surroundings, so full of tender memories for her ; she would suddenly
lose all sense of time and reality, would fancy herself back at
one of the old rendezvous, the Elena of those happy days.
Since nothing was altered in the *mise-en-scène* of their love,
why should their love itself be changed? She must of
necessity feel the profound charm of all these things which
once upon a time had been so dear to her.

And now the anguish of hope deferred created a fresh
torture for him. Minds that have the habit of imaginative
contemplation and poetic dreaming attribute to inanimate
objects a soul, sensitive and variable as their own, and recognise in all things—be it form or colour, sound or perfume
—a transparent symbol, an emblem of some emotion or
thought ; in every phenomenon and every group of pheno-
mena they claim to discover a psychical condition, a moral
significance. At times the vision is so lucid as to produce
actual pain in such minds, they feel themselves overwhelmed
by the plenitude of life revealed to them and are terrified by
the phantom of their own creation.

Thus Andrea saw his own dire distress reflected in the

aspect of the objects surrounding him, and as his own fond desires seemed wasting fruitlessly in this protracted expectation, so the erotic essence, so to speak, of the room appeared to be evaporating and exhaling uselessly. In his eyes these apartments in which he had loved and also suffered so much had acquired something of his own sensibility—had not only been witness of his loves, his pleasures, his sorrows, but had taken part in it all. In his memories, every outline, every tint harmonised with some feminine image, was a note in a chord of beauty, an element in an ecstasy of passion. The very nature of his tastes led him to seek for a diversity of enjoyment in his love, and seeing that he set out upon that quest as an accomplished artist and æsthetic it was only natural that he should derive a great part of his delight from the world of external objects. To this fastidious actor the comedy of love was nothing without the scenery.

From that point of view his stage was certainly quite perfect, and he himself a most adroit actor-manager; for he almost always entered heart and soul into his own artifice, he forgot himself so completely that he was deceived by his own deception, fell into the trap of his own laying, and wounded himself with his own weapons—a magician enclosed in the spells of his own weaving.

The roses in the tall Florentine vases, they too were waiting and breathing out their sweetness. On the divan cover and on the walls inscriptions on silver scrolls singing the praises of woman and of wine gleamed in the rays of the setting sun, and harmonised admirably with the faded colours of the sixteenth century Persian carpet. Elsewhere the shadow was deeply transparent and as if animated by that indefinable luminous tremor felt in hidden sanctuaries where some mystic treasure lies enshrined. The fire crackled on the hearth, each flame, as Shelley puts it, like a separate jewel dissolved in ever moving light. To Andrea it seemed that at that moment every shape, every colour, every perfume gave forth the essential and delicate spirit of its being. And yet *she* came not, *she* came not!

For the first time, the thought of her husband presented itself to him.

Elena was no longer free. Some months after her abrupt departure from Rome, she had renounced the agreeable liberty of widowhood to marry an English nobleman, Lord Humphrey Heathfield. Andrea had seen the announcement of the marriage in a society paper in the October following and had heard a world of comment on the new Lady Humphrey in every country house he stayed in during the autumn. He remembered also having met Lord Humphrey some half a score of times during the preceding winter at the Saturdays of the Princess Giustiniani-Bandini, or in the public salerooms. He was a man of about forty, with colourless fair hair, bald at the temples, an excessively pale face, a pair of piercing light eyes and a prominent forehead, on which a network of veins stood out. He had his name of Heathfield from that lieutenant-general who was the hero of the defence of Gibraltar and afterwards immortalised by the brush of Sir Joshua Reynolds.

What part had this man in Elena's life? What ties, beyond the convention of marriage, bound her to him? What transformations had the physical and moral contact of this husband brought to pass in her?

These enigmas rose tumultuously before him, making his pain so intolerable, that he started up with the instinctive bound of a man who has been stabbed unawares. He crossed the room to the ante-chamber and listened at the door which he had left ajar. It was on the stroke of a quarter to five.

The next moment he heard footsteps on the stair, the rustle of skirts and a quick panting breath. A woman was coming up hurriedly. His heart beat with such vehemence that—his nerves all unstrung by his long suspense—he felt hardly able to stand on his feet. The steps drew nearer, there was a long-drawn sigh—a step upon the landing—at the door—Elena entered.

'O Elena—at last!'

There was in that cry such a profound accent of agony endured, that it brought to Elena's lips an indescribable smile, mingled of pleasure and pity. He took her by her ungloved right hand and drew her into the room. She was still a little out of breath, and under her black veil a faint flush diffused itself over her whole face.

'Forgive me, Andrea! I could not get away any sooner—there is so much to do—so many calls to return—such tiring days! I hardly know where to turn. How warm it is in here! What a delicious smell!'

She was standing in the middle of the room—a little undecided and ill at ease in spite of her rapid and lightly spoken words. A velvet coat with Empire sleeves, very full at the shoulders and buttoned closely at the wrists and with an immense collar of blue fox for sole trimming, covered her from head to foot, but without disguising the grace of her figure. She looked at Andrea with eyes in which a curious tremulous smile softened the flash and sparkle.

'You have changed somehow,' she said; 'I don't quite know what it is—but round your mouth, for instance, there are bitter lines that used not to be there.'

She spoke in a tone of affectionate familiarity. The sound of her voice once more in this room caused him such exquisite delight that he exclaimed—'Speak again, Elena—go on speaking!'

She laughed. 'Why?' she asked.

'You know why,' he answered, taking her hand again.

She drew her hand away and looked the young man deep in the eyes. 'I know nothing any more.'

'Then you have changed very much.'

'Yes—very much indeed.'

They had both dropped their bantering tone. Elena's answer threw a sudden search-light upon much that was problematical before. Andrea understood, and with that rapid and precise intuition so often found in minds practised in psychological analysis, he instantly divined the moral attitude of his visitor, and foresaw the further development of the

coming scene.   Moreover, he was already under the spell of
this woman's fascination as in the former days, besides
being greatly piqued by curiosity.

'Will you not sit down?' he asked.

'Yes—for a moment.'

'Here—in this arm-chair.'

'Ah—*my* arm-chair!' she was on the point of exclaiming,
for she recognised an old friend, but she stopped herself in
time.

The chair was deep and roomy, and covered with antique
leather on which pale dragons ramped in relief, after the style
of the wall decorations of one of the rooms in the Chigi
palace.   The leather had taken on that warm and sumptuous
tone which recalls the background of certain Venetian por-
traits, or a fine bronze still retaining traces of former gilding,
or a piece of tortoiseshell with gleams of gold here and there.
A great cushion covered with a piece of a dalmatic of faded
colouring—of that peculiar shade which the Florentine silk
merchants used to call 'rosa di gruogo,' saffron red, contributed
to its inviting easiness.

Elena seated herself in it, placing on the tea-table beside
her her right hand glove and her card-case, a fragile toy in
polished silver with a device and motto engraven on it.   She
then proceeded to remove her veil, raising her arms high to
unfasten the knot, her graceful attitude throwing gleams of
changeful light on the velvet of her coat, along the sleeves
and over the contour of her bust.   The heat of the fire was
very strong, and with her bare hand, which shone transparent
like rosy alabaster, she screened her face from it.   The rings
on her fingers glittered in the fire-light.

'Please screen the fire,' she said, 'it is really too fierce.'

'What—have you lost your fondness for the flames?—and
you used to be a perfect salamander.   This hearth is full of
memories——'

'Let memory sleep,—do not stir the embers,' she interrupted him.   'Screen the fire and let us have some light.   I
will make the tea.'

'Won't you take off your coat?'

'No, I must go directly—it is late.'

'But you will be melted.'

She rose with a little gesture of impatience. 'Very well then—help me, please.'

As he helped her off with the mantle, Andrea noticed that the scent was not the same as the familiar one of old. However, it was so delicious that it thrilled his every sense.

'You have a new scent,' he said with peculiar emphasis.

'Yes,' she answered simply, 'do you like it?'

Andrea still held the mantle in his hands. He buried his face in the fur collar which had been next her throat and her hair—'What is it called?' he inquired.

'It has no name.'

She re-seated herself in the arm-chair within the circle of the firelight. Her dress was of black lace, on which sparkled a mass of tiny jet and steel beads.

The day was fading from the windows. Andrea lit candles of twisted orange-coloured wax in wrought-iron candlesticks, after which he drew a screen before the fire.

During this pause, both felt a certain perplexing uneasiness; Elena was no longer exactly conscious of the moment, nor was she quite mistress of herself. In spite of all her efforts she was unable to recall with precision her motives for coming here, to follow out her intentions—even to regain her force of will. In the presence of this man to whom, once upon a time, she had been bound by such passionate ties, and in this spot where she lived the most ardent moments of her life, she felt her reserve melting, her mind wavering and growing feeble. She was at that dangerously delicious point of sentiment at which the soul receives its every impulse, its attitudes, its form from its external surroundings as an aërial vapour from the mutations of the atmosphere. But she checked herself before wholly giving way to it.

'Is that right now?' asked Andrea in a low, almost humble voice.

She smiled without replying.   His words had given her inexpressibly keen delight.

She began her delicate manipulations—lit the spirit-lamp under the kettle, opened the lacquer tea-caddy and put the necessary quantity of aromatic leaves into the tea-pot, and finally prepared two cups.   Her movements were slow and a little hesitating, as happens when the mind is busied with other things than the occupation of the moment; her exquisite white hands hovered over the cups with the airiness of butterflies, and from her whole lithe form there emanated an indefinable charm which enveloped her lover like a caress.

Seated quite close to her, gazing at her from under his half-closed lids, Andrea drank in the subtle fascination of her presence.   Neither of them spoke.   Elena, leaning back in the cushions, waited for the water to boil, with her eyes fixed on the blue flame while she absently slipped her rings up and down her fingers, lost in a dream apparently.   But it was no dream; it was rather a vague reminiscence, faint, confused and evanescent.   All the recollections of the love that was past rose up in her mind, but dimly and uncertain, leaving an indistinct impression, she hardly knew whether of pleasure or of pain.   It was like the indefinable perfume of a faded bouquet, in which each separate flower has lost the vivacity proper to its colour and its fragrance, but from which emanates a common perfume wherein all the diverse component elements are indistinguishably blended.   She seemed to carry in her heart the last breath of memories already faded, the last trace of joys departed for ever, the last tremor of a happiness that was dead—something akin to a mist from out of which images emerge fitfully without shape or name. She knew not, was it pleasure or pain, but by degrees this mysterious agitation, this nameless disquiet waxed greater and filled her soul with joy and bitterness.

She was silent—withdrawn within herself—for though her

heart was full to overflowing, her emotion was pleasurably increased by that silence. Speech would have broken the charm.

The kettle began its low song.

Andrea on a low seat, with his elbow on his knee and his chin in his hand, sat watching the fair woman so intently that Elena, without turning, felt that persistent gaze upon her with a sense of physical discomfort. And while he gazed upon her he thought to himself that she seemed altogether a new woman to him—one who had never been his, whom he had never clasped to his heart.

And in truth, she was even more desirable than in the former days, the plastic enigma of her beauty more obscure and more enthralling. Her head with the low broad forehead, straight nose and arched eyebrows—so pure and firm in outline, so classically antique in the modelling—might have come from some Syracusan coin. The expression of the eyes and that of the mouth were in singular contrast, giving her that passionate, ambiguous, almost preternatural look that only one or two master-hands, deeply imbued in all the profoundest corruption of art, have been able to infuse into such immortal types of woman as the Mona Lisa and Nelly O'Brien.

The steam began to escape through the hole in the lid of the kettle, and Elena turned her attention once more to the tea-table. She poured a little water on the leaves; put two lumps of sugar in one of the cups, then poured some more water into the teapot and extinguished the lamp; doing it all with a certain fond care, but never once looking in Andrea's direction. By this time her inward agitation had resolved itself into such melting tenderness, that there was a lump in her throat and her eyes filled involuntarily; all her contradictory thoughts, all her trouble and agitation of heart, concentrated themselves in those tears.

A movement of her arm knocked the little silver card-case off the table. Andrea picked it up and examined the device: two true lovers' knots each bearing an inscription in English —*From Dreamland*, and *A Stranger here*.

When he raised his head, Elena offered him the fragrant beverage with a mist of tears before her eyes.

He saw that mist, and, filled with love and gratitude at such an unlooked-for sign of melting, he put down the cup, sank on his knees before her, and seizing her hand pressed his lips passionately to it.

'Elena! Elena!' he murmured, his face close to hers as if he would drink the breath from her lips. His emotion was quite sincere, though some of the things he said were not. He loved her—had always loved her—had never, never, never been able to forget her. On meeting her again, he had felt his passion rekindle with such vehemence that it had given him a kind of shock of terror—as if in one lightning flash he had witnessed the upheaval, the convulsion of his whole life.

'Hush—hush——' said Elena with a look of pain, and turning very pale.

But Andrea went on, still on his knees, fanning the flames of his passion by the images he himself evoked. When she had left him so abruptly, he had felt that the greater and better part of him went with her. Afterwards——never, never could he tell her all the misery of those days, the agony of regret, the ceaseless, implacable, devouring torture of mind and body. His wretchedness grew and increased daily till it burst all bounds and overwhelmed him utterly. Despair lay in wait for him at every turn. The mere flight of time became an intolerable burden. His regrets were less for the happy days gone by than for those that were passing all profitless for love. Those, at least, had left him a memory, these nothing but profoundest regret—nay, almost remorse. His life was preying upon itself, consumed in secret by the inextinguishable flame of one desire, by the unconquerable distaste to any other form of pleasure. Of all the fiery ardour of his youth nothing now remained to him but a handful of ashes. Sometimes, like a dream that vanishes at dawn, all the past, all the present would fade and fall away from his inner consciousness—like a tale that is told, a useless garment. Then he would remember the past no more, as a man newly risen from a long illness, a convalescent still overcome with stupor. At last he could forget—his tortured soul was sinking gently down to death.——But suddenly, out of the depths of this lethal tranquillity his pain had sprung up afresh, and the fallen idol was re-established higher than ever. She and she alone held every fibre of his heart captive beneath her spells, crushing out his intelligence, keeping the doors of his soul against any other passion, any sorrow, any dream to the end of all time——

He was lying of course, but his words were so fervid, his voice so thrilling, the clasp of his hands so fondly caressing that Elena was profoundly touched.

'Hush,' she said, 'I must not, dare not listen to you—I am yours no longer, I never can be yours again—never. Do not say these things——'

'No—listen——'

'I will not — good-bye — I must go now. Good-bye, Andrea,—it is late—let me go.'

She drew her hands out of the young man's clasp, and, successfully throwing off the dangerous languor that was creeping over her, she prepared to rise.

'Then why did you come?' he asked almost roughly, and preventing her from doing so.

Slight as was the force he used, she frowned. She paused before answering.

'I came,' she said in measured accents and looking her lover full in the eyes—'I came because you asked me. For the sake of the love that was once between us, for the manner in which that love was broken and for the long and unexplained silence of my absence I had not the heart to refuse your invitation. Besides, I wanted to say what I have said: that I am no longer yours—that I never can be again—never. That is what I wanted to tell you, honestly and frankly, to save you and myself all painful disillusionment, all danger or bitterness in the future.—Do you understand?'

Andrea bowed his head almost to her knee in silence. She stroked his hair with a familiar gesture of old.

'And then,' she went on in a voice that thrilled him to the heart's core—'and then—I wanted to tell you—that I love you—love you as much as ever: that you are still the heart of my heart and that I will be the fondest of sisters to you, the best of friends—do you understand?'

Andrea made no reply. She took his head between her hands and raised it, forcing him to look her in the face.

'Do you understand?' she repeated in a still lower, sweeter tone. Her eyes under the shadow of the long lashes were suffused with a pure and tender light, her lips were slightly open and trembling.

'No; you never loved me, and you do not love me now!' Andrea burst out at last, pulling Elena's hands from his temples and drawing away from her, for he was sensible of the fire that was kindling in his veins under the mere gaze of those eyes, and his regret at having lost possession of this fairest of women grew more bitter and poignant than before. 'No, you never loved me. You had the heart to strike your love dead at a blow—treacherously almost—just when it had reached its supremest height. You ran away, you deserted me, left me alone in my bewilderment, my misery, while I was still blinded by your promises. You never loved me—neither then nor now. And now, after such a long absence, so full of mystery, so silent and inexorable, after I have wasted the bloom of my life in cherishing a wound that was dear to me because your hand had dealt it—after so much joy and so much pain, you return to this room, in which every object is replete for us with living memories, and you say to me calmly—"I am yours no longer—good-bye." —Oh no—you do not love me.'

'Oh, you are ungrateful!' she cried, deeply wounded by the young man's incensed tone. 'What do you know of all that has occurred, or of what I have had to go through?—What do you know?'

'I know nothing, and what is more, I do not want to,'

Andrea retorted stubbornly, enveloping her in a darkling look in which burned the fever of his desire. ' All I know is that you were mine once—wholly and without reserve, and I know that body and soul I shall never forget it——'

' Be silent ! '

' What do I care for your sisterly affection ? In spite of yourself you offer it with your eyes full of quite another kind of love, and you cannot touch me without your hands trembling. I have seen that look in your eyes too often, you have too often felt me tremble with passion beneath your hands— I love you ! '

Carried away by his own words he grasped her wrists tightly and drew so close to her that she felt his hot breath on her cheek. ' I love you, I tell you—more than ever before,' he went on, slipping an arm about her waist to draw her to his kiss—' Have you forgotten—have you forgotten ? '

She pushed him forcibly from her and rose to her feet, trembling in every limb.

' I will not—do you hear ? '

But he would not hear. He came towards her with arms outstretched, very pale and determined.

' Could you bear,' she cried turning at bay at last, indignant at his violence, ' could you bear to share me with another ? '

She flung the cruel question at him point-blank, without reflection, and now stood looking at her lover with wide open frightened eyes, like one who in self-defence has dealt a blow without measuring his strength, and fears to have struck too deep.

Andrea's frenzy dropped on the instant, and his face expressed such overwhelming pain that Elena was stricken to the heart.

After a moment's silence—' Good-bye ! ' he said, but that one word contained all the bitterness of the words he refrained from saying.

' Good-bye,' she answered gently, ' forgive me.'

They both felt the necessity of putting an end, at least for

that evening, to this perilous conversation. Andrea affected
an almost over-strained courtesy. Elena became even gentler,
almost humble. A nervous tremor shook her continually.

She took her cloak from the chair and Andrea hastened to
assist her. As she did not succeed in finding the armholes,
Andrea guided her hand to it but scarcely touched her. He
then offered her her hat and veil. 'There is a looking-glass
in the next room if you would like——'

'No, thank you.' She went over beside the fireplace,
where on the wall hung a quaint little old mirror in a frame
surrounded by little figures, carved in so airy and vivacious a
style that they seemed rather ιo be of malleable gold than of
wood. It was a charming thing, the work doubtless of some
delicate artist of the fifteenth century and designed to reflect
the charms of some Mona Amorrosisca or some Laldomine.
Many a time in the old happy days Elena had put on her
veil in front of this dim, lack lustre mirror. She remembered
it again now.

On seeing her reflection rise out of its misty depths she
was stirred by a singular emotion. A rush of profound
sadness came over her. She did not speak.

All this time Andrea was watching her intently.

Her preparations concluded, she said, 'It must be very
late.'

'Not very—about six o'clock, I think.'

'I sent away my carriage. I would be very grateful if you
could send for a closed cab for me.'

'Will you excuse me then if I leave you alone for a
moment? My servant is out.'

She assented. 'And please tell the man yourself where to
go to—the Hotel Quirinal.'

He went out and shut the door behind him. She was
alone.

She cast a rapid glance around her, embracing the whole
room with an indefinable look that lingered on the vases of
flowers. The room seemed to her larger, the ceiling higher
than she remembered. She began to feel a little giddy. She

did not notice the scent of the flowers any longer, but the atmosphere of the room was close and heavy as in a hot-house. Andrea's image appeared to her in a sort of inter-mittent flashes—a vague echo of his voice rang in her ears. Was she going to faint?—Oh, the delight of it if she might close her eyes and abandon herself to this languor!

She gave herself a little shake and went over to one of the windows, which she opened, and let the breeze blow in her face. Somewhat revived by this she turned back into the room. The pale flame of the candles sent flickering shadows over the walls. The fire burned low but sufficed to light up in part the pious figures on the screen made of stained glass from a church window. The cup of tea stood where Andrea had laid it down on the table, cold and untouched. The chair cushion retained the impress of the form that had leaned against it. All the objects surrounding her breathed an ineffable melancholy, which condensed itself in a heavy weight upon Elena's heart, till it sank beneath the well nigh insupportable burden.

'*Mio Dio! mio Dio!*'

She wished she could make her escape unseen. A puff of wind inflated the curtains, made the candles flicker, raised a general rustle through the room. She shivered, and almost without knowing what she did, she called—

'Andrea!'

Her own voice—that name in the silence startled her strangely, as if neither voice nor name had come from her lips. Why was Andrea so long in returning? She listened. ——There was no sound but the dull deep inarticulate murmur of the city. Not a carriage passed across the piazza of the Trinità de' Monti. As the wind came in strong gusts from time to time, she closed the window, catching a glimpse as she did so of the point of the obelisk, black against the starry sky.

Possibly Andrea had not found a conveyance at once on the Piazza Barberini. She sat herself down to wait on the sofa and tried to calm her foolish agitation, avoiding all heart-searchings and endeavouring to fix her attention on external objects.   Her eyes wandered to the figures on the fire-screen, faintly visible by the light of the dying logs.   On the mantelpiece a great white rose in one of the vases was dropping its petals softly, languidly, one by one, giving an impression of something subtly feminine and sensuous.   The cup-like petals rested delicately on the marble, like flakes of snow.

Ah, how sweet that fragrant snow had been *then* ! she thought.   Rose-leaves strewed the carpets, the divan, the chairs, and she was laughing, happy in the midst of the devastation, and her happy lover was at her feet——

A carriage stopped down in the street.   She rose and shook her aching head to banish the dull weight that seemed to paralyse her.   The next moment, Andrea entered out of breath.

'Forgive me,' he said, 'for keeping you so long, but I could not find the porter, so I went down to the Piazza di Spagna.   The carriage is waiting for you.'

'Thanks,' answered Elena with a timid glance at him through her black veil.

He was grave and pale but quite calm.

'I expect my husband to-morrow,' she went on in a low faint voice.   'I will send you a line to let you know when I can see you again.'

'Thank you,' answered Andrea.

'Good-bye then,' she said, holding out her hand.

'Shall I see you down to the street ?   There is no one there.'

'Yes—come down with me.'

She looked about her a little hesitatingly.

'Have you forgotten anything ?' asked Andrea.

She was looking at the flowers, but she answered, 'Ah—yes —my card-case.'

Andrea sprang to fetch it from the table.   *'A stranger here ?'* he read as he handed it to her.

'No, my dear, a friend——'

Her answer was quick, her voice eager.   Then suddenly

with a smile peculiarly her own, half imploring, half seductive, a mixture of timidity and tenderness, she said : ' *Give me a rose.*'

Andrea went from vase to vase gathering all the roses into one great bunch which he could scarcely hold in his hands—some of them shed their petals.

'They were for you—all of them,' he said without looking at her.

Elena hung her head and turned to go in silence followed by Andrea. They descended the stairs still in silence. He could see the nape of her neck so fair and delicate where the little dark curls mingled with the gray-blue fur.

'Elena!' he cried her name in a low voice, incapable any longer of fighting against the passion that filled his heart to bursting.

She turned round to him with a finger on her lips—a gesture of agonised entreaty—but her eyes burned through the shadow. She hastened her steps, flung herself into the carriage and felt rather than saw him lay the roses in her lap.

'Good-bye! Good-bye!'

And when the carriage turned away she threw herself back exhausted and burst into a passion of sobs, tearing the roses to pieces with her poor frenzied hands.

CHAPTER III

So she had come, she had come! She had re-entered the rooms in which every piece of furniture, every object must retain some memory for her, and she had said—'I am yours no more, can never be yours again, never!' and—'Could you suffer to share me with another?'—Yes, she had dared to fling those words in his face, in that room, in sight of all these things!

A rush of pain—atrocious, immeasurable, made up of a thousand wounds, each distinct from the other and one more piercing than the other, came over him and goaded him to desperation. Passion enveloped him once more in a thousand tongues of fire, re-kindling in him an inextinguishable desire for this woman who belonged to him no more, re-awakening in his memory every smallest detail of past caresses and all the sweet mad doings of those days. And yet through it all, there persisted the strange difficulty in identifying that Elena with the Elena of to-day, who seemed to him altogether another woman, one whom he had never known, never held in his arms. The torture of his senses was such that he thought he must die of it. Impurity crept through his blood like a corroding poison.

The impurity which *then* the winged flame of the soul had covered with a sacred veil, had surrounded with a mystery that was half divine, appeared *now* without the veil and without the mystery as a mere carnal lust, a piece of gross sensuality. He knew that the ardour he had felt to-day in her presence was not Love—had nothing in common with Love—for when she had cried—'Could you suffer to share me with another?'—Why, yes, he could suffer it perfectly.

208

Nothing therefore—nothing in him had remained intact. Even the memory of his grand passion was now corrupted, sullied, debased. The last spark of hope was extinct. He had reached his lowest level, never to rise again.

He was seized by a terrible and frenzied desire to overthrow the idol that still persistently rose up lofty and enigmatic before his imagination, do what he would to abase it. With cynical cruelty, he set himself to insult, to undermine, to mutilate it. The destructive analysis he had already employed upon himself, he now turned upon Elena. To those dubious problems which, at one time, he had resolutely put away from him, he now sought the answer; of all the suspicions which had formerly presented themselves to him only to disappear without leaving a trace, he now studied the origin, found them justified and obtained their confirmation. But whereas he thought to find relief in this furious work of demolition, he only increased his sufferings, aggravated his malady and deepened his wounds.

What had been the true cause of Elena's departure two years before? There were many conflicting rumours at the time, and again when she married Humphrey Heathfield; but the actual truth of the matter was what he heard, quite by chance, among other scraps of society gossip, from Giulio Musellaro one evening as they left the theatre together, nor did Andrea doubt it for a moment. Donna Elena had been obliged to leave Rome for pecuniary reasons, to work some 'operation' which should extricate her from the serious embarrassments into which her outrageous extravagance had plunged her. The marriage with Humphrey Heathfield, who was Marquis of Mount Saint Michael and Earl of Broadford, and besides possessing a considerable fortune was related to the highest nobility of Great Britain, had saved her from ruin. Donna Elena had managed matters with the utmost adroitness and succeeded marvellously in steering clear of the threatening peril. It was not to be denied that the interval of her three years of widowhood had been none too chaste a

prelude to a second marriage—neither chaste nor prudent
—nevertheless, there was also no denying that Elena Muti
was a great lady——

'Ah, my boy, a grand creature!' said Musellaro, 'as you
very well know.'

Andrea said nothing.

'But take my advice,' his friend went on, throwing away
the cigarette which had gone out while he talked, 'do not
resume your relations with her. It is the same with love as
with tobacco—once out, it will not bear relighting. Let us
go and get a cup of tea from Donna Giulia Moceto. They
tell me one may go to her house after the theatre—it is never
too late.'

They were close by the Palazzo Borghese.

'You can,' answered Andrea, 'I am going home to bed.
I am rather tired after to-day's run with the hounds. My
regards to Donna Giulia—my blessing go with you!'

Musellaro went up the steps of the palace and Andrea
continued on his way past the Borghese fountain towards
the Trinità.

It was one of those wonderful January nights, cold and
serene, which turn Rome into a city of silver set in a ring
of diamonds. The full moon, hanging in mid-sky, shed a
triple purity of light, of frost, and of silence.

He walked along in the moonlight like a somnambulist,
conscious of nothing but his pain. The last blow had been
struck, the idol was shattered, nothing remained standing
above the ruins—this was the end!

So it was true—she had never really loved him. She had
not scrupled to break with him in order to contract a
marriage of convenience. And now she put on the airs of
a martyr before him, wrapped herself round with a mantle of
conjugal inviolability! A bitter laugh rose to his lips, and
then a rush of sullen blind rage against the woman came over
him. The memory of his passion went for nothing—all the
past was one long fraud, one stupendous, hideous lie; and
this man, who throughout his whole life had made a practice

of dissimulation and duplicity, was now incensed at the
deception of another, was as indignant at it as at some un-
pardonable backsliding, some inexcusable and inexplicable
perfidy. He was quite unable to understand how Elena
could have committed such a crime; he denied her all
possibility of justification, and rejected the hypothesis of
some secret and dire necessity having driven her to sudden
flight. He could see nothing but the bare brutal fact, its
baseness, its vulgarity—above all its vulgarity, gross, manifest, odious, without one extenuating circumstance. In short,
the whole matter reduced itself to this : a passion which was
apparently sincere, which they had vowed was profound and
inextinguishable, had been broken off for a question of money,
for material interests, for a commercial transaction.

'Oh, you are ungrateful! What do you know of all that
has happened, of all I have suffered!'

Elena's words recurred to him with everything else she
had said, from beginning to end of their interview—her words
of fondness, her offer of sisterly affection, all her sentimental
phrases. And he remembered, too, the tears that had dimmed
her eyes, her changes of countenance, her tremors, her choking
voice when she said good-bye, and he laid the roses in her lap.
'But why had she ever consented to come? Why play this
part, call up all these emotions, arrange this comedy? Why?'

By this time he had reached the top of the steps, and
found himself in the deserted piazza. Suddenly the beauty
of the night filled him with a vague but desperate yearning
towards some unknown good. The image of Maria Ferrès
flashed across his mind ; his heart beat fast, he thought of
what it would be to hold her hands in his, to lean his head
upon her breast, to feel that she was consoling him without
words, by her pity alone. This longing for pity, for a refuge,
was like the last struggle of a soul that will not be content to
perish. He bent his head and entered the house without
turning again to look at the night.

Terenzio was waiting up for him and followed him to the
bedroom, where there was a fire.

'Will the Signor Conte go to bed at once?' he asked.

'No, Terenzio, bring me some tea,' replied his master, sitting down before the fire and stretching out his hands to the blaze.

He was shivering all over with a little nervous tremor.

'The Signor Conte is cold?' asked Terenzio, hastening with affectionate interest to stir up the fire and put on fresh logs.

He was an old servant of the house of Sperelli, having served Andrea's father for many years, and his devotion for the son reached the pitch of idolatry. No human being seemed to him so handsome, so noble, so worthy of devotion. He belonged to that ideal race which furnished faithful retainers to the romance writers of old, but differed from the servants of romance in that he spoke little, never offered advice, and concerned himself with no other business than that of carrying out his master's orders.

'That will do very nicely,' said Andrea, trying to repress the convulsive trembling of his limbs and crouching closer over the fire.

The presence of the old man in this hour of misery and distress moved him singularly. It was an emotion somewhat similar to that which, in the presence of some very kind and sympathetic person, affects a man determined upon suicide. Never before had the old man brought back to him so strongly the recollection of his father, the memory of the beloved dead, his grief for the loss of a great and good friend. Never so much as now had he felt the want of that comforting voice, that paternal hand. What would his father say could he see his son thus crushed under the weight of a nameless distress? How would he have sought to relieve him—what would he have done?

His thoughts turned to the dead father with boundless yearning and regret. And he had not the shadow of a suspicion that in the very teachings of that father lay the primary cause of his wretchedness.

Terenzio brought the tea. He then proceeded slowly to

arrange the bed with a care and solicitude that were almost womanly, forgetting nothing, as if he wished to ensure to his master refreshing and unbroken slumbers till the morrow.

Andrea watched him with growing emotion. 'Go to bed now, Terenzio,' he said. 'I shall not want anything more.'

The old man retired and left him alone before the fire—alone with his heart, alone with his misery. Tortured by his inward agitation, he rose and began to pace the room. He was haunted by a vision of Elena, and each time he came as far as the window and turned, he fancied he saw her and started violently. His nerves were in such an overstrung condition that they only increased the disorder of his imagination. The hallucination grew more distinct. He stood still and covered his face with his hands for a moment to control his excitement, and then returned to his seat by the fire.

This time another image rose before him—that of Elena's husband.

He knew him better now. That very evening in a box at the theatre, Elena had introduced them to one another, and he had seized that opportunity to examine him attentively in detail with the keenest curiosity, as though he hoped to obtain some revelation, to draw some secret from him. He could still hear the man's voice—a voice of very peculiar tone, somewhat harsh and strident, with an interrogative inflection at the end of each sentence. Again he saw those pale, pale eyes under the great prominent forehead, eyes that at times assumed a hideous, glassy, dead look, and at others lit up with an indefinable gleam that savoured of madness. Those hands too, he saw—white and smooth and thickly covered with sandy yellow down, and with something obscene in their every movement; their way of raising the opera-glass, of unfolding a handkerchief, of reclining on the cushion in front of the box or turning over the pages of the libretto—hands instinct with vice.

Oh, horror! he saw those hands touching Elena, profaning her with their odious caresses.

The torture became insupportable. He rose once more,

went to the window, opened it, shivered under the biting breeze and shook himself. The Trinità de' Monti glittered in the deep blue sky, sharply outlined as if sculptured in faintly tinted marble. Rome, spread out beneath him, had a sheen as of crystal, like a city cut in a glacier.

The calm and sparkling cold brought his mind back to the realities of life and enabled him to recognise the true condition of his mind. He closed the window and sat down again. Once more the enigmatical aspect of Elena's character occupied him, questions crowded in upon him tumultuously, persistently. But he had the strength of mind to co-ordinate them, to attack th_.n one by one, with singular lucidity. The deeper he went in his analysis the more lucid became his mental vision, and he worked out his pyschological revenge with cruel relish. At last he felt that he had laid bare a soul, penetrated a mystery. It seemed to him, that thus he made Elena infinitely more his own than in the days of their passion.

What, after all, was this woman?—An unbalanced mind in a sensually inclined body. As with all who are greedy of pleasure, the foundation of her moral being was overweening egotism. Her dominant faculty, her intellectual axis, so to speak, was imagination—an imagination nourished upon a wide range of literature, connected with her sex and perpetually stimulated by neurotic excitement. Possessed of a certain degree of intellectual capacity, brought up in all the luxury of a princely Roman house—that papal luxury which is made up of art and history—she had received a thin coating of æsthetic varnish, had acquired a graceful taste, and, having thoroughly grasped the character of her beauty, sought by skilful simulation and a sapient use of her marked histrionic talents to enhance its spirituality by surrounding it with a delusive halo of ideality.

Into the comedy of human life she thus brought some highly perilous elements, and was thereby the occasion of more ruin and disaster than if she had been a *demi-mondaine* by profession.

Under the glamour of her imagination, every caprice assumed an appearance of pathos. She was the woman of fulminating passions, of suddenly blazing desire. She covered the lusts of the flesh with a mantle of ethereal flame, and could transform into a noble sentiment what was merely a base appetite.

Such was the scathing judgment brought by Andrea against the woman he had once adored. At the root of every action, every expression of Elena's love he now discovered studied artifice, an admirable natural gift for carrying out a pre-arranged scheme, for playing a dramatic part or organising a striking scene. He did not spare their most memorable episodes—neither the first meeting at the Ateletas' dinner, nor the Cardinal Immenraet's sale, nor the ball at the French Embassy, nor the sudden offer of her love in the red room at the Barberini palace, nor their farewells out in the country in the biting March blast. The magic draught which had intoxicated him then now seemed but an insidious poison.

Yet, in spite of it all, certain points perplexed him, as if in penetrating Elena's soul he had penetrated his own, and in the woman's perfidy had seen a reflection of his own. There was much affinity between their two natures. Therefore he *understood*, and little by little, his contempt changed to ironical indulgence. He was so thoroughly conversant with his own mode of procedure.

Then with cold lucidity, he mapped out his plan of campaign. He reviewed every detail of the interview that had taken place on New Year's Eve—more than a week ago —and it pleased him to re-construct the scene, but without the slightest indignation or excitement, only smiling cynically both at Elena and himself. Why had she come?—Simply because this impromptu *tête-à-tête* with a former lover, in the well-known place, after a lapse of two years, had tempted a spirit always on the lookout for fresh emotions, had inflamed her imagination and her curiosity. She thirsted to see into what new situations, new intrigues the dangerous game would lead her. She was perhaps attracted by the novelty of a platonic affection with a person who had already been the object of her sensual passion. As ever, she had thrown herself into the new part with a certain imaginative fervour. Also it was quite possible that, for the moment, she believed what she said, and that this illusory sincerity had furnished her with that deep tenderness of accent, those despairing attitudes, those tears. How well he knew it all! She had a sentimental hallucination as other people have a physical one. She forgot that she was acting a lie, was no longer conscious whether she were living in a world of truth or falsehood, of fiction or reality.

Now this was precisely the moral phenomenon which so constantly took place in himself. Therefore he could not reproach her without injustice. But the discovery very naturally deprived him of the hope of deriving any pleasure from her other than sensual ones. In any case, mistrust would poison all the sweetness of abandon, all soulful rapture. To deceive a confiding and faithful heart, dominate a soul by artifice, possess it wholly and make it vibrate like an instrument—*habere non haberi*—all this, doubtless, gives intense pleasure ; but to deceive, and know that one is being deceived in return, is a stupid and fruitless labour, a tiresome and aimless pursuit.

He must therefore work upon Elena to renounce the sisterly scheme and to return to his arms once more. He must regain possession of this beautiful woman, extract the utmost possible pleasure from her beauty and free himself for ever of this passion by reaching the point of satiety. But it was a task demanding prudence and patience. In that first interview, his ardour had availed him nothing. Obviously, she had founded her plan of impeccability on the grand phrase—'Could you endure to share me with another?' The mainspring of the great platonic business was a virtuous horror of divided possession. For the rest, it was just within the bounds of possibility that this horror was not feigned. Most women addicted to the practice of free love, if they do eventually marry, affect, during the early days of their marriage, a savage virtue, and make professions of conjugal fidelity with the most honest determination. Perhaps, therefore, Elena had been affected by this common scruple, in which case, nothing would be more ill-advised than to show his hand too boldly and offend against her new-found virtue. The better plan would be to second her spiritual aspirations, accept her as 'the fondest of sisters, the truest of friends,' intoxicate her with the ideal, be skilfully platonic and then make her glide imperceptibly from frank sisterly relations to a more passionate friendship, and from thence to the complete surrender of her person. In all probability these transitions would occur very rapidly. It all depended upon a wise adjustment of circumstances——

Thus Andrea Sperelli reasoned, sitting in front of the fire which had glowed upon Elena, laughing among the scattered rose leaves. A boundless lassitude weighed upon him, a lassitude which did not invite sleep, a sense of weariness, so empty, so disconsolate as to be almost a longing for death; while the fire died out on the hearth and the tea grew cold in the cup.

CHAPTER IV

HE waited in vain during the days that followed for the promised note to tell him when he might see Elena again——— So she did intend to make another appointment with him ; the question was—where ? At the Casa Zuccari again ? Would she risk such an imprudence a second time ? This uncertainty kept him on the rack. He passed whole hours in searching for some way of meeting her, of seeing her again. He went several times to the Hotel Quirinal in the hope of being received, but never once did he find her at home. One evening, he saw her again in the theatre with ' Mumps,' as she called her husband. Though only saying the usual things about the music, the singers, the ladies, he infused a supplicating melancholy into his gaze. She seemed greatly taken up by the arrangement of their house. They were going back to the Palazzo Barberini, her old quarters, but were having them much enlarged, and she was for ever occupied with upholsterers and decorators, giving orders and superintending the placing of the furniture.

' Are you going to stay long in Rome ? ' asked Andrea.

' Yes,' she answered—' Rome will be our winter residence.' Then, after a moment's pause—' You could give us some very good advice about the furniture. Come to the palace one of these days. I am always there from ten to twelve.'

He took advantage of a moment when Lord Heathfield was talking to Giulio Musellaro, who had just entered the box, to say to her, looking her full in the eyes.

' To-morrow ? '

218

'By all means,' she replied with perfect simplicity, as if she had not noticed the tone of his question.

The next morning, about eleven, he set off on foot to the Palazzo Barberini through the Via Sistina. It was a road he had often traversed before—and, for a moment, the impressions of those days seemed to come back to him, and his heart swelled. The fountain of Bernini shone curiously luminous in the sunshine, as if the dolphins and the Triton with his conch-shell had, by some interrupted metamorphose transformed themselves into a more diaphanous material— not stone, nor yet quite crystal. The noise of the building of new Rome filled all the piazza and the adjoining streets ; country children ran in and out between the carts and horses offering violets for sale.

As he passed through the gate and entered the garden, he felt that he was beginning to tremble. 'Then I *do* love her still?' he thought to himself—'Is she still the woman of *my dreams*?'

He looked at the great palace, radiant under the morning sun, and his spirit flew back to the days when, in certain chill and misty dawns, this same palace had assumed for him a look of enchantment. That was in the early times of his happiness, when he came away warm from her kisses and full of his new-found bliss ; the bells of Trinità de' Monti, of San Isidoro and the Cappuccini rang out the Angelus into the dawning day, with a muffled peal as if out of the far distance—at the corner of the street, fires glowed red round cauldrons of boiling asphalt—a little herd of goats stood against the white wall of the slumbering house——

These forgotten sensations rose up once more out of the depths of his consciousness, and, for an instant, a wave of the old love swept over his soul, for one moment he tried to imagine that Elena was still the Elena of those days, that his happiness had endured till now, that none of these miserable things were true. As he crossed the threshold of the palace, all this illusory ferment died away on the instant, for Lord Heathfield came forward to greet him with his habitual and somewhat ambiguous smile.

With that his torture began.

Elena appeared, and shaking hands cordially with him in her husband's presence, she said—'Bravo, Andrea! Come and help us, come and help us!'

She talked and gesticulated with much vivacity and looked very girlish in a close-fitting jacket of dark-blue cloth, trimmed round the high collar and the cuffs with black astrachan and fine black braiding. She kept one hand in her pocket in a graceful attitude, and with the other pointed out the various wall-hangings, the pictures, the furniture, asking his advice as to their most advantageous disposal.

'Where would you put these two chests? Look—Mumps picked them up at Lucca. These pictures are your beloved Botticelli's.—Where would you hang these tapestries?'

Andrea recognised the four pieces of tapestry from the Immenraet sale representing the Story of Narcissus. He looked at Elena, but could not catch her eye. A profound sense of irritation against her, against her husband, against all these things took possession of him. He would have liked to go away, but politeness demanded that he should place his good taste at the service of the Heathfields; it also obliged him to submit to the archæological erudition of 'Mumps,' who was an ardent collector and was anxious to show him some of his finds. In one cabinet Andrea caught sight of the Pollajuolo helmet, and in another of the rock-crystal goblet which had belonged to Niccolo Niccoli. The presence of that particular goblet in this particular place moved him strangely and sent a flash of mad suspicion through his mind.

So it had fallen into the hands of Lord Heathfield! The famous competition between the Countesses having come to nothing, nobody troubled themselves further about the fate of the goblet, and none of the party had returned to the sale after that day. Their ephemeral zeal had languished and finally died out and passed away, like everything else in the world of fashion, and the goblet had been abandoned to the competition of other collectors. The thing was perfectly natural, but at that moment it appeared to Andrea most extraordinary.

He purposely stopped before the cabinet and gazed long at the precious goblet on which the story of Venus and Anchises glittered as if cut in a pure diamond.

'Niccolo Niccoli!' said Elena, pronouncing the name with an indefinable accent in which the young man seemed to catch a note of sadness.

The husband had just gone into another room to open a cabinet.

'Remember—remember!' murmured Andrea, turning towards her.

'I do remember.'

'Then when may I see you?'

'Ah, when?'

'But you promised me——'

Lord Heathfield returned. They passed on into an adjoining room, making the tour of the apartments. Everywhere they met workmen hanging papers, draping curtains, carrying furniture. Each time Elena asked his opinion, Andrea had to make an effort before answering her, in order to disguise his ill-humour and his impatience. At last, he managed to seize a moment when her husband was occupied with one of the men to say to her in a low voice, unable any longer to conceal his chagrin—

'Why inflict this torture upon me? I expected to find you alone.'

Passing through one of the doors, Elena's hat caught in the portière and was dragged out of place. She laughed and called to Mumps to come and unfasten her veil. And Andrea was forced to look on while those odious hands touched the hair of the woman he desired, ruffling the little curls at the back of her neck, those curls which under his caresses had seemed to breathe out a mysterious perfume, unlike any other, and sweeter and more intoxicating than all the rest.

He hurriedly took his leave under pretext of being due at lunch with some one else.

'We shall move in here on the 1st of February,' Elena said to him, 'and then I hope you will be one of our *habitués.*'

Andrea bowed.

He would have given worlds not to be obliged to touch Lord Heathfield's hand.   He went away filled with rancour, jealousy and disgust.

CHAPTER V

AT a late hour that same evening, happening to look in at the Club, where he had not been for a long time, whom should he see at one of the card-tables but Don Manuel Ferrès y Capdevila. Andrea greeted him with effusion and inquired after Donna Maria and Delfina—whether they were still at Sienna—when they were coming to Rome.

Don Manuel, who remembered to have won several thousand lire from the young Count during the last evening at Schifanoja, and had recognised in Andrea Sperelli a player of the best form and perfect style, responded with the utmost courtesy and cordiality.

'They have been here some days already; they arrived on Monday,' he answered. 'Maria was much disappointed not to find the Marchesa d'Ateleta in town. I am sure it would give her the greatest pleasure if you would call on her. We are in the Via Nazionale. Here is the exact address.'

He handed one of his cards to Andrea and then returned to the game.

The Duke di Beffi, who was standing with a knot of gentlemen, called Andrea over to them.

'Why did you not come to Cento Celli this morning?' asked the duke.

'I had another appointment,' Andrea replied without reflecting.

'At the Palazzo Barberini perhaps?' said the duke with a shy laugh, in which he was joined by the others.

'Perhaps.'

'Perhaps, indeed?—why, Ludovico saw you go in.'

'And where were you, may I ask?' said Andrea turning to Barbarisi.

'Over the way, at my Aunt Saviano's.'

'Ah!'

'I don't know if you had better luck than we had,' Beffi went on, 'but we had a run of forty-two minutes and got two foxes. The next meet is on Thursday at the Three Fountains.'

'You understand—at the *Three* Fountains, not at the *Four*,' Gino Bommanaco admonished him with comic gravity.

The others burst into a roar of laughter which Andrea could not help joining. He was by no means displeased at their gibes; on the contrary, now that there was no truth in their suspicions, it flattered him for his friends to think he had renewed his relations with Elena. He turned away to speak to Giulio Musellaro, who had just come in. From a few strays words that reached his ear, he found that the group behind him were discussing Lord Heathfield.

'I knew him in London six or seven years ago,' Beffi was saying. 'He was Gentleman of the Bed-chamber to the Prince or Wales as far as I remember——'

The duke lowered his voice, he was evidently retailing the most appalling things. Andrea caught scraps here and there of a highly-spiced nature and, once or twice, the name of a newspaper famous in the annals of London scandal. He longed to hear more; a terrible curiosity took possession of him. His imagination conjured up Lord Heathfield's hands before him—so white, so significant, so expressive, so impossible to forget. Musellaro was still talking, and now said—

'Let us go—I want to tell you——'

On the stairs they encountered Albonico, who was coming up. He was in deep mourning for Donna Ippolita, and Andrea stopped to ask for details of the sad event. He had heard of her death when he was in Paris in November from Guido Montelatici, a cousin of Donna Ippolita.

'Was it really typhus?'

The wan and pale-eyed widower grasped at an occasion for pouring out his griefs, for he made a display of his bereavement as, at one time, he had made a display of his wife's beauty. He stammered and grew lachrymose and his colourless eyes seemed bulging from his head.

Seeing that the widower's elegy threatened to be somewhat long drawn out, Musellaro said to Andrea—

'If we don't take care, we shall be late.'

Andrea accordingly took leave of Albonico, promising to hear the rest of the funeral oration very shortly, and went away with Musellaro.

The meeting with Albonico had re-awakened the singular emotion—partly regret, partly a certain peculiar satisfaction— which he had experienced for several days after hearing the news of this death. The image of Donna Ippolita, half obliterated by his illness and convalescence, by his love for Maria Ferrès, by a variety of incidents, had reappeared to him then as in the dim distance, but invested with a nameless ideality. He had received a promise from her which, though it was never fulfilled, had procured to him the greatest happiness that can befall a man : the victory over a rival, a brilliant victory in the presence of the woman he desired. Later on, between desire and regret another sentiment grew up—the poetic sentiment for beauty idealised by death. It pleased him that the adventure should end thus for ever. This woman who had never been his, but to gain whom he had nearly lost his life, now rose up noble and unsullied before his imagination in all the sublime ideality of death. *Tibi, Hippolyta, semper!*

'But where are we going to?' asked Musellaro, stopping short in the middle of the Piazza de Venezia.

At the bottom of all Andrea's perturbation and all his varying thoughts, was the excitement called up in him by his meeting with Don Manuel Ferrès and the consequent thought of Donna Maria ; and now, in the midst of these conflicting emotions, a sort of nervous longing drew him to her house.

'I am going home,' he answered; 'we can go through the Via Nazionale. Come along with me.'

He paid no heed to what his friend was saying. The thought of Maria Ferrès occupied him exclusively. Arrived in front of the theatre, he hesitated a moment, undecided which side of the street he had better take. He would find out the direction of the house by seeing which way the numbers ran.

'What is the matter?' asked Musellaro.

'Nothing—go on,—I am listening.'

He looked at one number and calculated that the house must be on the left hand side, somewhere about the Villa Aldobrandini. The tall pines round the villa looked feathery light against the starry sky. The night was icy but serene; the Torre delle Milizie lifted up its massive bulk, square and sombre among the twinkling stars; the laurels on the wall of Servius slumbered motionless in the gleam of the street lamps.

A few numbers more and they would reach the one mentioned on Don Manuel's card. Andrea trembled as if he expected Donna Maria to appear upon the threshold. He passed so close to the great door that he brushed against it; he could not refrain from looking up at the windows.

'What are you looking at?' asked Musellaro.

'Nothing—give me a cigarette and let us walk a little faster; it is awfully cold.'

They followed the Via Nazionale as far as the Four Fountains in silence. Andrea's pre-occupation was patent.

'You must decidedly have something serious on your mind,' said his friend.

Andrea's heart beat so fast that he was on the point of pouring his confidences into his friend's ear, but he restrained himself. Memories of Schifanoja passed across his spirit like an exhilarating perfume, and in the midst of them beamed the figure of Maria Ferrès with a radiance that almost dazzled him. But most distinctly and more luminously than all the rest, he saw that moment in the wood at Vicomile, when she had flung those burning words at him. Would he ever hear such words from her lips again? What had she been doing —what had been her thoughts—how had she spent the days since they parted? His agitation increased with every step. Fragments of scenes passed rapidly before him like the phantasmagoria of a dream—a bit of country, a glimpse of the sea, a flight of steps among the roses, the interior of a room, all the places in which some sentiment had had its birth, round which she had diffused some sweetness, where she had breathed the charm of her person. And he thrilled with profound emotion at the idea that perchance she still carried in her heart that living passion, had perhaps suffered and wept, had dreamed and hoped.

'Well?' said Musellaro, 'and how is your affair with Donna Elena progressing?'

They happened to be just in front of the Palazzo Barberini. Behind the railings and the great stone pillars of the gates stretched the garden, dimly visible through the gloom, animated by the low murmur of the fountains and dominated by the massive white palace where in the portico alone was light.

'What did you say?' asked Andrea.

'I asked how you were getting on with Donna Elena.'

Andrea glanced up at the palace. At that moment he seemed to feel a blank indifference in his heart, the absolute death of desire—the final renunciation.

'I am following your advice. I have not tried to relight the cigarette.'

'And yet, do you know, in this one instance, I believe it would be worth while. Have you noticed her particularly? It seems to me that she has become more beautiful. I cannot help thinking there is something—how shall I express it?— something new, something indescribable about her. No, *new* is not the word. She has gained intensity without losing anything of the peculiar character of her beauty; in short, she is *more Elena* than the Elena of two years ago—the quintessence of herself. It is, most likely, the effect of her second spring, for I should fancy she must be hard on thirty. Don't you think so?'

As he listened, Andrea felt the dull ashes of his love stir and kindle. Nothing revives and excites a man's desire so much as hearing from another the praises of a woman he has loved too long or wooed in vain. A love in its death-throes may thus be prolonged as the result of the envy or the admiration of another; for the disgusted or wearied lover hesitates to abandon what he possesses or is struggling to possess in favour of a possible successor.

'Don't you think so?' Musellaro repeated. 'And, besides, to make a Menelaus of that Heathfield would in itself be an unspeakable satisfaction.'

'So I think,' answered Andrea, forcing himself to adopt his friend's light tone. 'Well, we shall see.'

BOOK IV

CHAPTER I

' MARIA, grant me this one moment of unalloyed sweetness!
Let me tell you all that is in my heart.'

She rose. ' Forgive me,' she said gently, without anger or
bitterness and with an audible quiver of emotion in her voice.
' Forgive me, but I cannot listen to you. You pain me very
much.'

'Well, I will not say anything—only stay—I implore
you.'

She seated herself once more. It was like the days of
Schifanoja come back again. The same matchless grace
of the delicate head drooping under the masses of hair as
under some divine chastisement, the same deep and tender
shadow, a fusion of diaphanous violet and soft blue, surround·
ing the tawny brown eyes.

' I only wanted,' Andrea went on humbly, ' I only wanted
to remind you of the words I spoke, the words you listened to
that morning in the park under the shadow of the trees, in an
hour that will always remain sacred in my memory.'

' I have not forgotten them.'

'Since that day my unhappiness has become ever deeper,
darker, more poignant. I can never tell you all I have
suffered, all the abject misery of that time: can never tell
you how often in spirit I have called upon you as if my last
hour had come, nor describe to you the thrill of joy, the
upward bound of my whole soul towards the light of hope, if,
for one moment, I dared to think that the remembrance of
me still lived in your heart.'

He spoke in the accents of that morning long ago; he

seemed to have regained the same passionate rapture: all his vaguely felt unhappiness rose to his lips. And she sat motionless, listening with drooping head, almost in the same attitude as on that day; and round her lips, those lips which she vainly sought to keep firm, there played the same expression of dolorous rapture.

'Do you remember Vicomile? Do you remember our ride through the wood on that evening in October?'

Donna Maria bent her head slightly in sign of assent.

'And the words you said to me?' the young man went on in a lower voice, but in a tone of suppressed passion and bending down to look into the eyes she kept steadfastly fixed upon the ground.

She raised them now to his—those sweet, patient, pathetic eyes.

'I have forgotten nothing,' she replied, 'nothing, nothing! Why should I hide my heart from you? You are good and noble-minded, and I have absolute trust in your generosity. Why should I act towards you like an ordinary foolish woman? I told you that evening that I loved you. Your question implies another one, I see that very well—you want to ask me if I love you still.'

She faltered for a moment and her lips quivered. 'I love you.'

'Maria!'

'But you must give up all claim upon my love, you must keep away from me. Be noble, be generous, and spare me the struggle which frightens me. I have suffered much, Andrea, I have borne much; but the thought of having to struggle with you, to defend myself against you, fills me with a nameless terror. You do not know at the cost of what sacrifices I have at last gained peace of heart; you do not know what lofty and cherished ideals I have been obliged to bid farewell to—poor ideals! I am a changed woman because I could not help it; I have had to place myself on a lower level.'

There was a note of grave, sweet sadness in her voice.

'In those first days after I met you, I abandoned myself to
the alluring sweetness, let myself drift with eyes closed to the
distant peril. I thought—he shall never know anything from
me, I shall never know anything from him. I had nothing
to regret and therefore I felt no fear. But you spoke—you
said things to me that no one had ever said before, and
then you forced my avowal from me. The danger suddenly
appeared before me, unmistakable, imminent. And then I
abandoned myself to a fresh dream. Your mental distress
touched me to the heart, caused me profound pain. "Impurity has sullied his soul," I thought to myself. "Oh, that I
had the power to purify it again! What happiness to offer
myself up as a sacrifice for his regeneration!" Your unhappiness attracted mine. I thought I might scarcely be able to
console you, but I hoped at least you might find relief in
having another soul to answer eternally *Amen* to all your
plaints.'

She uttered the last words with a face so suffused with
spiritual exaltation that Andrea felt a wave of half-religious
joy sweep over him, and his one desire, at that moment, was
to take those dear and spotless hands in his and breathe upon
them the ineffable rapture of his soul.

'But it cannot—it may not be,' she went on, shaking her
head in sad regret. 'We must renounce that hope for ever.
Life is inexorable. Without intending it, you would destroy
a whole existence—and more than one perhaps——'

'Maria, Maria! do not say such things!' the young man
broke in, leaning over her once more and taking one of
her hands with a sort of timid entreaty, as if looking for
some sign of permission before venturing on the liberty.
'I will do anything you tell me; I will be humble and
obedient, my one thought shall be to carry out your wishes,
my one desire, to die with your name upon my lips. In
renouncing you, I renounce my salvation, I fall back into
irremediable ruin and disaster. I have no words to express
my love for you. I have need of you. You alone are *true*
—you are Truth itself, for which my soul is ever seeking.

All else is vanity—all else is nought. To give you up is like signing my death-warrant. But if this immolation is necessary to your peace of mind, it shall be done—I owe it to you. Do not fear, Maria, I will never do anything to hurt you.'

He held her hand, but he did not press it. His voice had none of the old passionate ardour, it was submissive, disconsolate, heart-broken, full of infinite weariness. And Maria was so blinded by her compassion that she did not draw away her hand, but let it lie in his, abandoning herself for a moment to the unutterable rapture of that light contact—a rapture so subtle as hardly to have any physical origin—as if some magnetic fluid, issuing from her heart, diffused itself through her arm to her fingers and there flowed forth in a wave of ineffable sweetness When Andrea ceased speaking, certain words of his, uttered on that memorable morning in the park and revived by the recent sound of his voice, returned to her memory—'Your mere presence suffices to intoxicate me—I feel it flowing through my veins like blood, flooding my soul with nameless emotion——'

There was an interval of silence. From time to time, a gust of wind shook the window-panes and bore fitfully with it the distant roar of the city and the rumbling of carriage wheels. The light was cold and limpid as spring water; shadows were gathering thickly in the corners of the room and in the folds of the Oriental curtains; from pieces of furniture, here and there, came gleams of ivory and mother-of-pearl; a great gilded Buddha shone out of the background under a tall palm. Something of the exotic mystery of these things was diffused over the drawing-room.

'And what do you suppose is going to become of me now?' asked Andrea.

She seemed lost in perplexing thought. There was a look of irresolution on her face as if she were listening to two contending voices.

'I cannot describe to you,' she answered, passing her hand over her eyes with a rapid gesture, 'I cannot describe

to you the strange foreboding that has weighed upon me
for a long time past. I do not know what it is, but I am
afraid.'

Then, after a pause—'Oh, to think that you may be suffering, sick at heart,—my poor darling—and that I can do
nothing to ease your pain, may not be with you in your hour
of anguish—may not even know that you have called me—
Mio Dio!'

There was a quiver of tears in her breaking voice. Andrea
hung his head but did not speak.

'To think that my spirit will follow you always, always,
and yet that it may never, never mingle with yours, will
never, never be understood by you!—Alas, poor love!'

Her voice was full of tears and her mouth was drawn with
pain.

'Ah, do not desert me—do not desert me!' cried the
young man, seizing her two hands and half-kneeling at her
feet, a prey to overwhelming excitement—'I will never ask
anything of you—I want nothing but your pity. A little
pity from you is more—far more—to me than passionate
love from any other woman—you know it. Your hand
alone can heal me, can bring me back to life, can raise
me out of the slough into which I have sunk, give me back
my faith and free me from the bondage of those shameful
things that corrupt me and fill me with horror. Dear—dear
—hands!'

He bent over them and pressed his lips to them in a long
kiss, abandoning himself with half-closed eyes to the utter
sweetness of it.

'I can feel you tremble,' he murmured in an indefinable
tone.

She rose abruptly, trembling from head to foot, giddy,
paler still than on the morning when they walked together
beneath the flower-laden trees. The wind still shook the
panes; there was a dull clamour in the distance as of a
riotous crowd. The shrill cries borne on the wind from the
Quirinal increased her agitation.

'Go, Andrea—please go—you must not stay here any longer. You shall see me some other time—whenever you like, but go now, I entreat you——'

'Where shall I see you again?'

'At the concert to-morrow—good-bye.'

She was as perturbed and agitated as if she had been guilty of some grave fault. She accompanied him to the door of the room. When she found herself alone, she hesitated, not knowing what to do next, still under the sway of her terror. Her temples throbbed, her cheeks and her eyes burned with fierce intensity, while cold shivers ran through her limbs. But on her hands she still felt the pressure of that beloved mouth, a sensation so surpassingly sweet that she wished it might remain there for ever indelible like some divine impress.

She looked about her. The light was fading, things looked shapeless in the shadows, the great Buddha gleamed with a weird pale light. The cries came up from the street fitfully. She went over to a window, opened it and leaned out. An icy wind blew through the street; in the direction of the Piazza dei Termini, they were already lighting the lamps. Across the way, at the Villa Aldobrandini, the trees swayed to and fro, their tops touched with a faint red glow. A huge crimson cloud hung solitary in the sky over the Torre delle Milizie.

The evening struck her as strangely lugubrious. She withdrew from the window and seated herself again where she had just had her conversation with Andrea. Why had Delfina not returned yet? She earnestly desired to escape from her thoughts, and yet she weakly allowed herself to linger in the place where, only a few minutes ago, Andrea had breathed and spoken, had sighed out his love and his unhappiness. The struggles, the resolutions, the contrition, the prayers, the penances of four months had been wiped out, made utterly unavailing in one second of time, and she sank down more weary and vanquished than ever, without the will or the power to fight against the foes that beset her in her own heart, against the feelings that were upheaving her whole moral foundations. And while she gave way to the anguish and despair of a conscience which feels all its courage oozing from it, she still had the feeling that something of *him* lingered in the shadows of the room and enveloped her with all the sweetness of a passionate caress.

CHAPTER II

THE next day, she arrived at the Palazzo dei Sabini, her heart beating fast under a bunch of violets.

Andrea was looking out for her at the door of the concert-hall.

'Thanks,' he said, and pressed her hand.

He conducted her to a seat and sat down beside her.

'I thought the anxiety of waiting for you would have killed me,' he murmured. 'I was so afraid you would not come. How grateful I am to you! Late last night,' he went on, 'I passed your house. There was a light in one window—the third looking towards the Quirinal—I would have given much to know if you were up there. Who gave you those violets?' he asked abruptly.

'Delfina,' she answered.

'Did Delfina tell you of our meeting this morning in the Piazza di Spagna?'

'Yes—all.'

The concert began with a Quartett by Mendelssohn. The hall was already nearly full, the audience consisting, for the most part, of foreign ladies—fair-haired women very quietly and simply dressed, grave of attitude, religiously silent, as in some sacred spot. The wave of music passing over these motionless heads spread out into the golden light, a light that filtered from above through faded yellow curtains and was reflected from the bare white walls. It was the old hall of the Philharmonic concerts. The whiteness of the walls was unbroken by any ornament, with only here and there a trace of former frescoes and its meagre blue portières

238

threatening to come down at any moment. It had all the air of a place that had been closed for a century and opened again that day for the first time. But just this faded look of age, the air of poverty, the nakedness of the walls lent a curious additional flavour to the exquisite enjoyment of the audience, making their delight seem more absorbing, loftier, purer by contrast. It was the 2nd of February; at Monte-citorio the Parliament was disputing over the massacre of Dogali; the neighbouring streets and squares swarmed with the populace and with soldiers.

Musical memories of Schifanoja came back to the lovers, a reflected gleam from those fair autumn days illumined their thoughts. Mendelssohn's Minuet called up before them a vision of the villa by the sea, of rooms filled with the perfume of the terraced garden, of cypresses lifting their dark heads into the soft sky, of flaming sails upon a glassy sea.

Bending towards his companion, Andrea whispered softly : 'What are you thinking about?'

With a smile so faint that he hardly caught it, she answered : 'Do you remember the 22nd of September?'

Andrea had no very clear recollection of this date, but he nodded his head.

The Andante, calm, broad and solemn, dominated by a won-derful and pathetic melody, had ended in a sudden outburst of grief. The Finale lingered in a certain rhythmic monotony full of plaintive weariness.

'Now comes your favourite Bach,' said Donna Maria.

And when the music commenced they both felt an instinc-tive desire to draw closer to each other. Their shoulders touched; at the end of each part Andrea leant over her to read the programme which she held open in her hands, and in so doing pressed against her arm, inhaling the perfume of her violets, and sending a wild thrill of ecstasy through her. The Adagio rose with so exultant a song, soared with so jubilant a strain to the topmost summits of rapture, and flowed wide into the Infinite, that it seemed like the voice of some celestial being pouring out the joy of a deathless victory. The spirits of the audience were borne along on that irresistible torrent of sound. When the music ceased, the tremor of the instruments continued for a moment in the hearers. A murmur ran from one end of the hall to the other. A moment later, and the applause broke forth vehemently.

The lovers turned simultaneously and looked at one another with swimming eyes.

The music continued; the light began to fade; a gentle warmth pervaded the air, and Donna Maria's violets breathed a fuller fragrance. Seeing nobody near him whom he knew, Andrea almost felt as if he were alone with her.

But he was mistaken. Turning round in one of the pauses, he caught sight of Elena standing at the back of the hall with the Princess of Ferentino. Instantly their eyes met. As he bowed to her, he seemed to catch a singular smile on Elena's lips.

'To whom are you bowing?' asked Donna Maria, turning round too, 'who are those ladies?'

'Lady Heathfield and the Princess of Ferentino.'

She noticed a tremor of annoyance in his voice.

'Which of them is the Princess of Ferentino?'

'The fair one.'

'The other is very beautiful.'

Andrea said nothing.

'But is she English?' she asked again.

'No, she is a Roman. She was the widow of the Duke of Scerni, and now married again to Lord Heathfield.'

'She is very lovely.'

'What is coming next?' Andrea asked hurriedly.

'The Brahms Quartett in C minor.'

'Do you know it?'

'No.'

'The second movement is marvellous.'

He went on speaking to hide his embarrassment.

'When shall I see you again?' he asked.

'I do not know.'

' To-morrow ? '

She hesitated. A cloud seemed to have come over her face.

' To-morrow,' she answered, ' if it is fine I shall take Delfina to the Piazza di Spagna about twelve o'clock.'

' And if it is not fine ? '

' On Saturday evening I shall be at the Countess Starnina's——'

The music began once more. The first movement expressed a sombre and virile struggle, the Romance a memory full of passionate but sad desire, followed by a slow uplifting, faltering and tentative, towards the distant dawn. Out of this a clear and melodious phrase developed itself with splendid modulations. The sentiment was very different from that which animated Bach's Adagio; it was more human, more earthly, more elegiacal. A breath of Beethoven ran through this music.

Andrea's nervous perturbation was so great that he feared every moment to betray himself. All his pleasure was embittered. He could not exactly analyse his discomfort; he could neither gather himself together and overcome it, nor put it away from him; he was swayed in turn by the charm of the music and the fascination exercised over him by each of these women without being really dominated by any of the three. He had a vague sensation as of some empty space, in which heavy blows perpetually resounded followed by dolorous echoes. His thoughts seemed to break up and crumble away into a thousand fragments, and the images of the two women to melt into and destroy one another without his being able to disconnect them or to separate his feeling for the one from his feeling for the other. And above all this mental disturbance was the anxiety occasioned by the immediate circumstances, by the necessity for adopting some practical line of action. Donna Maria's slight change of attitude had not escaped him, and he seemed to feel Elena's gaze riveted upon him. What course should he pursue ? He could not make up his mind whether to accompany Donna Maria when she left the concert, or to approach Elena, nor could he determine where this incident would be favourable to him or otherwise with either of the ladies.

'I am going,' said Donna Maria, rising at the end of the movement.

'You will not wait till the end?'

'No, I must be home by five o'clock.'

'Do not forget—to-morrow morning——'

She held out her hand. It was perhaps the air of the close room that sent a flush to her pale cheek. A velvet mantle of a dull leaden shade, with a deep border of chinchilla, covered her to her feet, and amid the soft gray fur the violets were dying exquisitely. As she passed out, she moved with such a queenly grace that many of the ladies turned to follow her with their eyes. It was the first time that in this spiritual creature, the pure Siennese Madonna, Andrea also beheld the elegant woman of the world.

The third movement of the Quartett began. The daylight had diminished so much that the yellow curtains had to be drawn back. Several other ladies left. A low hum of conversation was audible here and there. The fatigue and inattention which invariably marks the end of a concert began to make itself apparent in the audience. By one of those strange and abrupt manifestations of moral elasticity, Andrea experienced a sudden sense of relief, not to say gaiety. In a moment, he had forgotten his sentimental and passionate pre-occupations, and all that now appealed to him—to his vanity, to his corrupt senses—was the licentious aspect of the affair. He thought to himself that in granting him these little innocent rendezvous, Donna Maria had already set her foot on the gentle downward slope of the path at the bottom of which lies sin, inevitable even to the most vigilant soul; he also argued that doubtless a little touch of jealousy would do much towards bringing Elena back to his arms and that thus the one intrigue would help on the other—was it not a vague fear, a jealous foreboding that had made Donna Maria consent so quickly to their next meeting? He saw himself, therefore, well on the way to a two-fold conquest, and he could not repress a smile as he reflected that in both adventures the chief difficulty presented itself under the same guise : both women professed a wish to play the part of sister to him ; it was for him to transform these sisters in something closer. He remarked upon other resemblances between the two—That voice ! How curiously like Elena's were some tones in Donna Maria's voice ! A mad thought flashed through his brain. That voice might furnish him with the elements of a study of imagination—by virtue of that affinity, he might resolve the two fair women into one, and thus possess a third, imaginary, mistress, more complex, more perfect, more *true* because she would be ideal——

The third movement, executed in faultless style, finished in a burst of applause. Andrea rose and approached Elena—

'Oh, there you are, Ugenta ! Where have you been all this time?' exclaimed the Princess — 'In the "pays du Tendre?"'

'And your incognita?' asked Elena lightly as she pulled a bunch of violets out of her muff and sniffed them.

'She is a great friend of my cousin Francesca's, Donna Maria Ferrès y Capdevila, the wife of the new minister for Guatemala,' Andrea replied without turning a hair — 'a beautiful creature and very cultivated—she was at Schifanoja with Francesca last September.'

'And what of Francesca?' Elena broke in—'do you know when she is coming back?'

'I had the latest news from her a day or two ago—from San Remo. Fernandino is better, but I am afraid she will have to stay on there another month at least, perhaps longer.'

'What a pity !'

The last movement, a very short one, began. Elena and the Princess occupied two chairs at the end of the room, against the wall under a dim mirror in which the melancholy hall was reflected. Elena listened with bent head, slowly drawing through her fingers the long ends of her boa.

The concert over, she said to Sperelli : ' Will you see us to the carriage ? '

As she entered her carriage after the Princess, she turned to him again—' Won't you come too ?   We will drop Eva at the Palazzo Fiano, and I can put you down wherever you like.'

' Thanks,' answered Andrea, nothing loath.   On the Corso they were obliged to proceed very slowly, the whole roadway being taken up by a seething, tumultuous crowd.   From the Piazza di Montecitorio and the Piazza Colonna came a perfect uproar that swelled and rose and fell and rose again, mingled with shrill trumpet-blasts.   The tumult increased as the gray cold twilight deepened.   Horror at the tragedy enacted in a far-off land made the populace howl with rage ; men broke through the dense crowd running and waving great bundles of newspapers.   Through all the clamour, the one word Africa rang distinctly.

' And all this for four hundred brutes who had died the death of brutes ! ' murmured Andrea, withdrawing his head from the carriage window.

' What are you saying ! ' cried the Princess.

At the corner of the Chigi palace the commotion assumed the aspect of a riot.   The carriage had to stop.   Elena leaned forward to look out, and her face emerging from the shadows and lighted up by the glare of the gas and the reflection of the sunset seemed of a ghastly whiteness, an almost icy pallor, reminding Andrea of some head he had seen before, he could not say where or when—in some gallery or chapel.

' Here we are,' said the Princess, as the carriage drew up at last at the Palazzo Fiano.   ' Good-bye—we shall meet again at the Angelieris' this evening.   Ugenta will come and lunch with us to-morrow ?   You will find Elena and Barbarella Viti and my cousin there——'

' At what time ? '

' Half-past twelve.'

' Thanks, I will.'

The Princess got out.   The footman stood at the carriage door awaiting further orders.

'Where shall I take you?' Elena asked Sperelli, who had promptly taken the place of the Princess beside her.

'Far, far away——'

'Nonsense—tell me now,—home?' And without waiting for his answer she said—'To the Palazzo Zuccari, Trinità de' Monti.'

The footman closed the carriage door and they drove off down the Via Frattina leaving all the turmoil of the crowd behind them.

'Oh, Elena—after so long——' Andrea burst out, leaning down to gaze at the woman he so passionately desired and who had shrunk away from him into the shadow as if to avoid his contact.

The brilliant lights of the shop windows pierced the gloom in the carriage as they passed, and he saw on Elena's white face a slow alluring smile.

Still smiling thus, with a rapid movement she unwound the boa from her neck and cast it over Andrea's head like a lasso, and with that soft loop, all fragrant with the same perfume he had noticed in the blue fox of her coat, she drew the young man towards her and silently held up her lips to his.

Well did those two pairs of lips remember the rapture of bygone days, those terrible and yet deliriously sweet meetings prolonged to anguish. They held their breath to taste the sweetness of that kiss to the full.

Passing through the Via due Macelli the carriage drove up the Via dei Tritone, turned into the Via Sistina and stopped at the door of the Palazzo Zuccari.

Elena instantly released her captive, saying rather huskily—

'Go now, good-bye.'

'When will you come?'

'*Chi sa!*'

The footman opened the door and Andrea got out. The carriage turned back to the Via Sistina and Andrea, still vibrating with passion, a veil of mist before his eyes, stood watching to see if Elena's face would not appear at the

window; but he saw nothing.   The carriage drove rapidly
away.

As he ascended the stairs to his apartment, he said to
himself—'So she has come round at last!'   The intoxication
of her presence was still upon him, on his lips he still felt
the pressure of her kiss, and in his eyes was the flash of the
smile with which she had thrown that sort of smooth and
perfumed snake about his neck.   And Donna Maria?—Most
assuredly it was to her he owed these unexpected favours.
There was no doubt that at the bottom of Elena's strange
and fantastic behaviour lay a decided touch of jealousy.
Fearing perhaps that he was escaping h┌. she sought thus to
lure him back and rekindle his passion.   'Does she love me,
or does she not?'   But what did it matter to him one way
or another?   What good would it do him to know?   The
spell was broken irremediably.   No miracle that ever was
wrought could revive the least little atom of the love that was
dead.   The only thing that need occupy him now was the
carnal body, and that was divine as ever.

He indulged long in pleasurable meditation on this
episode.   What particularly took his fancy was the arch and
graceful touch Elena had given to her caprice.   The thought
of the boa evoked the image of Donna Maria's coils, and so,
confusedly, all the amorous fancies he had woven round that
virginal mass of hair by which, once on a time, the very
school-girls of the Florentine convent had been enthralled.
And again he let his two loves melt into one and form the
third—the Ideal.

The musing mood still upon him while he dressed for
dinner, he thought to himself—'Yesterday, a grand scene
of passion almost ending in tears; to-day, a little episode of
mute sensuality—and I seemed to myself as sincere in my
sentiment yesterday as I was in my sensations to-day.   Added
to which, scarcely an hour before Elena's kiss, I had a
moment of lofty lyrical emotion at Donna Maria's side.   Of
all this not one vestige remains.   To-morrow, most assuredly
I shall begin the same game over again.   I am unstable as

water, incoherent, inconsistent, a very chameleon! All my
efforts towards unity of purpose are for ever vain. I must
resign myself to my fate. The law of my being is comprised
in the one word—*Nunc*—the will of the Law be done!'

He laughed at himself, and from that moment began a new
phase of his moral degradation.

Without mercy, without remorse, without restraint, he set
all his faculties to work to compass the realisation of his
impure imaginings. To vanquish Maria Ferrès he had
recourse to the most subtle artifices, the most delicate
machinations; taking care to deceive her in matters of the
soul, of the spiritual, the ideal, the inmost life of the heart.
In carrying on the two campaigns—the conquest of the new
and the re-conquest of the old love—with equal adroitness,
and in turning to the best advantage the chance circumstances
of each enterprise, he was led into an infinity of annoying,
embarrassing, and ridiculous situations, to extricate himself
from which he was obliged to descend to a series of lies and
deceptions, of paltry evasions, ignoble subterfuges and equi-
vocal expedients. All Donna Maria's goodness and faith and
single mindedness were powerless to disarm him. As the
foundation of his work of seduction with her he had taken a
verse from one of the Psalms :—*Asperges me hyssopo et mun-
dabor—lavabis me et super nivem dealbabor.* And she, poor,
hapless, devoted creature, imagined that she was saving a soul
alive, redeeming an intellect, washing away by her own purity
the stains that sin had left on him. She still believed im-
plicitly in the ever-remembered words he had spoken to her
in the park, on that Epiphany of Love, within sight of the
sea; and it was just in this belief that she found comfort and
support in the midst of the religious conflict that rent her
conscience; this belief that blinded her to all suspicion and
filled her with a soil of mystic intoxication wherein she opened
the secret floodgates of her heart and let loose all her pent-up
tenderness, and let the sweetest flowers of her womanhood
blossom out resplendently.

For the first time in his life, Andrea Sperelli found himself face to face with a *real* passion—one of those rare and supreme manifestations of woman's capacity for love which occasionally flash their superb and terrible lightnings across the shifting gray sky of earthly loves.   But he did not care a jot, and went on with the pitiless work which was to destroy both himself and his victim.

CHAPTER III

THE next day, according to their agreement at the concert, Andrea found Donna Maria in the Piazza di Spagna with Delfina, looking at the antique jewellery in a shop window. At the first sound of his voice she turned, and a bright flush stained the pallor of her cheek. Together they then examined the eighteenth-century jewels, the paste buckles and hair ornaments, the enamelled watches, the gold and ivory tortoise-shell snuff-boxes, all these pretty trifles of a by-gone day which afforded an impression of harmonious richness under the clear morning sun. Everywhere about them, the flower-sellers were offering yellow and white jonquils, double violets, and long branches of flowering almond. There was a breath of Spring in the air. The column of the Immaculate Conception rose lightly into the sunshine, like a flower stem with the *Rosa mystica* on its summit; the Barcaccia glistened in a shower of diamonds, the stairway of the Trinità opened its arms gaily towards the church of Charles VIII., the two towers of which stood out boldly against the blue cloud-flecked sky.

'How exquisite!' exclaimed Donna Maria. 'No wonder you are so deeply enamoured of Rome!'

'Oh, you don't know it yet,' Andrea replied, 'I wish I might be your guide'—she smiled—'and undertake a pilgrimage of sentiment with you this spring.'

She smiled again, and her whole person assumed a less grave and chastened air. Her dress, this morning, had a quiet elegance about it, but revealed the refined taste of an expert in style and in the delicate combinations of colour.

Her jacket, of a shade of gray inclining to green, was of cloth trimmed round the edge with beaver and opening over a vest of the same fur, the blending of the two tones—indefinable gray and tawny gold—forming a harmony that was a delight to the eye.

'What did you do yesterday evening?' she asked.

'I left the concert-hall a few minutes after you and went home; and I stayed there because I seemed to feel your spirit near me. I thought much. Did you not *feel* my thought?'

'No, I cannot say I did. I passed a very cheerless evening, I do not know why. I felt so dreadfully alone!'

The Contessa di Lucoli passed in her dog-cart, driving a big roan. Giulia Moceta, accompanied by Musellaro, passed on foot, and then Donna Isotta Cellesi.

Andrea bowed to each. Donna Maria asked him the names of the ladies. That of Giulia Moceta was not new to her. She recalled the day on which she heard Francesca mention it while looking at Perugino's Archangel Michael, when they were turning over Andrea's drawings at Schifanoja. She followed her curiously with her eyes, seized with a sudden vague fear. Everything connecting Andrea with his former life was distasteful to her. She wished that that life, of which she knew next to nothing, could be entirely wiped out of the memory of this man who had flung himself into it with such avidity and dragged himself out with so much weariness, so many losses, so many wounds—'To live solely in you and for you, with no to-morrow and no yesterday—without other bond or preference—far from the world——' Were not those his words to her? What a dream!

Matters of very different import were troubling Andrea. It was fast approaching the Princess of Ferentino's lunch hour.

'Where are you bound for?' he asked of his companion.

'Wishing to make the most of the sunshine, Delfina and I had tea and sandwiches at Nazzari's and thought of going up to the Pincio and visiting the Villa Medici. If you would care to come with us——'

He had a moment of painful hesitation. The Pincio, the Villa Medici, on a February afternoon—with her! But he could not well get out of the lunch; besides, he was desperately anxious to meet Elena again after yesterday's episode, for though he had gone to the Angelieris', she did not put in an appearance.

He therefore answered with an inconsolable air—'How wretchedly unfortunate! I am obliged to be at a lunch in a quarter of an hour. I accepted the invitation a week ago, but if I had known, I would have found some way of getting out of it—What a nuisance!'

'Oh, then you must go without losing a moment—you will be late.'

He looked at his watch.

'I can walk a little further with you.'

'Mamma, do let us go up the steps,' begged Delfina. 'I went up yesterday with Miss Dorothy. You should see it!'

They turned back and crossed the square. A child followed them persistently, offering a great branch of flowering almond, which Andrea bought and presented to Delfina. Blonde ladies issued from the hotels armed with red Bædekers; clumsy hackney coaches with two horses jogged past with a glint of brass on their oldfashioned harness; the flower-sellers thrust their overflowing baskets in front of the strangers, vociferating at the pitch of their voices.

'Will you promise me,' Andrea said to Donna Maria, as they began to ascend the steps—'will you promise me not to go to the Villa Medici without me? Give it up for to-day—please do.'

For a moment she seemed preoccupied by sad thoughts, then she answered: 'Very well, I will give it up.'

'Thanks!'

Before them the great stairway rose triumphantly, its sun-warmed steps giving out a gentle heat, the stone itself having the polished gleam of old silver like that of the fountains at Schifanoja. Delfina ran on in front with her almond-branch and, caught by the breeze of her movement, some of its faint pink petals fluttered away like butterflies.

A poignant regret pierced the young man's heart. He pictured to himself the delights of a sentimental walk through the quiet glades of the Villa Medici in the early hours of the sunny afternoon.

'With whom do you lunch?' asked Donna Maria, after an interval of silence.

'With the old Princess Alberoni,' he replied.

He lied to her once more, for some instinct warned him that the name Ferentino might arouse some suspicion in Donna Maria's mind.

'Good-bye, then,' she said, and held out her hand.

'No—I will come up to the Piazza. My carriage is waiting for me there. Look—that is where I live,' and he pointed to the Palazzo Zuccari, all flooded with sunshine.

Donna Maria's eyes lingered upon it.

'Now there you have seen it, will you come there sometimes —in spirit?'

'In spirit always.'

'And shall I not see you before Saturday evening?'

'I hardly think so.'

They parted—she turning with Delfina into the avenue, Andrea jumping into his brougham and driving off down the Via Gregoriana.

He arrived at the Ferentinos' a few minutes late. He made his apologies. Elena was already there with her husband.

Lunch was served in a dining-room gay with tapestries representing scenes after the manner of Peter Loar. In the midst of these beautiful seventeenth-century grotesques, a brisk fire of wit and sarcasm soon began to flash and scintillate. The three ladies were in high spirits and prompt at repartee. Barbarella Viti laughed her sonorous masculine laugh, throwing back her handsome boyish head and making free play with her sparkling black eyes. Elena was in a more than usually brilliant vein, and impressed Andrea as being so far removed from him, so unfamiliar, so unconcerned, that he almost doubted whether yesterday's scene had not been all a dream. Ludovico Barbarisi and the Prince of Ferentino aided and abetted the ladies; Lord Heathfield entertained his 'young friend' by boring him to extinction with questions as to the coming sales and giving him minute details of a very rare edition of the *Metamorphoses* of Apuleius—Roma, 1469—in folio, which he had acquired a day or two ago for fifteen hundred and twenty lire. He broke off every now and then to watch Barbarella, and then that gleam of dementia would flash into his eyes, and his repulsive hands trembled strangely.

Andrea's irritation, disgust, and boredom at last reached such a pitch that he was unable to conceal his feelings.

'You seem out of spirits, Ugenta,' said the princess.

'Well, a little, perhaps—Miching Mallecho is ill.'

Barbarisi at once overwhelmed him with importunate questions about the horse's ailments; and then Lord Heathfield recommenced the story of the *Metamorphoses* from the beginning.

The Princess turned to her cousin. 'What do you think, Ludovico,' she said with a laugh, 'yesterday, at the concert, we surprised him in a flirtation with an Incognita!'

'So we did,' added Elena.

'An Incognita?' exclaimed Ludovico.

'Yes, but perhaps you can give us further information. She is the wife of the new Minister for Guatemala.'

'Aha—I know.'

'Well?'

'For the moment, I only know the Minister. I see him playing at the Club every night.'

'Tell me, Ugenta, has she been received at court yet?'

'I really do not know, Princess,' Andrea returned with some impatience.

The whole business had become simply intolerable to him. Elena's gaiety jarred horribly on him, and her husband's presence was more odious than ever. But if he was out of temper, it was more with himself than with the rest of the company. At the root of his irritation lay a dim longing after the pleasure he had so lately rejected. Hurt and offended by Elena's indifference, his heart turned with poignant regret to the other woman, and he pictured her wandering pensive and alone through the silent avenues, more beautiful, more noble than ever before.

The Princess rose and led the way into an adjoining room. Barbarella ran to the piano, which was entirely enveloped in an immense antique caparison of red velvet embroidered with dull gold, and began to sing Bizet's Tarantelle dedicated to Christine Nilsson. Elena and Eva leaned over her to read the music, while Ludovico stood behind them smoking a cigarette. The Prince had disappeared.

But Lord Heathfield kept firm hold of Andrea. He had drawn him into a window and was discoursing to him on certain little Urbanese '*coppette amatorie*' which he had picked up at the Cavaliere Davila's sale, and the rasping voice with its aggravating interrogative inflections, the gestures with which he indicated the dimensions of the cups, and his glance—now dull and fishy, now keen as steel under the great prominent brow—in short, the whole man was so unendurably obnoxious to Andrea that he clenched his teeth convulsively like a patient under the surgeon's knife.

His one absorbing thought was how to get away. His plan was to rush to the Pincio in the hope of finding Donna Maria and taking her, after all, to the Villa Medici. It was about two o'clock. He looked out of the window at the glorious sunshine; he turned back into the room, and saw the group of pretty women at the piano, bathed in the red glow struck out of the velvet cover by a strong golden ray. With this red glow the smoke of the cigarette mingled lightly as the talking and laughter mingled with the chords Barbarelli Viti struck haphazard on the keys. Ludovico whispered a word or two in his cousin's ear, which the Princess forthwith communicated to her friends, for there was a renewed burst of laughter, ringing and deep, like a string of pearls dropping into a silver

bowl.   Then Barbarella took up Bizet's air again in a low
voice—

'Tra, la la—Le papillon s'est envolé—Tra, la la——'

Andrea was anxiously on the watch for a favourable
moment at which to interrupt Lord Heathfield's harangue
and make his escape.   But the collector had entered upon a
series of rounded periods, each intimately connected with the
other, without one break, without one pause for breath.   A
single stop would have saved the persecuted listener, but it
never came, and the victim's torments grew more unbearable
every minute.

'Oui!   Le papillon s'est envolé—Oui!   Ah! ah! ah! ah!'

Andrea looked at his watch.

'Two o'clock already!   Excuse me, Marquis, but I must
go.'

He left the window and went over to the ladies.

'Will you excuse me, Princess, I have a consultation at
two with the veterinary surgeons at my stables?'

He took leave in a great hurry.   Elena gave him the tips of
her fingers, Barbarella presented him with a *fondant*, saying—
'Give it to poor Mallecho with my love.'

Ludovico offered to accompany him.

'No, no—stay where you are.'

He bowed and left—flew down the stairs like lightning and
jumped into his carriage, shouting to the coachman—

'To the Pincio—quick!'

He was filled with a frenzied longing to reach Maria
Ferrès' side, to enjoy the delights which he had refused
before.   The rapid pace of his horses was not quick enough
for him.   He looked out anxiously for the Trinità de' Monti,
the avenue—the gates.

The carriage flashed through the gates.   He ordered the
coachman to moderate his pace and to drive through each of
the avenues.   His heart gave a bound every time the figure
of a woman appeared in the distance through the trees.   He
got out and, on foot, explored the paths forbidden to vehicles.
He searched every nook and corner—in vain.

The Villa Borghese being open to the public, the Pincio lay deserted and silent under the languid smile of the February sun. Few carriages or foot-passengers disturbed the peaceful solitude of the place. The grayish-white trees, tinged here and there with violet, spread their leafless branches against a diaphanous sky, and the air was full of delicate spider-webs which the breeze shook and tore asunder. The pines and cypresses—all the evergreen trees— took on something of this colourless pallor, seemed to fade and melt into the all-prevailing monotone.

Surely something of Donna Maria's sadness still lingered in the atmosphere. Andrea stood for several minutes leaning against the railings of the Villa Medici, crushed beneath a load of melancholy too heavy to be borne.

CHAPTER IV

In the days that followed, the double pursuit continued with the same tortures, or worse, and with the same odious mendacity. By a phenomenon which is of frequent occurrence in the moral degradation of men of keen intellect, he now had a terrible lucidity of conscience, a lucidity without interruptions, without a moment of dimness or eclipse. He knew what he was doing and criticised what he had done. With him self-scorn went hand in hand with feebleness of will.

But his variable humour, his incertitude, his unaccountable silences and equally unaccountable effusions, in short, all the peculiarities of manner which such a condition of mind inevitably brings along with it, only increased and excited the passionate commiseration of Donna Maria. She saw him suffer, and it filled her with grief and tenderness. 'By slow degrees I shall cure him,' she thought. But slowly and surely, without being aware of it, she was losing her strength of purpose and was bending to the sick man's will.

The downward slope was gentle.

In the drawing-room of the Countess Starnina, an indefinable thrill ran through her when she felt Andrea's gaze upon her bare shoulders and arms. It was the first time he had seen her in evening dress. Her face and her hands were all he knew. This evening he saw how exquisite was the shape of her neck and shoulders and of her arms too, although they were a little thin.

She was dressed in ivory-white brocade trimmed with sable. A narrow band of fur edged the low bodice and imparted an indescribable delicacy to the tints of the skin. The line of the shoulders, from the neck to the top of the arms, had that gracious slope which is such a sure mark of physical aristocracy and so rare nowadays. In her magnificent hair, arranged in the manner affected by Verocchio for his busts, there was not one jewel, not one flower.

At two or three propitious moments, Andrea murmured words of passionate admiration in her ear.

'This is the first time we have met in society,' he said to her. 'Give me a glove as a souvenir.'

'No.'

'Why not, Maria?'

'No, no. Be quiet.'

'Oh, those hands of yours! Do you remember when I copied them at Schifanoja? I feel as if I had a right to them; as if you ought to grant them to me; of your whole person they are the part that is most intimately connected with your soul, the most spiritualised, almost, one might say, the purest— Oh, hands of kindness—hands of pardon. How dearly I should love to possess at least a semblance of their form, some token to which their delicate perfume still clings. You will give me a glove before you leave?'

She did not answer. The conversation dropped. A short time afterwards, on being asked to play, she consented, and drawing off her gloves laid them on the music-stand in front of her. Her fingers, tapering and glittering with rings, looked very white as she drew off their delicate covering. On the ring finger of her left hand blazed a great opal.

She played the two Sonata-Fantasias of Beethoven (Op. 27). The one, dedicated to Giulietta Guicciardi, expressed a hopeless renunciation, told of an awakening after a dream that had lasted too long. The other, from the first bars of the *Andante*, described by its full smooth rhythm the calm that comes after the storm; then, passing through the disquietude of the second movement, opened out into an *Adagio* of luminous serenity, and ended in an *Allegro Vivace* in which there was a rising note of courage, almost of fervour.

Though surrounded by an attentive audience, Andrea felt

that she was playing for him alone. From time to time, his eyes wandering from the fingers of the pianist to the long gloves hanging from the music stand, which still retained the form of those hands, still preserved an inexpressible charm in the small opening at the wrist where, but a short time ago, a tiny morsel of her soft flesh had been visible.

Maria rose amidst a round of applause. She left the piano, but she did not take away her gloves. Andrea was tempted to steal them.—Had she not perhaps left them for him?—But he only wanted one. As a connoisseur in amatory matters has said, a pair of gloves is a totally different thing from a single one.

Led back to the piano by the insistence of the Countess Starnina, Maria removed her gloves from the desk and placed them in a corner of the keyboard, in the shadow. She then played Rameau's Gavotte—*the Gavotte of the Yellow Ladies*—the never-to-be-forgotten dance of Indifference and Love.

Andrea regarded her fixedly with a little trepidation. When she rose, she took up one of her gloves. The other she left in the shadowy corner of the piano—for him.

Three days afterwards, when astonished Rome had awakened to find itself under a covering of snow, Andrea received a note to the following effect—

' *Tuesday,* 2 *p.m.*—To-night, between eleven and twelve o'clock, you will wait for me in a carriage in front of the Palazzo Barberini, outside the gates. If by midnight I am not there, you can go away again.—*A stranger.*'

The tone of the note was mysterious and romantic. Was it in remembrance of the 25th of March two years ago? Lady Heathfield seemed particularly fond of the use of carriages in her love affairs. Had she the intention of taking up the adventure at the point where it broke off? And why —*A stranger*? Andrea could not repress a smile. He had just come back from a visit to Maria—a very pleasing visit—and his heart inclined, for the moment, more to the Siennese than to the other. His ear still retained the sound of her sweet and gentle words as they stood together at the window and watched the snow falling soft as peach or apple blossom on the trees of the Villa Aldobrandini, already touched with the presentiment of the coming Spring.   However, before going out to dinner, he gave very particular orders to Stephen.

Eleven o'clock found him in front of the palace, devoured by impatience and curiosity.   The novelty of the situation, the spectacle of the snowy night, the mystery and uncertainty of it all, inflamed his imagination and transported him beyond the realities of life.

Over Rome, on that memorable February night, there shone a full moon of fabulous size and unheard of splendour. In that immense radiance, the surrounding objects seemed to exist only as in a dream, impalpable, meteoric, and visible at a great distance by virtue of some fantastic irradiation of their own.   The snow covered the railings of the gateway, concealing the iron and transforming it into a piece of open-work, more frail and airy than filigree; while the white-robed Colossi supported it as oaks support a spider's web.   The garden looked like a motionless forest of enormous and mis-shapen lilies all of ice; a garden under some lunar enchant-ment, a lifeless paradise of Selene.   Mute, solemn and massive the Palazzo Barberini reared its great bulk into the sky, its most salient points standing out dazzlingly white and casting a pale blue shadow as transparent as light.

He waited, leaning forward on the watch; and under the fascination of that marvellous spectacle, he felt the spirits that wait on love awake in him, that the lyric summits of his sentiment began to gleam and glitter like the frozen shafts of the gateway under the moon.   But he could not make up his mind which of the two women he would prefer as the centre of this fantastic scenery: Elena Heathfield robed in imperial purple, or Maria Ferrès robed in ermine.   And as he lingered pleasurably over this uncertainty of choice, he ended by mingling and confounding his two anxieties—the real one for Elena and the imaginary one for Maria.

A clock near by struck in the silence with a clear vibrating sound, and each stroke seemed to break something crystalline in the air. The clock of the Trinità de' Monti responded to the call, and after that the clock of the Quirinal—then others faintly out of the distance. It was a quarter past eleven.

Andrea strained his eyes towards the portico. Would she dare to traverse the garden on foot? He pictured the figure of Elena in the midst of all this dazzling whiteness, then, in an instant, that of Donna Maria appeared to him, obliterating the other, triumphant over the whiteness, *Candida super nivem*. This night of moonlight and snow then was under the dominance of Maria Ferrès as under some invincible actual influence. The image of the pure creature grew symbolically out of the sovereign purity of the surrounding aspect of things. The symbol re-acted forcibly on the spirit of the poet.

While still watching to see if the other one would come, he gave himself up to a vision suggested by the scene before him.

It was a poetic, almost a mystic dream. He was waiting for Donna Maria—she had chosen this night of supernatural purity on which to sacrifice her own purity to her lover's desire. All the white things about her, cognisant of the great sacrifice about to be accomplished, were waiting to cry *Ave* and *Amen* at the passage of their sister. The silence was alive.

And behold, she comes! *Incedit per lilia et super nivem.* She comes, robed in ermine; her tresses bound about with a fillet; her steps lighter than a shadow; the moon and the snow are less pale than she—*Ave!*

A shadow, azure as the light that tints the sapphire, accompanies her. The great mis-shapen lilies bend not as she passes; the frost has congealed them, has made them like the asphodels that illumine the paths of Hades. And yet, like those of the Christian paradise, they have a voice and say with one accord—*Amen.*

So be it—the Beloved glides on to the sacrifice. Already

she nears the watcher sitting mute and icy, but whose eyes
are burning and eloquent. And on her hands, the dear
hands that close his wounds and open the doors of dreams,
he presses his kiss.—So be it.

Then on her lips, the dear lips that know no word of false-
ness, he lays his kiss. Released from the fillet, her hair
spreads like a glorious flood in which all the shadows of the
night put to flight by the moon and the snow seem to have
taken refuge. *Comis suis obumbrabit tibi, et sub comis peccavit.
Amen.*

And still the other did not come! Through the silence,
through the poetry, the hours of men sounded again from the
towers and belfries of Rome. A carriage or two rolled noiselessly past the Four Fountains towards the Piazza or crawled
slowly up towards Santa Maria Maggiore; and each street-
lamp shone yellow as a topaz in the light. It seemed as if
the night, reaching its highest point, had grown more
luminously radiant. The filigree of the gateway twinkled
and flashed as if its silver embroideries were studded with
jewels. In the palace, great circles of dazzling light shone on
the windows like diamond florins.

'What if she does not come?' thought Andrea to himself.

The flood of lyric fervour that had passed over his soul at
Maria's name had submerged the anxiety of his vigil, had
appeased his desire and calmed his impatience. For a
moment, the thought that she would not come only made
him smile. But the next, the anguish of uncertainty
began again worse than ever, and he was tortured by the
vision of the joys that might have been his, here in the warm
carriage where the roses breathed so sweet an atmosphere.
Besides which, his sufferings were further increased, as on
New Year's Eve, by a sharp touch of wounded vanity; it
annoyed him particularly that his delicate preparations for a
love scene should thus be wasted and useless.

In the carriage, the cold was tempered by the pleasant
warmth diffused by a metal foot-warmer, full of hot water.
A bunch of white roses, snowy, moonlike, lay on the bracket

in front of the seat. A white bear-skin covered his knees. Everything pointed to an intentional arrangement of a sort of *Symphonie en blanc-majeur.*

The clocks struck for the third time. It was a quarter to twelve. The vigil had lasted too long—Andrea was growing tired and cross. In Elena's apartments, in the left wing of the palace, there was no light but that which came from outside. Was she coming? And if so, in what manner? Secretly? Under what pretext? Lord Heathfield was certainly in Rome—how would she explain her nocturnal absence? Once more the soul of the former lover was torn with curiosity; once more jealousy gnawed at his heart and carnal passion inflamed him. He thought of Musellaro's derisive suggestion about the husband, and he determined to have Elena again at all costs, both for pleasure and for revenge. Oh, if only she would come!

A carriage drove through the gates and into the garden. He leaned forward to look at it. He recognised Elena's horses and caught a glimpse inside of the figure of a woman. The carriage disappeared into the portico. He remained perplexed. She had been out then? She had returned alone? He fixed a scrutinising gaze upon the portico. The carriage came out, passed through the garden and drove away towards the Via Rasella; it was empty.

It wanted but two or three minutes to midnight and she had not come!

It struck the hour. A bitter pang smote the heart of the deluded watcher. She was not coming.

Unable to see any cause for her having missed the appointment, he turned upon her in sudden anger; he even had a suspicion that she might have wished to inflict a humiliation, a punishment upon him, or else that she had merely indulged in a whim in order to inflame his desire afresh. The next moment he called to the coachman—

' Piazza del Quirinale.'

He yielded to the attraction of Maria Ferrès; he abandoned himself once more to the vaguely tender sentiment which, ever since his visit in the afternoon, had left, as it were, a perfume in his soul and suggested to him thoughts and images of poetic beauty.   The recent disappointment, proving, as he considered, Elena's malice and indifference, urged him more strongly than ever towards the love and goodness of the other.   His regret for the loss of so beautiful a night increased, under the influence of the vision he had dreamed just now.   And, truth to tell, it was one of the most enchanting nights Rome had ever known ; one of those spectacles that oppress the human soul with deep sadness, because they transcend all power of admiration, all possibility of human expression.

The Piazza del Quirinale, magnified by the all-pervading whiteness, lay spread out solitary and dazzling, like an Olympian acropolis above the silent city.   The edifices surrounding it reared their stately proportions into the deep sky ; Bernini's great portal to the royal palace surmounted by the loggia offered an optical delusion by seeming to detach itself from the building and stand out all alone in all its unwieldy magnificence, like some mausoleum sculptured out of a meteoric block of stone.   The rich architraves to the Palazzo della Consulta were curiously transformed by the accumulated masses of snow.   Sublime amidst the uniform whiteness, the colossal statues seemed to dominate all things. The grouping of the Dioscuri and the horses looked bolder and larger in that light ; the broad backs of the steeds glittered under jewelled trappings, there was a sparkle as of diamonds on the shoulders and the uplifted arm of each demi-god.

An august solemnity flowed from the monument.   Rome lay plunged in a death-like silence, motionless, empty—a city under a spell.   The houses, the churches, the spires and turrets, all the confusion and intermingling of Christian and Pagan architecture, resolved itself into one unbroken forest between the heights of the Janiculum and the Monte Mario, drowned in a silvery vapour, far off, infinitely immaterial, reminding one a little of a lunar landscape, calling up visions of some half extinct planet peopled by shades. The dome of St. Peter's, shining with a peculiar metallic lustre in the blue atmosphere looked gigantic and so close that one might have thought to touch it. And the two youthful Heroes, sons of the Swan, radiant with beauty in the vast expanse of whiteness as in the apotheosis of their origin, seemed to be the immortal Genii of Rome guarding the slumbers of the sacred city.

The carriage stopped in front of the palace and remained there for a long time. The poet was once more absorbed in his impossible dream. And Maria Ferrès was quite near, was perhaps watching and dreaming also, perhaps she too felt the grandeur of the night weighing upon her heart and crushing it in vain.

Slowly the carriage passed her closed door, while the windows reflected the full moon gazing at the hanging gardens of the Villa Aldobrandini where the trees looked like aërial miracles. And as he passed, the poet threw the bunch of roses on to the snow before Donna Maria's door in token of homage.

CHAPTER V

'I saw—I guessed—I had been at the window for a long time, unable to tear myself away from the fascination of all that whiteness. I saw the carriage pass slowly in the snow. I felt that it was you, before I saw you throw the roses. No words can describe to you the tenderness of my tears. I wept for you from love and for the roses out of pity. Poor roses! It seemed to me that they were alive and must suffer and die in the snow. I seemed to hear them call to me and lament like human creatures that have been deserted. As soon as your carriage had disappeared, I leaned out of the window to look at them. I was on the point of going down into the street to pick them up. But a servant was still in the hall waiting up for some one. I thought of a thousand plans but could find none that was practicable. I was in despair—You smile? Truly, I hardly know what madness had come over me. I watched the passers-by anxiously, my eyes full of tears. If any one of them had trodden on the roses, he would have trampled upon my heart. And yet in all this torment I was happy, happy in your love, in the delicacy of your passionate homage, in your gentleness, your kindness.—When, at last, I fell asleep, I was sad and happy together; the roses must have been nearly dead by that time. After an hour or two of sleep, the sound of spades upon the pavement woke me up. They were shovelling away the snow just in front of my door. I listened; the noise and the voices continued till after daylight and filled me with unutterable sadness!—Poor roses! But they will always live and bloom in my heart. There are certain memories that can perfume a soul for ever—Do you love me very much, Andrea?'

She hesitated for a moment, and then—'Do you love only me? Have you forgotten all the rest? Do all your thoughts belong to me?'

Her breath came fast and she was trembling.

'I suffer—at the thought of your former life,—the past of which I know nothing—of your memories, of all the marks left upon your soul, of that in you which I shall never understand, never possess. Oh, if I could but wipe it all out for you! Incessantly, Andrea, I hear your first, your very first words. I believe I shall hear them at the moment of my death——'

She panted and trembled, shaken by the force of all-conquering passion.

'Every day I love you more, every day more!'

He intoxicated her with words of honied sweetness; he was more fervent than herself; he told her of his visions in the night of snow and of his despairing desire and some plausible story of the roses and a thousand other lyric fancies. He judged her to be on the point of yielding—he saw her eyes swim in melting languor, and on her plaintive mouth that nameless contraction which seems like an instinctive dissimulation of the physical desire to kiss; he looked at her hands, so delicate and yet so strong, the hands of an archangel, and saw them trembling like the strings of an instrument, expressing all the anguish of her soul. 'If, to-day, I could succeed in stealing even the most fleeting kiss from her,' he thought, 'I should find myself considerably nearer the goal of my desires.'

But, conscious of her peril, she rose hastily with an apology and, ringing the bell, ordered tea and sent to ask Miss Dorothy to bring Delfina to the drawing-room.

'It is better so,' she said, turning to Andrea with the traces of her agitation still visible in her face; 'forgive me!'

And from that day she avoided receiving him except on Tuesday and Saturday when she was at home to every one.

Nevertheless, she allowed Andrea to conduct her on long peregrinations through the Rome of the Emperors and the Rome of the Popes, through the villas, the museums, the churches, the ruins. Where Elena Muti had passed, there Maria Ferrès passed also. Often enough, the sights they visited suggested to the poet the same eloquent effusions which Elena had once heard. Often enough, some recollection carried him away suddenly from the present and disturbed him strangely.

'What are you thinking of at this moment?' Donna Maria would ask him, looking him deep in the eyes with a shade of suspicion.

'Of you—always of you!' he answered. 'I am sometimes seized with curiosity to look into my own soul to see if there remains one tiny particle that does not belong to you, one smallest corner still closed to your light. It is an exploration made for you, as you cannot make it for yourself. I may say with truth, Maria, that I have nothing more to give you. You have absolute dominion over me. Never, I think, in spirit has one human being possessed another so entirely. If my lips were to meet yours my whole life would be absorbed in yours—I believe I should die of it.'

She had full faith in his words, for his voice lent them the fire of truth.

One day, they were in the Belvedere of the Villa Medici and were watching the gold of the sun fade slowly from the sky while the Villa Borghese, still bare and leafless, sank gently into a violet mist. Touched with sudden melancholy she said:

'Who knows how many times you have come here to feel yourself beloved?'

'I do not know,' he answered, like a man lost in a dream, 'I do not remember. What are you saying?'

She was silent. Then she rose to read the inscriptions written on the pillars of the little temple. They were, for the most part, written by lovers, by newly-married couples, by solitary dreamers. All expressed some sentiment of love,

grave or gay ; they sang the praises of a beauty or mourned
a lost delight; they told of some burning kiss or ecstasy of
languor; they thanked the ancient wooded glades that had
sheltered their love, pointed out some secret nook to the
happy visitor of the morrow, described the lingering charms
of a sunset they had watched. All of them, whether lovers or
married, under the fascination of the eternal feminine had
been seized with lyric fervour in this little lonely Belvedere to
which they ascended by a flight of steps carpeted with moss
as thick as velvet. The very walls spoke. An indefinable
melancholy emanated from these unknown voices of vanished
lovers, a sadness that seemed almost sepulchral, as if they had
been epitaphs in a chapel.

Suddenly Maria turned to Andrea. ' You have been here
too,' she said.

' I do not know,' he answered again, looking at her in the
same dreamy way as before, ' I do not remember. I remember nothing. I love you.'

She read, written in Andrea's hand, an epigram of Goethe's,
a distich, the one beginning—*Sage, wie lebst du?* Say, how
livest thou ? *Ich lebe!* I live ! ' And were it mine to live a
hundred, hundred years, my only wish would be that to-
morrow should be as to-day.' Underneath this there was
a date: *Die ultima februarii* 1885, and a name: *Helena
Amyclæ.*

' Let us go,' she said.

The canopy of branches cast deep shadows over the little
moss-carpeted stairway.

' Will you take my arm ? ' he asked.

' No, thank you,' she replied.

They went on in silence. The heart of each was heavy.

Presently she said—' You were very happy two years
ago.'

And he, persisting in his tone of reverie—' I do not know
—I do not remember.'

In the green twilight, the path was mysterious. The
trunks and branches of the trees were coiled and interlaced

like serpents ; here and there a leaf gleamed through the
shade like an emerald green eye.

After a interval of silence, she began again—'Who was
that Elena?'

'I do not know, I have forgotten. I remember nothing
but that I love you. I love none but you. I think only
of you. I live for you alone. I know nothing, I wish for
nothing but your love. Every fetter that binds me to my
former life is broken. Now I am far from the world, utterly
lost in you. I live in your heart and in your soul ; I *feel
myself* in every throb of your pulse ; I do not touch you, and
yet I am as close to you as if I held you in my arms, pressed
to my lips, to my heart. I love you and you love me ; and
that has been for ages and will last for ages, to all eternity.
At your side, thinking of you, living in you, I am conscious
of the infinite—the eternal—I love you and you love me. I
know nothing else—I remember nothing else.'

On all her sadness, all her suspicions, he poured out a
flood of warm fond eloquence. And she listened, standing
straight and slender in front of the balustrade that runs round
the wide terrace.

'Is it true ? is it true?' she repeated, in a faint voice like
the echo of a moan out of the depth of her soul—'is that
true ?'

'Yes, it is true—and that alone is true. All the rest is
a dream. I love you and you love me. I am yours as you
you are mine. I know you to be so absolutely mine that I
ask for no caress ; I ask for no proof of your love. I can
wait. My dearest delight is to obey you. I ask for no
caresses, but I can feel them in your voice, in your eyes,
your attitudes, your slightest movement. All that comes to
me from you intoxicates me like a kiss, and when I touch
your hand I know not which is greater, the rapture of my
senses or the exaltation of my soul.'

He lightly laid his hand on hers. She trembled, drawn by
a wild desire to throw herself upon his breast to offer him, at
last, her lips, her kiss, herself. It seemed to her—for she

believed blindly in Andrea's words—that by so doing, she would bind him to her finally with an indissoluble bond. She felt that she was going to swoon, to die. It was as if the tumults of passion from which she had already suffered swelled her heart and increased the present storm; as if, into this one moment of time were gathered all the varying emotions she had experienced since she first knew this man. The roses of Schifanoja bloomed again among the shrubs and laurels of the Villa Medici.

'I shall wait, Maria. I shall be true to my promises. I ask nothing of you. I wait and look forward to the supreme moment. That moment will come, I know it, for the power of love is invincible. And all your fears, all your terrors will vanish; and the communion of the body will seem to you as pure as the communion of the soul; for all flames are alike in purity.'

He clasped Maria's ungloved hand in his. The gardens seemed deserted. From the palace of the Accademia came not a sound, not a voice. Clear through the silence, they heard the lisp of the fountain in the middle of the esplanade; the avenues stretched away towards the Pincio, straight and rigid as if enclosed between two walls of bronze, upon which the gilding of the sunset still lingered; the absolute immobility of all things suggested the idea of a petrified labyrinth; the reeds round the basin of the fountain were not less motionless than the statues.

'I feel,' said Donna Maria, half-closing her eyes, 'as if I were on one of the terraces at Schifanoja—far, far away from Rome—alone—with you. When I shut my eyes, I see the sea.'

Born of her love and of the silence, she saw a vision rise up before her and spread wide under the setting sun. Andrea's gaze was upon her; she said no more, but she smiled faintly. As she uttered the two words—'with you' —she closed her eyes, but her mouth seemed suddenly to grow luminous as if on it were concentrated all the splendour veiled by her quivering lids and her eyelashes.

'I feel as if none of these things existed outside of my consciousness, but that you had created them in my soul, for my delight. I am profoundly affected with this illusion each time I stand before some spectacle of beauty and you are at my side.'

The words came slowly, with pauses in between, as if her voice were the halting echo of some other voice imperceptible to the senses, imparting to her words a singular accent, a tone of mystery, revealing that they proceeded from the innermost depths of her heart ; they were no longer the ordinary imperfect symbols of thoughts, they were transformed into a more intense means of expression, transcendant, quivering with life, of infinitely ampler signification.

> ' And from her lips, as from a hyacinth full
> Of honey-dew, a liquid murmur drops,
> Killing the sense with passion, sweet as stops
> Of planetary music heard in trance.'

Andrea thought of Shelley's lines. He repeated them to Maria, feeling the contagion of her emotion, penetrated by the charm of the hour and the scene.

'Never, in my hours of loftiest spiritual flights, have I attained to such heights. You lift yourself above my sublimest dream, shine resplendent above my most radiant thoughts ; you illumine me with a ray that is almost brighter that I can bear.'

She stood up straight and slender against the balustrade, her hands clasping the stone, her head high, her face more pallid than on the memorable morning when they walked beneath the flowering trees. Tears filled her half-closed eyes and glittered upon her lashes, and as she gazed before her, she saw the sky all rosy-red through the mist of her tears.

The sky seemed to rain roses as on that evening in October when the sun, sinking behind the hill at Rovigliano, lit up the deep pools in the pine-wood. The Villa Medici, eternally green and flowerless, received upon the tops of its rigid arboreal walls this gentle rain of innumerable petals showered down from the celestial gardens.

She turned to go down. Andrea followed her. They walked in silence towards the stairway; they looked at the wood that stretched between the terrace and the Belvedere. The light seemed to stop short at the entrance to it, where stood the two guardian statues, unable to pierce the further gloom; and the trees looked as if they spread their branches in a different atmosphere, or rather in some dark waters at the bottom of the sea, like giant marine plants.

She was seized with sudden terror. Hastening towards the steps, she ran down five or six and then stopped, dazed and panting. Through the silence, she heard the beating of her heart like the roll of distant thunder. The Villa Medici was no longer in sight; the stairway was enclosed between two walls, damp and gray and with grass growing in the cracks, gloomy as a subterranean dungeon. She saw Andrea lean down swiftly to kiss her on the lips.

'No, no, Andrea—no!'

He stretched out his hands to draw her to him, to hold her fast.

'No!'

Wildly she seized one of his hands and carried it to her lips; she kissed it twice—thrice, with frenzied passion. Then she fled down the steps to the gate like a mad creature.

'Maria! Maria! Stop!'

They stood together before the closed gate, pale, panting, shaken, trembling from head to foot, gazing at one another with wide distraught eyes, their ears filled with the throb of their mad pulses, a sense of choking in their throats. Then suddenly, with one impulse, they were in each other's arms, heart to heart, lips to lips.

'Enough—you are killing me,' she murmured, leaning, half fainting, against the gateway, with a gesture of supreme entreaty.

For a moment, they stood facing one another without touching. All the silence of the Villa seemed to weigh upon them in this narrow spot enclosed in its high walls like an

open tomb. High above them sounded the hoarse cawing
of the rooks gathering on the roofs of the palaces or crossing
the sky. Once more, a strange fear possessed Maria's heart.
She cast a terror-stricken glance up at the top of the walls.
Then, with a visible effort she said quickly :

'We can go now ; will you open the gate !'

And, in her uncontrollable haste to get away, her hand
met Andrea's on the latch of the gate.

As she passed between the two granite columns and under
the jasmin, Andrea said—'Look, the jasmin is just going to
blossom !'

She did not turn but she smiled—a smile that was infinitely sad because of the shadow cast upon her heart by
the sudden recollection of the name she had read in the
Belvedere. And while she walked through the mysterious
gloom of the avenue, and she felt his kiss flame in her blood,
a ruthless torture graved deep into her heart, that name—oh,
that name !

CHAPTER VI

LORD HEATHFIELD opened the great book-case containing his private collection, and turning to Sperelli—

'You should design the clasps for this volume,' he said; 'it is in quarto and dated from Lampsacus, 1734. The engravings seem to me extremely fine. What do you think?'

He handed Andrea the rare volume, which was illustrated with erotic vignettes.

'Here is a very notable figure,' he continued, pointing to one of the vignettes—'something that was quite new to me. None of my erotic authors mention it.'

He talked incessantly, discussing each detail and following the lines of the drawing with a flabby white finger, covered with hairs on the first joint and ending in a polished, pointed nail, a little livid like the nail of an ape. His voice grated hideously on Sperelli's ear.

'This Dutch edition of Petronius is magnificent. And here is the *Erotopægnion* printed in Paris, 1798. Do you know the poem attributed to John Wilkes, *An Essay on Women*? This is an edition of 1763.'

The collection was very complete. It comprised all the most infamous, the most refinedly sensual works that the human mind has produced in the course of centuries to serve as a commentary to the ancient hymn in honour of the god of Lampsacus, *Salve! Sancte pater.*

The collector took the books down from their shelves and showed them in turn to his ' young friend,' never pausing in his discourse. His hands grew caressing as he touched each volume bound in priceless leather or material. A subtle smile played continually round his lips, and a gleam as of madness flashed from time to time into his eyes.

'I also possess a first edition of the Epigrams of Martial —the Venice one, printed by Windelin of Speyer, in folio. This is it. The clasps are by a master hand.'

Sperelli listened and looked in a sort of stupor that changed by degrees into horror and distress. His eyes were continually drawn to a portrait of Elena hanging on the wall against the red damask background.

'That is Elena's portrait by Frederick Leighton. But now, look at this ! The frontispiece, the headings, the initial letters, the marginal ornaments combine all that is most perfect in the matter of erotic iconography. Look at the clasps ! '

The binding was exquisite. Shark-skin, wrinkled and rough as that which surrounds the hilts of Japanese sabres covered the sides and back; the clasps and bosses, of richly silvered bronze, were chased with consummate elegance, and were worthy to rank with the best work of the sixteenth century.

'The artist, Francis Redgrave, died in a lunatic asylum. He was a young genius of great promise. I have all his studies. I will show them to you.'

The collector warmed to his subject. He went away to fetch the portfolio from the next room. His gait was some-what jerky and uncertain, like that of a man who already carries in his system the germ of paralysis, the first touch of spinal disease; his body remained rigid without following the movement of his limbs, like the body of an automaton.

Andrea Sperelli followed him with his eyes till he crossed the threshold of the room. The moment he was alone, un-speakable anguish rent his soul. This room, hung with dark-red damask, exactly like the one in which Elena had received him two years ago, seemed to him tragic and sinister. These were, perhaps, the very same hangings that had heard Elena say to him that day, 'I love you.' The book-case was open, and he could see the rows of obscene books, the bizarre bindings stamped with symbolic decorations. On the wall hung the portrait of Lady Heathfield side by side with a copy of Sir Joshua Reynolds's Nelly O'Brien. And the two women looked out of the canvas with the same, self-same piercing intensity, the same glow of passion, the same flame of sensual desire, the same marvellous eloquence; each had a mouth that was ambiguous, enigmatical, sibylline, the mouth of the insatiable absorber of souls ; and each had a brow of marble whiteness, immaculately, radiantly pure.

'Poor Redgrave!' said Lord Heathfield, returning with the portfolio of drawings. 'There was a genius for you. There never was an erotic imagination to equal his. Look! look! What style ! What profound knowledge of the potentialities of the human figure for expression.'

He left Andrea's side for a moment in order to close the door. Then he returned to the table in the window and began turning over the collection under Sperelli's eyes, talking without a pause, pointing out with that ape-like finger the peculiar characteristics of each figure.

He spoke in his own language, beginning each sentence with an interrogative intonation and ending with a monotonous, irritating drop of the voice. Certain words lacerated Andrea's ear like the sound of filing iron or the shriek of a steel knife over a pane of glass.

And the drawings passed in review before him, appalling pictures which revealed the terrible fever that had taken hold upon the artist's hand, and the terrible madness that possessed his brain.

'Now here,' said Lord Heathfield, 'is the work which inspired these masterpieces. A priceless book—rarest of the rare ! You are not acquainted with Daniel Maclisius ?'

He handed Andrea the treatise : *De verberatione amatoria.* He had warmed more and more to his subject. His bald temples were flushed, and the veins stood out on his great forehead ; every minute his mouth twitched a little convulsively and his hands, those detestable hands, were perpetually on the move, while his arms retained their paralytic immobility. The unclean beast in him appeared in all its brazen ugliness and ferocity.

'Mumps! Mumps! are you alone?'

It was Elena's voice. She knocked softly at one of the doors.

'Mumps!'

Andrea started violently; the blood rushed to his head and drew a veil of mist before his eyes, and there was a roar in his ears as if he were going to be seized with vertigo. In the midst of the fever of excitement into which he had been thrown by these books, these pictures, the maddening discourses of his host, a furious instinct ose out of the blind depths of his being, the same brutal impetus which he had already experienced on the race-course after his victory over Rutolo amid the acrid exhalations of his steaming horse. The phantasm of a crime of love tempted and beckoned to him: to kill this man, take the woman by force, wreak his brutal will upon her, and then kill himself. But it passed rapidly as it had come.

'No, I am not alone,' answered the husband, without opening the door. 'In a few minutes I shall have the pleasure of bringing Count Sperelli to you—he is here with me.'

He replaced the book in the book-case, closed the portfolio and carried it back into the next room.

Andrea would have given all he possessed not to have to undergo the ordeal that awaited him, and yet it attracted him strangely. Once more, he raised his eyes to the crimson wall and the dark frame out of which Elena's pallid face looked forth, that face with the haunting eyes and the sibylline mouth. A penetrating and continuous fascination emanated from that imperious image. That strange pallor dominated tragically the whole crimson gloom of the apartment. And once again he felt that his miserable passion was incurable.

'Will you come into the drawing-room?' asked the husband, reappearing in the doorway perfectly calm and composed. 'Then, you will design those clasps for me?'

'I will try,' answered Andrea.

He was quite unable to control his inward agitation. Elena looked at him with a provocative smile.

'What were you doing in there?' she asked him, still smiling in the same manner.

'Your husband was showing me some unique curiosities.'

'Ah!'

There was a sardonic sneer upon her lips, a manifest mocking scorn in her voice. She settled herself on a wide divan covered with a Bokhara carpet of faded amaranthine hues on which languished great cushions embroidered with spreading palms of dull gold. Here she leaned back in an easy, graceful attitude, and gazed at Andrea from under her drooping eyelids, while she spoke of trivial society matters in a voice that insinuated its tones into the young man's heart, and crept through his blood like an invisible fire.

Two or three times, he surprised a look which Lord Heathfield fixed upon his wife—a look that seemed surcharged with all the infamies he had stirred up just now. Again that criminal thought sped through his mind. He trembled in every fibre of his being. He started to his feet, livid and convulsed.

'Going already?' exclaimed Lord Heathfield. 'Why, what is the matter?' and he smiled a singular smile at his 'young friend.' He knew well the effect of his books.

Sperelli bowed. Elena gave him her hand without rising. Her husband accompanied him to the door, where he repeated in a low voice—'You won't forget those clasps?'

As Andrea stood in the portico, he saw a carriage coming up the drive. A man with a great golden beard nodded to him from the window. It was Galeazzo Secinaro.

In a flash, the recollection of the May Bazaar came back to him, and the episode of Galeazzo offering Elena a sum of money if she would dry her beautiful hands, all wet with champagne, on his beard. He hurried through the garden and out into the street. He had a dull confused sense as of some deafening noise going on inside his head.

It was an afternoon at the end of April, warm and moist.

The sun appeared and disappeared again among the fleecy slow-sailing clouds. The languor of the sirocco lay over Rome.

On the pavement in front of him in the Via Sistina, he perceived a lady walking slowly in the direction of the Trinità. He recognised her as Donna Maria Ferrès. He looked at his watch; it was on the stroke of five; only a minute or two before the accustomed hour of meeting. Maria was assuredly on her way to the Palazzo Zuccari.

He hastened forward to join her. When he reached her side, he called her by name.

She started violently. 'What? You here? I was just going up to you. It is five o'clock.'

'It wants a minute or two yet to the hour. I was hurrying on to receive you. Forgive me.'

'But you seem quite upset and very pale. Where were you coming from?'

She frowned slightly, regarding him fixedly through her veil.

'From my stables,' Andrea replied, meeting her look unblushingly as though he had not a drop of blood left to send to his face. 'A horse that I thought a great deal of has been hurt in the knee—the fault of the jockey—and now it will not be able to run in the Derby on Sunday. It has annoyed and upset me very much. Please forgive me. I over-stayed the time without noticing it. But it is still a few minutes to five.'

'It does not matter. Good-bye. I am going back.'

They had reached the Piazza del Trinità. She stopped and held out her hand. A furrow still lingered between her brows. With all her great sweetness of temper, she occasionally had moments of angry impatience and petulancy that seemed to transform her into another creature.

'No, Maria—come, be kind! I am going up now to wait for you. Go on as far as the gates of the Pincio and then come back. Will you?'

The clock of the Trinità de' Monti began to strike.

'You hear that?' he added.

She hesitated for a moment.

'Very well, I will come.'

'Thank you so much! I love you.'

'And I love you.'

They parted.

Donna Maria went on across the piazza and into the avenue. Over her head, the languid breath of the sirocco sent a broken murmur through the green trees. Subtle waves of perfume rose and fell upon the warm, damp breeze. The clouds seemed lower; the swallows skimmed close to the ground; and in the languorous heaviness of the air there was something that melted the passionate heart of the Siennese.

Ever since she had yielded to Andrea's persuasions, her heart had been filled with a happiness that was deeply fraught with fear. All her Christian blood was on fire with the hitherto undreamed-of raptures of her passion, and froze with terror at her sin. Her passion was all-conquering, supreme, immense, so despotic that for hours sometimes it obliterated all thought of her child. She went so far as to forget, to neglect Delfina! And afterwards, she would have a sudden access of remorse, of repentance, of tenderness, in which she covered the astonished little girl's face with tears and kisses, sobbing in horrible despair as over a corpse.

Her whole being quickened at this flame, grew keener, more acute, acquired a marvellous sensibility, a sort of clairvoyance, a faculty of divination which caused her endless torture. Hardly a deception of Andrea's but seemed to send a shadow across her spirit; she felt an indefinite sense of disquietude which sometimes condensed itself into a suspicion. And this suspicion would gnaw at her heart, embittering kisses and caresses, till it was dissipated by the transports and ardent passion of her incomprehensible lover.

She was jealous. Jealousy was her implacable tormentor; not jealousy of the present but of the past. With the cruelty

that jealous people exercise against themselves, she would
have wished to read the secrets of Andrea's memory, to
find the traces left there by former mistresses, to know—to
know——. The question that most often rose to her lips
if Andrea seemed moody and silent was, 'What are you
thinking about?' And yet, at the very moment of asking
the question, a shadow would cross her eyes and her
spirit, an inevitable rush of sadness would rise out of
her heart.

To-day again, when he turned up so unexpectedly in the
street, had she not had an instinctive movement of suspicion?
With a flash of lucidity, the idea had leapt into her mind
that Andrea was coming from the Palazzo Barberini, from
Lady Heathfield.

She knew that Andrea had been this woman's lover; she
knew that her name was Elena; she knew also that she was
the Elena of the inscription—'Ich lebe!' Goethe's distich
rang painfully in her heart. That lyric cry gave her the
measure of Andrea's love for this most beautiful woman.
He must have loved her boundlessly!

Walking slowly under the trees, she recalled Elena's appearance in the concert-hall and the ill-disguised uneasiness
of the old lover.   She remembered her own terrible agitation
one evening at the Austrian Embassy when the Countess
Starnina said to her, seeing Elena pass by—'What do you
think of Lady Heathfield? She was, and is still, I fancy, a
great flame of our friend Sperelli's.'

'Is still, I fancy.' What tortures in a single sentence!
She followed her rival persistently with her eyes through the
throng, and more than once her gaze met that of the other,
sending a nameless shiver through her.   Later on in the
evening, when they were introduced to one another by the
Baroness Bockhorst, in the middle of the crowd, they merely
exchanged an inclination of the head.   And that perfunctory
salutation had been repeated on the rare occasions on which
Maria Ferrès had joined in any social function.

Why should these doubts and suspicions, beaten down and

stifled under the flood of her passion, rise up again now with so much vehemence? Why had she not the strength to repress them or put them away from her altogether? The least touch brought them up to the surface as lively as ever.

Her distress and unhappiness increased with every moment. Her heart was not satisfied; the dream that had risen up within her on that mystical morning under the flowering trees in sight of the sea, had not come true. All that was purest and fairest in that love had remained down there in the sequestered glades in the symbolical forest that bloomed and bore fruit perpetually in contemplation of the Infinite.

She stood and leaned against the parapet that looks towards San Sebastianello. The ancient oaks, their foliage so dark as almost to seem black, spread a sombre artificial roof over the fountain. There were great rents in their trunks filled up with bricks and mortar like the breaches in a wall. Oh, the young arbutus-trees all radiant and breathing in the light! The fountain, dripping from the higher into the lower basin, moaned at intervals, like a heart that fills with anguish and then overflows in a torrent of tears; oh, the melody of the Hundred Fountains in the laurel avenue! The city lay as dead, as if buried under the ashes of an invisible volcano, silent and funereal as a city ravaged by the plague, enormous, shapeless, dominated by the cupola that rose out of its bosom like a cloud. Oh, the sea, the tranquil sea!

Her uneasiness increased. An obscure menace emanated from these things. She was seized with the feeling of terror she had already experienced on so many occasions. Across her pious spirit there flashed once more the thought of punishment.

Nevertheless, the recollection that her lover awaited her, thrilled her to the heart's core; at the thought of his kisses, his caresses, his mad endearments, her blood was on fire and her soul grew faint. The thrill of passion triumphed over the fear of God. She turned her steps towards her lover's house with all the palpitating emotion of her first rendezvous.

'At last!' cried Andrea, gathering her into his arms, and drinking the breath from her panting lips.

He took one of her hands and held it against his breast.

'Feel my heart. If you had stayed away a minute longer, it would have broken.'

But instead of her hand, she laid her cheek upon it. He kissed the white nape of her neck.

'Do you hear it beat?'

'Yes, and it speaks to me.'

'What does it tell you?'

'That you do not love me.'

'What does it tell you?' repeated the young man, biting her neck softly and preventing her from raising her head.

She laughed.

'That you love me.'

She removed her cloak, her hat and her gloves, and then went to smell the bouquets of white lilac that filled the high Florentine vases like those of the *tondo* in the Borghese Gallery. Her step on the carpet was extraordinarily light, and nothing could exceed her grace of attitude as she buried her face in the delicate tassels of bloom.

She bit off the end of a spray, and holding it between her lips—

'Take it,' she said.

They exchanged a long, long kiss in among the perfume.

He drew her closer and said with a tremor in his voice, 'Come.'

'No, Andrea—no; let us stay here. I will make the tea for you.'

She took her lover's hand and twined her fingers into his. 'I don't know what is the matter with me. My heart is so full of love that I could almost cry.'

The words trembled on her lips; her eyes were full of tears.

'Oh, if only I need not leave you, if I could stay here always!'

Her heart was so full that it lent an indefinable sadness to her words.

'When I think that you can never know the whole extent of my love! That I can never know yours! Do you love me? Tell me, say it a hundred, a thousand times—always—you love me?'

'As if you did not know!'

'No, I do not know.'

She uttered the words in so low a tone that Andrea hardly caught them.

'Maria!'

She silently laid her head on Andrea's breast, waiting for him to speak, as if listening to his heart.

He regarded that hapless head, weighed down by the burden of a sad foreboding; he felt the light pressure of that noble, mournful brow upon his breast, which was hardened by falsehood, encased in duplicity as in a cuirass of steel. He was stirred by genuine emotion; a sense of human pity for this most human suffering gripped him by the throat. And yet this agitation of soul resolved itself into lying words and lent a quiver of seeming sincerity to his voice.

'You do not know!—Your voice was so low that it died away upon your lips; at the bottom of your heart something protested against your words; all, all the memories of our love rose up and protested against them. Oh! *you do not know* that I love you!——'

She remained leaning against him, listening, trembling, recognising or fancying that she recognised in his moving voice the accents of true passion, the accents that intoxicated her and that she supposed were inimitable. And he went on speaking, almost in her ear, in the silence of the room, with his hot breath on her cheek and with pauses that were almost sweeter than words. '—To have one sole thought, continually, every hour, every moment——not to be able to conceive of any happiness but the transcendent one that beams upon me from your mere presence——to live throughout the day in the anticipation—impatient, restless, fierce—of the moment when I shall see you again, and, after you have gone, to caress and cherish your image in my heart,——to believe in you alone, to swear by you alone, in you alone to put my faith, my strength, my pride, my whole world, all that I dream and all that I hope——'

She lifted her face all bathed in tears. He ceased to speak, and with his lips arrested the course of the warm drops that flowed over her cheeks. She wept and smiled, caressing his hair with trembling hands, shaken with irrepressible sobs.

'My heart, my dearest heart!'

He made her sit down and knelt before her without ceasing to kiss her lids. Suddenly he started. He had felt her long lashes tremble on his lips like the flutter of an airy wing. Time was, when Elena had laughingly given him that caress twenty times in succession. Maria had learned it from him, and at that caress he had often managed to conjure up the image of *the other*.

His start made Maria smile; and as a tear still lingered on her lashes—'This one too,' she said.

He kissed it away, and she laughed softly without a thought of suspicion.

Her tears had ceased, and, reassured, she turned almost gay and full of charming graces.

'I am going to make the tea now,' she said.

'No, stay where you are.' The image of Elena had suddenly interposed between them.

'No, let me get up,' begged Maria, disengaging herself from his constraining arms. 'I want you to taste my tea. The aroma will penetrate to your very soul.'

She was alluding to some costly tea she had received from Calcutta which she had given to Andrea the day before.

She rose and went over to the armchair with the dragons in which the melting shades of the *rosa di gruogo* of the ancient dalmatic continued to languish exquisitely. The little cups of fine Castel-Durante Majolica still glittered on the tea-table.

While preparing the tea, she said a thousand charming things, she let all the goodness and tenderness of her fond heart bloom out with entire freedom ; she took an ingenuous delight in this dear and secret intimacy, the hushed calm of the room with all its accessories of refined luxury. Behind her, as behind the Virgin in Botticelli's *tondo*, rose the tall vases crowned with sprays of white lilac, and her archangelic hands moved about among the little mythological pictures of Luzio Dolci and the hexameters of Ovid beneath them.

'What are you thinking about?' she asked Andrea, who was sitting on the floor beside her, leaning his head against the arm of her chair.

'I am listening to you. Go on !'

'I have nothing more to say.'

'Yes, you have. Tell me a thousand, thousand things——'

'What sort of things?'

' The things that you alone know how to say.'

He wanted Maria's voice to lull the anguish caused him oy *the other* ; to animate for him the image of *the other*.

'Do you smell that?' she exclaimed, as she poured the boiling water on to the aromatic leaves.

A delicious fragrance diffused itself through the air with the steam.

'How I love that !' she cried.

Andrea shivered. Were not those the very words—and spoken in her very tone—that Elena had used on the evening she offered him her love? He fixed his eyes on Maria's mouth.

'Say that again.'

'What?'

'What you just said.'

' Why ?'

'The words sound so sweet when you pronounce them— you cannot understand it, of course. Say them again.'

She smiled, divining nothing, and a little troubled, even a little shy, under her lover's strange gaze.

'Well then—I love that !'

' And me ? '

' What ? '

' And me ?——you——'

She looked down puzzled at her lover writhing at her feet, his face haggard and drawn, waiting for the words he was trying to draw out of her.

' And me ?——'

' Ah ! you——I love you——'

' That is it ! That is it !——Say it again—again——'

She did so, quite unsuspecting. He felt a spasm of inexpressible pleasure.

' Why do you shut your eyes ? ' she asked, not because of any suspicion in her mind, but to lead him on to explain his emotion.

' So that I may die.'

He laid his head on her knee and remained for some minutes in that attitude, silent and abstracted. She gently stroked his hair, his brow—that brow behind which his infamous imagination was working. Shadows began to fill the room, and the fragrance of the flowers and the aromatic beverage mingled in the air ; the outlines of the surrounding objects melted into one vague form, harmonious, dim, unsubstantial.

Presently she said : ' Get up, dearest, I must go. It is getting late.'

' Stay a little longer with me,' he entreated.

He drew her over to the divan where the gold on the cushions still gleamed through the shadows. There he suddenly clasped her head between his hands and covered her face with fierce hot kisses. He let himself imagine it was the other face he held, and he thought of it as sullied by the lips of her husband ; and instead of disgust, was filled with still more savage desire of it. All the turbid sensations he had experienced in the presence of this man now rose to the surface of his consciousness, and with his kisses these vile things swept over the cheeks, the brow, the hair, the throat, the lips of Maria.

'Let me go—let me go,' she cried, struggling out of his arms.

She ran across to the tea-table to light the candles.

'You must be good,' she said, panting a little still, and with an air of fond reproof.

He did not move from the divan, but looked at her in silence.

She went over to the side of the mantelpiece, where, on the wall, hung the little old mirror. She put on her hat and veil before its dim surface, that looked so like a pool of dull and stagnant water.

'I am so loath to leave you this evening!' she murmured, oppressed by the melancholy of the twilight hour. 'This evening more than ever before.'

The violet gleam of the sunset struggled with the light or the candles. The lilac in the crystal vases looked waxen white. The cushion in the arm-chair retained the impress of the form that had leaned against it.

The clock of the Trinità began to strike.

'Heavens! how late! Help me to put on my cloak,' exclaimed the poor creature, turning to Andrea.

He only clasped her once more in his arms, kissing her furiously, blindly, madly, with a devouring passion, stifling on her lips his own insane desire to cry aloud the name of Elena.

At last she managed to gasp in an expiring voice—

'You are drawing my life out of me.' But his passionate vehemence seemed to make her happy.

'My love, my soul, all, all mine!' she said.

And again, blissfully—'I can feel your heart beating—so fast, so fast.'

At last, with a sigh, 'I must go now.'

Andrea was as lividly pale and convulsed as if he had just committed a murder.

'What ails you?' she asked with tender solicitude.

He tried to smile. 'I never felt so profound an emotion,' he answered.

'I thought I should have died.'

He took the bouquet of flowers from one of the vases and handed it to her and went with her towards the door, almost hurrying her departure, for this woman's every look and gesture and word was a fresh sword-thrust in his heart.

'Good-bye, dear heart!' said the hapless creature to him with unspeakable tenderness. 'Think of me.'

CHAPTER VII

ON the morning of the 20th of May, as Andrea Sperelli was walking along the Corso in the radiant sunshine, he heard his name called from the doorway of the Club.

On the pavement in front of it was a group of gentlemen amusing themselves by watching the ladies pass and talking scandal. They were Giulio Musellaro, Ludovico Barbarisi, the Duke of Grimiti, Galeazzo Secinaro, Gino Bomminaco, and two or three others.

'Have you heard what happened last night?' Barbarisi asked him.

'No, what?'

'Don Manuel Ferrès, the Minister for Guatemala——'

'Well?'

'Was caught red-handed cheating at cards.'

Sperelli retained his self-command, although some of the men were looking at him with a certain malicious curiosity.

'How was that?'

'Galeazzo was there and was playing at the same table.'

Secinaro proceeded to give him the details.

Andrea did not affect indifference, he listened with a grave and attentive air. At the end of the story, he said, 'I am extremely sorry to hear it.'

After remaining a minute or two longer with the group, he bowed and passed on.

'Which way are you going?' asked Secinaro.

'I am going home.'

'I will go with you part of the way.'

They went off together in the direction of the Via de' Condotti. The Corso was one glittering stream of sunshine

from the Piazzo di Venezia to the Piazzo del Popolo.   Ladies
in light spring dress passed along by the brilliant shop-
windows—the Princess of Ferentino with Barbarella Viti
under one big lace parasol; Bianca Dolcebuono; Leonetto
Lanza's young wife.

'Do you know this man—this Ferrès?' asked Galeazzo
of Andrea, who had not spoken as yet.

'Yes, I met him last year at Schifanoja, at my cousin
Ateleta's.   The wife is a great friend of Francesca's.   That
is why the affair annoys me so much.   We must see that it is
hushed up as much as possible.   You will be doing me the
greatest favour if you will help me about it.'

Galeazzo promised his assistance with the most cordial
alacrity.

'I think,' said he, 'that the worst of the scandal might be
avoided if the Minister sends in his resignation to his Government without a moment's delay.   That is what the President of
the Club advised, but Ferrès refused last night.   He blustered
and did the insulted.   And yet the proofs were there, as clear
as daylight.   He will have to be persuaded.'

They continued on the subject as they walked along.
Sperelli was grateful to Secinaro for his assistance, and the
intimate tone of the conversation predisposed Secinaro to
friendly confidences.

At the corner of the Via de' Condotti, they caught sight of
Lady Heathfield strolling along the left side of the street past
the Japanese shop-windows, with her undulating, rhythmic,
captivating walk.

'Ah—Donna Elena,' said Galeazzo.

Both the men watched her, and both felt the glamour
of that rhythmic gait.

When they came up to her, they both bowed but passed on.
They no longer saw her, but she saw them; and for Andrea
it was a form of torture to have to walk beside a rival under
the gaze of the woman he desired, and feel that those piercing
eyes were perhaps taking a delight in weighing the merits of
both men.   He compared himself with Secinaro.

Galeazzo was of the bovine type, a Lucius Verus with golden hair and blue eyes; while amid the magnificent abundance of his golden beard shone a full red mouth, handsome, but without the slightest expression. He was tall, square-shouldered and strong, with an air of elegance that was not exactly refined, but easy and unaffected.

'Well?' Sperelli asked, goaded on by a sort of madness. 'Are matters going on favourably?'

He knew he might adopt this tone with a man of this sort.

Galeazzo turned and looked at him half surprised, half suspicious. He certainly did not expect such a question from him, and still less the airy and perfectly calm tone in which the question was uttered.

'Ah, the time that siege of mine has lasted!' groaned the bearded prince. 'Ages simply—I have tried every kind of manœuvre but always without success. I always came too late, some other fellow had always been before me in storming the citadel. But I never lost heart. I was convinced that sooner or later my turn would come. *Attendre pour atteindre.* And sure enough——'

'Well?'

'Lady Heathfield is kinder to me than the Duchess of Scerni. I shall have, I hope, the very enviable honour of being set down after you on the list.'

He burst into a rather coarse laugh, showing his splendid teeth.

'I fancy that my doughty deeds in India, which Giulio Musellaro spread abroad, have added to my beard several heroic strands of irresistible virtue.'

'Ah, just in these days that beard of yours should fairly quiver with memories.'

'What memories?'

'Memories of a Bacchic nature.'

'I don't understand.'

'What, have you forgotten the famous May Bazaar of 1884?'

'Well, upon my word, now that you remind me of it, the third anniversary does fall on one of these next days. But you were not there—who told you?'

'You want to know more than is good for you, my dear boy.'

'Do tell me!'

'Bend your mind rather to making the most skilful use of this anniversary and give me news as soon as you have any.'

'When shall I see you again?'

'Whenever you like.'

'Then dine with me to-night at the Club—about eight o'clock. That will give us an opportunity of seeing after the other affair too.'

'All right. Good-bye, Goldbeard. Run!'

They parted in the Piazza di Spagna, at the foot of the steps, and as Elena came across the square in the direction of the Via due Macelli to go up to the Quattro Fontane, Secinaro joined her and walked on with her.

The strain of dissimulation once over, Andrea's heart sank within him like a leaden weight. He did not know how he was to drag himself up the steps. He was quite assured that, after this, Secinaro would tell him everything, and somehow this seemed to him a point to his advantage. By a sort of intoxication, a species of madness, resulting from the severity of his sufferings, he rushed blindly into new and ever more cruel and senseless torments; aggravating and complicating his miserable state in a thousand ways; passing from perversion to perversion, from aberration to aberration, without being able to hold back or to stop for one moment in his giddy descent. He seemed to be devoured by an inextinguishable fever, the heat of which made all the germs of human lust lying dormant in the hidden depths of his being flourish and grow big. His every thought, his every emotion showed the same stain.

And yet, it was the very deception itself that bound him so strongly to the woman he deceived. His mind had adapted itself so thoroughly to the monstrous comedy that he

was no longer capable of conceiving any other way of satisfy-
ing his passion. This incarnation of one woman in another
was no longer a result of exasperated desire, but a deliberate
habit of vice, and now finally an imperious necessity. From
thenceforth, the unconscious instrument of his vicious imagination had become as necessary to him as the vice itself.
By a process of sensual depravity, he had almost come to
think that the real possession of Elena would not afford him
such exquisite and violent delight as the imaginary. He was
hardly able to separate the two women in his thoughts. And
just as he felt that his pleasure would be diminished by the
actual possession of the one, so his nerves received a shock if
by some lassitude of the imagination he found himself in the
presence of the other without the interposing image of her
rival.

Thus he felt crushed to the earth at the thought that Don
Manuel's ruin meant for him the loss of Maria.

When she came to him that evening, he saw at once that
the poor thing was ignorant as yet of her misfortune. But
the next day, she arrived, panting, convulsed, pale as death.
She threw herself into his arms, and hid her face on his
breast.

'You know?' she gasped between her sobs.

The news had spread. Disgrace and ruin were inevitable,
irremediable. There followed days of hideous torture, during
which Maria, left alone after the precipitate flight of the
gamester, abandoned by the few friends she possessed, persecuted by the innumerable creditors of her husband, bewildered by the legal formalities of the seizure of their effects,
by bailiffs, money-lenders and rogues of all sorts, gave evidences of a courage that was nothing less than heroic,
but failed to avert the utter ruin that overwhelmed the
family.

From her lover she would receive no assistance of any
kind; she told him nothing of the martyrdom she was
enduring even when he reproached her for the brevity of her
visits. She never complained; for him she always managed

to call up a less mournful smile; still obeyed the dictates of
her lover's capricious passion, and lavished upon her ruthless
destroyer all the treasures of her fond heart.

Her presentiments had not deceived her. Everything was
falling in ruins around her. Punishment had overtaken her
without a moment's warning.

But she never regretted having yielded to her lover; never
repented having given herself so utterly to him, never be-
wailed her lost purity. Her one sorrow—stronger than
remorse, or fear, or any other trouble of mind—was the
thought that she must go away, must be separated from this
man who was the life of her life.

'My darling, I shall die. I am going away to die far from
you—alone—all alone—and you will not be there to close my
eyes——'

She smiled as she spoke with certainty and resignation.
But Andrea endeavoured to kindle an illusive hope in her
breast, to sow in her heart the seeds of a dream that could
only lead to future suffering.

'I will not let you die! You will be mine again and for a
long time to come. We have many happy days of love before
us yet!'

He spoke of the immediate future.—He would go and
establish himself in Florence; from there he could go over
as often as he liked to Sienna under the pretext of study—
could pass whole months there copying some Old Master or
making researches in ancient chronicles. Their love should
have its hidden nest in some deserted street, or beyond the
city, in the country, in some villa decorated with rural
ornaments and surrounded by a meadow. She would be
able to spare an hour now and then for their love. Sometimes she would come and spend a whole week in Florence,
a week of unbroken happiness. They would air their idyll
on the hillside of Fiesole in a September as mild as April, and
the cypresses of Montughi would not be less kind to them
than the cypresses of Schifanoja.

'Would it were true! Would it were true!' sighed Maria.

'You don't believe me?'

'Oh yes, I believe you; but my heart tells me that all these sweet things will remain a dream.'

She made Andrea take her in his arms and hold her there for a long time; and she leaned upon his breast, silently crouching into his embrace as if to hide herself, with the shiver of a sick person or of one who seeks protection from some threatening danger. She asked of Andrea only the delicate caresses that in the language of affection she called 'kisses of the soul' and that melted her to tears sweeter than any more carnal delights. She could not understand how in these moments of supreme spirituality, in these last sad hours of passion and farewell her lover was not content to kiss her hands.

'No—no, dear love,' she besought him, half repelled by Andrea's crude display of passion, 'I feel that you are nearer to me, closer to my heart, more entirely one with me, when you are sitting at my side, and take my hand in yours and look into my eyes and say the things to me that you alone know how to say. Those other caresses seem to put us far away from each other, to set some shadow between you and me——I don't know how to express my thought properly—— And afterwards it leaves me so sad, so sad—I don't know what it is——I feel then so tired—but a tiredness that has something evil about it——!'

She entreated him, humbly, submissively, fearing to make him angry. Then she fell to recalling memories of things recent and passed, down to the smallest details, the most trivial words, the most insignificant facts, which all had a vast amount of significance for her. But it was towards the first days of her stay at Schifanoja that her heart returned most fondly.

'You remember? You remember?'

And suddenly the tears filled her downcast eyes.

One evening Andrea, thinking of her husband, asked her—
'Since I knew you, have you always been *wholly* mine?'

'Always.'

' I am not speaking of the soul——'

' Hush !——yes, always wholly yours.'

And he, who had never before believed one of his mistresses on this point, believed Maria without a shadow of doubt as to the truth of her assertion.

He believed her even while he deceived and profaned her without remorse ; he knew himself to be boundlessly loved by a lofty and noble spirit, that he was face to face with a grand and all-absorbing passion, and recognised fully both the grandeur of that passion and his own vileness. And yet under the lash of his base imaginings he would go so far as to hurt the mouth of the fond and patient creature, to prevent himself from crying aloud upon her lips the name that rose invincibly to his ; and that loving and pathetic mouth would murmur, all unconscious, smiling though it bled—

' Even thus you do not hurt me.'

CHAPTER VIII

It wanted but a few days now to their parting. Miss Dorothy had taken Delfina to Sienna, and then returned to help her mistress in the last and most trying arrangements and to accompany her on the journey. In the mother's house in Sienna the truth of the story was not known, and Delfina of course knew nothing. Maria had merely written that Don Manuel had been suddenly recalled by his government. And she made ready to go—to leave these rooms, so full of cherished things, to the hands of the public auctioneers who had already drawn up the inventory and fixed the date of the sale for the 20th of June, at ten in the morning.

On the evening of the 9th, as she was leaving Andrea, she missed a glove. While looking for it she came upon a volume of Shelley, the one which Andrea had lent her in Schifanoja, the dear and affecting book in which, before the excursion to Vicomile, she had underlined the words

> 'And forget me, for I can *never*
> Be thine.'

She took up the book with visible emotion and turned over the pages till she came to the one which bore the mark of her underlining.

'*Never!*' she murmured with a shake of the head. 'You remember? And hardly eight months have passed since.'

She pensively turned over a few more leaves and read other verses.

'He is our poet,' she went on. 'How often you promised to take me to the English Cemetery! You remember, we were to take flowers for his grave. Shall we go? You might take me before I leave. It will be our last walk together.'

'Let us go to-morrow,' he answered.

The next evening, when the sun was already declining, they went in a closed carriage ; on her knees lay a bunch of roses. They drove along the foot of the leafy Aventino and caught a glimpse of the boats laden with Sicilian wine anchored in the port of Ripa Grande.

In the neighbourhood of the cemetery they left the carriage and went the rest of the way to the gates on foot and in silence. At the bottom of her heart, Maria felt that not only was she here to lay flowers c.. the tomb of a poet, but that in this place of death she would weep for something of herself irreparably lost. A *Fragment* of Shelley, read in the sleepless watches of the night echoed through her spirit as she gazed at the cypresses pointing to the sky on the other side of the white wall.

> ' Death is here, and Death is there,
> Death is busy everywhere ;
> All around, within, beneath,
> Above, is death—and we are death.
>
> Death has set his mark and seal
> On all we are and all we feel,
> On all we know and all we fear—
>
> First our pleasures die, and then
> Our hopes, and then our fears : and when
> These are dead, the debt is due,
> Dust claims dust—and we die too.
>
> All things that we love and cherish,
> Like ourselves must fade and perish.
> Such is our rude mortal lot :
> Love itself would, did they not——'

As she passed through the gateway she put her arm through Andrea's and shivered.

The cemetery was solitary and deserted. A few gardeners were engaged in watering the plants along by the wall, swing-

ing their watering-cans from side to side with an even and
continuous motion and in silence.

The funeral cypresses stood up straight and motionless in
the air; only their tops, gilded by the sun, trembled lightly.
Between the rigid, greenish-black trunks rose the white tombs
—square slabs of stone, broken pillars, urns, sarcophagi.
From the sombre mass of the cypresses fell a mysterious
shadow, a religious peace, a sort of human kindness, as limpid
and beneficent waters gush from the hard rock. The un-
changing regularity of the trees and the chastened whiteness
of the sepulchral monuments affected the spirit with a sense
of solemn and sweet repose. But between the stiff ranks of
the trees, standing in line like the deep pipes of an organ, and
interspersed among the tombs, graceful oleanders swayed their
tufts of pink blossom; roses dropped their petals at every
light touch of the breeze, strewing the ground with their
fragrant snow; the eucalyptus shook its pale tresses—now
dark, now silvery white; willows wept over the crosses and
crowns; and, here and there, the cactus displayed the glory
of its white blooms like a swarm of sleeping butterflies or an
aigrette of wonderful feathers. The silence was unbroken
save by the cry, now and then, of some solitary bird.

Andrea pointed to the top of the hill.

'The poet's tomb is up there,' he said, 'near that ruin to
the left, just below the last tower.'

She dropped his arm and went on in front of him through
the narrow paths bordered with low myrtle hedges. She
walked as if fatigued, turning round every few minutes to
smile back at her lover. She was dressed in black and wore
a black veil that cast over her faint and trembling smile a
shadow of mourning. Her oval chin was paler and purer
than the roses she carried in her hand.

Once, as she turned, one of the roses shed its petals on the
path. Andrea stooped to pick them up. She looked at him
and he fell on his knees before her.

'*Adorata!*' he exclaimed.

A scene rose up before her, vividly as a picture.

'You remember,' she said, 'that morning at Schifanoja when I threw a handful of leaves down to you from the higher terrace? You bent your knee to me while I descended the steps. I do not know how it is, but that time seems to me so near and yet so far away! I feel as if it had happened yesterday, and then again, a century ago. But perhaps, after all, it only happened in a dream.'

Passing along between the low myrtle hedges, they at last reached the tower near which lies the tomb of the poet and of Trelawny. The jasmin climbing over the old ruin was in flower, but of the violets nothing was left but their thick carpet of leaves. The tops of the cypresses, which here just reached the line of vision, were vividly illumined by the last red gleams of the sun as it sank behind the black cross of the Monte Testaccio. A great purple cloud edged with burning gold sailed across the sky in the direction of the Aventino—

> 'These are two friends whose lives were undivided.
> So let their memory be, now they have glided
> Under their grave ; let not their bones be parted
> For their two hearts in life were single-hearted.'

Maria repeated the last line. Then, moved by a delicate inspiration—'Please unfasten my veil,' she said to Andrea.

She leaned her head back slightly so that he might untie the knot, and Andrea's fingers touched her hair—that magnificent hair, in the dense shadow of which he had so often tasted all the delights of his perfidious imagination, evoked the image of her rival.

'Thank you,' she said.

She then drew the veil from before her face and looked at Andrea with eyes that were a little dazed. She looked very beautiful. The shadows round her eyes were darker and deeper, but the eyes themselves burned with a more intense light. Her hair clung to her temples in heavy hyacinthine curls tinged with violet. The middle of her forehead, which was left free, gleamed, by contrast, in moonlike purity. Her features had fined down and lost something of their materiality through stress of love and sorrow.

She wound the veil about the stems of the roses, tied the two ends together with much care, and then buried her face in the flowers, inhaling their perfume. Then she laid them on the simple stone that bears the poet's name engraved upon it. There was an indefinable expression in the gesture, which Andrea could not understand.

As they moved away, he suddenly stopped short, and looking back towards the tower, 'How did you manage to get those roses?' he asked.

She smiled, but her eyes were wet.

'They are yours—those of that snowy night—they have bloomed again this evening. Do you not believe it?'

The evening breeze was rising, and behind the hill the sky was overspread with gold, in the midst of which the purple cloud dissolved, as if consumed by fire. Against this field of light, the serried ranks of the cypresses looked more imposing and mysterious than before. The Psyche at the end of the middle avenue seemed to flush with pale tints as of flesh. A crescent moon rose over the pyramid of Cestius, in a deep and glassy sky, like the waters of a calm and sheltered bay.

They went through the centre avenue to the gates. The gardeners were still watering the plants, and two other men held a velvet and silver pall by the two ends, and were beating it vigorously, while the dust rose high and glittered in the air.

From the Aventine came the sound of bells.

Maria clung to her lover's arm, unable to control her anguish, feeling the ground give way beneath her feet, her life ebb from her at every step. Once inside the carriage, she burst into a passion of tears, sobbing despairingly on her lover's shoulder.

'I shall die!'

But she did not die. Better a thousand times for her that she had!

CHAPTER IX

Two days after this, Andrea was lunching with Galeazzo Secinaro at a table in the Caffè di Roma. It was a hot morning. The place was almost empty; the waiters nodded drowsily among the buzzing flies.

'And so,' the bearded prince went on, 'knowing that she had a fancy for strange and out-of-the-way situations, I had the courage to——'

He was relating in the crudest terms the extremely audacious means by which he had at last succeeded in overcoming Lady Heathfield's resistance. He exhibited neither reserve nor scruples, omitting no single detail, and praising the acquisition to the connoisseur. He only broke off, from time to time, to put his fork into a piece of juicy red meat, or to empty a glass of red wine. His whole bearing was expressive of robust health and strength.

Andrea Sperelli lit a cigarette. In spite of all his efforts, he could not bring himself to swallow a mouthful of food, and with the wine Secinaro poured out for him, he seemed to be drinking poison.

There came a moment at last, when the prince, in spite of his obtuseness, had a qualm of doubt, and he looked sharply at Elena's former lover. Except his want of appetite, Andrea gave no outward sign of inward agitation; with the utmost calm he puffed clouds of smoke into the air, and smiled his habitual, half-ironical smile, at his jocund companion.

The prince continued: 'She is coming to see me to-day for the first time'

'To you—to-day?'

' Yes, at three o'clock.'

The two men looked at their watches.

'Shall we go?' asked Andrea.

'Let us,' assented Galeazzo rising. ' We can go up the Via de' Condotti together. I want to get some flowers. As you know all about it, tell me—what flowers does she like best?'

Andrea laughed. An abominable answer was on the tip of his tongue, but he restrained himself and replied unmoved—

' Roses, at one time.'

In front of the Barcaccia they parted.

At that hour the Piazza di Spagna had the deserted look of high summer. Some workmen were repairing a main water-pipe, and a heap of earth dried by the sun threw up clouds of dust in the hot breath of the wind. The stairway of the Trinità gleamed white and deserted.

Slowly, slowly, Andrea went up, standing still every two or three steps, as if he were dragging a terrible weight after him. He went into his rooms and threw himself on his bed, where he remained till a quarter to three. At a quarter to three he got up and went out. He turned into the Via Sistina, on through the Via Quattro Fontane, passed the Palazzo Barberini and stopped before a book-stall to wait for three o'clock. The bookseller, a little wrinkled, dried-up old man, like a decrepit tortoise, offered him books, taking down his choicest volumes one by one, and spreading them out under his eyes, speaking all the time in an insufferable nasal monotone. Three o'clock would strike directly ; Andrea looked at the titles of the books, keeping an eye on the gates of the palace, while the voice of the bookseller mingled confusedly with the loud thumping of his heart.

A lady passed through the gates, went down the street towards the piazza, got into a cab, and drove away through the Via del Tritone.

Andrea went home. There he threw himself once more on his bed, and waited till Maria should come, keeping himself in a state of such complete immobility, that he seemed not to be suffering any more.

At five Maria came.

'Do you know,' she said, panting, 'I can stay with you the whole evening—till to-morrow. It will be our first and last night of love. I am going on Tuesday.'

She sobbed despairingly, and clung to him, her lips pressed convulsively to his.

'Don't let me see the light of another day—kill me!' she moaned.

Then, catching sight of his discomposed face, 'You are suffering?' she exclaimed. 'You too—you think we shall never meet again?'

He had almost insuperable difficulty in speaking, in answering her. His tongue clove to the roof of his mouth, the words failed him. He had an instinctive desire to hide his face from those observant eyes, to avoid her questions at all cost. He was neither capable of consoling her nor of practising fresh deceptions.

'Hush!' he whispered in a choking, almost irrecognisable voice.

Crouching at her feet, he laid his head in her lap and remained like that for a long time without speaking, while she laid her tender hands upon his temples and felt the wild, irregular beating of his arteries. She realised that he was suffering fiercely, and in his pain forgot all thought of her own, grieving now only for his grief—only for him.

Presently he rose, and clasped her with such mad vehemence to him that she was frightened.

'What has come to you! What is it?' she cried, trying to look in his eyes, to discover the reason of his sudden frenzy. But he only buried his face deeper in her bosom, her neck, her hair—anywhere out of sight.

All at once, she struggled free of his embrace, her whole form convulsed with horror, her face ghastly and distraught as if she had at that moment torn herself from the arms of Death.

That name! That name!—She had heard that name!

A deep and awful silence fell upon her soul, and in it there suddenly opened one of those great gulfs into which the whole universe seems to be hurled at the touch of one thought. She heard nothing more. Andrea might writhe and supplicate and despair as he would—in vain.

She heard nothing. Some instinct directed her actions. She found her things and put them on.

Andrea lay upon the floor, sobbing, frenzied, mad.

He was conscious that she was preparing to leave the room.

'Maria! Maria!'

He listened.

'Maria!'

He only heard the sound of the door closing behind her—she was gone.

CHAPTER X

AT ten o'clock in the morning of June 20th the sale began of the furniture and hangings belonging to His Excellency the Minister Plenipotentiary for Guatemala.

It was a burning hot morning. Summer blazed already over Rome. Up and down the Via Nationale ran the tramcars, drawn by horses with funny white caps over their heads to protect them against the sun. Long lines of heavily-laden carts encumbered the road, while the blare of trumpets mingled with the cracking of whips and the hoarse cries of the carters.

Andrea could not make up his mind to cross the threshold of that house, but wandered about the street a long time, weighed down by a horrible sense of lassitude, a lassitude so overwhelming and desperate as to be almost a physical longing for death.

At last, seeing a porter come out of the house with a piece of furniture on his shoulder, he decided to go in. He ran rapidly up the stairs. From the landing already he could hear the voice of the auctioneer.

The sale was going on in the largest room of the suite—the one in which the Buddha had stood. The buyers were gathered round the auctioneer's table. They were, for the most part, shopkeepers, second-hand furniture dealers and the lower classes generally. There being little competition in summer when town was empty, the dealers rushed in, sure of obtaining costly articles for next to nothing. A vile odour permeated the hot air exhaled by the crowd of dirty and perspiring people.

Andrea felt stifled. He wandered into the other rooms, where nothing had been left but the wall hangings, the curtains, and the portières, the other things having been collected in the sale room. Although he was walking on a thick carpet, he heard his footsteps as distinctly as if the boards had been bare.

He found himself presently in a semicircular room. The walls were deep red, with here and there a sparkle of gold, giving the impression of a temple or a tomb, a sad and mysterious sanctuary fit for praying in, or for dying. The crude, hard light blazing in through the open windows seemed like a violation.

He returned to the auction room. Again he breathed the nauseating atmosphere. He turned round, and in a corner of the room perceived the Princess of Ferentino and Barbarella Viti. He bowed and went over to them.

' Well, Ugenta, what have you bought ? '

' Nothing.'

' Nothing ? Why, I should have thought you would buy everything.'

' Indeed, why ? '

' Oh, it was just an idea of mine—a romantic idea.'

The princess laughed and Barbarella joined in.

' We are going. It is impossible to stay any longer in this perfume. Good-bye, Ugenta—console yourself ! '

Andrea went to the auctioneer's table. The man recognised him.

' Does the Signor Conte wish for anything in particular ? '

' I will see,' Andrea answered.

The sale proceeded rapidly. He looked about him at the low faces of the dealers, felt their elbows pushing him, their feet touching his, their horrid breath upon him. Nausea gripped his throat.

' Going—going—gone ! '

The stroke of the hammer rang like a knell through his heart and set his temples throbbing painfully.

He bought the Buddha, a great carved cabinet, some china,

some pieces of drapery. Presently he heard the sound of voices, and laughter, and the rustle of feminine skirts. He turned round to see Galeazzo Secinaro entering, accompanied by Lady Heathfield and followed by the Countess Lucoli, Gino Bomminaco and Giovanella Daddi. They were all laughing and talking noisily.

He did his best to conceal himself from them in the crowd that besieged the auctioneer's table. He shuddered at the thought of being discovered. Their voices and laughter reached him over the heads of the perspiring people through the suffocating heat. Fortunately the gay party very soon afterwards took themselves off.

He forced himself a passage through the closely packed bodies, repressing his disgust as well as he could, and making the most tremendous efforts to ward off the faintness that threatened to overcome him. There was a bitter and sickening taste in his mouth. He felt that from the contact of all these unclean people he was carrying away with him the germs of obscure and irremediable diseases. Physical torture mingled with his moral anguish.

When he got down into the street in the full blaze of noonday, he had a touch of giddiness. With an unsteady step, he set off in search of a cab. He found one in the Piazza del Quirinale and drove straight home.

Towards evening, however, a wild desire came over him to revisit those dismantled rooms. He went upstairs and entered, on the pretext of asking if the furniture he had bought had been sent away yet.

A man answered him : the things had just gone, the Signor Conte must have passed them on his way here.

Hardly anything remained in the rooms. The crimson splendour of the setting sun gleamed through the curtainless windows and mingled with the noises of the street. Some men were taking down the hangings from the walls, disclosing a paper with great vulgar flowers, torn here and there and hanging in strips. Others were engaged in taking up and rolling the carpets, raising a cloud of dust that glittered in the sunlight. One of them sang scraps of a lewd song. Dust and tobacco-smoke mingled and rose to the ceiling.

Andrea fled.

In the Piazza del Quirinale a brass band was playing in front of the royal palace. Great waves of metallic music spread through the glowing air. The obelisk, the fountain, the statues looked enormous and seemed to glow as if impregnated with flame. Rome, immense and dominated by a battle of clouds, seemed to illumine the sky.

Half-demented, Andrea fled ; through the Via del Quirinale, past the Quattro Fontane and the gates of the Palazzo Barberini with its many flashing windows and, at last, reached the Cassa Zuccari.

There the porters were just taking his purchases off a cart, vociferating loudly. Several of them were carrying the cabinet up the stairs with a good deal of difficulty.

He went in. As the cabinet occupied the whole width of the staircase, he could not pass. So he had to follow it, slowly, slowly, step by step, up to his door.

THE END

Triumph of Death - Gabriele D'Annunzio

"D'Annunzio's 1894 novel of obsessive passion, in chillingly stylish translation. The two protagonists, Giorgio and Ippolita, are classic thwarted lovers, strangely transported from the Romantic Age, where they surely belong, to the era of trains and telegraph messages. In true Gothic fashion they agonise, torn between the fascination of love and the horror of inevitable decay; they share transports of joy and agonies of melancholy, and generally stagger about emoting madly and behaving badly. Given the recurring suicide motif, the title's a bit of a giveaway. But all is not formula, and D'Annunzio smartly subverts the Gothic genre with touches of vivid observation and realism".

Time Out

The Torture Garden - Octave Mirbeau

The Torture Garden begins as a conventional narrative, a drawing room discussion, the subject however is murderers and their role in society. It then develops into a tale of decadent sensuality before reaching the exquisitely beautiful Chinese Garden, the scene of the most violent and horrific tortures imaginable.

"The Torture Garden set Paris cynically shivering with a new sensation. This garden of tortures is the most cruel book in contemporary fiction. It was conceived by the Torquemada of sadism to show the cruelty and injustice of all governments. The Chinese were selected as masters of the most exquisite tortures. It demands strong nerves to read it once through; a rereading would seem incredible."

James Huneker

The Dedalus Book of Decadence: Moral Ruins
- edited by Brian Stableford

The Decadent Movement which flourished in the 1890s produced some of Europe's most striking and exotic works of literature. The Decadents, convinced that civilization was in a state of terminal decline, refused to rebel as the Romantics had, but set forth instead to cultivate the pleasures of calculated perversity and to seek the artificial paradise of drug-induced hallucination.

In MORAL RUINS Brian Stableford describes the colourful history of the Decadent ideal, and provides two samplers of Decadent poetry and prose, encapsulating the spirit of the French and English Movements. The French sampler includes nine stories which have never been translated into English before and displays a fuller spectrum of French Decadent writings than has been presented previously.

The Dedalus Book of Decadence exhibits the mordant wit, eroticism and moral perversity of Decadence as it takes the movement into the 1990s.